For Alyssa
Be afraid
Do it Anyway

DAUGHTER OF SHATTERED SKIES

BOOK ONE IN THE SHATTERED TRILOGY

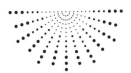

SARA DELAVERGNE

D1519899

Daughter of Shattered Skies is a work of fiction. Names, characters, places, and incidents either are the product of the author's imagination, or are used fictitiously. Any resemblance to actual persons, living or dead, events, or locales is entirely coincidental.

© 2021 Sara DeLaVergne

ASIN / B09BXF93CW / eBook

ISBN / 9798521770144 / Paperback

ISBN / 9798478507107 / Hardcover

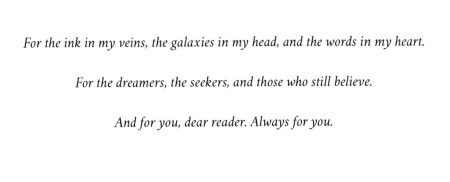

For the ink in my veins, the galaxies in my head, and the words in my heart.

For the dreamers, the seekers, and those who still believe.

And for you, dear reader. Always for you.

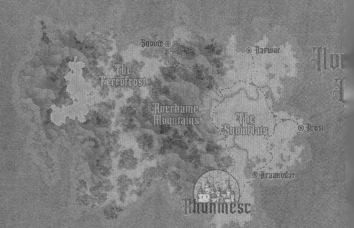

The Salt Ice

The Almystrou Ocean

Savvir

Narwar

Nor

The Ferrofrost

Averhame Mountains

The Snowfans

Irost

Hraamvdar

Rhunmesc

The Lanzauve Sea

The Lands of Ellorhys

Eastern
Lothian Jungle

The
Rasten Sea

Sorair

Western
Lothian Jungle

Straits of
Voyage

Straits of
Voyage

Aera Uino

Belxac ⊗

Hypis ⊗

Alwey ⊗

Uel ⊗

Ares

Hokaan ⊗

The
Ascahh

Rosvia ⊗

Rizan
Mountains

Battle of
Ares

Tarkham ⊗

Espera

Wildrine
Mountains

BaelForta

Lyth
River

Nazarvon ⊗

The
Northern
Glass

The
Southern
Glass

Kinhallow

The Glass Coast

The
Southern
Seas

PART I
DAWN OF THE EVENTIDE

YEAR 3317

1

ISSARIA

Cloaked in black velvet, the petite figure sprinted from shadow to tree trunk, zig-zagging through the orchard. The dizzying dapple of moonlight filtering through pale branches above looked the same on her cloak as on the grass beneath her feet. There one moment and gone the next, she was a phantom among the trees.

Pause.

Pressed against the gnarled trunk, Princess Issaria cast a glance over her shoulder. Violet eyes darted from shadow to shadow, surveying the ground she had covered: the expanse of orchard that stood between her and the Annex where she had slipped out of the Crystal Palace and onto the grounds. She searched the night for movement, for any flicker of light that could betray a pursuer. Even at nine years old she knew to wait, and expect that she's being watched, followed and even hunted.

She bit back a giggle. Elon was *so* overprotective. Nothing ever happened in Espera, but he still made her learn how to check if she was being followed, how to disappear into a crowd, and how to tie and untie at least dozen different types of knots, among other useless things. He still treated her like she was such a little kid even though she was *practically* already Empress. If she made it outside the palace tonight without getting caught, she was going to tease him so bad!

But it was also Elon she had to outwit.

Overhead, silver leaves fluttered back and forth against a knot of branches, blotting out the faint grey light from the crescent moon. The aroma of apple blossom was heavy in the air, sickeningly sweet as she leaned against pale white trunks of the Mythos-touched trees. She continued to search the shadows for signs of movement, but beneath her fingertips she felt it. *Mana*—the magical lifeblood of the tree just beneath its bark. These saplings were only transplants, coronation gifts to her parents from the neighboring kingdom of Ares, where the original grove grew. It was said that the trees were a gift from Baelfor, the Terran Mythos who carved the world, to the Kings of the Daybreak City. It was obvious the trees were peculiar, with pale trunks and silver leaves, but it wasn't until the purple blossoms gave way to golden apples did the King of Ares realize the greatness of the gift the Mythos had bestowed upon his city.

Issaria wasn't talented with magic herself, but she could at least feel the presence of magic in a thing like a steady, flowing river, and these trees were flush with terran energy.

When she was satisfied that Elon had not followed her this far yet, assuming he was already aware that she was not taking a stroll down to the kitchen for a late night snack as she'd told her chambermaid to tell him in the likely event that he came searching, Issaria pulled her hood down over her face and dashed back into the shadows. Elon, cadet or not, was probably hot on her trail already and determined to catch her before she snuck out into the city.

Going through the orchard was a straight shot to the passageway —a secret staircase carved inside the crystalline geode formations that surrounded the palace like a protective wall. The path was meant to be an escape route for the Imperials if ever there was a siege on the palace, but Issaria knew her family was loved and respected as the saviors of the realm. The passage was antiquated by the time her parents ushered in the new dynasty, despite the fact that it had been forged out of the spilled blood of both Imperial Mythos, Aurelia of the Light and Obsidia of the Dark.

The sisters, though only sisters in name for they were sculpted from the very essence of the Cosmos, could have lived forever, reigning the kingdoms of Ellorhys in peace. But it was not written in the stars. Perhaps Aurelia should have read the signs, the distance that had grown between them like the very oceans themselves. Envy blackened Obsidia's heart when the magicians began to revere the day and only debauchery and darkness crept through the night. Corrupted against her cosmic sister, Obsidia enacted horrific black magic to sacrifice Aurelia and her mortal spouse, harvesting her cosmic power for her own nefarious gain.

The ridiculous Evernight. Eternal darkness for the whole of Ellorhys. If the curse had taken hold, Issaria wasn't sure if there would even *be* an Ellorhys. Everything needs the light. The plants, the animals...how could her ancestor be so short-sighted when she was *of the Cosmos?*

Though they were young and untested, Umbriel, daughter of Obsidia, and Helios, son of Aurelia, rose up and joined their magic together to harness near-Cosmic fury and defeat the power-crazed witch. Thus, they solidified their hold on the Imperial rule.

And since then, Issaria was likely the biggest issue the Elysitao line had known. Rambunctious Princess Issaria, her magic so catastrophic she was never even enrolled in the Academies with the other magicians. Instead she was given private tutors in the palace to hide the family's secret. Her mother told her constantly that her magic had to awaken when she was old enough, as it did for all Imperials, but Issaria had heard her parents whispering in the night when they thought she'd gone to sleep.

She was *inept.*

Shaking the thought from her head, she smirked to herself as she dashed forward, slinking from shadow to shadow like a stealthy cat, spinning herself around toward the wall before continuing on. Magic might not be her talent, but Issaria knew she was good at plenty of other things, like dancing, and she loved reading *about* magic, *and* she was learning Alchemy from Elon, even if he didn't know he was teaching her. She just had to watch and remember what ingredients he selected. Memorization was easy if she read something enough times.

As she pressed herself against another trunk and peered up into the blossom laden branches, she liked to think she was good at sneaking around too. The apple trees, in full bloom and bursting with pale flowers stood like luminous moonlit soldiers defending the palace from the harsh expanse of the Glass beyond the northern walls.

The *Glass*.

Issaria shuddered at the thought of its pitching dunes and sharp, glittering edges. Strange to believe the expanse it covered was once a desert. Rolling dunes of soft black sand south of Hinhallow once expanded nearly the entire western coast of Ellorhys. Now, as far as the eye could see, a jagged and uninhabitable ocean of blackish-purple glass stretched into the distant horizon.

Nothing survived out there. No plants. No animals. It was truly a wasteland, a scar on Ellorhys that marked the end of dark times. From her towers within the crystal palace, Issaria had thought it looked as though the ocean had been frozen in time, jagged and razor sharp after being harrowed by salt wind off the Lanzauve Sea for five hundred years.

Shaking the fearful thought from her head, Issaria sprang off the tree and used the momentum to propel her into the final sprint. Ahead, she identified the crystal formation she was searching for and—

"I hope," an ethereal, motherly voice echoed around her, "you're not thinking of using that staircase, my sweet moon drop?"

Issaria spun, looking for the source of the familiar voice, but it came from nowhere, and everywhere. "Aunt Cate?"

Ever-regal in a shimmering floor-length gown of black silk Countess Hecate Messorem, her mother's younger sister, stepped into view, just ahead of her in the trees. Her dark eyebrows arched inquisitively as she folded clasped hands before her, a vision of understanding. "Are you sneaking out to the Star Festival?" Her full lips parted in smile and the twinkle in her silver-blue eyes made Issaria think her aunt already knew the answer was yes.

"How did you know?"

Hecate laughed, a light, trilling snicker as she emerged from shadow into shimmering moonbeams. Silver light crowned the curls of her raven hair through the branches. "I didn't, but Elon Sainthart did, as always." She tipped her head to the left, a bemused expression on her face. "I only had to determine the where," she teased. She dipped back into shadow and appeared several feet away, closer to the crystal formation that hid the staircase. "Luckily, I possess magic unlike those of common magicians," she began, fading back into velvet, "and am able to reach my destination much quicker," she finished, appearing back where she began.

"That's clever," Issaria said, shifting her weight to one foot and crossing her arms over her chest. "But if that were true Elon would have caught me by now."

Hecate eyed a thicket of trees behind her, and Issaria turned again, peering into the darkness behind her. "You followed her this far, Cadet. If you were going to stop her you would have by now." Hecate appeared to be talking to the arbor's many trees until Elon emerged from the darkness and stepped into view, looking sheepish as he ruffled his coppery curls.

He was tall and lanky, having hit his growth spurt this summer, but Issaria knew how swift and skilled he was with the sword that hung on his hip. He kept his emerald gaze on the dewy grass underfoot. "I would have stopped her," he began, but Aunt Cate cut him off with a wave of her hand.

"Oh, come now, boy. The whole court knows how you two are together. Issaria would have convinced you to go with her. So, both of you. . ." She took a breath and nodded once, seeming to assure herself more than the children that this was a sound decision, "Just go. Two hours, no more. At midnight, I will see you both back here, yes? Our little secret?"

Both children nodded, grins spread wide across their faces.

"Wonderful. Then enjoy the festival, children," she said, and they rushed past her, eyes alight with the possibilities of the Star Festival.

Seven days of celebration were hosted in the capitol city to honor the anniversary of the first Imperials, the Primordial Magicians Aurelia and Obsidia. Fashioned in the likeness of mortal magicians, they were sent by the Ethereal Mythos, Dovenia and her consorts, Chronos and Essos, and flew across the Cosmos to Ellorhys on a shooting star to liberate magicians from the oppression and corruption of the Elemental Mythos. It was the heat from their comet that left the Glass in its wake as their star impacted into the site that would later become the crystal palace. It was this Starfall, as the event became known, that rendered the Elemental Mythos extinct, and gave their magic to everyone in Ellorhys...if they survived the Godsplague.

Aurelia and Obsidia had restored balance through equal parts gift and curse. They righted wrongs and triumphed over evil while exacting a blood toll on the land. Such were the ways of Mythos, and the first imperials were more Mythos than magician. Primordial, her mother said, the divine right to rule. Something *other*.

Her parents were nothing like that.

And neither was she.

Issaria and Elon rounded the crystal hiding the staircase leading *inside* the wall and surrounding the palace. Elon took the lead, his hand on the hilt of his sword, the princess on his heels.

"Princess Issaria?"

She stopped just short of vanishing into the facets of the crystal cluster. "Yes, Aunt Cate?" she asked, looking over her shoulder at her beloved countess.

Hecate's hands wrung together at her chest, and her face creased with worry as she said, "Keep your hood up, and Mythos willing, do be safe."

Issaria smiled and nodded. "Of course. I have Elon with me. He'd never let anything happen," she replied confidently.

It was true. Four years her elder, Elon aspired be the captain of her personal guard one day, her *Sanguinem Defendier*, as his adoptive father was to her own father, Imperial Emperor Helios. Already, he took his nomination from Soren Sainthart very seriously and tailed the princess wherever she went. Issaria was just glad he still treated her like she was his friend.

Aunt Cate smiled and nodded. "Of course. Go on then. Two hours! Don't make me regret letting you go, moon drop."

"Two hours," Issaria confirmed before following Elon into the staircase. The pair descended into the passage, zigging right, zagging left, following the sharp spiral of the staircase as it routed itself around passages used by the soldiers defending the crystal palace. Issaria kept one hand on Elon's back while he navigated the pitch-black corridor by touch.

"Do you," Elon's voice was gentle in the pitch dark, "want to try a *Radiata?*"

Issaria bit her lip. As a Terra magician, Elon was unable to harness light for them. A *Radiata* should have been a simple spell to illuminate, even children could use them if they were fire magicians, and certain storm magicians could sustain a spark. Born of Imperial blood, Issaria should have been able to harness all dimensions of the four elemental magics, but she hadn't attempted the spell since she burned her tree-house to the ground three years ago. She could access her mana, but it was unstable, volatile and disastrous, often resulting in injury and destruction.

"If you don't want to try it I could use a Lux," he offered, recanting his first idea.

"NO—no. If... if you feel safe I could give it a try?"

Elon stopped short.

Issaria walked straight into his backside. "Ow! Elon—" Then she felt his hand on her shoulder.

In the dark, he patted down her arm until his fingers found her hand. He entwined his hand in hers and squeezed it tight. "Princess, I will *never* fear you." He paused, and Issaria felt her heart hammering in her chest. "Or your power."

The silence in the darkness was deafening. She wished she could see his face and get some sort of read on what he meant. Was this only because Soren had nominated him as her *defendier* and her father had joyously agreed? Was it because he...cared for her?

Heat rushed into her face and suddenly, she was glad for the darkness. She knew he didn't think of her that way; she was just a kid to him. His little sister, even, given the age difference between them. But to her, Elon Sainthart was *everything*—which was even more upsetting when she thought of how her parents were considering a betrothal to the prince of Hinhallow on her behalf. Princess Issaria wished nothing more than to grow up and fall in love with Elon, her stable boy turned knight-in-shining-armor, make him her Emperor Consort, and rule Ellorhys in peace and prosperity like her parents before her.

Just as she wondered if she was supposed to say something, Elon broke the silence with a bleating laugh before finishing, "If I'm to die in this tunnel in some fireball of yours, then that's just how I go!"

"Elon!" Issaria scowled and launched a blind fist into the darkness, glancing the playful punch off his arm. "That's not funny! It could really happen!"

"I know. I remember the treehouse, *and* half the orchard going up in flames!" he exclaimed, squeezing her hand again. "But seriously." His voice dropped all tone of amusement and she felt his breath on the top of her head. He had closed the distance between them. "I trust you, Issa," he whispered. "Give the spell a try if you feel confident."

She lingered there, feeling his exhale ruffling her bangs as she considered the offer. Did she feel confident? Not after his joke. But then...could she feel the aura from the stars and the moon even hidden away inside the tunnel? Magic was said to be strongest during the Sacred Rites of the year, the seasonal festivals celebrating the cosmic changes, and Starfall, signifying the new year, would be the most powerful of all.

But if magic was stronger, that also meant it would be stronger for *her*. Even harder to control than normal. Issaria pressed her hand into Elon's chest to distance him again. "No. Not tonight. Let's just get to the festival."

"Suit yourself." Rolling the moment off, Elon started down the passage again, only releasing her hand when he was certain she was following him again. "Now which one is the Lux?" he mused aloud as he snapped open a loop on his tactical belt and considered the contents of the shattersphere. She heard a gentle rattle before the charcoal sparked into blazing embers against the Solarium inside the glass bulb.

As the illumination began to glow red-orange, Issaria felt her heart skip a beat as the satisfied smirk on his face came into view. He was happy to be able to use one of his alchemic creations and proud of the successful result. The recipe was an easy one, and while many magicians used Lux, only the alchemists made them and this one Elon had created himself. She'd memorized the recipe as he weighed the ingredients nearly two moons ago.

"Right, well now that we can see, we'll be there in no time," he said as they navigated the twisting passageway.

Like the palace, the crystals that bordered it were purple in color, shifting from deep plum, near black even, where it was thickest to a sheer lilac at its thinnest parts, allowing more light to pass through. The shift of light played across the planes of the crystal casting hesitant shadows and shimmers, changing the shape of the passage from one step to the next. First one thinks there is a left ahead, and then you realize that doorway was a trick of the light, and the tunnel continues to the right. Issaria realized that perhaps traversing this path by touch was easier, when a glint of light ahead lifted her gaze from beyond the gentle glow of the Lux enclosed in Elon's fist.

"C'mon, Elon, hurry up! I see the exit!"

"Okay, okay," he said, but his pace didn't change.

Issaria huffed. He never hurried anything.

Unable to extinguish the light, Elon stuffed the Lux into a pocket of his tunic, the glow dim like a captured star through the weave of the linen. They lingered in the mouth of the passageway before Elon put a finger to his lips, reminding her to remain silent. She resisted the urge to roll her eyes, having been thoroughly lectured on safety and stealth her entire life, but instead obeyed and leaned back into the darkness of the jagged stairway. Elon stepped out into the night, and peered around the edge of the cluster of crystal that hid the doorway from view. When he was satisfied the way was clear, he waved her forward, took her hand and led her down the final staircase, appearing to walk down the outside of the wall on invisible stairs and out into the night.

2

ELON

They emerged from between the hedges dividing two elegant cottages in a neighborhood burrow of Espera and took to the cobblestone streets. Down the tree-lined path, they came to the crest of a hill, giving them a full view of the rolling hills of the seaside city. The houses, like most of the buildings in Espera, featured domed rooftops polished in various metallic hues, giving the skyline a jewel-laden appearance amongst the trees and cobbled streets. Street lamps glowed at regular intervals in burrows on the distant hill, illuminating corners of homesteads like shifting ghosts among the silhouettes of trees. Beside him, Issaria sighed contentedly at the sight and he cast her a sideways glance.

You could tell just by looking at her how much she loved everything about her gentle, vibrant, Celestial City. She wasn't some pampered princess who kept to her towers. Issa loved her people, the energy and texture of Espera. Being among them, one of them, Elon saw a side of the princess he was certain only he knew.

"I can't believe Countess Hecate let you go," he mused, breaking up the sound of summer crickets singing in the starry night.

"Really? Aunt Cate loves me," Issaria replied, surprised, then added more candidly, "Then again, I think she likes the mischief I get into.

Whenever Mother and Father scold me for my," she threw air quotes up with her fingers as she mimicked her father's deep, scolding voice, "*antics*," before continuing on as herself, "I always catch her hiding a smile from them."

Elon was silent for a moment and then said, "Mother and Father. Like you're just some village girl." If only.

Issaria grinned. "Tonight, I *am* a simple village girl."

He examined her pointedly. Could she pass as a village girl? Her eyes were a dead give away. Only the Imperial family, those descended from Aurelia had those entrancing purple eyes; Imperial Emperor Helios, bronzed skin and golden haired, also bore the imperial eyes. By luck or chance, Issaria's sable hair was inherited from her mother's side, and was a fairly common color. She had dressed subtly in a short indigo chiton, a linen dress commonly worn in the warm southern cities. Her cloak was black, and fastened at her throat with a simple alloy clasp, and the oversized hood shadowed her brilliant irises. For being the pinnacle of royalty, she had learned to obscure herself quite well.

Elon scoffed. Her Ethereal Grace, the Imperial Princess Issaria Elysitao, walking the streets—city streets that would be filled with foreigners celebrating the country's most sacred of festivals in the capitol—with only a *teenage cadet* to protect her. "If that's the case, a village girl would raise suspicions enjoying a festival with her hood up. Put it down." She did. He considered her again, then nodded and said, "Take the comb out of your hair. Leave it long and wild. Let the curls hide your eyes."

Issaria stared at him, her violet gaze blank. "That what the hood was for, rock head."

Elon rolled his eyes. "Yes, let's just shout from the roof tops that we want to hide who you are."

She freed the alloy butterfly comb from her hair, spilling her tangle of spirals around her shoulders, framing her face in raven-colored tresses. Elon held her gaze a little longer than usual before he swallowed and said, "Yes. This should do just fine. Stay by my side, and don't look anyone in the eye; only look at what people are doing."

He offered her his hand, and she took it, falling into line like his little sister. Issamarya and Elyott, well-worn identities created to protect her.

As the pair neared the city's bazaar, multi-colored paper lanterns strung tree-to-tree cast a flickering glow across the cobbled street. Sounds from the festival's crowd began to overtake the crickets, and when they rounded the next corner, they could see the glow of the festival over the rooftops. Thunderous drums battled rhythms against the flighty trills and arpeggios of an Aresian flute. The music swelled in the air, bringing with it the syrupy sweet aroma of *surrepan*, a sticky bun from Rhunmesc that Issaria loved, and the laughter and cheers of the festival goers.

Issaria squeezed Elon's hand as they shouldered their way into the crowd and began meandering the labyrinth of spice mongers, wine sellers and crafts-magicians showing their trade in textiles, alloys, housewares, and more. The vibrant colors and cacophony of sounds had Issaria tugging on his hand as she wended through the crowd, likely thrilled to be set free from the palace. They could hear the clang of bells as games of strength and agility were won, the bartering of prices, how many Metals each product was worth. At an intersection of tents and stalls, Issaria released him and weighed the leather pouch tied to her zoster, feeling the coins within. Likely an insane amount of Metals for a girl her age to be carrying.

Eyes wide and cheeks rosy, she looked up at him and rattled off in one overexcited breath, "I want to buy some sweets, and play the fish-catching game, and watch a beastmaester performing with their familiar!"

"All right, let's play some games first. We can cut through over here."

They passed by a Rhunish merchant selling fur cloaks from the far north, something alluring and elegant, but much too heavy for the temperate climate of the southern cities. Another stall brought flashy daggers and knives forged in Sorair, while the next booth offered samplings of wines from the vineyards in Ares. Issaria barely glanced at the tent selling spit-roasted boar from Hinhollow, but Elon's mouth watered at the savory scent of garlic, watercress and rosemary mingling with the smoky tang of meat. Meat was a rare treat in Espera, as it mostly came from the forests beyond the Glass. Fish and vegetation were the staple diet of the Esperian citizens, while the outer villages farmed. For the Star Festival, all the delicacies from the cities of Ellorhys were brought to the capitol. The boar in that tent was probably alive that morning.

"Oh! Over there!" Issaria slipped her hand from Elon's grip and wove between the perusing patrons.

"Issamarya!" Elon elbowed around a Rhunish man wielding an entire roasted leg of wild boar like a club as he wandered between merchant's booths.

The barrel-bellied merchant rose from his stool in the back where he was threading beads onto an alloy wire. "Blessed be, little miss," he said in a gruff voice.

"You can't slip away from me like that!"

She had raced over to a gauzy booth draped in sheer silks from Hinhallow and traced her fingers along the glittering baubles and crafted jewelry bearing precious stones and gems. On a wooden shelf next to an array of prayer candles, colorful stone carvings of the Elemental Mythos were arranged in a neat array of colors and poses. Naia the ocean nymph diving deep; Zephyrus the great storm bird with winds outstretched; Fiery Tarlix prowling the dunes of the Ascalith, the flames of his mane whipping in the desert winds; lumbering Baelfor, the forest-sower with all the plants and creatures of Ellorhys living in the forest on his back.

"I'm sorry Elyott," she began, establishing their identities since it was clear the merchant might remember them later. "I just saw the shinys and I…" she finished with a shrug.

Frustrated, but knowing now was not the time, he shook his head, and rolled his eyes. A peeved sibling. She leaned over the table, allowing her bangs and hair to obscure her eyes from the Hollowvanian's curious stare. "Oh these are very pretty," she commented, running her fingers across the display of rings, and soon the merchant was watching her hands for theft instead of her face. A flicker of pride lit in his chest. He'd taught her that move.

"I like this one though." She pulled a delicate strand of alloy studded with iridescent pearls and little glass beads that reflected light in little prisms from the table and laid it across her wrist, admiring it against her ivory skin. "How much for the bracelet?"

"Good eye, little miss! Pretty thing for a pretty girl," the craftsmagician said, stepping into his secondary role as a salesman as well as an artisan. "I harvested those pearls from the mouth of the Cyth myself!" he boasted, tucking his thumbs into the wide crimson zoster at his waist. "But, I'm afraid that one is a Gold and three Silvers," he finished solemnly, shaking his head in disappointment.

Elon took the bracelet from Issaria's wrist and examined the craftsmanship up close. He was looking at the welding between the alloy links, the way the pearls were secured by tiny screws, and that the glass beads dangled securely. All metalwork in Ellorhys was to be done by the forge, not magic, by Imperial Law to prevent the tampering or forgery of Metals. It was easy to be fooled into buying shoddy craftsmagic, but Elon was not only a cadet and skilled soldier, he was an Alchemist, a specialized type of craftsmagician and his scrutiny was ruthless. After threading link by link in front of his keen eye, Issaria smiled when he handed it back to her with a short nod. "It's a good piece, sir. You're the magician who crafted it?"

The merchant puffed up his chest. "I am!"

"If Elyott says it is good work, then it is worth the Metals," Issaria said as she pulled the thick coins from her purse.

The merchant's eyes were wide as the princess handed him the currency. He took the money, hands trembling as his mind worked out the equation before him. Elon fastened the clasp around her wrist, and they turned to leave.

"My Lady," the merchant whispered in awe, "Pray-tell, your Grace?" When neither of the children replied, he continued, "Which house does this generous patronage come from?"

Issaria, having kept her eyes low, glanced to Elon, seeking his approval. Elon narrowed his eyes, and examined their surroundings before giving her a very subtle nod. In response Issaria met the merchant's waving gaze with her vivid violet eyes—he gasped—all the confirmation he needed.

"Keep it a secret until we leave the festival, though?" she asked, innocent as a lamb.

With the subtlest of bows, a slight inclination of his head, the merchant grinned and whispered, "Of course, Princess. Yes, of course." And Elon knew he would. He'd brag about it in the next port, of course, but he would keep his tongue while in Espera. "I am honored to have been blessed by your generosity. Had I known it was you upon your arrival, you could have had anything you wanted for nothing!" He hesitated a moment then said, "Would you take anything else with you today? A statuette of yourself, perhaps? I carved it by hand to ensure your likeness, though you are much lovelier than your portrait provided." Flattery poured from his lips as he turned his back to them to search his stores for the trinket.

While the merchant was busy, they slipped back into the crowd, slowing only when they were several stalls away and rounding a corner between the shop stalls and the gambling stalls. Colorful banners announced games of chance and displayed prizes of elementia stones and Metals. For the children they offered rows of toys, puzzles, or bags of assorted candies. The princess's eyes glistened with the beauty of it all.

"Oh Elon! Please say we can play a game!" Issaria shouted, her excitement for a prize overtaking her senses.

"Issamarya," Elon growled, reminding her of their identities. She cringed and he continued, "I'm not sure if Father gave us enough metals to play too many games, but I'm sure we can play at least one." His expression softened and he said, "Go ahead and pick a game, Issa, but only one. I want to go see at least one duel before we have to go home. I think some of the Imperial Guards might participate this year."

Issaria nodded, agreeing to the schedule for their remaining time. "But which one?" she pondered as they perused the stalls, passing by ring-toss games and target games that challenged a magician's precision but rewarded raw chunks of elementia on leather cords as a reward. Ahead of them a crowd gathered beneath a bright blue banner framed by two large, wobbling globes of water in which live fish were swimming happily. Stock for the *Chartarete*, the paper-net game from Rhunmesc, as written on the banner. The game, though it required no magic to play, offered a lunafish as the prize to the child who could scoop a fish into a jar before their paper net tore.

"That one!" She squealed, pointing to the stall before grabbing Elon's sleeve and rushing him along. Intentionally, he leaned backward against her, slowing her progress. "C'mon, *Elyott*," she urged, remembering to use his alias.

"I can't. Gravity—it's too powerful!"

"Fine!" She released her grip on his tunic sleeve. "You can catch up," Issaria quipped as she darted across the aisle of booths to the Chartarete stall before a meandering crowd of tourists intersected the aisle.

Elon snapped back to attention as he lost sight of her. "Hey! Issaria, I didn't—I was just messing with you!"

He tried to elbow his way into the clogged corridor, but the burly group of Hollowvanians were rowdy and drunk from the tasting stalls. Crowded around a test of strength that offered a hundred silver Metals to the magician who could lift a massive polished boulder of jade, they cheered on one of their compatriots as he assumed a squatting position to heft the ore onto his shoulders, unaware that they were blocking his path. "Excuse me, I just need to—no, that's fine, I'll just go over—Ouch!"

He managed to elbow his way through and limped over to where Issaria was crouched between the other children, deep in concentration with a paper net in one hand and a glass jar in the other. She leaned over the basin of water, at least a dozen black and white spotted lunafish swimming lazily before her. Elon smiled as she lowered the mouth of the jar toward the water careful not to spill the water inside back into the basin, poised to catch the fish she intended to scoop.

In a quick flick of her wrist, she dipped the paper net into the water, startling the group of lunafish. The surface of the water erupted into ripples and splashes as panicked fins breached the surface trying to escape. "Oh!" Issaria jumped and rocked back on her heels to keep her balance. Wet and giggling, she looked up at him and smiled before asking, "One more time?"

"Once more."

Without moving from her crouched position, Issaria reached into her purse and pulled out three copper Metals and handed it to one of the game's three attendants, who traded the coins for a second paper net. Resuming her position above the fish, Issaria was focused on the game.

Elon let his eyes wander. A bored brother looking for the next entertaining thing to do while his sister tried for a fish. The rowdy Hollowvanians had moved on down the row to another game booth and were again cheering on another of their friends while sloshing drinks on themselves. In the next booth over a group of girls his own age were celebrating a victory in a racing game, jumping up and down. He turned and observed the path down which they'd come. Magicians milled back and forth, eating surrepan or drinking wine, no one in particular paying them any attention. He turned his attention back to his charge.

She had a fresh paper net in her hand, and he had the distinct feeling she had snuck another try from the attendant while his back was turned. The devious girl.

"We have a winner!" Another attendant shouted across the tent, drawing his attention past the groups of children and parents around fish-filled basins.

"Yay! You did it, Zaid!" a mother cheered across the game tent as her chubby boy managed to get a lunafish into his jar. The attendant took the boy's jar and secured a lid on it before tying a short blue ribbon around the rim, making a makeshift handle for him to carry his new pet.

Elon's breath caught in his throat.

Beyond the happy family were a pair of men who wore their hoods up, looking just as suspicious as he thought it would. And they were staring at Issaria.

Elon had to be imagining it. He was paranoid. They were just foreigners watching the games. He looked back down at the princess, and then back to the men, who were now talking to each other, sinister scowls on their faces.

The hairs on his arms stood on end. He was not imagining it.

He stepped back from Issaria, behind the family to their left, to watch the pair. They pointed at her. He was certain one was reaching inside his cloak for a weapon. If they noticed him, they didn't seem to realize he was a problem.

"Cosmos above!" Issaria cursed as she failed to catch a lunafish again, splashing her chiton more than she had the first two times.

He had to get her out of here. Fast.

Elon took a breath and stepped up, crouching behind the princess. "Okay, okay. Let an old pro show you how it's done, Issamarya," he said as he took the copper Metals from his pocket and handed them off for a paper net. "You see, the trick is," he started loudly as he let Issaria hold the net, then he took her hand in his. He leaned in close to her, and when his mouth inches from her ear, he whispered, "Don't panic. Don't look. Keep smiling. Keep watching the fish."

"What's going on?"

"We have trouble. I have to get you back to the palace. We have to go now. As soon as we finish this game, we're going to move slowly, calmly, like we are *not* being followed. Head toward the south entrance, and we will loop back through the burrows to the staircase when I'm certain we've lost them."

"And if they catch us?"

Elon didn't respond. Instead, he dipped the paper net into the basin and tried to flip a fish into the jar in Issaria's waiting hand. "Oh no!" he exclaimed as the paper net tore and the fish slipped back into the basin. "Guess I'm not as much of a pro as I thought," he finished lamely as he pulled Issaria to her feet. "Let's go watch some duels!"

They had just begun moving toward the festival's south entrance, when the bells tolled out over the city. Around them, the confusion of the siren evaporated the joy from the crowd and panic set in. Issaria looked to Elon, her luminous complexion now moon-white as the sharp peal of the siege siren hushed the festival, foreigners and Esperians alike. Confusion echoed through the crowd, how was there a siege? This was the Star Festival, and nothing was amiss!

But the children knew better. This was no accident. The siren was old spell magic, a ward left on the palace, on the whole city, after Aurelia was slaughtered at her sister's hand. The Black Arts was the only thing that would trigger it.

Shouts and screams began to resound from the pockets of people littering the festooned bazaars.

"Damnit," Elon cursed as he grabbed her hand and charged ahead.

They bobbed and weaved through the stricken crowd, ducking between stalls and behind merchants and patrons alike as they backtracked through the festival, trying to stay ahead of the men Elon had seen. Sticking to the sides of buildings and keeping to the shadows as much as they were able to, they kept their heads down when they came to cross-streets. Intermingled with large groups of festival patrons trying to flee the bazaar back to the safety of homes and rooms at the inns, Elon and Issaria ducked between the tents, sliding between the colorful canvas sheets that divided the tasting tents. Decadent smells of festival foods wafted around them, festival joys forgotten in the frenzy. Issaria wrinkled her nose. Underneath the smell of saltwater candies from Hinhallow, and lavish cakes from Ares, the stench of burning was strong, and several columns of black smoke billowed into the sky from around the city.

"What do we do, Elon?" Issaria asked, her voice strained with panic.

"We have to go back to the palace, but if the palace is compromised, we might be walking into a trap."

"We have to go back! My parents are in there! Your. . ." she hesitated before finishing, "Soren is there."

He nodded once, his brow furrowed, emerald eyes distant as he calculated their next moves. "We have to be careful when we get inside, but I think I know a way. We still have to lose the goons, or at least delay them long enough for us to—" Over her shoulder, the men rounded the corner of the tasting stalls grabbing every frantic black-haired woman and girl they saw. "They're desperate to find you now. They don't care who sees them."

"Elon!" Issaria began but Elon hushed her with one look.

"I will not let anything happen to you," he said as he grabbed her wrist again, the familiar and welcome notion becoming more of a panicked response. "But right now, we have to go." He was already dragging her through the hysterical crowd as she struggled to gain her bearings.

"I need my hands! Can you keep up?" he shouted to be heard above the commotion.

"Yes! Just go!" Issaria snatched her hand back from him and kept close as they weaved through the chaos.

In tandem, they ran through the fleeing crowd, Elon in the lead, fidgeting with his tactical belt as they ran, trying to formulate the correct composition to use. Overhead, the resounding wail of the siege siren stopped, but the echo lingered over the city like a banshee's wail, haunting long after it had faded. They looked to the towers of the palace, glittering with the lights from the chambers within. What-ever had set the sirens off was done, but they night was far from over.

Several blocks from the bazaar Elon Sainthart and Princess Issaria slumped, chests heaving and breath ragged, against the alley walls between a popular armory and an equally acclaimed jeweler on the southern edge of Espera. Beyond the shops lay the boardwalk, and the docks before giving way the Southern Sea. The chaos of the festival fires was a dull roar over the rolling ocean waves crashing into the boardwalk. From here it was a straight shot to the Temple.

Elon edged to the corner of the building and peeked around the corner, estimating the distance they had to sprint. While most of the festival was celebrated in the bazaar, the path to the Temple of Aurelia from the festival was illuminated by the same strings of paper lanterns, little solarium hearts flickering in the breeze. The crossroads with the lanterns was at least a hundred yards away.

Not a soul was in sight, but he knew not to trust his eyes.

"We should just go now. Forget the—"

"Shh!" Elon's hand flew over Issaria's mouth, silencing her.

"You rottin' numbskull. You sed she was over e're! Ain't nothin' over e're but storefronts!"

"She is! I saw the two of 'em come through that alley into this here square," the second replied. "They came through here, I swear it!"

The voices were getting closer.

"Then where they at? Where they gone?"

Issaria sucked in a breath as the first man came into view. He stood several feet from the mouth of the alley, in the courtyard of the shopping burrow through which they'd come. If he looked to his left, he would see them for certain.

"Why don't you look for a change? The bleedin' princess wasn't suppose to be this hard to kill! She's a kid for Mythos sake." The second man stepped into view, facing their direction, but the first man turned to face him, and his broad stature obscured his shorter associate's view of the alley.

"Yer tellin' me. I thought I'd be home counting my Metals by now."

The pair were silent for a moment. Issaria and Elon held their breath.

"You think she made it back to the palace?"

"Better hope not," the first man replied. "C'mon. Let's search the square. You say she came this way? I believe ye. Let's root the little bitch out."

Issaria whimpered.

The men turned, and there were only moments to react.

"There!" The first one pointed. "Get her!"

Pushing Issaria up to her feet he shoved her ahead of him, as the assassins charged down the narrow alley. A fireball charred the side of the armory as Elon slipped around the corner, tossing a gleaming shattersphere over his shoulder.

The bulb hit the cobblestone at the feet of the assailants.

Silver foam bubbled from within, expanding like a dense cloud. It swallowed their feet first, slowing their momentum, until it reached their torsos where the metallic shine faded to a flat grey.

"What in the Cosmos is this?" Elon heard one of them exclaim, dumbfounded by his transmutation.

Hot on Issaria's heels, he shouted, "Go, go, go!" but he wished he could have seen their faces as the seemingly gentle foam hardened into a rock-like substance, stopping them in their tracks.

Issaria needed no encouragement. She was at end of the last shop on the row, already soaring over the top of the hedge, the hem of her cloak dragging across the white blossoms, scattering petals behind her like snowflakes. She reached the temple, and darted into its open gates.

Elon skidded around the corner and started toward the cavernous opening in the crystal tower that served as the doorway to the temple, its great alloy doors permanently swung open in welcome to those who would seek the guidance of the Mythos.

"Over here!" Issaria hissed, and he spun around, frantic eyes scanning the shadows for her figure.

She had pressed herself against the wall behind the gate, nearly invisible in the thick shadows.

"I got them caught up in a swift-stick foam I cooked up from some silex and a lightning based zephryrite elementia—" he caught himself and shook his head. "It won't stop them for long. We have a head start for now." He started toward the temple again. "Let's vanish while we still can."

The Temple of Aurelia, formerly the Temple of Mythos, was an annex of the palace, a small spire of crystal that never made it into the palace's overall design due to its place outside the walls. Its moniker changed to bear Aurelia's name after Obsidia fell from grace. Her name, her dark magic, and anything associated with it was shunned, and it seemed magicians and Imperials alike sought to erase her memory from history. Even Countess Hecate's moon magic was feared, often confused with Obsidia's dark magic, though Elon had never seen her perform more than a parlor trick or two with it. He wasn't sure she was all that powerful, even if she was an Imperial.

The temple's courtyard was dark, and the temple inside the spire darker still. Across the threshold, the room opened into a wide semi-circle, with an aisle of pillars guiding visitors toward the back of the temple. Sections of the hall were illuminated by the glow of votives in the four alcoves carved into the walls, and sconces hung in intervals around the congregation hall. Each vestibule was a smaller chapel, glittering with candles lit in prayer, one for each of the Elemental Mythos. In the back, on a dais behind an altar was an immense, white marble statue of Aurelia. A lithe, long haired woman with hands outstretched, palms up toward the cosmos. A gentle smile turns up at the corners of her mouth. Originally, she had shared the central dais with a black marble statue of equal magnificence, but like everything that represented Obsidia, it too had been destroyed.

At Aurelia's massive marble feet were offerings left in prayer: fresh bouquets of flowers, among others in various stages of wilt, pillar candles with herbs and spells imbedded into their wax, and a wide variety of raw gemstones, crystal clusters, and metals. Tribute left for the Mythos above and below. Behind the massive likeness of the Mythos of Light, a waterfall poured down from a glorious carving of a stormy sky in the crystal ceiling far above.

The sight of it brought Elon back to the last time they'd been here together. Being privy to the workings of the city, a younger and more mischievous princess had learned that this particular waterfall was a recycled and purified product of a filtering system to cleanse the city's water, and descends straight down through the floor into a massive basin. Submerged deep at the bottom of this basin the largest Aquathyst they'd ever seen had been enchanted to feed the city's springs, bathing houses, public wells, and multiple decorative fountains in the burrows of the city with clean, fresh water of the purest source.

It was a glorious swimming hole if one could brave the leap.

The roar of the waterfall was quieted in the sacred space by an ancient *obice*, a powerful sound barrier meant to soften the echo of the torrent, and so it sounded as though a mere stream of water were pouring down from the temple's ceiling. Rainfall.

Together, Elon and Issaria crossed the veil of the barrier spell, and the roar of the waterfall was unleashed upon them. Deafening. Mist dotted their skin as they crept along the rim of the splash pool, the polished incline in the floor that served as the drain through which the waterfall plunged. Careful to hug the wall, they inched behind the waterfall so that they were obscured from view if the assassins were to come into the temple.

Elon looked to Issaria and told her to jump, but the words were drowned out by the eternal echo of the waterfall, caged in its own barrier of silence. Frustrated, he pointed to Issaria and then pointed to the drain.

She had to jump first.

Swallowing hard, she sat down on the rim and let the icy spray drench her legs as she peered over the edge. The last time they made this jump, the impact had taken the wind from her lungs and Elon had pulled her from the pool and breathed for her until she coughed up the water she'd swallowed. She looked back up at him, eyes wide, and he knew she was remembering too. He'd made her promise to never come back here. Not like this.

Issaria swallowed hard and quirked the left side of her mouth into a reluctant smirk before shoving herself into the darkness below.

The waterfall swallowed her.

Elon crouched on the rim of the pool and waited for her to surface. The seconds ticked by and still she hadn't breached the surface. Heart in his throat, Elon feared that he'd land on her if he jumped too soon, or perhaps if he waited too long she'd drown anyway.

And then he saw her face breach the surface, a pearl amidst the black. Issaria reached a hand out of the water to signal his attention, and moments later he plunged over the rim. The fall pulled Elon's terror from his chest for a few exhilarating seconds before he splashed down into the reservoir, pushed deep into the pool by the immense pressure of the waterfall. Eyes closed, Elon kicked hard to free himself from the churning water.

Elon broke the surface closer to the shore of the underground lake, and Issaria paddled over. "Are we safe?" she asked as she swam toward him.

Down in the basin, the waterfall echoed against itself in a deafening roar. The rippling pool glistened in the darkness, harnessing light from the open portal high above to reflect upon the ceiling of the cave and illuminate the space in pale light. Elon's eyes darted around the cavern. After adjusting to the darkness, he began to define the space of the massive grotto. The shore was on the other side of the pool from where they treaded water and rose like a cliffside out of the basin. The last time they were here the reservoir level was much higher, and they had merely flopped out of the water like gutted fish.

Elon and Issaria looked between each other and the ceiling before breaking into hysterical giggles that ricocheted around the cavern like the laughter of ghosts.

But the dark reality of their narrow triumph silenced them, and they locked eyes, the somber mood gripping them both. "Let's get moving. Should the assassins follow us, we want to be long gone by the time they get here," Elon said as he jerked his thumb over his shoulder. "That climb doesn't exactly look like a cakewalk."

They swam to the edge of the pool and looked up the steep incline at the side of the basin. It was a ten, maybe fifteen-meter vertical ascent on wet, slippery crystal. Elon looked to Issaria and then back to the wall. "I'll climb up and get a rope—"

"I can do it," Issaria said resolutely.

"It's not that I don't think you can—"

"I know the palace could be dangerous, but I have to know Elon. I have to see for myself what made the siren sound." The desperation in her voice cut through his concern for her safety. "I'll listen to everything you say. I won't make a peep and if we see anything that makes us think the palace isn't safe…we'll run away together," she promised.

Elon didn't say anything but instead took her in. Her chin barely crested the surface, and her breath rippled the water in front of her face. Her eyes were locked on his in fierce determination. Her jaw was set. He knew that look. If he left her here she would just climb up on her own and go into the palace by herself. "Fine. But if we see *anything*, we're out of here. I'm not letting anything happen to you. We'll regroup and figure something out based on what we learn."

Issaria gave him a curt nod before she reached up and found her first hand hold in the crystal. Beside her, Elon found purchase as he heaved his sopping body out of the water and began to climb.

"Here, I've got you," Elon said as he hauled his legs over the top. He crouched, leaning over the side, and gripped her wrist to pull her up as he snagged her waist with his other hand. Collapsing into a heap, the pair rolled over onto their backs and stared up at the shimmering light reflected on the cavern ceiling.

Elon was on his feet first. "Remember—"

"I know, I know," Issaria huffed as she followed him toward the staircase that would lead up and into the palace. "Anything and we're out of here," she recited his command. "I promise. Just…help me find out what's happening."

3

ISSARIA

The staircase from the reservoir emptied into a long dark tunnel that Issaria and Elon sprinted down. Their ragged breaths echoed around them mimicking their own terrified heartbeats, a mockery magnified in their ears. When they reached the end of the corridor, they emerged from behind a woven tapestry in the storehouses in the cellars beneath the kitchens. This particular room housed the kindling and was stacked wall to wall with thick logs and barrels of solarium crystals.

Elon scouted ahead as they wended through the storerooms. He peered around corners and into the adjacent chambers housing wine, cured meats, barrels of grains, and jars of preserved fruits and vegetables. Issaria followed a distance behind, watching and waiting. Keeping her promise to mind his orders.

At the end of the hall, he waved her forward, and Issaria darted down the hall to meet him. Tentatively, the pair crept up the stairs, their ears keened for any sounds to indicate the status of the palace, but their hearing was only met with the stoic crackle of fire in the hearths.

The kitchens were empty. Black smoke churned up the flue as the contents of stewpots and loaves of bread charred in the fire.

Exchanging stricken glances, they raced through the abandoned kitchens, their fear of what they would find propelling them deeper into the bowels of the palace.

By the time they emerged from a stairwell in the servant's corridors of the Grand Hall, silent tears were streaming down Issaria's face as they shoved through the doors and into the palace's throne room. They had yet to encounter a single soul. No guards were at their posts. No staff were wandering the halls. They had anticipated seeing something, but they hadn't prepared for *nothing*.

She pushed into the Grand Hall from the servant's hall running along the side of the space, and stopped short.

The expansive hall carved into the central pillar of the Crystal Palace was packed with the palace staff, the chefs and cooks still caked in flour, maids in their pajamas roused from their sleep. Soldiers taken from their posts and others from the barracks, some with sleep in their eyes, and more wobbled where they stood, drunk from the festival. Issaria glanced at Elon, confused as to the ragtag assembly of Imperial personnel. They had emerged in the back of the hall, in a door built to be obscured so that servants could cater palace events without disturbing the guests. As intended, they had arrived unseen, and the door closed firmly behind them.

Without waiting for Elon's command, Issaria raced around the back of the crowd, searching for a part in the sea of people to catch sight of who stood before on the dais before them all. At last, in the center of the hall, the aisle formed, having cleared a path for a glittering carpet of black up to the dais at the front of the hall where her parents' twin thrones, carved from the meteor that brought Aurelia and Obsidia to Ellorhys, sat empty.

Her pulse echoed in her ears as the staff in the back began to recognize her.

"That's the princess, innit?" a portly servant asked, elbowing his tall friend.

"Oy! That's the princess!" someone shouted, bringing a clamor into the hall as people began confirming her presence among them.

"They didn't catch her!"

31

"Thank the Cosmos!"

"Blessed be!"

Issaria was halfway up the aisle when her aunt stepped into view, looking nothing like herself, disheveled in linen pajamas, crimson blood splattered across the pale fabric. A sword sheathed around her waist and a plate of armor across her chest, completed the strange attire. Her black hair was frazzled, and she looked as though she'd been asleep recently, but Issaria knew only hours ago she'd been dressed in regal finery and dancing from shadow to shadow bidding their curfew.

The fire in her ice blue eyes was real even from a distance.

Issaria lingered in the aisle. Elon drew up beside her, one hand on the princess's shoulder, the other on a small glass bulb on his belt.

"Aunt Cate?" She asked, ashamed in the way her voice wavered.

"Mythos Above! Princess Issaria, it *is* you!" Hecate rushed down the aisle to meet her. "Oh, thank the Cosmos you're alive!" She folded Issaria into a tight embrace, smooshing the side of her face into the cool alloy of her breastplate. "I thought for certain they had gotten to you as well." Hecate pulled back and held her hand up to her lips. "Oh, Issaria...I'm so sorry."

"Where are my parents?" Issaria asked, her voice tight, barely a whisper.

The silence in the hall could have filled an abyss. The eyes of the palace staff, soldiers and sleepy-eyed magistrates visiting from other cities fell heavily upon her. Aunt Cate looked around at the crowd and shook her head. "Issaria...lets go somewhere priv—"

"Are—are they d—dead?" she croaked, her voice breaking like sheets of ice in a spring-thawed river.

Hecate fixed her gaze on her niece and after a steadying breath that shook her chest, she said, "Yes, my sweet. The Emperor and Empress are dead."

Issaria was silent as the words washed over her.

The world seemed to fall away, and deep in her heart, a cold voice she'd never heard before whispered, *This too, shall be avenged. I swear it will be so.*

Dazed and disoriented, she allowed herself to be reclaimed against the cold alloy of her aunt's breastplate. Fat tears rolled down her cheeks and she felt her face flush. "What are we going to do now, Aunt Cate?" she meant to ask, but her question pitched into a bawling wail that carried through the hall.

Whispers sparked through the frightened magicians like black-powder set alight, their panic louder than their joy in announcing her survival.

"Princess Issaria is a *child*."

"Imperial or not, she is not suited to rule the empire so soon!"

"King Akintunde will eat her alive!"

Issaria wrapped her arms around Aunt Hecate's neck and locked them there. Tears streaked down her face as she gasped for breath between heavy, ragged bellows. Hecate sank to the floor with her niece in her arms, but Issaria may have been holding a statue for all the warmth that she felt from the embrace. Cold rage was etched on her aunt's features as she stroked Issaria's snarled matte of wet curls.

"And Sir Soren?" Elon inquired softly. "Is he—"

"Died defending the Imperial Emperor Helios, as was his sworn duty," Hecate snapped, then softened when she added, "He was dead before I arrived. I am sorry for your loss, Sainthart." She paused, then finished loudly, her voice projected across the hall, "As I am sorry to mourn the loss of so many good magicians on this sacred night."

"How?" Elon asked.

"Assassins posing as servants for Mythos knows how long," Hecate spat, disgust evident as she released her grip on her niece and left Issaria to cling, still bawling, to her pajama pant leg, the hem of which was soaked for inches with scarlet as she rose to her feet. "I…I killed them myself. I'm only sorry that I wasn't there sooner." Gingerly, she reached out for her niece again, and touched the girl's head without leaning down too far. "Princess Issaria…Moondrop. I am so sorry I couldn't spare you this horror."

Countess Hecate righted herself and her fury blazed anew. "So sorry that you are forced to endure this unjust sorrow. Your inno-cence ripped away before your very eyes. I am also regretful of the fact that so many brave magicians were senselessly—*thoughtlessly* executed in cold blood to get to the Imperial emperor and empress, *asleep* in their chambers!"

The image conjured by Aunt Cate's words rotted away at her memories. Her mother's sweet face flecked with blood, would smile no more. Lilac eyes stared lifeless at the forest frescoed ceiling they had once lain beneath and pointed out all the animals hidden within. Her father's golden hair soaked with crimson—so much crimson it pooled like tar underneath their bodies. Sheets and dreams stained scarlet. Issaria's chest felt like it were collapsing in on itself and she gasped for breath between heavy sobs.

This couldn't be happening right now. Tonight *couldn't* have been the last time she'd see them, bicker with them, and storm off knowing they knew she'd do it anyway. The last time she'd hear her mother ask her for patience, the last time she'd be cross with her father for telling her she didn't need to go to the festival so late into the night. There was a fist closing around her heart, squeezing so hard she thought it might pop.

She'd been cross with them. And now they were gone.

And she didn't even say goodnight or goodbye...or I love you.

"This was an act of war!" one soldier roused from the barracks shouted.

"Who sent the demons?" a woman cried in question.

"They were good folk! They didn't deserve to go out like this!"

"What will happen to the city?" Gasps and terror seeped across the gathered magicians like a fresh plague.

"They must be coming for us!"

"War is coming!"

"What will we do?"

Scattered screams pierced the mounting fear. In waves, the staff lurched for the exits.

"I WILL RULE!" Hecate's voice boomed, and a ripple of silence rushed over the crowd as they all turned their attention back to their only remaining adult monarch.

Issaria pulled away from her aunt and looked up at her from her crumpled, tear-stained seat on the floor. She hiccuped and sniffed, wiped at her eyes with her trembling hands until her crying had slowed to slow solitary tears sliding silently down her scarlet cheeks.

Hecate's face softened, and she laid a hand on her niece's head again in an effort to console her. "Temporarily," she said when she was sure the crowd had fallen quiet. She stepped past Issaria, and stood her ground between the crowd of magicians on either side of the aisle. "Until Imperial Princess Issaria is of age to take the crown herself, I will guide her and nurture her in my beloved sister's place. I will rule the City of Espera as Empress Regent," Hecate paused for a beat too long then said, "but I will *only* rule the Celestial City of Espera. One of the cities beyond our borders has violated a great trust within our empire and sent assassins to live among us, to *befriend* us. It was a vile sort of cunning I cannot condone."

"What are you saying, Imperial Count—" Magistrate Niroula, a Storm Magi and diplomatic representative from Rhunmesc stopped when Hecate flashed him the fury in her arctic eyes. "Empress Regent?" he squeaked out instead.

"I will not rule such barbarians!" she proclaimed, as the transparent layer of crystal that formed the skylight ceiling high above shattered, sending shards raining down as a single ultraviolet lightning bolt cracked down from the Cosmos. Issaria, Elon, and the closest magicians scrambled backwards to escape the blast.

Frozen lightning called *cosmic filament* crackled and arced through the air around Hecate as she summoned the deepest parts of her mana, gaining access to the mythical primordial magic Imperials were said to possess. Amplified by the newfound and unforetold depth of her mana, she was unhinged, uncaged. Hecate's eyes bled into black from her pupils until the whole of her eyes were dark obsidian stones, reflecting light like diamonds. "I will ensure that no one has the power to harm my family again," her voice boomed, but her lips did not move. "I will do what must be done, as it should have been long ago."

Screams and shouts erupted from the gathered crowd. People closest to the exits began to filter out through the grand arching double-doors in the back of the hall. Those from the front pushed back against the walls to avoid the filaments as they sparkled and surged in orbit around the new empress regent as her amplified state of being levitated her off the ground.

"Aunt Cate!" Issaria shouted from where she crouched on the ground, using her bare arms as a shield against the growing maelstrom of Hecate's dark magic. "What are you doing?"

"What I must to protect you, my sweet moonbeam." Hecate's voice softened, but the volume of her telepathic voice shook the palace itself. "I will bring the Eventide, an eclipse of my own making to bring my protective darkness to the Crystal City." Her proposal, like her concerns for her niece, seemed to come from everywhere, but she did not utter a word. "A darkness that I control, a darkness that will not end with my family's death ever, ever again."

"Eventide?" Issaria looked to Elon, who's horrified eyes were glued past Hecate to the night sky beyond the chamber's now obliterated ceiling.

"You are the last Imperial, and must be cherished so." Hecate, still caught in the tempest of her dark affinity with the night, seemed not to hear the fear in their voices. "I will protect you with all that I am, in penance for failing my dear sister and the Imperial emperor." She returned her attention to the sky, ignoring Issaria's cries below.

Hecate's curse could be heard across the City, "*Lucaelest corpori termasolis!*"

"What is she doing, Elon?"

"The moon! She's taken control of it!"

Issaria wrenched her gaze away from her aunt to the moon. Previously a thin crescent in nebulous star-filled sky, it grew fat and full overhead, transforming through phases that should have taken a month to transpire.

It was unnatural.

By the time the moon was whole, illuminating the palace with its pearlescent face, the only ones left in the Great Hall to bear witness to Hecate's mournful madness were Princess Issaria and Elon Sainthart.

"It's forbidden to alter the Cosmos, Aunt Cate! It's Black Magic!" Issaria begged, "*Please,* Aunt Cate! Don't do this!"

"*Vestra mutare,*" Hecate plowed along with her solitary *cantus,* entranced by her own power. "*Aeturnum obscuratus!*"

In what should have been the wee hours of the morning, when the sun should have crept over the horizon and bathed the land in light, the moon hung low over the southern horizon like a forgotten lure bobbing in the ocean. The indigo sky studded with the same stars that had shined on the festival for centuries remained above them.

The Eventide, a portion of the planet eternally turned toward the dark night of the moon, had fallen.

PART II
A STIRRING IN THE COSMOS

YEAR 3326

4
CALIX

Sunlight beamed through the dayburnt branches of the emaciated forest grove as the broad, crimson-hooded figure led his horse on foot. Prince Calix held the tawny beast's reins loosely in one gloved hand as they navigated the old riverbed. Cracked and dry, the red clay shattered into a scaly, winding bed of dust and dirt that cut an easy path through the scraggly bramble of the copse-dotted countryside. His hood was pulled up to shield him from the brutal rays beating down on him from overhead, but the beads of sweat trickling down his back in rivulets made him want to tempt a summer breeze and remove the protective covering.

But he knew better that to let the heat cook his senses.

He reached for the leather flask lashed to his horn of his horse's saddle, and pulled the cork from the bladder with his teeth, spitting it out so that it swung back and forth on its tether like a pendulum as he tilted his head back, mouth open and ready to receive. . .

A few measly drops of warm water.

Calix swallowed hard, the grit in his throat grinding on itself. He coughed into one hand and with the other, he turned the leather pouch upside down, as if letting whatever water remained fall to the parched earth were better than it being empty.

Nothing happened, and Calix held in a groan.

Sensing his disappointment, his horse nickered then hung her head in order to graze at any withered vegetation that was within reach. As if there was any to be had.

"The city limits are just over the next rise, Arietes," Calix said aloud, assuring his weary steed of the short distance left in their journey instead of himself.

The horse gave no reply, opting to lip futilely at the barren earth instead. Prince Calix sighed and used the hem of his hooded cloak to blot the beads of sweat stinging his eyes. He looked out over the parched valley, branches barren of all but the most stubborn of snarled coverage. He sighed again, this time, in mourning. When he was a boy, this valley was a lush green forest whistling in a refreshing summer zephyr. The river bed through which he walked had flowed slow and fat in this grove, a swirling eddy where he and his companions had lazed away summer days not much cooler than this blistering night.

So much had changed since those peaceful, easy times.

When was the last time Ellorhys had seen a sunset paint the sky with hues of orange and red as the inky evening rose up in the south? When would he once again see the near forgotten constellations of the Cosmos? Would he ever enjoy those simple pleasures again, or would the memory fade, replaced with the bloodthirsty crusade of his father's Celestial Alliance? So bent on the destruction of the Evernight Witch, they failed to lend permanent aid to a failing country, a starving people. Supplies and stores were going to run out eventually.

Had the Mythos forsaken them? Left them to rot on this sunbaked scrap of land, waiting for the red sand of the Ascalith to swallow them whole as the black sands of the Glass had threatened to centuries ago? How much longer did they have before the sun scorched them from the face of Ellorhys?

At last, Prince Calix and his horse plodded wearily to the top of the forlorn valley's last knoll. Skinny trees rattled like bones in the balmy breeze. He shielded his eyes against the glare and looked out over the rolling hills that made up the expansive network of farms on the outskirts of Hinhallow. Dozens of little thatched cottages dotted the arrays of feeble crops. Short stalks bore tiny ears of corn, pea pods with one pea, if any at all. Potatoes rotted in the earth and fruit spotted on the branches, often becoming a feast for the flies instead of a bite for a hungry child. In the distance, surrounded by a bustling city and framed by the glinting western sea, the great spires of the city's white castle rose up to support the gilded onion domes that pierced the sky.

More for his father's expectations than pride, Calix mounted Arietes, slinging his weight clumsily over the saddle. The beast shifted back and forth underneath him, prancing hooves kicked up clouds of dust from the beaten trail that emerged from the woods. He patted the mare's sleek black mane and cooed to comfort and encourage the exhausted creature.

"Easy there, Arietes. Easy does it. You're okay, everything's okay. Shh."

When the horse stilled and accepted that she indeed had the strength to carry him, she whinnied and shook her head, her mane flipping from side to side as her natural energy returned. Prince Calix guided his horse into an easy trot along the trail that would turn into a dirt road through the farmland, and then to a street through the bustling city to the white stone castle he called home.

"We'll be home by midnight," he announced, patting the horse's neck as they passed through the countryside. Even though the sun was high in the midday sky, Calix estimated by the lack of people about in the countryside that it was late by the Ellorhys hour.

Once, the white granite fortress overlooked the seaside City and warded the bountiful countryside whilst boats fished the harbor. Now the opulence of the shimmering domes seemed oppressive, too glamorous as it dominated the desiccated landscape. He knew, though it might not show by casting a wary eye upon the skyline, life within the castle was strained as well. No one could claim it was near as much as his people's suffering, and it pained him to admit that, but tensions were high in the Court of the Flame as the Ballentines struggled to provide for their City.

King Akintunde Ballentine, his father, had summoned an emergency faction of Terran Magistrates from the other cities, but only five of the requested fifty had arrived. The botanists were stretched thin between the struggling cities as many of their ranks had fled to their homes, abandoning their posts to save themselves and their loved ones, if they were able. The Magi that did come, struggled to tend to the thousands of acres of farmland by themselves. He cast a resentful glare at his gloved hands.

It was not the first time he regretted having been born of Tarlix's flame.

If only he had Baelfor's Blessing instead, he would have nurtured the land and the harvest alongside the botanists. But that wasn't the case, and it seemed even Tarlix had turned his back on him, now that the *Sanguinignis Fervent*, the Bloodfire Fever, was slowly consuming his hands from the inside out each time he channeled his mana and ignited his fire talent. Calix clenched his hand into a fist. The strength of his mana was too intense for his mortal magician flesh to contain, and thus it fed on him. Over time, his hands charred black like torched kindling each time he summoned his armament magic.

Lately, the prince had taken to wearing gloves to hide the extent of the damage. At first, he only had nightmares about it happening. And then, one morning he left to scout game trails in the mountains, he saw the red-hot coals beneath the black. Embers glowed within, the heat seeping out through the fissures that had formed at his joints. His hands, exposed to the most heat as they held his flaming scimitars, were the most ravaged of all.

But now the illness and its eventualities seemed like small pains compared to the plight of not just Hinhallow, but of the whole of Ellorhys. Cursed to eternal day while the accursed Glass and the Southern Seas languished in the protective darkness of lavish night thanks to the Evernight Witch Hecate and her black magic. His heart ached for his desperate people. Rumors had reached the Celestial Alliance that the Wildrine Mountains were resistant to the drought that was slowly sapping the realm of life. The prospect that animals migrated there gave way to reasoning as to why none of the hunting parties in Hinhallow could find any game in a fortnight. After a Council meeting his father did not invite Calix to attend, the king volunteered his son, the White City's champion, to charter an expedition to confirm the rumors before flocks of starving refugees wasted away on a quest for naught.

Calix was sorry that his return heralded a poor report. The rumors were just that. The mountains that rimmed the northern border and shielded the ailing vale of the Hollovanian empire from the red sands beyond their peaks were scarce of wildlife, save a skinny squirrel he'd seen preening its wiry tail in a shabby evergreen tree.

He dreaded seeking his father's audience in the morning, but tonight, he looked forward to putting up Arietes in a stable with enough oats and hay for two horses, scrubbing off the stench of his week, and sleeping until the chambermaids woke him with breakfast.

CRIMSON CLOAK SLUNG OVER ONE SHOULDER, PRINCE CALIX CROSSED the courtyard from the stables to the south tower, intent on making it to his chambers without seeing any of the staff. Solarium sconces lit the spiral stone staircase that led to the various floors of the castle. The darkness of the tower washed over him as he closed the heavy wooden door behind him. Sweat-drenched patches on his tunic felt like ice, and he resisted the urge to drop to his knees like a child and press his face and chest to the cool stone walls.

Calix emerged from the stairs into the luxurious dark wood study that served as the reception area to his private chambers, tossed his filthy cloak onto a chaise by his desk, and grimaced when his yellow eyes fell upon Kaddin, one of his father's many attendants.

The small, blond youth dressed in a gold and crimson page uniform, Ballantine's house colors, seemed to be dozing in an armchair near the expansive slate hearth nestled between floor-to-ceiling bookcases against the far wall. He must have sat there for a while, as the clusters of solarium crystals were to provide light in the chamber without warmth, but the king's aide jumped to his feet when the door to the tower banged into the frame behind the prince.

"Oh! It's you!" The boy snatched his crimson beret from atop his head and sunk into a deep bow. "Prince Calix, you've returned!"

"I have, Kaddin. Late for the hour of messages, is it not?"

"A thousand apologies, I know you must be tired from your journey, and I had told the king not expect you until the morning—"

"Kaddin," Calix quipped. "The message?"

"King Akintunde summons your presence in the Blue Room at the moment of your return from the Wildrines," the messenger recalled on command. "The Celestial Alliance deliberates their next move since the day before last. They have only stopped to break their fast and restore the *somnus*."

"Reckless, Father. Reckless," Calix muttered and shook his head, striding away from the messenger. His father was impetuous, forcing the Magistrates to carry on under enchantment like that—nothing, not even the false hope placed upon his campaign was worth the duress. Especially when he knew they would come to no further resolution on the refugee problem. He strode past Kaddin in the parlor and threw open the alloy doors that protected his personal quarters before continuing past the various rooms.

"Prince Calix, where..." Kaddin began from where he lingered at the threshold. "Where are you going?"

Calix paused halfway to the bath chamber. "To wash. Father can't possibly mean for me to come before the Alliance covered in—"

"King Akintunde," the messenger started again, causing Prince Calix to turn, "summons your presence post haste, your Grace." The poor boy quivered in his boots at the prince's yellow gaze fell upon him. "I'm...I'm sorry. I was told—"

"It's fine, Kaddin," Calix spat as he trudged back the way he'd come, elbowing past the young messenger and through the parlor.

It wasn't until he was down the staircase and past the western solars, stomping his way through the portico that lead past the library, that he began to feel guilty over how he muscled past the page. Kaddin was just his father's lackey, a fool seeking only to please the king, probably pressured into the role by his status-climbing parents to gain Ballentine favor. Calix slowed his gait and ran a gloved hand through his sweat-greased ebony hair.

Taking a deep, steadying breath, he languished in the speckled shadow of a dried shrub of climbing vine that used to bloom with the most fragrant roses he'd ever seen. He had to temper his irritation before he arrived before the Alliance. They were the most powerful gathering of magicians in Ellorhys, save those who defected to the realm of Evernight and they all looked to the King of Hinhallow for guidance in these troubled times.

Without further delay, Calix strode across the stone courtyard and into the Blue Room, a squat tower on the Northeastern perimeter of the castle. The circular chamber was so named for the blue petals of glass that formed the smaller dome atop the cupola at the center of the cathedral ceiling. With an eternal day, the chamber was submerged in a thick ultramarine haze.

The heavy doors ground against the floor as he flung them open and strode into the meeting illuminated in a beam of bright white daylight before the doors slammed closed behind him. Eight men and women sat around a round table, blinking into the hue of the room. Four were members of the court, diplomats from the Cities of Ellorhys, three were military officials from the various branches of Hinhallow's armed forces, and the last was King Akintunde Ballentine. All but one rose from where they sat around circular wooden table when the silhouette in the door was revealed to be the prince.

When his eyes adjusted to the dim spheres of amber light cast from the solarium chandelier suspended overhead, Calix found his father seated at the farthest end of the chamber. He clasped his fist over his heart and bowed. "I'm sorry for my tardiness, my Lords, Father. I have only just returned from my campaign in the mountains when I was fortunate enough to receive Kaddin's urgent summons."

"Prince Calix!" Magistrate Auric Alesio, an *altumaegus*, one of the highest ranked magicians within the Magistrate, asked from across the table. "How fared your journey?" The storm magi's pitch complexion seemed to be a reflection of his devastating talent. He was

47

one of five elected to hold the position and council the Magistrate Guild. He was a good ally to have, and perhaps a frightening enemy as well, as Auric was rumored to be a powerful beastmaester. Calix had never seen the power himself, and for that he was thankful.

Nothing was more terrifying than magic that thought for itself.

"Not so well, I'm afraid. The game has gone from the mountains as well," Calix replied as he started around the table toward his father.

Major Silfa Tilak, a sun-bronzed Terran magistrate serving as the Captain of the Archers, reached out to land an awkward pat on his shoulder, releasing a cloud of dust from his tunic as he said, "Your dedication to the realm is most admirable, your Highness." Calix always liked him. Silfa had an agreeable nature and was always pleased with the kingdom.

"Good of you to join us, my boy," King Akintunde's voice boomed over the greetings of the magistrates and generals of the Celestial Alliance. The greying monarch leaned back in his high-backed chair, his hands resting on the yellow zoster restraining the growing girth of his belly.

Once he had been feared. His appearance on any battle field, nearly seven feet tall and straddling his ebony warhorse with flaming sword held aloft like the dawn on the horizon—inevitable—terrified his adversaries. The Warlord of the West was an icon. His head was half shaved to brandish elaborate black tattoos across his scalp, one of them being a crown, an image that became clear as his father turned his head to the side. In old age, his black beard striped sliver and his belt had been taken out quite a bit as years of lavish life caught up to the aging monarch. But Calix still revered his father. The man had overtaken half the realm to maintain his hold on the Western quarters, and before the Evernight Curse altered the natural course of Ellorhys, the people had been well fed, protected, and pleased with the Ballentine reign.

"Please, sit at my side," his father said, even though no such seat was available.

From either side of the King, white-haired Magistrate Nicora Firstfrost and brooding General Jareid Valente, a diplomatic stand-in for King Tayman Wintersea of Rhumesc and the commander of the Hallowvanian Battalion respectively, locked eyes with one another, each hesitant as to whom was expected to forfeit their seat to the prince. Though elderly, her fair face creased with wrinkles like the shifting tide of an avalanche, Magi Nicora made to stand when General Jareid jolted from his chair before she could rise fully.

"Please, Councilors, don't trouble yourselves on my account," Calix protested, and without hesitation, the general seated himself again. "I have traveled long and far this evening and would seek to retire to my chambers at your behest, my liege."

"Of course, of course," King Akintunde began, "But first, the Celestial Alliance has only just agreed upon the trial that will be set forth before you, so your arrival is serendipitous indeed, Prince Calix."

"Trial," echoed Calix.

"To prove your worth to the Alliance, and to me, as the Crown Prince of the White City."

Calix's mouth felt as dry as the riverbed he'd walked earlier as the ascension announcement washed over him. He must still have dust or a pebble from his trek wedged in his ear. "Father, are you..."

"When you return from this campaign, we will have a gala, and celebrate your Crowning," Akintunde confirmed, nonchalantly stroking his pointy grey beard. "I will remain king until the end of my days. The Imperials could not take the city crowns from our forefathers, and king is not a title you relinquish, but rather one that you take to your grave. However," Akintunde mused as he exchanged knowing glances with the councilors at the table, "we *all* agree it is high time that Hinhallow begins to look to *you* for leadership, instead of an old magician like me."

Maybe it was just the glee stirring in his stomach, but Calix would even say his father's fiery eyes shone with pride. "I—I'm honored by your pledge of confidence, Father," he stammered, unprepared for such a momentous announcement.

As the eldest of the Ballantine children by seven years, he always thought he would be named the heir to the kingdom, but he had anticipated the nomination at a family dinner, before his mother, and siblings. Were they privy to this proclamation as well? He had imagined the praise and celebration his family would bestow on him as they speculated on the shining moments of his upcoming reign. Instead, he was covered in dust, sweaty, exhausted and probably more than a little rank.

"Don't be honored just yet, son," Akintunde cautioned. "The trial before you is a lengthy and laborious one, and even then, should you be named as my heir, the sacrifice needed for a glorious reign has only just begun. You've performed a great many feats and tasks for the Celestial Alliance, and for the benefit of Hinhallow. It is *because* of the skills you've demonstrated time and time again that we have assigned your trial, for the good of *all of Ellorhys.*"

Prince Calix held back a smug scoff and instead said, "Council. Father. I have trained my whole life for this privilege. I am ready to prove my worth to the Celestial Alliance, to Hinhallow, and most of all, to you, Father," he declared, thumping his fist on his chest. "What is it that I must do?"

Blue light bled quiet black shadows into the chamber as clouds passed over the sun, casting a moment of brief relief from the blistering heat upon the City. Light returned, spilling through the blue dome like clouds of gold as King Akintunde answered the Prince's question.

"You must assassinate the Imperial Princess. Get the Witch too, if you can, but we all agree that her protégé. . ." King Akintunde hissed and shook his head, "We simply cannot afford for her to claim the crown and reinforce the curse. The young Imperial must die."

5

ISSARIA

"Princess Issaria!" Magistrate Caltac Kholozzo snapped his charcoaled fingers, sparking a flickering flame that he held before her dazed expression. "Are you even listening?" The ancient scholar held her gaze, unamused and expectant, wiry white eyebrow arched over his one golden eye.

"I...umm..." Issaria, in fact, had not been listening. Her cheeks flushed as she shook her head. Blinking, she raised her amethyst eyes to meet her professor's singular gaze.

Magi Caltac had been monologuing the formula for a basic healing ointment, novice Terra magic, when she heard the affable voices of the Initiates gathering in palace yard. The arching door of the library-like Annex was propped open behind her, a failed attempt to coax a late summer breeze into the dimly lit and incredibly stuffy classroom. By the time Magi Caltac was reviewing the proper technique in applying ointment to the patient, Issaria could hear the sharp clang of blades. The Initiates were running sword drills in the courtyard just beyond the breezeway. She was so focused on distinguishing one voice from the others that she had completely tuned out the lesson.

"The *Mandatum?*" he asked for the spell spoken to awaken the combined healing properties of the herbs within the salve. For the second time, she realized. He peered at her with his one good eye, and she felt her nerve shutter under its weight. He might have lost the other to the *Fervent*, but she was certain the remaining eye worked well enough for the both of them.

"Are you really sure you want me to try that?" Issaria began, trying to wile her way out of attempting the spell which she knew would either accidentally ignite the patient's hair, Magistrate Caltac, or maybe even the Annex itself. It wouldn't be the first time. And then the *real* lecture would begin. She could already hear him droning on, about how healing spells are complex; and no one element held mastery over the mystic art of healing. "It's just that..." Did she dare? She bit her lip before blurting out, "Elon is in the yard. He's been training and he's to join the Imperial Guard today. If he does well, I mean."

They both knew what that meant to Elon Sainthart. After being orphaned in the Esperian countryside after his parents and younger sister were trapped inside their home, one of many, devastated in a village blaze, Elon found his place in house Sainthart, earning Soren's love as a son. The night the assassins came, hundreds died fleeing the chaos, Soren among them, and Elon was orphaned all over again. Elon Sainthart taking his adopted father's place among the Imperial Guard as the youngest recruit at twenty-two was a great honor and a sacred rite of passage. More, as he had petitioned the Empress Regent to be placed as the head of the princess' own personal unit of the guardsmen now that she was to be eighteen next month, it was another step toward becoming her *Defendier*. The palace was abuzz with the verdict: Empress Regent Hecate had agreed, but only on the condition that he undergo the same rigorous initiation trials as the other magicians seeking to join the Imperial Guardsmen.

"Ah! A most momentous moment indeed!" he proclaimed, clapping his hands together once. A tiny array of sparks and popping sizzles, a miniature fireworks display, glittered in the air above his hands. "We better not distract him, then. He is honing his skills as you should your own," Magi Caltac said briskly. His mustache wiggled over his lip as he spoke. Issaria wasn't certain she'd ever seen his mouth. "Why is it that you are so afraid of your own talent?"

"I'm not...afraid of my power so much as I don't want to clean up the mess after," she started, then returned his affronted stare with her own arched eyebrow. "We both know that I know the spell. Stop acting like I don't. I just don't want to singe your caterpillar-eyebrows off when I fail at it again," Issaria snapped with a knowing smirk that melted Magi Caltac's disappointment into bemused curiosity.

"If you know it, then *recite it.*" His mustache curled around his lips in a snarl.

Issaria sighed. The old man was going to make her do it again.

Rolling her eyes, she stood and paused to adjust the *zoster*, silk belt, that cinched the waist of her chiton, as if she had all the time in the world. She then detailed, from memory, her own definition of the spell, "A *Sanatiture* is a type of Terran spoken spell, subcategory *mandatum,* being a one-word command to elicit a desired result. When paired with the right herbs and applied to the affected area in a salve or ointment it stimulates a rejuvenation of energy, helping a body combat mild sickness, injury, and infection."

It was useful and complex. She had learned the process to procure and produce the light grey-green gritty paste that was to be considered as the ointment and anchor for the Terran magic to affect the body down to the very annunciation of the spell—*Sa-na-tit-oo-ree* — and the way to hold one's hand above the paste to channel their mana into it. She could recall this spell and countless others across the nine schools of magic, even though each attempt to use her own power ended in utter failure, and more often than not, flames.

"Very good! I am pleased you know it." He turned his back to her and strode from her tabletop to the demonstration table where their patient, a small brown rabbit, waited inside a wicker basket. "The rabbit was caught by a palace hound. Unfortunately for the dog, it lost its dinner when the kitchen maid's daughter saw the scuffle," Magi Caltac explained as he beckoned her to the table. He huffed, a little irritation in his voice as he said, "Abihail wouldn't stop her wailing out in the yard so I went out there and told the girl I would heal the thing if she ceased the racket." He turned from the rabbit to her, a smile on his withered face. "What I failed to mention was that by I, I meant you, Princess Issaria. It will be good to tell her that the princess herself saw to the healing of her pet."

"I *really* don't think that's a great idea," Issaria said again, unable to shake the idea that perhaps Abihail might cry one more time when the princess's out-of-control magic mutilated her bunny. She resisted the urge to look over her shoulder at the open doors. She could still hear the bite of steel on steel as the Initiates endured more of the Imperial Guard's rigorous initiation trials. Even if they passed it was not a guarantee that they would be allowed on the elite and select guard. Not without the Emperor's approval after the affirmation of their skill.

Of course, there was no Imperial Emperor now. Daylight saw to that, Issaria thought bitterly.

"One try. Issaria, you have the ability, you only need to find and control the flow of mana within you." He snatched his wand, a polished zephyrite crystal infused with storm magic, a relic that allowed his lessons to be illuminated in air, from her table top and turned his back on her. "I cannot heal this animal alone. I am fire, I do not have the necromancy talent."

In the air, he drew out a river, connected to a pond. The yellow lines glowed and crackled as they hung there, and Magi Caltac gestured to the drawing. "Imagine this is the well of your mana, the magical talent within you. Being Imperial, you, like your parents and your Mythos ancestors have mana of unforetold depths." With the wave of a hand over the hovering drawing, he erased the bottom of the lake, and like a berg on the Salt Ice, he gave it a vast depth, increasing the bottom of the lake several inches lower than it had been before, until it looked more like a drinking glass than any lake Issaria had seen. "Only the Imperials are capable of harnessing this great power and mastering all nine elemental talents."

"I can't harness *anything*, Magi," Issaria said, exasperated with the old Magician's lectures.

"Until now."

"Now? What's so special about now?"

"Perhaps nothing, or perhaps everything. Only *trying* will determine the measure of the moment." Magistrate Caltac gestured to the streaks of light lingering in the air behind him. "Think of your talent like the lake and river. To harness the power of the river, you must channel the lake to one outlet. Picture a funnel in your head, sift through the elements and call forth your Terran magic. Hold it in your hands like a living thing, and then....release the spell with your heart, not your mind."

Taking a deep breath, Issaria rounded the corner of her table and joined her tutor at the front of the room. Her eyes flicked to the open doorway only once as she removed the top from the wicker basket that contained the injured rabbit. Exposed to light, the rabbit began to scramble in the basket. Issaria reached in and scooped the small animal into her hands. She held it to her chest until it stopped squirming and she could feel his terrified tremble against her breast. "Shh. It's okay, little one," she cooed, meeting the Magistrate's golden eye. In the same soft voice, she added, "Mythos above, if I hurt this animal I will not be happy." Her violet eyes did not waver.

Issaria's heart was soft when she thought of the creatures of Ellorhys, subject to the wars and laws magicians set forth in their world. Many suffered or were now extinct due to the Daylight and Eventide. If they could not make it past the Timeline, they often died of dehydration, starvation, or exposure. Even the Timeline was not guarantee of survival. Most enchantments kept the chill at bay, but Issaria knew the world outside the celestial city was changing. Unlike animals, Magicians were more resilient and for the most part, stayed in their Daylight Cities thriving on magic while the Imperials and those loyal to them remained within the protection of the Eventide.

The rabbit squirmed against her, and Issaria continued to stroke its ears as she unraveled the haphazard bandages along the animal's hindquarters to expose the puncture wounds from the dog. From the ceramic jar on the demonstration table, she took a fat glob of the healing ointment she'd brought to the lesson as her home study and smeared it on the visible wounds. Almost immediately, the rabbit began to still, feeling the soothing effect of the paste. When the rabbit was placid, she laid him out on the table so that she could see the entire wound, an oblong trail of bloody holes from the dog's fangs pocking the rabbit's brown hide. She covered them all in the green smear, making sure to think only of the sinew knitting back together seamlessly, fractured bones that were crushed in powerful jaws setting, of pooling blood receding back to whence it came.

Eyes closed, she reached deep inside herself and touched her mana, feeling the surge of her own ability, a beacon of effervescence, fizzing inside her—her *mana*, the lifeblood of her magical talents. It rippled through her like electricity, pulsing from her heart. Issaria pulled back when she felt Magi Caltac's charred hand on her shoulder.

"Steady," his voice wavered, and she knew he could feel the mana within her trying to break free. "Find the Terran magic, not the storm," he coached.

In her mind's eye, she pictured it like a spring within her soul, bubbling up from her heart like a shimmering mist of stars. It pulsed, and she felt its breath as if it were alive.

I am alive. *Within you.*

Her eyes snapped open and Issaria jerked her hand back from the rabbit as if she'd been shocked. "What did you say?"

"Gently now, you've opened the door. If you're not carefu—"

But it was too late.

The door to her mana was open and the woman's voice had broken her focus. The air around them crackled with static electricity, the tiny hairs on her arms stood on end. The incandescent storm summoned by her magic crackled through the air like rogue lightning. Panicked, the rabbit kicked off the table with surprising strength for one so wounded and scurried to the nearest dark corner and tried to smother itself against the crystalline wall.

"Rein it back in! Reach for it, align with your power!" Magi Caltac shouted over the sizzle and pops of her unhinged might. "Tame this power and it will recognize you as its master!"

"I'm *trying!*" Issaria shouted, her arms flung wide in the center of the room, calling her magic back to her like a flickering flame in a snowstorm. White bled across her vision as she retreated inside her mana again, fearful of who she would find dwelling inside that shimmering chasm within herself, but determined to control the hurricane of energy she was unleashing before she killed someone.

Tentatively, she searched for the tether to her own chaotic abilities. She touched her mana and felt the rush of magic flow through her much like the river Magi Caltac had illustrated with his wand. There was so much power to be had here. *Unforetold depths* echoed in her mind, but she doubted Magi Caltac, even with all his might as a seasoned Magistrate, realized just how true that statement was. This was no mere lake. Issaria was floating in an endless sea of cosmos, eternal and unending, all the might in the world at her fingertips. She was a mere instrument of its will. It was exhilarating. Intoxicating. *Addicting.*

She could have lived in that moment forever, could have let her power rip the fabric of the world with her cosmic might...but she took a steadying breath and calmed herself. Her thunderous heartbeat hammered against her ribcage. It was so easy to succumb to it. The temptation was there. There were *no* limits. No wonder Aunt Hecate so easily harnessed the moon. She would not cower so easily before her enemies, nor her own talents. Only harnessing the moon had been *restraining* herself. Issaria thought she might understand more of her Aunt's insane concept of protection—nay the *punishment* of using the moon to anchor the planet in rotation, forcing an unending day over the northern hemisphere.

As if it heard her and acknowledged her terror, her magic began to ebb, pulled back from a raging typhoon to a retreating tide. Around her, the jagged volts of crepitant electricity fizzled into iridescent sparks and embers that burned away before hitting the chamber's floor.

And then she felt it.

The second heartbeat alongside her own.

Soon, Sanguinem Descendia, *soon I will awaken, and my Mythos might will be your burden to bear no longer.*

Issaria opened her eyes, and looked around, expecting Aunt Cate, or another woman standing with her and Magi Caltac in the Annex. But they were alone, save the rabbit who cowered in a corner near an upturned table.

"Are you all right, Magi?" Issaria asked as her vision cleared.

Magistrate Caltac rose from where he had taken shelter behind his desk, dusting himself off and picking up stray sheets of parchment, though the floor was littered with them while dozens more swirled lazily to the floor like blossoms shed in the spring. Nothing was aflame, thank the Cosmos, but chairs and books had been toppled, shards of glass from shattered vials and jars littered the floor like errant stars, their contents blown astray by her storm. "Quite all right, though I daresay, that was frightening. Your eyes, Princess..." He hesitated a moment then whispered, "Your eyes were glowing."

Trembling, Issaria nodded in agreement. "I couldn't see, Magi, it was all white. I could only feel power." She neglected to mention the woman's voice, frightened by what Magi Caltac would tell her about it.

He put his hands in the sleeves of his white Magistrate robes, bringing together crimson and gold filigree stitching on the sleeves like two fiery meteors colliding. He steadied his golden eye on her. "I confess, my child. I have never seen that happen to an Imperial before. Not your Aunt Hecate. Nor your gentle mother Umbriel, or your illustrious father Helios."

"Are you saying my magic is...different?" She already knew the answer was yes. There was *someone* living inside her mana. She tried to still her heartbeat, afraid it would betray her silence on the matter, but if her mentor could hear its deafening roar, he gave no indication.

"I'm saying your powers are..." he trailed off, reaching one fire-blackened hand, the sacrifice of all fire Magicians who channeled through their limbs, up to stroke his bushy white beard. He took his time considering the word he chose and when he settled on, "Untapped."

"Untapped?"

Magi Caltac nodded and approached her, placing his hands on her shoulders. Issaria knew this to be a moment the Magistrate considered important, an exchange of wisdom between more than just student and pupil. "I believe we can learn to control the power. It is fearsome and ferocious indeed, but I believe it can be as gentle as you, dear Princess. I believe you can tame it, ride it like the dragon it is and be the most glorious of all Imperial Empresses that have ever been." As he finished, tears shimmered in his golden eye. "Ellorhys has need of you; I know you feel it too."

"In Daylight?" It was true, she had been curious of late and had probed Aunt Cate about what was happening in Daylight, the hemisphere of the planet the Empress Regent cursed to an eternal sequence of scorching days. Aunt Cate had been furious with her inquiry, asking if Issaria, her own flesh and blood, feared her power like the weak magicians that started this mess, the cowards who sent assassins as friends among them. Hecate offered the crown to Issaria right then and there, thrust it upon her and told her if she could do a better job, she was welcome to it.

The idea of reigning frightened Issaria, as she thought herself unready to lead a population and make decisions that effected the lives of hundreds of thousands of Magicians, and she knew her Aunt used that fear against her, but still she backed down. She explained that she had only been concerned about the condition of her true realm, something her aunt had been toying with as the name for their campaign when Issaria assumed the throne and unified the cities under the Imperial reign once more. Now, she asked the same question of her teacher.

"Magi Caltac, what happened in Daylight when Aunt Cate anchored the moon to Espera?"

"Daylight. Eventide." Magi Caltac gave a heavy sigh and turned away from her. He paced to the window and she considered him for a moment. He suddenly looked much more tired than he had in years and Issaria wondered how close he was to the end of his lifespan. He knew her parents a great many years and had been teaching her all her life. An Imperial life was at least twice that of a normal Magician, but his frail shoulders sagged, seeming to bear the weight of his years and her question. "The balance of our realm has never been in day or night, but in the equilibrium the moon grants us. It is the true anchor for our planet, and when it is stationary as it is cursed to be...it cannot balance the planet as it should."

"And this balance...it could be restored?"

"I believe it can. With you."

She steadied herself before she addressed the other question that eroded her heart, "I wouldn't have to restore balance if the Daylight Cities didn't orchestrate to kill my parents in the first place. Were they not benevolent and kind as you said? Were they not beloved by all? How could something that changed *physics* have happened if it was truly the Golden Dynasty?"

Years of silence on the matter hung between them. The weight of the realm was always expected to rest on her shoulders, but now it was divided. Issaria knew in her heart that Daylight would *never* accept her now that they'd been forced to suffer at their hand for near to a decade. Unity across Ellorhys would come only at great cost. Aunt Cate spoke of expansion, dominating the Daylight Cities and furthering the peace and prosperity of the Imperial reign. As Empress, only Issaria had the divine right to rule, and Aunt Cate expected to see the kings and queens of the Daylight cities kneel before her or be crushed beneath their Imperial might.

Was that truly the *only* path left before her? This was nothing of what she wanted for the realm she once hoped to protect. At this rate all that would be left of Ellorhys would be a scorched wasteland not unlike the Glass.

Magi Caltac took a deep breath and settled his hands on the belt of his white scholars' robes. The golden embroidery on the collar of the garment brought out his eye from his grizzled, bearded face. "My blessed child. You ask a large question for such a short time that we have left for lessons today. Next time we will explore your inquiry more, yes? What I can tell you right now is that Empress Regent Hecate suffered great loss that day. Her sorrow and rage gave her access to primordial magic unparalleled in supply. Her mana was endless in those moments, and she changed more than just the balance of the planet, I'm sure." He curled his mustache and stroked his beard, leaving charcoal smears from his fire-blackened fingertips in the white hair. "I am a believer that your Aunt did what she thought she must in order to protect you, but also herself." Magi Caltac tucked his hands into the sleeves of his robes. "You'd do well to remember that. It wasn't until you returned to the Palace that we finally knew the assassins hadn't found you as well, Princess. Those were a few very hopeless and harrowing hours."

Again, the clang of metal on metal ricocheted down the breezeway and into the Annex. Her eyes flicked to the doorway and Magi Caltac gave a rare, warm smile. "For your home study you will attempt to bottle a raincloud. A small one. Manipulating air pressures is about feeling the currents rather than seeing them. I believe it may be more in tune with the part of your mana that wishes to be released. Collect a beaker and stopper from the storage supply and the scrolls from the archives." He looked about the disaster of a classroom. "If they're still there." When Issaria didn't move for a beat, he finished, "You're dismissed, Princess. You may see to your soldier now."

Relief that she would not have to perform more magic extinguished her curiosity and she bowed slightly before crossing the room to the wooden cabinet against the far wall to gather her materials. She cast one glance over her shoulder to make sure that her tutor wasn't still watching her. Pleased to see he had refocused his attention on the rabbit, Issaria snuck a few *extra* supplies into her bag. "Thank you, Magi Caltac, for your wisdom," she said as she crossed the room with a glass cylinder with a round glass stopper in hand. "As always," she continued as she pulled two scrolls from the bookshelves, "you have given me much to consider."

"Of course, your Imperial Grace. Thank you for your mind," he said as he knelt and began coaxing the frightened rabbit from the corner with soft kissing noises.

Issaria deposited the materials gathered as well as her own class supplies from her table into a woven satchel and shouldered it before returning to the front of the room. Magi Caltac had the rabbit stretching to sniff his hand. She took several steps backward down the aisle between tables, as if the classroom ever held more students than just herself, before saying, "See you on the morrow, Magi!" Gleefully she exited the overheated and still catastrophically disorganized Annex with the knowledge that along with her supplies, she had also taken from his stores an Aquathyst cluster and a leather flask, both of which would help her execute the scheme formulating in her head.

The old magician barely acknowledged her departure as the rabbit had deemed him trustworthy and tentatively hopped into the Magi's charcoaled hands. Caltac stood, and returned to the demonstration table, cradling the rabbit against his chest. Gently, he pressed his fingers into the creature's fur, examining its skeletal structure, and feeling where its wounds were. "Well, that can't be right," he murmured to himself as he set the rabbit into the basket to get a closer look at him.

The rabbit hopped around the basket, sniffing the enclosure at every angle, and Caltac was amazed to see shiny pink scar-tissue peek through the open patches of fur where the dog's fangs had been. The bones that were broken had set, the muscle that had been torn was mended, and the punctured flesh was sealed over with new skin.

Magistrate Caltac looked from the rabbit to the doorway through which the princess had vanished in a flurry of silken skirts and raven hair.

6

ELON

Elon spun and felt the air come off the blade as he avoided the swift slice. His feet knew the steps as if it were a dance he'd learned long ago. He grunted, his own sword meeting the strike. Moonlight glittered off the silver alloy of the blunted practice swords, but all the same, these weapons could leave brutal bruises. He braced the blunt of the blow and pushed his opponent's longsword back.

Rhori, his sparring partner, laughed as he jumped back and paced around him, his blue-grey eyes glinting at the challenge of their match. "Almost had you there, Sainthart," he taunted.

"You wish," Elon replied as he deftly whirled his sword back into an offensive position.

He lunged forward, feigned left until he was certain he had baited his quarry. Rhori leaned in, his stance pivoted.

Elon redirected to the right. He heard his opponent's surprised gasp as he found his exposed side with too much ease. Poised for the final blow, he leaned into his attack—

"Yeah Elon! Take him out!" Her voice cut through him like a beam of light in the darkness.

His attack faltered, if only for a second.

But it was enough for Rhori to take the advantage: he sidestepped Elon's clumsy blade and knocked the weapon from his grasp with a short swing of his own sword. A jab of his elbow into Elon's shoulder blade was all it took to put him face first in the dirt.

"And you're dead," Rhori said, pointing the tip of his blunted sword at Elon's back. He extended his hand to help Elon to his feet and sighed. "I hate to say it but if you're dead, she's dead. Situationally speaking and all." Elon locked forearms with Rhori to get back on his feet as another sparring pair edged closer.

Elon snatched his broadsword from the ground just before Roane Wetherwood stepped on the hilt. Elon spared a glance for his match, Flynt Petramut, and decided that Flynt would lose, as his left side was slower to react, and Roane would surely exploit that weakness. He turned and joined Rhori and they side stepped their way through the dwindling matches on the lawn, each pair that had ended their duel lingering around the edges with the other Initiates, spectating the remaining bouts.

Rhori ran a hand through his shaggy blond hair. "Not only did you embarrass yourself in front of your girl—"

"Princess Issaria is not—"

"Not your girl. I know. We know. We *all* know." Exasperated Rhori paused for a beat before resuming his jovial amble, "Not only did you embarrass yourself in front of your *princess*, but if this were a real battle? You got her killed too. All because she shouted your name."

Elon cast a glance to Issaria, who was grimacing apologetically from where she stood beneath the rose-covered breezeway that overlooked the palace yard. The flowered walkway bridged the Annex, where the Imperial Princess took her private lessons, to the rest of the palace. His heart warmed to see her crowned in moonbeams as white rose petals fell into her midnight curls. However it was far later in the day than was usual for her to be in this wing of the palace. It would not have been the first time her afternoon observations of the Empress Regent attending the requests of the people had been cancelled, but he noted the flush on her cheek and he was glad to see her smiling after her lessons with the old magistrate.

"Specialist Sainthart. Corporal Galeryder." Commander Galen addressed them as they approached. "Good spar, you two. However, that was a poor finish for you both. Galeryder, you didn't earn that victory, nor should you savor it. Sainthart," he barked, turning his dark eyes on Elon. "I expect better from you where *she* is concerned. If you expect me to take your recommendation for *Defendier* to the Empress Regent, that is."

"Yes, sir. Won't happen again, sir."

"It won't." Galen's deadpan tone rooted Elon to the spot. "I've been informed this was your final test as Initiates. The Selection will happen in due course but you two...are to be elsewhere when the Empress addresses the assembled."

Elon felt the color drain from his face. Beside him, he felt Rhori freeze in place, as if he could go unnoticed in this moment if he didn't move. Their crimson haired Commander Galen Acontium was no joking man. Clad daily in full battle regalia of menacing black armor studded with shiny blue Aquathyst crystals to enhance his elemental power, the commander was an intimidating figure to approach on any day. And today, he held the weight of every hour of practice, every sleepless night of research and formulas, every *ounce* of effort Elon had put into qualifying for the Initiate trials in the palm of his seldom unclenched fist. He'd endured the intellect and academic testing, the magical battles against one Initiate from each element and conquered them all with his Alchemic creations. This battle of blades had been the final test and....Elon gulped.

He held the Commander's weighted stare as he began, "Sir, if you think I've failed in some way—"

"Failed?" he echoed, his eyebrow arched. His grimace battled the amusement in his voice. He didn't give Elon a chance to reply before he shook his head, dismissing their conversation. "Specialist, the Imperial princess is late for a meeting with her most illustrious aunt. See to it that she knows she is tardy, would you?" The request sounded simple enough, but the ice in the commander's eyes made the hairs on the back of Elon's neck stand on end as he gave a curt nod. Seemingly satisfied with his obedience, Acontium looked away, over his shoulder toward the remaining Initiates still locked in battle on the grass. "When the princess is on her way, go get yourselves cleaned up, then report to the map room in the Council Chambers. I will meet you there to discuss your...*future* in the ranks of the Imperial Guard."

Maybe it was Elon's heart punching his ribs, but he was certain that the commander's voice dripped with apathy at mention of their meeting. He forced himself to nod and turn from his superior officer and not show that he was horrified to have failed the Trials. He had taken only two steps away from the yard when he heard the commander say with irritation biting his tone, "Galeryder, don't make me give an order twice."

"Yes, sir!" Rhori chirped, probably too eager for the dismissal.

Elon slowed his pace until Rhori caught up with him. He looked up from the scuffed tips of his boots in the trampled grass, turned a pale yellow without sunlight for close to a decade now, as they made their way across the yard toward the Annex and the princess. He swallowed. How was he to face her knowing he'd already he'd failed to uphold the most sacred promise he intended to make?

"It'll be all right, Elon," Rhori said under his breath before smiling, and saluting with a closed fist over his heart. "Princess, it's so good to see you. I hope the Cosmos have been favoring you as of late. Though by the blush on your cheeks, I dare hope you're thinking of me?"

Elon shot his friend a venomous look but held his tongue as Issaria rolled her eyes at the impetuous flirt.

"Oh Rhori," Issaria chided. "Have you no shame? You know Liara would have my head if I even so much as *glanced* in your direction," she said, referencing the pretty laundress that Rhori had been tumbling the past several moons. The princess was a darling among the palace staff, whomever remained had been employed since her parents' time—and it was well known that she was friends with most of the ladies in her service.

She turned her radiant purple gaze upon Elon and he felt himself pale. He had failed her for the first time. He didn't know what to say to her.

"I'm so sorry, Elon, about the bout. I didn't mean to distract you, I was just so pleased to see you...in action."

Was it his imagination or was she blushing?

"It's all right," Elon replied. "It was only one match. Rhori had to beat me sometime."

Rhori slugged him in the arm. "I'll have you know I would have beaten you even if she hadn't distracted you." It might have been true. Rhori's skill with a blade nearly rivaled his own. "Although, we do come bearing a message, Princess," he added, looking to Elon for support.

"A message from whom?" Issaria asked.

"Commander Acontium," Elon replied. "He bid us to remind you of your tardiness for a meeting with the Empress Regent. She will be awaiting you." He tried to sound confident but he was certain that Empress Regent Hecate had expected perfection from him. She would settle for nothing less. As the commander said, nothing less would do where Issaria was concerned.

Not after that night. Not when they'd come so close to losing her too.

Issaria huffed. "I *just* finished with Magi Caltac. Can't I have a moment that isn't scheduled?" She shook her head and sighed. "Well, I'll get there when I get there, I suppose. Especially after that lesson."

Both Elon and Rhori knew that meant she'd had yet another incident with her magic, and neither asked any further questions of her. Elon was glad there wasn't smoke billowing out of the Annex again. Maybe this time old Caltac had been drenched, or flowers sprouted in his beard. He had to shave his whole beard last time *that* little pop of power showed itself.

"Come now, Princess," Elon began, "your aunt is expecting you, and now the commander knows you've been here. You know how he and the Empress Regent are." The Commander was the Empress Regent's *Sanguinem Defendier.* Elon had always thought it strange they had taken the sacred oaths so soon after the assassinations, as if she had always had Galen selected as her chosen warrior in the event she ever was called to rule Ellorhys. The thought was nearing treason, and

Elon kept it to himself. "We also have a prior engagement to get to," he finished.

Issaria frowned, but Elon knew her defeated face as she chewed her bottom lip. "I'll see you later, Elon?" she asked, expectant.

He felt his face growing hot as Rhori cast him a sideways glance. "Of course. I shall fetch you for supper."

Anger flashed across her face. "Fetch me for supper? Rock head!" she cursed before sticking out her tongue at him. Issaria stormed off into the palace, her cloak swirling behind her.

Elon only hoped she was going to find her aunt before he dug himself a deeper hole. He held back a groan. Now she was mad at him on top of it all.

Rhori slapped him on the back as they crossed the lawn and around the western side of the palace was the barracks where Elon and many of the other Initiates were housed. "That did not go in your favor, my friend. Maybe I should give you some pointers with the ladies, eh?"

"I told you, it's not like that between the princess and me."

"You know the only person who believes that is you, and perhaps maybe the princess herself, right?"

Elon snapped his head in his friend's direction, eyes narrowed, a scowl across his face. "I'm so glad you find our torment amusing."

"Oh Sainthart..." Rhori began as he slung an arm around Elon's shoulders. They turned from the breezeway and headed for the barracks. "You've got it bad for her, huh?"

"I'd rather not speak of this," he replied before brushing Rhori's arm off himself. "It's not appropriate, all things considered."

"I suppose you're right," Rhori conceded as they passed the cavernous crystal space that served as the mess hall, and then descended down into the stone hallways of the sub-levels. There was enough space for each squadron of soldiers serving on the Palace Guard, the Imperial Guard, and *still* there was room to house several legions of Esperian soldiers beneath the palace.

"What do you think the commander wants to see us about?" Rhori asked, changing the subject to their impending doom just as they came to their squad's hall.

"By his tone I can't imagine that it's anything good."

"Well, whatever it is," Rhori clapped him on the shoulder before heading a down the hall toward his own room. "We will face it together."

ELON HAD ONLY BEEN IN THE COUNCIL CHAMBERS ONCE, AND THAT WAS when he was a boy and Soren had brought him before Imperial Emperor Helios and Empress Umbriel to declare he was claiming the Elon as his ward, his son in place of a bloodheir. To be summoned there now, by the commander, for his dismissal from the ranks of the Guard made Elon's stomach churn.

Long arched hallway lit at intervals with sconces gave way to a heavy pair of alloy doors framed by two black marble solarium sconces, their glowing geodes cast shifting shadows on the crystal walls like flames.

"Does it have to be so...creepy in here?" Rhori asked.

"I think it's part of her ambiance," Elon murmured. This part of the palace was technically part of the Empress Regent's personal quarters and was forbidden unless one had business to attend to with the Empress Regent herself, and he didn't want to offend her.

Together, they pushed through the double doors, and into the council chamber.

Centered beneath a chandelier was a large carved crystal table that took his breath away. Large, maybe thirty, even forty meters across, a rough-hewn circle in shape, the table gave way to a great basin carved deep into its center was a scale replica of the continents and islands of Ellorhys in alarming detail.

He had not seen the table since he was a boy and while it had felt massive and awe inspiring then, that was nothing compared to how he felt before it now. He took in the great northern continent of Rhunmesc; it was nearly as large as the southern continent itself.

Luckily the City only retained up to the Averhame Mountains as their territory, claiming that the north was too wild even for them. Elon had scoffed at the time but now as he gazed past those miniature peaks and beyond the depths of the Ferrofrost and *still* he had not lain eyes on the edge of the Salt Ice on the northern shore, he realized how true that claim of wilderness must be.

From across the chamber, next to the large picture window over-looking the Bay of Prisms and the shipping and docks burrow of Espera, Commander Acontium watched them arrive with a look that Elon could only describe as smug satisfaction. It did nothing to ease his nerves.

"Good. You've arrived. Now we're only waiting on two more before we may begin," Commander Galen said from where he stood.

Elon glanced around the room, taking a tally. Around the carved table stood three soldiers he called friends from the Initiate Trials. Both Roane and Flynt stood shoulder to shoulder, though Flynt was now sporting a bloody nose jammed-up with some scrap linen and a fair black eye to match. Beside them stood Xenviera Lightizner, a dually-aligned storm magician whose armament magic was deadly and adaptable. He'd seen her summon a shield of wind to ward off a barrage of arrows and then fire a bolt of lightning that decimated her opponents. The girl was not one to mess with. She stood tall, jutted her chin out, and kept her hands clasped behind her back. Her long inky hair was back in a tight ponytail, and she kept her expression neutral even though her dark eyes brightened when he caught her eye.

She was pleased to see them. But why? What did she know that he didn't? Elon's mouth went dry.

From a second set of double doors set into an alcove on the western side of the chamber, Empress Regent Hecate entered. Her raven hair was coiled in braids and piled atop her head in an elaborate display that framed the sparkling silver diadem she wore as Empress Regent. Her glacial gaze assessed the room, meeting every pair of eyes within before she stepped aside and allowed Princess Issaria to cross the threshold.

At once, the soldiers, Elon included, sank to bended knees until the Empress Regent swept past them and went to Commander Acontium, still by the window. They whispered together there, and Elon found his attention turning to Issaria. He'd seen her little more than an hour ago, but something had changed. She kept close to her aunt and trailed her like a shadow across the chamber. She kept her eyes to the floor, avoided his gaze. He narrowed his eyes. She chewed her lower lip and somehow found a way to look from the floor, all the way up to the ceiling without looking at him.

She was up to something.

He was certain he'd know her "I've got a secret" face anywhere. He hadn't seen it in years, but the memories of their youthful escapades across the city were never far from his heart.

"Initiates!" Commander Acontium barked, and even though all five of the soldiers in the room were already standing, they straightened, and clasped hands behind their backs at attention. "You've been brought here today because it has been determined through your own aptitude, dedication, and merit that you are worthy." The room was so silent he thought he could hear the stars twinkle. The commander offered a rare smile and said, "Your Grace," turning over the floor to the Empress Regent.

In tandem, Hecate and Issaria stepped toward them. Empress Regent Hecate reached out and took Issaria's hand. "You all know that the Princess's eighteenth birthday is nearly upon us. In a little over a moon's time, she will be crowned and her true reign can begin." Pride swelled in the Empress Regent's voice as she turned her gaze upon her niece. "You all know how precious Issaria is to me. To all of Espera, and the realm over."

Overwhelmed with emotion, the Empress Regent had to clear her throat and turned aside to dab at her eyes. She gathered her composure and met the eyes of each soldier at the table before she continued, "Over the past few years, you have been trained, tested, and evaluated," she began, "but not by the Commander, or by myself, as you have been led to believe."

All eyes were on Hecate, expectant, but it was Issaria who said, "The choice of who would serve on my Imperial Guard has always

71

been mine. The first choice I make as Imperial Empress." Breaking from her aunt's hand, Issaria took her place at the head of the table. When she lifted her eyes, Elon knew her parents would have been proud. She looked as much an empress as her mother ever did.

"Come forward," she said. "Receive my invitation."

He could hardly believe his ears, even as Roane and Rhori lead of their little lines of soldiers around the head of the table, forming a semi-circle around the Princess. This was a meeting between the six of them, it seemed, the commander and Empress Regent bearing witness with placid smiles on their faces.

"The Trials have come to an end at last. I have selected you five from the pool of Initiates to be anointed as my Imperial Guard, should you accept—"

"All right!" Flynt pumped his fist in the air. Roane shoved an elbow into his ribs, collapsing him into a fit of coughs. "I mean to say, I accept, your Imperial Radiance?" He offered a slanted smile that made Issaria struggle to conceal her own grin, and Xenviera rolled her eyes. They were all well accustomed to Flynt's roughness by now.

"I accept," echoed Xenviera.

"As do I," Roane said.

After a moment of tight-lipped smirking, Issaria cleared her throat and continued, "I have brought you together to offer you places in the Imperial Guard, yes, but also, to bear witness to a sacred pledge." Her amethyst eyes locked on his, and she knelt before him and offered up her palms.

He wasn't being dismissed at all, and his foolish nerves melted to gold in his stomach.

"Elon Sainthart." With his name on her lips, she looked up at him from bended knee and asked the one question he'd longed to hear since the day he realized the wild child in the stable with straw in her hair and mud up to her knees—the girl who made him smile for the first time after his family perished—was Issaria Elysitao.

"I offer you my bloodoath, the sacred role of *Sanguinem Defendier.* Do you accept my life as your own? Will you bind your blood with mine and protect me until your dying breath?"

Always, forever, the answer was a resounding yes. He would give her everything, every last breath in his body if it would keep her on this planet one more day. If only so he didn't have to be without her.

"Issa—Princess Issaria." Breathless, Elon brought her to her feet. He hardly had the words to tell her—not here. Not in front of all these people. The words he had for her would have to wait for a different time. "I have strived for this day ever since Soren took me in and showed me what true loyalty means to a man. He charged me with his name, and his legacy is my greatest honor to uphold."

Her smile wavered, her prismatic gaze shimmered with tears and at once he knew he'd botched it. He should have spoken about her, their friendship and his loyalty to *her*. This claim to the Sainthart mantle of Imperial Guardian was not what she wanted to hear, not from him, despite their audience. Still, she did not falter, not now when there was an audience. If Hecate had taught Issaria one thing, it was always to maintain control when a weakness might be betrayed. She continued on, her voice steady as she broke her gaze away. "I am pleased, Commander Sainthart, but the only oath I wish you to swear is one of the most arcane magic, under the light of the next full moon." She looked to the other Initiates. "Will you all swear to obey Commander Sainthart, my chosen *Defendier,* as if his word was my own?"

Without hesitation, one by one, they all sank to bended knee, heads bowed.

"We all knew that Sainthart would be your chosen," Xenviera admitted, looking up from where she knelt. "We wouldn't have it any other way, Princess."

"It is an honor to be bound to you, Princess Issaria," Rhori confirmed.

"We take our vows with pride," Flynt said.

"Then it is written in the Cosmos. On the full moon, we shall bind ourselves, and when I am eighteen, I will ascend the throne with you as my Guard. Blessed be our eternal bond," Issaria declared.

Commander Acontium and Empress Regent Hecate clapped politely from where they observed by the window.

Elon fell back, leaving the other Initiates—the other *Imperial Guards*, he thought—to converse freely with the Princess, Regent and Commander. *Imperial Guard.* He puffed out his chest a little, feeling his pride again. Issaria's forsaken eyes flashed in his memory and he deflated, knowing he should have said something about how much he cared for her. He swallowed. It wasn't permitted. He could never...

He looked to where she stood, talking to Xenviera who stood nearly a full head taller than her. Braced with a deep, head-clearing breath, he made a second promise to her. He would never see that disappointment on her face again.

One by one the new guards filed out through the long hallway behind him, faces bursting with pride and smiles. Hecate and Commander Galen had exited silently through the western doors at some point during the conversations.

And then they were alone.

Issaria stood near the window, moonlight highlighting her black curls in silver. Her back was to him, though he was sure she knew he was there.

He took a step toward her. "Princess—"

"How many times do I have to tell you?"

Elon froze. "Tell me what?"

"Call me *Issaria*. You used to before all this nonsense. I thought we were friends." Anger bit into her voice and held him rooted in place. "When did that change, Elon?"

"Nothing changed," he protested, but he knew exactly what she meant. *He* had changed. He had to change how he acted toward her, how he lived, breathed, *existed* for her. His infatuation had been painfully obvious and after Soren's death...

She was still the reason he lived and breathed but it was bigger than Issaria now. It was bigger than himself, bigger than his feelings for her, and how they could *never* be—not while she was who she was.

You have to let her go, for her own good, the Empress Regent had said. He'd never be worthy, not in the way it mattered, and he had to let her go. Deter her girlhood crush. *Don't encourage her, Sainthart.*

She turned to face him, silver tears rimming her eyes. "If all I am is an oath to you…" Issaria closed her eyes and swallowed before she found the strength to say, "If all I am is an Oath, a mantle to some name that you think you need…Elon, I thought I meant more to you!" She blurted out the words, then spun on her heels and dashed from the chamber, leaving him alone with the world carved into a tabletop and his own self-loathing.

7

ISSARIA

Issaria waited until the guards outside her chambers switched at midnight. Elon had been there at the guard change for the evening. As always, he stayed until midnight then switched off with another guard, usually one of the other Initiates who had passed the intellectual exams last year. Feeling only slightly guilty that she'd picked a fight with Elon, she waited beside the door, listening to the new attendant settle into his post.

At least fifteen minutes had passed since Elon exchanged evening pleasantries with his replacement. Rhori, perhaps, maybe Flynt. She couldn't be sure without opening the door, and that was not happening. Either way, Elon needed to believe tonight was just another quiet night, any ordinary night under the Eventide, even if they were quarreling.

Partially, it was true. She *was* upset he chose to declare for his name instead of her...but what did she really expect? She swallowed the thought and settled her resolve again, for probably the hundredth time that night. She picked the fight on purpose, so that he would leave her to cool down and she could execute her plan without drawing too much attention to herself. If she were caught and it looked as though she just slipped out to get some distance, maybe they wouldn't ask where she went. At least until she decided what to do with whatever she learned at the end of her quest.

She needed to do this now, before the binding ritual. She wasn't sure what it would really...*feel* like to be linked to Elon. How close would they really be? Would he be able to read her mind, or at least, her intentions? Would he know how much she's always loved him? Or that there was a voice, a *something* inside her mana?

Issaria recalled her father, Helios, saying that Soren Sainthart was more than just his *Defendier*, but his most loyal and trusted friend. Helios sat a young Issaria on his knee and told her that the greatest bond she would ever know would be the loyalty and love of her *Defendier*, that they would always know what she needed just by looking into her heart. That bond seemed magical and wonderful at the time, but now, Issaria was an adult, and a bond that *intimate* sounded terrifying when she'd never even been kissed.

All the pageantry of the Trials was because Issaria's time to ascend the throne was nearly upon them. She would be crowned as the new Imperial Empress in a little more than a month's time, and Issaria still didn't know what type of Empress she would be. Adrift in a sea of questions, she grasped for answers to mysteries that no one wanted to speak of: What was happening in Daylight? Who killed her parents and to what end? Surely this was not the world they wished to create.

With that in mind, should she *really* conquer—no, it was *unification*, Aunt Cate said. Conquering was for warmongers like Akintunde Ballentine of Hinhallow. *You cannot conquer what is yours by divine right, moon drop.*

Regardless of the words she used, Aunt Cate still sought vengeance for the assassinations. She pushed Issaria to continue her protest against the Daylight Cities. She bid Issaria to conquer, ravage, and claim until all of Ellorhys bowed before them.

But what of her parent's legacy? The Golden Dynasty, while brief, had always been thought of as the most peaceful time in Ellorhys, making the assassination of the emperor and empress all that more horrific as the nation descended back into war following their deaths. War couldn't be the only way.

She was running out of time and she had to know for herself. Issaria was going to see Daylight once and for all.

By now, Elon would probably be in his quarters in the barracks, getting ready to settle in for some hard-earned rest. He'd endured a brutal gauntlet today and over the past few weeks of Trials. He earned his place among the Guard for himself. She smiled to herself, proud of him, then shook her head.

He was going to be *furious* when he found her missing in the morning.

Issaria crept across her chambers to her bed where the final items for her journey laid in wait for her. Already dressed for travel as much as she could be: a pale linen blouse, and her hair was tied back in a modest ponytail. Her bangs and loose wisps around her face kept her purple gaze obscured in the moonlight. The soft, tawny trousers gave way to bare feet— better for sneaking on the polished crystal.

She slung a sack across her back. Inside she packed wool socks and a pair of knee-high leather boots to slip into once she'd escaped her chambers, the Aquathyst stolen from Magi Caltac's stores to produce water for her journey, and a linen napkin tied around some bread and cheeses stolen from the evening snack she had requested her Mistress of Household, Safaia, to bring her earlier. She felt terrible lying to her friends about what she wanted to do, about where she was going, but their ignorance had to be believable, or else she was certain they'd be dismissed from the staff. Aunt Cate had done worse for less when Issaria's safety was concerned.

She took a black hooded cloak from where it was draped on the back of lounge chaise by the balcony and wrapped it around her with a snap, securing the clasp at her throat before pulling the oversized hood up to hide her face.

It wasn't much, but she didn't plan to be gone long, just until the following evening maybe, and she had even thought to leave a note this time! Poor Safaia would be in for a rough morning when she found the letter and Issaria's chambers empty. Without so much as a click from the locks as she gripped the doorknobs, Issaria flung the double doors open into the late summer night.

She crossed the balcony and looked out over the palace grounds. Her balcony was a great vantage point; she could see nearly the entire palace yard save for the far eastern quadrant, which housed the main gates to the grounds, as it was blocked by the monolithic pillar of the main palace halls. From the stables tucked against the far western wall, to the arbor of silver-leafed Gracelings beneath her balcony, nothing looked amiss. Beneath her, the fruit was nearly plump enough to pick, but the Harvest Season wouldn't begin until after her birthday.

She craned her neck and strained to listen for the echoes of conversation from the guards as they made their rounds in the yard.

Right on schedule, she heard muffled voices like rushes of wind at first, but then they grew as the pair of guards rounded a crystal cluster on the western side of the palace that Issaria knew to be the Annex, where Magi Caltac was probably snoring like a grizzly in his chambers on the second floor.

"Well, then he said to me—you won't believe this—he said that she controlled his body with water," one guard said, his voice filled with awe and fear as they approached beneath her.

"Controlled his body, you say?" The other chuckled. "Sounds like an old star-tale if you ask me. Ain't no way a water magician can control someone's body with water. I should know. I'm a water magician." He slapped the other guard on the back, rattling his armor. "Kid, you're listening to too many drunks in the taverns."

"You don't get it, Zorovic. The lady ain't no ordinary magician. She's a witch. She uses the black arts," the first guard insisted. "That's what he told me. That she uses this water witch to make sure things happen the way she wants them to."

"The black arts? Ha! Now I know you got this from a drunk," Zorovic guffawed as the pair came to wait beneath her balcony. "Look, kid, I'm a hundred and seventy-three. I've been a guard at this palace since I was sixty-eight. I've seen a lot of things, but I assure you, the Empress Regent does *not* have a witch on her council that can control people with water. That is just preposterous. I knew her before, I see her now, *and* I know her Guard as well as her council.

She's a good woman and a devoted ruler for someone who was never supposed to wear the crown."

"But what if—"

"What you're saying could be considered treason," Zorovic cautioned.

The pair fell silent. Issaria held her breath. She wasn't sure what they were talking about, but this Zorovic fellow seemed to be a veteran of the Guard while the other seemed to be a gullible novice, falling for all sorts of fantastical rumors.

"You're right. Yaxin probably had one too many that night. Maybe let his mouth get away from him."

"His imagination too, it seems," Zorovic said. "C'mon. Let's get back to the gates. Let the hounds roam until the dawn shift. I'll tell you about the water magicians that built the ice palace of Rhunmesc. Now *that* is a water magi work of wonder..." Their voices faded as they rounded the corner and vanished around the eastern side of the palace.

Hounds? Heart hammering in her chest, Issaria swallowed at the mention of the palace hounds. They would scent her on the grounds and bay at the guards until they followed them to her. She needed to move much faster than she originally thought. She swallowed her outrage at that guard's lack of discretion with his words as she sucked in a breath of air and hoisted herself up onto the railing, straddling it with one leg on either side. Rumors like that were easily dispelled when uttered by drunks, but a palace Guard had a reputation to uphold! She shook her head as she tossed the length of sheets and blankets she'd knotted together over the railing. To help her scale down the side of the tower, it was secured to one of the thick, crystal columns that supported the balustrade and flapped lazily against reflective palace wall, descending to about eight meters above the ground, just above any guard's heads should they pass this way unscheduled.

Winding the sheet around the length of her arm and underneath her to wrap around her leg on the opposite side of her body, she thought she could control the speed of her descent and not require too much strength on her part. The return journey would be much easier, she planned to walk up to the front gate with a smile and an apology for her absence. Steadied on the lip of the balcony, her toes were the only thing touching the crystal when she leaned back and judged the fall from this height at about sixty-five meters. Maybe more.

"Okay," she said aloud, letting out the breath she'd been holding. "Let's just take this nice and slow…" Issaria eased her weight from her trembling toes to her makeshift escape rope, trusting the fabrics to hold her. The knots tightened as she let her rope take the brunt of her weight, but they held. Pride surged within her as she began the awkward shimmy-shift of letting gravity help her rappel down the side of the palace.

She maintained a slow pace and bounced gently off the side of the palace with each increment of the descent taken. Halfway down, she heard the distinct *shhhhhhhrrrrrrrrrrrrrp* of tearing fabric.

Gravity claimed her. Issaria dared not scream as she plunged several meters. She clenched her eyes, unable to watch the ground fast approaching.

She jerked to a halt and smacked against the palace. Her skull rattled off the crystal, sending stars cascading across her vision. She groaned, glad she didn't bite her tongue off, and cast her eyes upward to see what malfunctioned.

Above her, the bedsheet had ripped, but the knot tying it to the sheet before it held strong. For now. Much closer to the ground now, Issaria shimmied down the rest of the makeshift rope before dropping silently to the grass below. She pressed her back to the palace, letting the shadow of her balcony cloak her movements as she paused to jam her dew-dampened feet into the thick socks before lacing up her leather boots. With her pack beneath her cloak, supplies tucked inside, she stole across the palace yard, and disappeared into the shadows of the arbor before the hounds were even out of their kennels.

✳ ✴ ✳

SLIPPING OUT OF THE PALACE HAD BECOME SECOND NATURE TO ISSARIA. She's done it many times as a child, but then her parents were murdered, and Aunt Hecate cast the Eventide upon Espera to protect the last of the Imperials.

She spent many years following her Aunt's guidance, terrified of what lay beyond her Aunt's fierce protection. It seemed her bloodline was cursed by regicide. First Obsidia, corrupted by Khaos, murdered her sister to steal her magic and cast the world into darkness. Thank the Cosmos Issaria's parents were able to unite their magic to defeat her before she was able to enact her plan. And then her beloved parents, genuine heroes in their own right, were *dead*. An Imperial assassination.

Issaria put a hand to her throat and rubbed her collar bone. She wondered who would try to kill her and if, or when, they would be successful. Over the years her aunt had told her when attempts on her life were made. Even invited her to look her would-be assassins in the eye when they were caught, but she'd never accepted. She didn't want to meet a person who would kill her on an order without meeting her, knowing her, but still prepared to claim her life. Despicable.

Getting out of the palace, it seemed, was still a simple task. Getting in was supposed to be another story. Aunt Cate had interrogated each member of the staff in the weeks and months that followed her parent's deaths. Many were deemed unfit for service and were dismissed. Since then, the palace staff had been thin but effective, if not always the most efficient. Unused chambers and hallways went unkempt, dust accumulating on floors and bedding that awaited visiting diplomats and royals that would never come.

Espera had changed in the years since, and not just because their little corner of the world now existed entirely in night.

Heels clacked against the cobblestones as she walked through the mist coming in off the sea. At the docks, fisherman loaded nets and baskets into their boats by lantern light. Worn planks groaned under Issaria's steps, and the men looked up from their tasks, eyes tracking her to the last boat on the pier where she stopped.

"I heard that I could buy passage to the Baelforia on your vessel," she said to the man who knelt in the single-masted sloop before her.

His hands remained busy, tying knots in his net to mend the holes ripped the previous night as he said, "Three silvers will get you to the shore. Make it gold, and you've got my silence as well."

Issaria considered for a moment what this man's silence meant. Others bartered passage with this man to escape her aunt's reign. Many feared her power and thought that life outside the Eventide was better than life within it. "How about five gold pieces, and you also retrieve me and return me here when you return from your outing? I will be waiting where you leave me."

The man stiffened, his back to her. "You'd be the first to come back."

"Then we have a deal?"

The man stood and turned to her. "Six pieces and we have an accord." He extended his hand before her, to seal the agreement, not to collect the coins.

"Six pieces," she echoed and placed her hand in his, a single shake to seal the bargain.

THE BAELFORIA WAS ALIVE WITH SOUND AS ISSARIA TOOK HER FIRST tentative step from the moonlit beach where she had been dropped off by the fisherman. She had watched until he rowed into open water and unfurled the pale blue sail on his sloop to take him further out into the Gulf. When he was gone, just a speck of lantern light tossed on the night-black sea, she turned her back on the southern horizon and headed into the trees.

Fallen leaves and moss carpeting the forest floor cushioned her footfalls as the soft echo of ocean waves was traded for the chirrup of birds, now accustomed to the night, as they flitted from branch to branch heralding the princess' arrival to their sacred wood. Steadying herself with a deep breath, Issaria cast one glance over her shoulder as the beach vanished into the thicket behind her. There was no turning back now unless she wanted to swim back to Espera. She wasn't *too far* from the Timeline, she estimated by the map. Quick sail around the bay, and then a brisk walk through the woods. Perhaps only half a day's walk as the crow flies, and then she would see for herself what eight years of constant, berating sunlight would do to a landscape. To people she still felt responsible for, even if some vile Daylighters had taken her family from her. The sins of the few did not merit the punishment of the many, not to Issaria.

Ancient limbs creaked as they swayed against the star-strewn sky. Moonlight sifted through the treetops, casting ripples across the varied leaves of jade, emerald, and evergreen. As she ventured deeper into the first forest, the initial clamor of life dissipated. Silence overtook her, leaving her with only her own breathing and the crisp crunch of the leaf-litter underfoot.

Branches broke just beyond her field of vision, and she snapped her head in the direction of the noise, peering into the darkness. She was not alone in this sacred forest; she knew she would not be. Many creatures roamed this wood before the Eventide, and many more had migrated to the safety of its grove since. It would have been irrational to say that all the creatures in Ellorhys had been identified. Gritting her teeth, Issaria glared into the shadows. Silent, she dared whatever lingered just out of sight to face her. But nothing happened, and her wild imagination set her cheeks aflame. Issaria continued through the trees.

It was midmorning, as judged by the stars overhead, when she stopped to break her fast. Choosing a spot where she could see the sky and the constellation of Tarlix, bearing the Vitalief, the planet's sacred heart of fire represented by the brightest star in the sky, Issaria snacked on soft cheese as she recalled the legends of the cosmos.

Tarlix, the fire Mythos, was chosen by the Ethereal Mythos to carry a heart blessed with the covenant of life to the core of their planet. The image she imagined transposed over the scattered star points across the sky was a fierce and handsome warrior mid-stride, bearing a heart ablaze in his hand held before him, guiding one south to the Celestial City—Espera. She sat for a while, staring at the sky until the southern star symbolizing the heart had vanished into the canopy.

It was time to move on.

Issaria gathered her belongings and drank again from the Aquathyst crystal, glad the magic instilled within it was intention-bound and needed only a hope and a prayer. Distilled water dripped like a spigot until she'd had her fill, then dripped twice more for extra measure before she dropped the damp blue stone into her pack. Issaria bound her remaining food in the napkin again, much smaller a bundle now, she noted. She over-ate as she stargazed. Scolding herself, Issaria set off again into the trees, keeping that southern star to her back as she went.

Hours later, the princess was stomping through the brush. Her footfalls descended with rage and trampled the underbrush. Her face was scraped from having to scale a small cliffside in order to save her from backtracking only Mythos knows how far. Her knees were skinned and bleeding from the gorge where a skinny sapling had loosed its roots while Issaria braced her weight, sending her skidding yards before she reclaimed her purchase and continued her ascent. This trek wasn't supposed to be this…this *difficult.*

She'd pictured a serene walk through the woods until she was blinking into the sunshine like a fawn new to the world. She would have turned back by now but stubbornness kept her going. Elon's rage was already guaranteed; she may as well have something to show for it after the way she snapped at him yesterday.

Issaria sought answers and Mythos be damned, she was going to get them if it killed her. At this point, she was so deep in the Baelforia even she didn't know where she was anymore. The trees here were thick, the forest floor was a maze of exposed roots. Some were as wide as she was tall. Massive trunks shot up fifteen and twenty meters before splitting thick branches and blotting out the sky, save a few sifting moonbeams that made Issaria feel like she walked the ocean floor instead of in a forest.

Seething with frustration and maybe more than a little self-hatred, she tromped through the underbrush, catching her tattered cloak on every other briar bush. Issaria continued that way, her stubbornness propelling her forward, or maybe sideways. She wasn't sure. She probably should have told Elon her plan; it was so stupid to come out here alone. If she'd only told him the truth he probably would have wanted to come with her, to help her find the answers to the questions that plagued her.

The ground beneath her boots quaked. Birds took wing from trees that shuddered with the vibrations of whatever approached. Tremors loosed her balance and she fell as the earth cracked open before her, releasing a brilliant shine of green light. Issaria threw her arm up to shield her eyes as bones and saplings, pebbles, dirt, and an assortment of creeping insects surged from the chasm in the glen.

Jade light charged the fragments and leaped between stones and boulders, lashing the chunks together until a creature began to take shape before her. Taller than any magician she'd seen by the height of at least two full-grown men, the colossal being radiated a soft, shifting halo of emerald light from the glowing nerve-like network of vines that held the thing's shape. It stood on two legs like a person, but they were thick, cylindrical and each foot could have flattened a man, or at least half of one.

It was all manner of earthen things. Moss still grew on the sharp ridges of boulders and rocks that formed the broad torso. Saplings ridged its spine like a lion's mane. Branches extended from its head like a forest of antlers toward the canopy. The green leaves withered, fell, budded, blossomed and greened before her eyes, going through seasons of life on his back as he stood before her. Her mouth hung open as she took it in.

She knew she should run.

She should be afraid.

But it was the massive Terran monster's eyes that rooted her before it.

Deep pools of glowing golden-green light spiraled in the crevasses between the pebbles and rocks that formed its elongated face. In the depths of its eyes, she saw a kinship. She felt the adoration, and dare she say, devotion as the creature gazed upon her.

It would not hurt her, she knew. It had come here...no. It was *already* here. She had come to it. To...to him.

Her mana swelled inside her, wanting to answer the call, to speak his name and break the spell on her sleeping mind.

The name was on her lips, a trembling question that she dared to ask. "Baelfor?"

The Elemental Mythos only said one word.

"Aurelia."

Issaria's mana erupted at the name, white light crackled from within her, far beyond the princess' control. Terror gripped her before she felt nothing at all.

8
CALIX

Prince Calix walked through the dark and ancient forest, flipping his dagger easily in his hand. He caught the handle each time even as his gaze was fixed on the Vitalief, the southern star. More than half the morning had passed since he crossed the Timeline from day into night. The prince basked in glorious relief of night for the first time in eight years. *However,* he growled, it was ridiculous that he had to take this route. He'd taken a ship from Hinhallow to Ares, around the northern tip of the continent, through the Norvenello Ocean. He'd found safe harbor in Ares, on the Timeline and the closest city to Espera. He should have just taken a horse across the Razor, the foot trail along the River Cyth bordering the Glass and the Baelforia—

He stopped walking.

He wasn't certain when as he'd been lost in thought, but the forest had fallen silent. The birds had stopped chirping, the crickets ceased to sing. Small creatures that scampered through the undergrowth seemed to have all found their burrows and nests and even the wind seemed to know not to disturb this moment.

Calix reached for his belt and pulled a second dagger, shifted his stance, ready to attack at the slightest—

A blinding flash of light had him blinking spots away as he whirled towards the source. After a moment, his vision cleared enough for him to see that not too far off his path was an eerie purple glow just... lingering in the trees. He waited and watched in silence until spots no longer danced across his vision.

Quiet and low, he stalked toward the light, his hood pulled up over his head and his crimson cowl up to cover his lower face. Fever-black hands itched to summon his scimitars, but the armament magic was too iconic of the Prince of Hinhallow, so he tightened his grip on his alloy daggers. All anyone or anything would see would be his blades and his eyes. He pressed his back to the trunk of the closest tree. It was thicker than some of the buildings in Hinhallow, and he edged around it slow as he scanned the bramble and branches above for sentries. Tentative, he peered around the column of gnarled grey bark, then sucked in a breath that made his teeth cold.

In the clearing beyond he saw...well he wasn't sure what he saw. Calix gazed upon something beyond magic. Something archaic and made of legends.

A woman, with pure white hair and brilliant violet eyes that smoldered with incandescent light that made his eyes burn to behold. She flew—floated in an opaque aura of purple light before a massive golem of stone, bone, and petrified wood. Her white hair floated behind her as if it obeyed no gravity but its own. The woman hovered in midair, the train of her radiant white dress brushing against the ferns in the glen, and *still* the monster towered over the Ethereal Lady.

A small forest grew on the creature's back, and small birds chirruped in the branches of trees that thickened their trunks and felled their leaves in moments. It held an other-worldly aura all its own, but the green bands of light that entwined the massive sections of boulders seemed to be the very magic that bound its form together, whereas the woman in the air...she was *made* of starlight and magic. He could taste her power in the air around them. Whatever this beast was that garnered this cosmic lady's intervention—

"Aurelia," the creature spoke, its voice rolling through Calix like an avalanche. *"Too long has Ellorhys awaited your return."*

He could hardly believe his ears. He lay mortal eyes upon the Imperial Mythos of Light herself. Aurelia was…Calix's mouth went dry. Well, first off, she was supposed to be dead. But more than that, she was the answer to all the prayers on all the altars in all the temples in Ellorhys. Her light, her goodness would return the balance of night and day to the planet. Perhaps the land could recover from the damage done in the past eight years.

Calix leaned forward, strained to hear her reply to the terran titan.

I am here now, Baelfor. Aurelia's voice was light as songbirds in the summer. He heard her voice in his head without her speaking a word. The smile on her face was one of bitterness and regret. *All will be well but, you know as well as I that I am not yet returned. My vessel has almost cycled through the eclipse of the Saros curse. Only then may I walk Ellorhys again.*

"I feel the bonds of destiny that tether you to this world. You feel it too; even in your weakened state, you must." Baelfor's voice shook the young trees that grew around them. Frail leaves broke free from their branches at his breath. *"The land aches for balance. It will not long survive the darkness upon it. The covenant will shatter without Tarlix tending it. He was not supposed to be gone this long. The Vitalief grows dark."*

Calix crept forward, entranced by the scene before him. He was witnessing divine prophecy. He'd never taken himself for a believer in that sort of thing, but seeing them here, now? Two ancient powers were in the Baelforia the same day as himself. Learning of their return to Ellorhys since their extinction? It was either uncanny luck or providence.

A branch snapped underfoot, and their attention was on him. The gravity of their collective radiance had him kneeling, bowing over to save his sight. To have them look upon him directly was like staring into a thousand suns.

"Good of you to join us," Baelfor grumbled at him. They were expecting him? *"Though you look rather silly with all that power cooped up in that weak mortal flesh."*

"Who, me?" Calix croaked at their recognition.

Baelfor. Aurelia's voice was clipped. *Time is short. She will know when*

I awaken, and then there will be no time to waste. *Her influence is already hooked deep into her descendia. Raise the others, and when I am reborn from my vessel I will join you for the yielding.*

The Terran Mythos, larger now than he had been when Calix stumbled upon their secret meeting, seemed to understand he had been dismissed. Sparing a final glance at Calix as he trailed moths behind him, the giant golem lumbered from the glen. Each step shook the trees around him, and leaves spiraled down around him until the shadows of the forest named for his existence swallowed him, and even his green light no longer lingered in the air like a spring rain.

The woman's purple aura remained like a thick fog upon them.

Prince Calix Ballentine. His daggers clattered to the forest floor. She knew his name. *Long have I wished to look upon your face.*

What?

"Ethereal Lady," he said, hoping to honor her with the name he had called her in his head. "I did not mean to intrude upon your meeting with the Elemental. Please, forgive my transgression."

Rise, son of the first flame, for I have called you here, as I have brought her to meet you. To learn she can trust one who would be her enemy.

Calix trembled, he was not afraid to admit it, as he rose, and lifted his eyes to gaze upon her beauty again. "Her?" he echoed, confused, for he was alone in the glen.

My vessel will soon be in great danger, for if I am here, then the Darkness that Consumes is as well. Even in rebirth, I will not be as strong as he without drinking from the Celestial Spring.

"The Vera Caelum?" Prince Calix looked upon the woman with moonbeam colored hair and wanted to laugh. "Isn't that an old star-tale?"

It is not. There is a temple in the sky where the Ethereal Mythos laid their heads while the Elementals toiled and sculpted the continents. Within the halls of this sacred space is a spring that is fed by the very cradle of life itself, the place where even Dovenia, Chronos, and Essos draw their primordial strength. It is where I was born of them and told to drink. I must drink again, or this body will fail to contain me. She gave him a sad smile. *Not unlike the blight of the fervent upon you.*

Calix pounded a fist over his heart and dared to look her in her star-fire eyes. Like looking at the sun, colorful stars burst across his vision as he beheld her glory. "If you seek the spring, my Lady, I will find it. I swear it so."

Yes, you who are born of the original flame are the only one suited to this task. But you must wait for me, as you have these long years. I am not yet awakened, and as such, am not ready for the journey.

"If not now, then when? When should I seek this Temple of Life?"

We shall seek it together, my Prince. My vessel will come to you when the time is near, but she will wear the guise of another as I wear her face as my own. For now, know that the truth will set her free, as she has already begun to tip the scales toward balance.

"Who is this *she* of which you speak, Ethereal Lady? Who is your vessel, and how will I know her?" Calix demanded, his voice much bolder than he felt before her radiant light and divine presence. His knees shook but his voice did not.

At once, the light radiating from her extinguished, leaving them in the darkness of the night. She hovered still, her purple eyes glowing, white hair suspended around her as though she were adrift under the sea. Then, slowly, she descended. Her eyes began to dull, and her hair seeped black from the root until it was all sable and curls. She was no longer a glowing Mythos of Light, but a black-haired girl, laid gently on the forest floor, blinking, and holding her head.

He stared at her from where he stood, rooted to the spot, one hand on the trunk of the tree he'd rounded to enter the grove. As if she sensed his presence in the clearing with her, she turned toward him, panic evident on her pale face. "What…what happened?"

"Issaria Elysitao?" He almost didn't believe his own voice. She was scratched and bleeding and looked almost nothing like the pampered witch he sought, but he would know those legendary violet eyes anywhere.

They widened at her name. Scrambling to her feet she pulled up her hood as if it could still hide her identity. "Do I know you?" she asked, voice full of challenge but without denial.

He chuckled. Mythos be damned. He understood now, at least part of what the glowing lady had said. "I'm not going to hurt you," he announced, and was surprised to find that despite his original quest, he meant it.

"Gee, that's reassuring," she retorted as she stepped back a few paces. "Forgive me if I don't quite believe you, seeing as I just woke up from whatever you did to me."

"Did to you?" Calix echoed, almost laughing. "I didn't do anything to you, *Princess.*" Beneath his own cloak he felt his belt for his dagger, but they were in the leaves behind him. He almost felt vulnerable, except that he was a Prince of Hinhallow, and a fire magician, and this princess had never once seen him in combat, despite how clearly powerful her magic was.

"How..." She paused for a moment, then said, "How far from the Timeline am I, stranger?"

"You're going to Day?" He didn't hide the shock in his voice. "Why?"

"Because..." The princess's face fell. "Because I need to see for myself."

"See the destruction you and the Evernight Witch have cursed us to?" He hissed.

She looked to the ground, the hood of her cloak obscuring her eyes, but Calix could see the downward pull of her mouth. After a moment she said, "Yes."

"Well, no need to go so far, your *Imperial Highness.*" Calix let his distaste for this girl seep into his words. "I can tell you all about it."

For a moment, hurt flashed across her face before she schooled it into a placid expression of mild curiosity. "Did I do something to earn your hostility?" She gestured around them. "As far as I'm aware, I was looking at Baelfor and then you bashed me over the head—"

"Bashed you over the head?" Calix was affronted. "I did no such thing!"

"Then what happened to me just now? Where is Baelfor?" Princess Issaria shouted at him, and he drew back. "Why don't I remember anything after her voice?"

And for the first time, he heard the panic in her voice. He saw the fear etched on her face in the crease of her brow, the desperation in her purple eyes.

She didn't know what lived inside her.

Somehow, she was unaware that she was a vessel for something— no, some*one* cosmic.

"I saw a light in the trees." He pulled down his cowl, exposing his face to her as he spoke. "I'm on my way to Espera and I saw a flash, and I came in this direction to see…"

He let his sentence trail. How did he explain what he saw when she could still be the enemy? He'd been raised to despise her. Sent to kill her even, but here she was, innocent as a doe. How bizarre. His crown and his father were depending on Calix ending her life and he knew he wouldn't do it.

"Princess, Ellorhys burns in the unforgiving light of the sun. I can only imagine what the tides have done to Espera's harbors now that the Salt Ice melts and even proud Rhunmesc finds themselves seeking aid. Your aunt has sentenced the land to drought and famine with her accursed night, and it is time you heard the truth of the evil you call Empress."

"Evil?" The princess scoffed. "Aunt Cate is not—"

"Aunt Cate?" He forced himself to laugh. Such a domestic title for one so despicable. "Aunt Cate?" he repeated again, shaking his head. "The one you hold so high in regard is probably going to kill you for that crown, just like she murdered your parents."

"Liar!" she spat. "How dare you speak such lies!" She stalked toward him, anger radiating off of her. "My aunt is not a witch! She is protecting me—protecting Espera! The Eventide…" The princess closed the space between them in a few angry paces. "The Eventide is the only way. I'm the last of us. She promised me…" She was out of breath, her face flushed as she came right up to him and jabbed a finger into his sternum repeatedly, causing him to step back with each forceful accusation. "And who are *you* to claim to know such things? A bandit? Some farmer's son? You're clearly from Daylight. You've probably never even met her. You know nothing of my parents, or of Aunt Cate!"

Calix considered for a moment as he looked down at this girl—no, he could see now that while she was petite, she was definitely not a child. And a woman's fury raged on her scraped and flushed face. Wild black hair peeked out from beneath her hood, some leaves stuck in the snarl of her curls. She braced her hands on her hips as she met his eyes with her own unwavering stare.

What would this princess do if she knew who he was or why he was sent here?

I have called you here, as I have brought her to meet you. To learn she can trust one who would be her enemy.

The Ethereal Lady's voice echoed in his head. Wasn't he sent here by his father and the Celestial Alliance? Suddenly, he wasn't so sure the order came from them alone. And what *did* happen to Issaria? Aurelia was dead. Long gone. Murdered by her sister in some black arts ritual sacrifice to harvest her magic—horrific, really. But he'd seen her mere moments ago, and Princess Issaria, his target, was her vessel.

Something great was afoot in the ancient wood, and Calix would be damned if he was going to stand in the way of the Cosmos.

The truth will set her free.

"I was sent here by the Celestial Alliance to kill you, Princess."

9
ISSARIA

Issaria held the stranger's golden gaze. She wasn't quite sure she heard him right. He wore black, but his pants and tunic were trimmed with gold embroidery, she noted, and the crimson cowl that had hidden his *very* handsome, slightly stubbled face, was silk. His skin was bronzed and baked from endless hours in the sun. Even his sweat smelled different, hot and dusty, as if he might never be clean of the shimmer of sand on his skin. But under that, he smelled of...sandalwood and jasmine. He may have been a hired blade, but he was well off, suggesting he earned his keep, and then some, on the edge of a blade. Not only was he from Daylight, but this man was from Hinhallow.

And he was here to kill her.

"Well, not here, specifically, I suppose," the man continued on, "They sent me to Espera to kill you, and perhaps your beloved aunt if I am able, but I suppose it is more than luck that our paths crossed a bit early."

She thought of the rock-titan, the light and then...she was certain she'd heard the voice again, felt her mana rising up, unwelcome, and unsummoned. Then she was blinking into the moonlight and suddenly this man was standing in the clearing with her. Yes. Yes, it did seem like more than luck that they had found each other. "If you're supposed to kill me," she began, as she pulled back her hood, "why tell me?" She didn't know why she wasn't running, or why...she didn't feel afraid.

"Because I've had a change of heart."

She blinked up at him. "What? Why?"

"Because you seek the truth of the Evernight Witch, your aunt's actions, do you not?" A light danced in the stranger's eyes that hadn't been there before. "Consider your search over. I come bearing the truth."

They stood like that for a moment. The forest chattered around them as they held each other's gaze. Issaria searched for a hint of betrayal on his face, some indication that he lied. But there was no tremor along the sharp angle of his jaw, nor in his eyes that shifted like embers. Save for the daggers that glinted in the underbrush behind him, he seemed to bear her no ill will. Resentment, maybe, by how he'd chastised her, but even that seemed too strong a word now.

"You don't trust me?"

"You said you were sent to kill me, rock head. Would *you* trust you?"

He laughed. A genuine guffaw as he tipped his head back toward the canopy and cackled like a crow. "No, I suppose I wouldn't." He turned and gathered his daggers from the leaves behind him before turning back to her. "It was Baelfor. He told me not to harm you. So I shall obey." He didn't meet her eyes as he spoke of the Mythos, and she knew he wasn't being entirely truthful with her, but she felt it in her gut that he truly meant her no harm. Not any longer, anyway. Perhaps he was only a skilled liar and she'd soon find a blade in her back.

"I didn't know assassins were devout."

"Maybe I'm not just an assassin. Kind of like you're clearly not *just* a princess."

"Who...who are you?"

"Who I am doesn't matter," the man insisted. "I come bearing the truth you seek, and more. I was sent to kill you because the Celestial Alliance believes you corrupt, under your aunt's influence." He held her gaze a beat longer than necessary before he added, "I can see now that isn't true and I will bring this knowledge back to my...the council."

She furrowed her brow. "And just like that, you're going to spare me?"

He arched his eyebrows in amusement. "Would you rather I didn't?"

A blush crept up her neck, and she was glad for the heavy cover of the trees, as the darkness would hide her embarrassment. "No, thank you...and thank you again, for sparing me," she said, as she realized she had come into the forest—a dark and dangerous forest without so much as a butter knife to protect herself. She felt like an idiot of the highest caliber. Elon would be *furious*.

She thought for a moment then asked, "You said...that my aunt had killed my parents?" She shook her head. "That's not true. I was there that night. It was assassins posing as palace staff. Aunt Cate was the one who stopped them."

Images from that night flashed over and over in her head. The empty kitchens, bread charred in the hearth. The lack of staff in the corridors. The blood on Aunt Cate's sword, and—wait. Why did Aunt Cate even *have* a sword? Issaria knew she wouldn't have needed one to dispose of the traitors.

"Was it?" he asked, his voice even as he sheathed his blades at his sides. "Or is that what she wanted you all to see?"

His words sent a chill down her spine.

"It's not true," Issaria said again, but it came out as a whisper and even she wasn't convinced.

She'd seen Hecate that evening in the arbor. She swore to meet her at midnight. Why would Aunt Cate, whom she'd never seen in all her days wear anything other than the most elegant of gowns, be caught in her nightclothes? How had those servants lived among them for years before they struck? And why on *that* night? How did the assassins know to look for her at the festival when, by all accounts, she was tucked into her bed down the hall from her parent's room? And with that in mind...how did she get found so *easily*? Even Elon had questioned that. Had it been dumb luck that the assassins Daylight hired found her deep within the festival bazaar when it should have taken them much longer to locate her?

There were so *many* unanswered questions about that night. Things that her aunt…could not or…would not answer.

"If you still seek it, I will walk with you to the Timeline. You've got another several hours' trek though. I was planning on sleeping in the forest before crossing into Espera."

Issaria's face must have betrayed her dismay at the distance she still had yet to cross to see beyond the Timeline because the assassin brushed passed her and then stopped. "Come. I'll walk you home and I will tell you of what I know, of Ellorhys and what happens in the Daylight."

Southern star before them, they began the journey back through Baelforia. Issaria glanced at him, taking in his strong jaw and the cording of muscle in his neck. He was taller than Elon by a few inches at least and was broader by far. He wore the two daggers on his hips, but it was his charred hands that had captured her attention.

They were black as night well past his sleeves, she could tell. The damage of the *fervis* was extensive. He was a fire magician, and probably one that wielded some sort of weapon with those fire-blackened hands. His fever had claimed his hands far more than Magi Caltac's charred fingertips, who looked like he'd dipped his digits in black ink, although the old man *had* lost an eye to the fever as well in some epic story unbeknownst to herself.

Strangely, she trusted the assassin not to hurt her, even after he admitted he had been dispatched to end her. After the trouble she had getting this far, she was strangely glad to have the company on the way back home. Without him, she may not have made it back to the beach before the fisherman returned, and then she'd be stranded, or she'd have to swim back.

"If you won't tell me who you are, at least tell me what to call you, or else this will be a very long and awkward walk, calling you Mr. Assassin."

They continued on in silence, single file through the tall grasses, following the path that Issaria had bent in the forest on her way toward the timeline. He had sworn to give her the truth, but maybe he wouldn't give that sort of truth. Just as she was about to ask a different question he said, "You can call me Blaze." She snorted, and he glared at her over his shoulder, his molten eyes gleaming. "It's an alias! It's obviously not my real name."

"I should hope not."

"Well, what would you have said? It's not like I had a lot of time to think about it," he huffed.

Issaria bit back a laugh at his defensiveness before replying, "Issamarya."

"Issamarya? That's actually quite good."

She shrugged. "It's an identity I've used since I was a girl. My friend and I used aliases when we snuck out of the palace."

"For some reason I never pictured the Imperial Princess of Espera sneaking out of the palace," he mused aloud as they continued through the forest. Creatures of the night twittered around them. "Then again, having met you here in the Baelforia perhaps I underestimated you, Princess. How did you get here, anyway? There's no way Hecate would allow you to see what her curse has wrought upon Ellorhys."

"Like I said, I snuck out of the palace." Issaria was quiet for a moment before she added in a whisper, "I snuck out of the palace the night my parents were murdered too. Only Aunt Cate knew where I went; she caught me on my way out."

"The kings and queens of the Cities swore under a blood oath that they did not order an assassination on the Imperial Emperor and Empress," Blaze said. "Most were insulted they were asked, but readily agreed to the spell." He waited a while before he added, "They're all still alive, as you know."

"She was the only one who knew I wasn't in the palace, and still… they found me and my companion at the Star Festival."

Blaze was silent as they cut sideways across a steep incline. He braced himself against the trunks of sturdy saplings, and offered his hand to help balance her as she followed his path. "That is suspicious, Princess. I shouldn't have to tell you that."

"Tell me about Daylight. Is it as bad as you said? Drought and famine? What is the alliance you mentioned? The ones that hired you to...what will you tell them about me?"

Blaze waved her down with a blackened hand. "One question at a time, Princess." Saffron eyes roamed her face before he said, "Do you want me to clean that gash on your face? It's rather...gruesome."

Her hand twitched at her side, wanting to caress her throbbing cheek, but resisted. "I'll be fine. Tell me about the Day."

He hesitated, his eyes flicking between her own and the side of her face before he shrugged and said, "It's bad in Daylight, as you call it. To us, its just Ellorhys. As it always has been and will never be again. It wasn't terrible at first, in fact, I recall King Akintunde saying that a little sunlight would be good for the fields." Blaze scoffed and shook his head. "And he was right, for a time. We had a good year, harvests were bountiful, the warmth truly had done the work for the season, as the season never changed."

He almost laughed, she could hear the chuckle catch in his throat and turn into venom as he continued, "But then the sun never set, and things started to die. Now the seas are too warm for fishing, and the earth crumbles in the savage heat. Herds starve, and the game has all migrated south. The Ascalith's borders have started to expand as well; it could be another black sands event if things keep shriveling up and turning to dust." His voice still held that bitterness from when they first spoke and he accused her of being evil. Blaze looked back at her and said, "There are refugees coming to the city every day, seeking answers." He pursed his lips and said, "Some demand justice for the curse."

"And...this Celestial Alliance," Issaria tried out the name, rolling it around on her tongue. "The Celestial Alliance sent you to kill me and my aunt, perhaps sentencing you to your own execution in the process...all for justice?" She closed her eyes for a moment, feeling the hatred Blaze had shown her upon their initial meeting and understanding it. He had every right.

She did nothing to help them. Nothing to stop it.

"The Celestial Alliance is a gathering of the remaining Monarchs in Ellorhys. King Akintunde is the chairman and founder. He formed the alliance as a resistance against the Evernight Witch."

"Why do you call her that? The Evernight Witch." Issaria couldn't mask the disgust in her voice. "She's the Empress Regent, holding my crown for me until I am old enough to rule."

Moonlight filled their path, silver light flooding the brush and undergrowth in the clearing between trunks. They were getting smaller, but still, these massive trunks reached eight or ten feet in the air before their branches extended skyward.

"I know this is heavy, but your aunt, Hecate is…she's evil, Princess. Evil. She killed her sister—your mother, as well as your father. May her soul never find peace in the Cosmos after such an atrocity."

Hearing it aloud made her blood run cold. And he made the statement with such…conviction. There was no doubt in Blaze that her aunt was a cold-blooded murderer. And since he was an assassin by trade…he would know, wouldn't he?

"My order to assassinate you was to eliminate the threat of eternal darkness after Hecate's death. Without you there would be no heir to continue Obsidia's campaign of Evernight."

Issaria shook her head. "No, this isn't an Evernight. Not…not yet." She swallowed before confessing to the assassin's back, "She calls this the *Eventide*. But…she wants me to create the Evernight when I am Empress. I am to conquer the other cities as revenge for my parent's death."

The assassin turned around. Tears brimmed her lashes as she clenched her eyes, unable to meet his golden gaze for fear of what she would see there. "I don't believe that's what my parents would have wanted though," she said at last.

"Ellorhys is dying. Hecate is a witch, evil as they come, and she will stop at nothing to rule the land, just as her mother before her. This Eventide as you call it? It is the same dark magic that Obsidia wished to curse Ellorhys with and you are a blind fool if you do not see it."

Issaria thought of the Evernight her great aunt, the Dark Witch

Obsidia, had sought to unleash upon the continents. Obsidia harnessed the black arts to kill her sister and steal her primordial power. With the magic of two Mythos, she tried to cover Ellorhys with darkness. Issaria thought the story implied she covered the land with evil but...what if darkness just meant...eternal night?

Her face flushed at her naivety. Had she really been that foolish?

"If you do not bend to her will, Princess, she will have you killed. I guarantee it." She opened her eyes at his voice and found that he was looking at her not with hatred or fear, but with sorrow in his eyes. "She likely has already tried, if you have come this far for the truth instead of falling in line with her ideals and..." He stopped and looked away.

"And what?"

"And if she knows what power you wield."

She stared at him, blank faced across the grove. A breeze tugged on her hair, pushing loose tendrils across her face as it carried the scent of the mountains, pine and snow, through the trees. She could smell the night, crisp and dark around her. "I don't have any power," she said at last.

"We both know that isn't true, Princess," Blaze said, his stare unwavering. Not a challenge, just...the truth.

"What happened to me before...before I woke up?" Issaria asked. She'd heard the woman's voice again, when the light surrounded her. She'd said...what had she said? Her head ached as she thought about it. The voice inside her mana...it *reacted* to Baelfor. He said...

Issaria thought her heart would stop in her chest as the voice whispered in her head.

He had given her a name.

What had he called her?

Blaze walked past her and several steps into the next grove before he said, "One day soon, Hecate will turn on you. She must know the power you possess, and she will kill you for it. Perhaps she will fear it, or maybe she will seek it for herself in some dark ritual." His voice was sharp as he kept his back to her. "You don't have to make it so easy for her."

"What?"

"Come back to Hinhallow with me. I have...connections. You can fight her. Stand with the Alliance, with Hinhallow, and fight her."

Issaria scoffed, looking away from his earnest offer, his palms held open in supplication. "You say fight her like it's so easy, but I hate to tell you, *Blaze*, that I'm no warrior. I take dance lessons. I have soldiers that fight to win a place in my guard. I attend councils only when my aunt believes the content of the meeting will further my knowledge. Mundane issues are...her pleasure to take care of so that I may pursue my studies," Issaria repeated mechanically as she began to realize each answer was a line fed to her by her aunt in response to her own prodding questions. Her throat tightened around her words. "I have no power like you. I'm...I'm broken or something. I have been for years," she confessed, afraid to meet his gaze and see the pity across his beautiful face. "I was hidden," she finished.

The assassin turned back and closed the distance between them, the toes of his boots only inches from hers. She felt the weight of his hand on her shoulder before he gently squeezed, as if willing her to meet his gaze. But she refused and stared instead at the supple leather of his boots and the leaves giving way to soft green moss beneath their soles. "I've seen your power. You...you changed."

Her face paled and her lips trembled as she met his eyes, searched his tanned face for traces of the truth. "What do you mean, I *changed?*" She watched his jaw clench as he wrestled with himself. "Please... Blaze." The ache in her voice surprised herself, but she held his golden gaze. "I've...I'm telling the truth when I say I'm no good at magic. I don't have power that I can wield, it's too wild for me to safely control. But lately..." She dare not finish her sentence. It was too dangerous. Too... strange.

"When I stumbled across the purple light, I saw the titan you spoke of, with the green light in his eyes," Blaze said, his voice gravel. "And I saw a woman hovering in the air in this...glow of light. The light was coming from her."

"Where was I if Baelfor was there? I must have been laying right..."

"She wasn't you. But she knew who I was, who I am. She spoke to me and told me she called us both here, and then she *became* you."

Issaria's mouth went dry, and her face was flushed with heat. "What does that mean?"

"The woman I saw had white hair like moonlight, and…" Blaze stopped and shook his head.

"And what?" She closed the distance between them and took hold of his sleeve. "Please, tell me."

"Her eyes…"

"They were glowing," Issaria finished for him.

Blaze's eyes widened. "You've done this before."

"Yes. No." Issaria shook her head. "Maybe. Maybe but not…not the white hair."

"You have a dangerous gift, Princess."

"I…I think I know that."

They walked a long while before either of them attempted conversation again. Trees grew thinner, shorter, and smaller as they crossed small hills and crunched leaves underfoot. Underbrush grew thicker, and more saplings sprouted between the more established trees. The assassin passed his own canteen to her, and she accepted without a thought and drank deeply, thanking him each time he passed it to her along their journey.

Blaze was helping her down a rocky incline, his hand clasped on hers, when he said, "She doesn't want to give you the crown. She won't. She killed your parents for it, and I believe she meant to kill you that night too. However you managed to escape, you foiled her plan that night."

"How can you say such things?"

"Because I trust that the magic was true when the monarchs swore oaths to the Cosmos. They would have died if they had told an untruth in the face of such bloodmagic. King Akintunde would have died the moment the lie touched his lips. I was there that day, Princess. No one lied." When they were silent for a few moments and the song of the forest birds and insects had filled the space between them, he added, no more than a whisper between them, "You must learn to control the power before it controls you. I know something of that battle. It will not be easy."

"I don't know whats happening to me," she whispered, her voice trembling. "I don't know how to be this person you wish I was, running off to fight a war I never asked for. I'm just...I'm useless. I always have been."

"Perhaps I should kill you after all."

The assassin's words chilled her, but it was the cool breeze that played salt across her skin that made her realize how close to the beach they had come in the hours since they began walking toward Espera. If he truly wanted to kill her now, he had walked her right to her city's doorstep to accomplish his task. Maybe the fisherman who she'd bartered with would even find her body this close to the shore, if he was kind enough to look for her when she never returned.

"When I was a boy, my father used to tell me that we are born with our destinies written in the Cosmos and when it comes time for us to earn our future, we will find that we have all the weapons we need if only we have the courage to use them. And when I asked him if he was ever afraid of the future, he said, 'Life is not about being fearless, but having the courage to overcome our limitations. Be afraid. But then you must do it anyway.'"

Issaria was silent for a while before she nodded, acknowledging the words between them. "I can't just leave. Not yet. I need to know for certain."

He stalked several paces back into the trees before saying, "When you have the truth you seek, you have allies in Hinhallow. The prince will see to it that you are received warmly when you find yourself at the gates to the white palace."

"The prince?" she echoed incredulously. The last time she'd thought of him...she'd been a girl and had overheard her parents talking of an offer they'd received from Hinhallow. A marriage offer for the eldest prince and the only Imperial Princess. "What business of his am I?"

Blaze merely shrugged. "I dwell within the palace. He is an... associate of mine. When I tell him you're not under the Witch's influence as they've all believed, he will be very pleased. When you find your way to the white palace, ask for me at the gate."

"The palace?" Issaria asked hating how ignorant she must seem. She turned to back to the depths of the Baelforia and to face the would-be-assassin. "Who are you?"

His eyes gleamed in the moonlight as he smirked and pulled his hood up to hide his face. "Ask for Blaze, and the guards will bring you to me. I'll make sure they know my new alias," he said with a chuckle.

"And you can't tell me your real name?"

He shook his head, golden eyes glittering with delight at her curiosity being denied. "Truly, it is too dangerous for you to know me as you are now. You're not ready for the journey my name would set you on."

Issaria rolled her eyes, trying to believe he was just enjoying torturing her as some form of flirting. She gave him her best glower.

"It's nice to meet you at last, Princess. I'm glad I didn't have to kill you. You're much too lovely." He turned and walked back the way they came, not sparing a backward glance to see her face flush crimson at his words.

She stood in the forest for a while after his departure, both making sure he wasn't going to linger and steadying herself for her return. If what he said was true, her aunt was incredibly dangerous. *She likely has already tried.* There had been assassination attempts, or so she had been told. Perhaps those were assassins sent by Daylight kings and queens seeking to finish what they started, as Aunt Cate claimed. Or perhaps...

Issaria swallowed hard. She didn't want to consider the alternative. Blaze had no real reason to lie to her, not when his entire purpose for being in the Baelforia in the first place was to find her in Espera and end her life.

He'd had no way of knowing she'd be here.

She had no way of knowing she'd be here. She'd only decided yesterday afternoon.

When the sounds of the wild forest around her fully resumed their normal cadence, Issaria turned and made her way toward the scent of the sea. She emerged from the trees to see the fisherman's morning blue sails glowing in the light of a lantern on the bow as he rowed up to the shore to retrieve her.

"Aye, see you made it out alive. I was wondering if I'd made a mistake leaving a young thing like yourself to wander the Ancient Woods alone," the sea-worn old man said as she climbed into his little rig and they pushed back out into the bay. "Little worse for wear, though. Forest put up a fight, did it?"

Issaria grimaced as she nodded. "It certainly did." Elon was going to kill her for her long absence, but Aunt Cate might actually kill her for her defiance.

PRINCESS ISSARIA SWAGGERED UP TO THE FRONT GATE OF THE CRYSTAL Palace, looking worse for wear, she knew, but in one piece, and her guilty conscience hoped that last bit mattered for something. The guards turned the massive gears to open the alloy gates

"Princess Issaria! You've returned!" a guard exclaimed from the parapet.

"I'll summon a healer at once!" another said at the sight of her.

"No!" she cried before coughing and starting again, "No, that won't be necessary. I'm quite all right."

"But your hair—"

"Forget about her hair. Look at her face!"

"Oh the Empress will not be pleased. She's been looking for you all day."

"I *said* I'm fine," Issaria pushed, her voice declaring the command to stay more than her words. "I will see my aunt, but first I have need of a messenger."

"If it pleases you, Princess Issaria, I will carry your message." Basl, a younger brown-haired boy with a freckled face and a squat nose whom she recalled being related to some Chancellor or other stepped forward.

From the back of the group of gathered soldiers and palace staff, another young boy departed from the group, and Issaria resisted the urge to curse. He would be one of her aunt's messengers and would surely bring news of her return to Hecate's ears. Withholding her grimace, she nodded at Basl. "Very well. I need you to let Captain Sainthart know that I have urgent need of an audience with him and that I will be coming to his quarters post-haste."

"At once, Princess," Basl said as he turned from her and dashed across the palace yard toward the barracks on the far side of the grounds.

As the messenger vanished around the side of the palace, Issaria swept up the long road to the courtyard and up the stairs to the doors, where the guards pulled open the massive arched doors so she could enter the grand foyer. A cavernous, crystal pillar hollowed out and bedecked with solarium chandeliers and sconces like fireflies encased in amber. From the balcony of the grand staircase, Hecate stood with the missing messenger.

Issaria fought to keep her legs moving in their casual gait as she would have after any successful misadventure. "Good evening, Aunt Cate!"

Her Aunt's icy eyes narrowed in her direction, clearly conveying her displeasure, before she slid her glare to the blonde youth. "You are dismissed. Thank you for bringing me news, but it seems you are hardly necessary." At once, the messenger retreated down the hallway. "Princess Issaria."

Issaria had the good grace to cower as her Aunt turned her heated glare upon her. "I didn't realize you'd be cross with me, Aunt Cate," she said as she ascended the left curve of the ornate imperial style staircase. When she reached the landing she inclined her head, a sign of respect. It was Hecate herself who told Issaria never to bow, not fully. But it was her father who told her that she was the very Cosmos themselves. *You bow to no one, my little star.*

"I just went to clear my head. A lot is happening very fast and I…" she sighed. "I can't help but think of what my parents would have said…what wisdom they would have offered me as I come of age."

It was a shallow ploy, she knew. She hadn't actually spoken to Aunt

Cate about her parents in at least five, maybe six years. But her knees were quaking, and she had to at least *try* to account for her resistant behavior these past few months. All the lessons she turned her nose at, disagreeing openly like a blind fool to the dagger hidden behind such a loving back.

"And if I told you that the Harbor Master sent word that a young girl matching the esteemed crystal princess's description was seen boarding a boat known to ferry traitors?" Hecate's voice was scathing, the accusation clear.

"I would tell you I know nothing of the association, I only wished...to stretch my legs and clear my head...and hope that their spirits would commune with me from across the Cosmos." She took a tentative step toward her aunt, and reached out, letting her clammy hand fall just short of her aunt's arm. "Aunt Cate, what is it that you think I've done?"

Hecate held her gaze for longer than Issaria felt comfortable with, knowing what Blaze told her. "I fear that you will turn against me, moon drop," she seemed to confess at last. "I fear that weak-minded magicians who cannot understand my fear of the extinction of Imperial Magicians will corrupt your opinion of the Eventide. We *must* protect what is our right, or they will overthrow us and all will be for naught. We use the skills we are given, in what little ways we can."

"Auntie." Issaria offered her fearsome guardian a gentle, forgiving smile. "I know you have protected me with all of your power ever since..." She let genuine tears shimmer in her eyes, the wish for those wise words truer than she cared to admit. "I would *never* betray you, or your love."

As if sent to answer her prayers for escape, Issaria's stomach growled. The gurgle echoed across the foyer, and she only fought to contain her laugh for a moment before the light returned to Hecate's eyes.

"Go on," Hecate said as she rolled her eyes. "Your adventure was more arduous than you thought, it seems?" She reached up and removed a thorny branch from the snarl of her hair.

Issaria bobbed her head. "I was staring at the sky and I tripped."

She stuck out her tongue and shrugged. "It was down a hill…which might have been more of a cliff?"

"See to it that you get to the infirmary or have one of your ladies send for a healer." She petted Issaria on the head. Three swift, soft raps. Like she truly *were* a pet. One of the palace hounds, perhaps. "Along with you now, go satisfy that hunger." She offered a smile that felt neither kind nor familiar. "I'll see you for breakfast on the morrow."

"Yes, Aunt Cate. Goodnight!" she called as she retreated down the hall toward the kitchens.

She was halfway down the hall, when her aunt's voice reached her from where she still stood on the landing of the stairs. "Did you find what you were looking for? The wise counsel you sought?"

Tiny hairs on Issaria's neck stood on end as she turned in the darkened hall. She had paused in the deep shadow between sconces where the purple crystal of the palace seemed as black as obsidian. She shook her head and gave a woeful smile. "Silent as stars, I'm afraid."

"I know they are proud of you and your spirit, my sweet," Hecate's voice was syrupy thick as she added, "They will be watching over you from the Cosmos on your coronation day, I'm sure of it."

She inclined her head, thankful for the sentiment even as she contemplated what double meaning there might have been in her words. "Sleep well, Auntie," Issaria bid again, wondering if Hecate realized she'd failed to call her Empress the entire conversation.

10

ELON

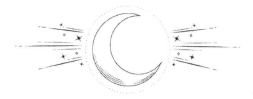

She has returned, Captain," Basl said as he stood in the doorway of Elon's chambers.

The messenger's words washed over him in a mixture of relief that gave way to instant anger. Issaria had been gone an *entire* day. No one even knew when she escaped her room. He'd been a fool to think her mischievous look before the announcement had been about keeping the secret of the new Imperial Guard. She deceived him and likely picked a fight just to put some distance between them. She was too clever for her own good. He just hoped she was all right.

"Where?"

"The front gate, Sir."

"She just walked right—" He stopped himself and shook his head before laughing a little. "Of course she just walked up to the gates. Why wouldn't she?" Elon mused. The page shifted in front of him and he asked, "Does the Empress Regent know of her return?"

"I believe so, Captain. Another messenger departed from the gate when she identified herself. It would be a wise assumption to say that they bore word to her Imperial Majesty. She has been most concerned about the princess's disappearance."

"Right. I'll be right there." He rose from his seat. "See to it that she goes straight to her chambers."

"Actually, Captain, Princess Issaria wished me to tell you that she has an urgent need of an audience with you and that she would be here as soon as she was able."

Basl's words settled Elon right back into his chair. "Fantastic. Suppose I'll just wait some more then."

The messenger grimaced and bowed himself out the door, leaving Elon staring at the woodgrain as if it would make time go faster. As soon as she was able. But when would that be? After a snack from the kitchens? After she'd had a long soak in the tub? His face heated at the thought and he immediately found the alloy hinges on the door much more interesting than they'd been before.

After what felt like an eternity, the door to his barracks swung open again to reveal a dirty, scraped up Princess Issaria, her cloak in tatters and mud up to her knees. Leaves stuck out of her wild tangle of curls. A heinous gash marred the side of her face; the wound was dirty and she needed a healer immediately. Her eyes met his, and the anger in his stomach guttered like a flame in a hurricane. A radiant smile broke across her face, the garish cut on her cheek began to bleed again.

"I'm back."

"Well, I'd ask if you're okay but that's apparent by you standing here," Elon started as he rose from the small wooden desk. "Though you've clearly seen better days. You didn't stop for a bath before you came? You're filthy, and you need a healer. Your face is going to scar. You look like you fought a bear." He couldn't conceal the anger in his voice as he said, "And on top of everything, its improper for you to be here, Princess."

"What is it with everyone and telling me I need a healer?"

"Princess...have you seen your face?"

She closed the door and turned the lock, but kept her back to him. She stood at the door, listening for longer than he taught her to. "I don't have time for improper or a healer, and after what I just went through, I do not care about my face."

"What's going on?"

Her paranoia was palatable, but he highly doubted she didn't care about the massive dirt and pebble encrusted scrape that spanned the left side of her face from jaw to temple. Elon crossed his room and took a tin of healing salve, a small bottle of cleansing water, and a clean hand towel from a cabinet above a small brass wash basin.

"We need to take the bloodoath. Sooner rather than later. I need my *Defendier*," Fear edged her voice and Elon's irritation at her evaporated.

"Where have you been." It wasn't a question. He sat her on the edge of his bed and he knelt before her, turning her face to the right so that he could see the expanse of the wound.

"I wanted to see Daylight for myself—"

"Issaria, are you insa—" She hissed as he dabbed a clean towel soaked with the pungent cleansing water to the crusty scratches. "Sorry."

"I didn't get very far," she said through gritted teeth. Dirt and pebbles freed themselves from the scrapes and fresh blood beaded up when he blotted the towel across her cheek. "I didn't actually make it to the Timeline."

"Why did you come back? If you didn't make it there, I mean." He tried to keep his tone steady as he focused his attention on cleaning he wound. She didn't answer immediately, but instead her eyes glazed over, as if the answer were so very far away. He continued his pattern of brushing debris from her wound and blotting with the towel and cleaning solution.

Issaria was...spooked. Whatever had her so rattled, he didn't want to make it worse. With the scrape on her cheek cleaned of the debris, crimson beads of blood dotted the slashes across her pale flesh.

"I saw Baelfor in the woods," she whispered, casting haunted eyes in his direction at last as she held her head in place for him.

He stared at her for a moment before shaking his head again. "If you're just going to lie I don't—"

"I'm not lying, Elon." She pushed herself up from his bed and strode past him, trembling fingers fussing with the clasp on her cloak.

"I saw a...a titan of rock and trees erupt from the forest floor. It was him." Issaria paced while she spoke, stopping near his desk to drape her cloak across the back of his chair before continuing her path around his room. "I was...probably another half day's journey from the Timeline. I was ill-prepared for the trek." Mud caked her boots, and her riding trousers were torn at the knees. He tried not to think of how she could have died in the woods and no one would have been able to find her. "I was very frustrated when I found him. He... Baelfor." She looked him in the eye at the mention of the extinct Mythos name. "It was Baelfor, and he came *out of the ground*, Elon."

"Out of the—"

"I was so lost. I knew I made a huge mistake going out there without you, and then the ground started to shake. It opened up and there was this green light. And then this...this creature started to form out of all the rock and earth and trees were...growing *years* on its back. I watched the seasons speed by as they grew—as Baelfor grew."

Elon no longer believed she was lying. Issaria's eyes were more than just haunted. She was...enlightened, maybe even radiating with some secret knowledge others only dared imagine.

"He spoke to me and called me..."

"What? What did he call you?" Elon grabbed her arm and forced her to look at him.

She shook her head and the terror in her eyes was real as she whispered, "I don't know. The name...the word or whatever...it made my magic...I blacked out."

"What happened to you? You left a note that said you'd be back soon and not to worry. I worried, Issaria! I worried a lot." He couldn't help his voice from rising to a near yell. He dropped her wrist, affronted with himself and his conduct toward her. He turned and went to the desk where he'd been when she arrived and sank into the wooden chair. "You...you were gone much longer than usual. Longer than you should have been." He sighed and hung his head in his hands. "You can't just leave me behind like that. How am I supposed to protect you if you don't tell me when you need me?"

He hated the desperation in his voice.

"Elon…" Issaria's voice was soft as she crossed the room and knelt before him, her head bowed between his knees, as if she begged for his blessing, or forgiveness like some lowly peasant. Her voice wavered as she whispered, "Elon, there is something…happening to me that I don't understand," she began but seemed unable to finish her thoughts aloud.

What could possibly be so terrible, so wrong that Issaria, *his* Issaria would hold back? In all the years he had known the princess, she had never restrained herself from sharing her mind with him. He admired the wild fire of her spirit; it burned bright as any star and twice as fierce. Yes, sometimes he wanted to scream at her until his throat burned with the thousands of ways she found to push his buttons… but she also surprised him with what she absorbed, and often proved that she was a lady of many talents.

Issaria was many things, and he knew his feelings toward her ran deeper than he cared to admit, but she had never kept something from him that weighed upon her heart enough to bring her to her knees.

"*I don't understand*, Issaria," Elon urged her, his own hoarse murmur barely a whisper above hers. "Please. Of all magicians, you and I?"

He lifted her chin with his fingertips, and as always, was amazed by the softness of her skin compared to the calluses on his own flesh. Her usually bright eyes glistened with desperation and fear and he felt some levy inside him shatter.

"Issaria. *Princess,* I am devoted to you. In all ways, whatever you need from me, whatever you desire." Violet eyes had gone wide, and for the first time in a long time, Elon was close enough to her to see the faint smattering of freckles scattered across the bridge of her nose and witness the rosy blush that heated her cheeks. "I should have said it earlier, but I didn't want to admit it to everyone else before I'd said it to you first. I've already said yes. Soren…"

He wanted to look away, but her lips parted as if she wanted to speak and he plowed on, unable to stop the flood now that it had begun. "Soren may have charged me with his mantle, but I happily take it for *you.*" Elon licked his lips and swallowed the desire to crush his mouth against hers. "Ever since I met you in the stables all those years ago, I have belonged to you." Restraint of the most stoic variety kept him from doing more than pressing his forehead against hers as he finished, "You needn't fear anything from me, Issa. I exist for you. I know I'm just an orphan from the vale but, as long as you'll have me, I am yours."

Elon kept his eyes closed as he concluded his declaration, and he hoped she could feel his honesty in his words. Issaria did not pull away from him, although his hand had long fallen to his lap for fear he would tilt her lips to his and—

"There is a voice inside my mana. She speaks to me of the power I have. She says it isn't mine. It's hers and that I…I wont have to bear it for much longer."

His mind went blank. He didn't dare breathe as her brow trembled against his.

"The titan of stone. He was all earth and rock and trees—" Her eyes darted around the room as if she could still see him before her. Issaria took a deep breath, seeming to know she rambled about something he couldn't begin to conceive. "Baelfor. He called me by a name and then…I blacked out. When I woke up, I wasn't alone in the grove, but it wasn't the Mythos with me."

Elon jerked back, and his eyes snapped open. "Are you okay?"

She nodded. "I am. But I could have not been very easily. The man that stood before me in the woods knew who I was instantly."

He scoffed. "That's not hard to do, Issaria. Your eyes are Imperial Violet. They're impossible to mistake. Who was it? The man."

She glared at him and he found he was relieved to see more than terror in her eyes. Her wild spirit wasn't so easily broken. Not yet—not ever. He wouldn't allow it.

"He was an assassin, Elon." He opened his mouth to exclaim his outrage, but the princess pressed her fingertips to his lips, and he stilled beneath her touch. "The Cosmos brought us together in that grove. He knew it as much as I did. He relinquished the claim on my life because he spoke with Baelfor as well." Her hand fell away and she shook her head. "He said a lot of things I'm still sorting out, but he said I changed *into* myself when he stumbled across...a woman with white hair and glowing eyes."

"Changed into yourself?" Elon parroted.

"He said he saw a glowing purple light in the trees as he was on his way to Espera on a mission to eliminate me, and when his presence was revealed, the woman dismissed the Mythos and," she paused, taking a steadying breath before she said, "she was floating."

"That's impossible. Even storm magi can't control the currents enough to float. Not steadily, anyways."

"Well, she was. And then I suppose she...changed into me and I came-to in the clearing..." She shrugged as she settled back on her heels before him. "I guess the experience changed his mind about killing me, and instead he confessed, then told me about the truth I wanted to see for myself as he walked me back through the Baelforia."

Elon's anger simmered as he imagined some handsome stranger walking the princess through the woods like a romantic escort. It was naive of her to trust the man, but he knew his anger was more than irritation at the princess's lack of concern for her own wellbeing. "And what truth did this *assassin* reveal?" he growled through gritted teeth.

Issaria looked over her shoulder at the closed door before looking back to Elon. She beckoned him closer with her finger and he obliged, leaning in as she brought her lips to his ear.

Her whisper was barely breath in his ear but he heard the words like she'd screamed them.

"Aunt Cate is going to kill me."

THIS WAS AN *INSANE* PLAN. HE WAS INSANE, HE HAD TO BE, TO BE DUMB enough to risk this.

He had a paper-thin excuse for his presence in the Empress Regent's private council chambers. The only sane thing about this plot was that the princess was safe in her chambers, sleeping *for real* this time. After she told him of her suspicions, he had brought her back to her chambers and summoned Safaia, Isida, and Daphnica, her hand-maidens, to get her cleaned up.

Once she was in the safety of her room, Elon stood guard as Issaria's handmaidens filled the carved tub in her bathing chambers with steaming water. He ignored the fact that she bathed just beyond the crystal between them, and instead focused on sweeping the rooms for any indication that Issaria would not be safe here. When he was satisfied the princess was not in danger, he took up his place beside her door. She emerged from the bath, clean of dirt, blood and leaves but still scraped and scabbed.

Isida, one of the Princess's handmaidens and tailor, fussed over her tattered cloak and riding clothes, complaining that she'd just have to make the next one imbued with some alloyed fibers to resist tearing, maybe a healing charm embroidered into the stitching. Safaia, her Mistress of Household, tended to the princess's wounds. Safaia was a skilled chef, preparing the princess's meals herself, but she was also a talented herbalist and healer and had aided them in healing the princess, and even himself many times before. Each of the girls on Issaria's retinue had dual roles. Even Daphnica, the tall redhead lingering on the edge of the chamber near the door who seemed at first glance only to clean and maintain the princess's chambers, was a talented Fire Magi and warrior assigned to protect her as a last resort.

As the maids fussed over her, healing her wounds with glowing green terran magic, Issaria continued to tell him of the truths from Daylight the assassin called Blaze had bestowed upon her, letting her trusted hands bear witness to her misadventure. Later in the evening, after hugs were given and mild scolding had been admonished, the handmaidens were dismissed, and Elon found himself alone with her again. Issaria had beckoned for Elon to stay until she was asleep. Tucked into the plush silk of her bed, Issaria revealed one more truth to him. She wanted him to find out if what the assassin said was true.

He was the only one she trusted, and this matter could not wait.

Elon did not disagree.

So he found himself creeping through the shadows in an area of the palace he'd seldom been before to seek proof of a threat to

Issaria's life. His heart hammered in his chest as Issaria's conviction and worries about Hecate's behavior, both past and present spurred him into action. He wasn't sure if he would learn anything of value, but he had to start somewhere, and he had no time to waste. At best, he could rummage through whatever was left within her private chambers. He wasn't exactly expecting to find a hand-written confession to her crimes but…maybe there was something. At worst, if the room was occupied, he hoped he would be able to listen in on whatever was discussed so late at night.

He emerged from the stairwell that led to the council chamber. Light shifted in the gap between the heavy alloy doors and the gleaming crystal floor at the far end of the hall. Oh lucky day, it was occupied. Hecate was kind enough not to post guards, so Elon took it upon himself and slunk down the hall toward the door. Pressed against the cold crystal walls of the arched corridor, he edged closer and closer.

A faint ringing in his ears began. He could already hear the muffled din of voices from beyond the doors but could not distinguish what they said. He pressed on until he squatted outside the door with black spots dancing wild in his peripheral vision. Ears buzzing with an unsourced sound. He found himself unable to stop from falling to his knees. It took all his control to keep his ragged breathing quiet.

Back. He had to get back.

The crushing pressure was too much, as if darkness had swallowed him whole and he could feel the *weight* of it on top of him, as if he'd never get out from underneath it. Elon staggered back to the stairwell, away from the door and the immense weight of eternal black. He crossed the threshold and down two steps before his ears popped, as if he'd suddenly come up for air too quick.

The pressure was gone. Vanished, as if it had never been there.

It was a ward, he realized. And a dark one, full of malice at that. Hecate had protected her chambers well. He'd need to find another way to get inside that chamber and hear what was going on inside.

Elon sat on the top step, peering through the slightly ajar door, watching the light beneath the door for hours. He gleaned that there were definitely multiple people in the room. Three, maybe four, more depending on if they remained seated elsewhere or not. They were passionate: at times when he thought he could hear the echoes of shouting, he also felt the static pulse of the pressure touch upon him like a second skin before evaporating like morning fog—slowly at first, then all at once it was only a lingering mist.

Elon rubbed a crick in his neck and shook out the arm he'd been leaning on. His eyes were gritty with prolonged focus. Usually that only happened when he was alchemizing.

The door to the council chamber opened, and Basl the messenger ran out, pale faced and sweating in the glow from the room beyond. Elon saw inside as the door swung inward: Hecate, hands clasped before her, Commander Acontium and a man Elon knew to be Malek Wardlaw, a councilor only in name. He was a representative from the Guild of Shadow and Bone, a network of magicians who would and could do just about anything you wanted, even murder someone—for a price. The door shut behind Basl as he dashed toward the stairwell door, a scroll clutched in his fist so tight his knuckles were white and the scroll crunched.

Lucky day, indeed. Elon didn't let himself celebrate, but rather pulled himself up and pressed back into the shadow of the stairs, descending back where Basl would not be seen from either entrance. Above him, the stairwell door opened, and a swath of light lanced across the stairs as Basl's heavy footsteps started down the stairs toward where he lay in wait with a dagger in his fist and a hand at the ready.

Basl rounded the corner, brown hair obscuring his vision as his eyes focused on the slick stairs before him. Elon clonked him right in the skull with the handle of his dagger before he knew what was happening. The poor messenger dropped like a sack of oats, his hands uncurling from around the scroll as Elon propped him up on the stair. It bore a white wax seal, embossed with a skull and a candle—a known sigil for the Guild of Shadow and Bone. A message from Malek then.

Elon broke the seal and unfurled the parchment.

It was blank.

Basl was carrying a blank message? His stomach dropped. Basl was a decoy. Elon whirled back to the doorway, expecting an ambush, to be seized by Imperial Guard, maybe even Acontium himself...but nothing happened.

But the parchment was blank. Elon flipped it over, and over in his hands. It was blank, but Basl's demeanor said that it was something important. Crucial. He was nervous about carrying it.

It wasn't blank, Elon realized.

It was spelled. Perhaps to be read by a specific item, or after an incantation was read, or...well, it could be any manner of things. Maybe it needed a blood sacrifice under a full moon. They *were* a guild of assassins and thieves after all. How Hecate had permitted them to exist—

It all made sense in retrospect, didn't it? She permitted them to exist because she employed them. Perhaps *multiple* times.

It made him sick, how naive they'd all been. How willing, like sheep to the slaughter.

The options were just too vast for him to narrow it down on his own. He looked down at the unconscious messenger and sighed. He was probably going to regret involving him, but this kid might be his best shot at this scroll.

He hefted him up over his shoulder and descended the stairs.

Back in his room, Elon strapped Basl to a chair and held a vial of puce-colored sulfur chunks under his nose to rouse him. The messenger groaned as he came to. Frantic, he glanced around the small barrack room, saw Elon and the array of tools and blades lain out carefully across his desk and bed, and immediately began squirming and pleading.

"Please, I don't know anything. I never know anything. They bring me in there and I just—I don't know what happens!"

"You don't know what happens?" Elon scowled and the messenger squealed.

"No, you don't understand! I can never remember what they talk about! The Empress Regent says its for security but—but I have these *dreams*...where I do things, tell them things that I wish I didn't—"

"Did you tell them the princess came to see me earlier?"

Basl frowned. "I...I might have?"

Elon wanted to roar at him, but he only turned his back to the messenger, and examined an alloy hunting dagger with a serration near the hilt. He had moved from the hunting knife to a long, thin needle-like device he used to measure granular ingredients with immense precision when he said, "You're not very helpful, Basl." He selected a rather sharp obsidian knife from his desktop and turned back to Basl, his gaze unrelenting.

"I'll tell you anything you want to know, please, please. Just ask me what you want and I'll tell you—"

"Why is the message blank?"

Basl blinked. "That one was blank? Blank ones go to the sleepers—the ones who pretend to be someone they're not."

"Who?"

He shook his head, blue eyes frantic. "I can't remember! I don't know where I was supposed to go, I was just—I hold the scroll, and I know who its for."

"How do I read it?"

"It depends who it was for."

"If I were to give you the scroll would you know where you were going with it?"

"I'm not sure. I've never been interrupted before," Basl said.

"Worth a try, then," Elon said aloud as he placed the roll of parchment into the messenger's restrained wrist. "Well? Anything?"

Basl's hand spasmed, fingers splaying before clenching white-knuckled around the scroll again. His blue eyes glazed over.

"Basl? Where are you going with the message? Do you know how I can read it?" Elon prodded.

"I was coming... here with it. To the barracks. Not this room. But one... like it," Basl replied monotonously and vaguely.

All the rooms in the barracks, save those for commanding officers or the suites known as family units, were pretty much identical.

"Who is the sleeper in the barracks."

Basl only shrugged. "I'm not sure. But he has a chunk of that," he pointed with his free hand to the shining black dagger forgotten in Elon's other hand, "on top of the other ones I brought him."

Elon held up the obsidian knife. "He has this? Obsidian?"

Basl nodded eagerly, happy to please him. "Yes. A chunk of it."

"Fantastic." Elon prized back Basl's fingers one by one until he reclaimed the parchment. "You've been a real gem, Basl. I'm almost sorry about this."

"Sorry about—"

Elon clocked him upside the head with another alloy hilt, rendering him unconscious. He knew this solution was only temporary. The messenger's allegiance couldn't be trusted. He'd have to find a more permanent solution for the kid sooner rather than later, but right now...

Right now Elon had a spelled message to decipher.

He turned back to his desk and spread the scroll out, clearing the space from his idle threats toward Basl at the same time. He weighted the ends of the scroll with a burlap pouch filled with charcoal and a copper-rimmed magnifying glass. Holding the obsidian blade the horizontally, he hovered it a hair's breadth above the parchment.

Nothing happened.

No words unfurled from smoke and shadow. Nothing seared itself into the parchment like a brand. No hidden messages unfurled across the page.

Elon looked back over his shoulder at the unconscious messenger.

It was worth a shot.

The chair scraped across the floor as Elon positioned it before the desk. He unbound Basl's hands from the chair, but re-bound them around the handle and tip of the obsidian dagger, and then back to the desk itself. No sense in risking getting stabbed by a frightened boy.

The meat of Basl's palms rested against the parchment itself, as it appeared that the spell was somehow associated with physical contact with the item by approved personnel only.

Still, nothing happened. Elon was contemplating using the sulfur chunks to wake him again, in case being conscious was also some rule imbedded into the magic, when the obsidian dagger shifted in the light—light that had not altered since Elon had shut himself in the room with the unconscious messenger.

And then it was there, projected like a black aurora across the ceiling of the room.

SON OF SHADOWS,

Our esteemed patron's patience has run out. Issaria is awakening and must be put down before the seal shatters completely. You will know when the time is right to eliminate the princess. A word of caution: Aurelia will protect her vessel if she feels threatened. Do not give the Mythos the chance.

Be swift. Keep your cover, if you can. If not, eliminate the witnesses.

Walk with graceful death, my son.

ELON TORE THROUGH THE PALACE, HOPING THAT ALL THE TIME HE'D taken to unlock this scroll hadn't cost him dearly when the order came from elsewhere after the delay. He was halfway to Issaria's chambers when the whole palace shuddered and a tremendous boom popped off in the distance.

Once.

Twice. Three times. Again and again. Elon blocked it out, refusing to count more explosions—for that's what they were. Explosions in the city.

He was out of time, and he only hoped he could salvage a little of the disaster that was unfurling around him.

11

ISSARIA

The crystal palace shook, rattling the chandelier in her room and chattering the windows in their casings. The quake's tremors made the princess stir, drowsy and tangled in her gossamer sheets, but it was scent of smoke that jolted her awake and sent her across her chambers. Breathless, she wrenched the doors to her balcony open and hurled herself against the balustrade, nearly knocking the wind from herself as she cast her gaze to the east, straining to see the city.

Bile caught in her throat at what she glimpsed in the burrows of her beloved Celestial City.

Red and orange flames rose in pillars, billowing from beyond the walls of the Crystal Palace. Screams pierced the night as the black smoke churned thick spirals in the wind, shrouding the palace in an acrid black fog that choked her senses and seared her eyes. Espera was a burning backdrop against the pale sickle of the crescent moon. Her people were dying.

Her nightgown swirled around her legs as she sprinted from her chambers, to what end, she wasn't entirely sure. Bare feet slapped against the crystal as she tore through her sitting room and into the corridor. Her guards were gone from their posts, the antechamber to her chambers was dark, even the solarium sconces had been dimmed. Issaria did not stop to wonder where they were. She thundered down the stairs two at a time, jumping the last several steps between landings.

"Issaria!" Elon's voice reached her from further down the stairwell.

"Elon!" she called out as if it would summon him to her location, and a moment later he was standing on the landing before her, face flushed and wearing same clothes she'd seen him in earlier, though now he was heavily laden with weapons. His scabbard hung on his belt and a dagger had joined it along with a slew of his shatterspheres, only a few of which Issaria could identify, but she knew enough about them to know Elon was to be considered a highly dangerous man in that moment.

"Praise the Cosmos," he exclaimed, out of breath as he closed the distance between them. Elon ran frantic hands down her frame, pet her hair, and pulled her into a hug before he let go of her. "We have to get out of here." Sweat beaded on his neck, one hand held his drawn sword, and he swept his copper hair out of his green eyes.

"There's a fire in the city—"

"It's a distraction meant to sow fear and chaos," Elon said as he seized her wrist and dragged her behind him. "You were right. Blaze was right." Issaria's knees nearly gave out at his words, but Elon continued to drag her behind him, unwilling to relent his pace down the stairwell. "We're out of time, Issa. Hecate's assassin is coming for you. Tonight. Right now maybe, I don't know how much advance warning this is. We have to flee."

"What?" Issaria wasn't sure she heard him correctly. Her pulse echoed in her ears, drowning out everything but the fear threatening to choke her.

"I went to her chambers while you were sleeping and intercepted a messenger with a kill order," Elon said as they emerged from the stairwell. He drew her against the wall, hiding in the shadows between the sconces carved into the crystal walls.

Down the hall, an array of soldiers had emerged from one of the many armories in the palace. They were armed to the teeth with alloy blades, pikes and shields and they turned at the crossroads of the east and west wings of the palace toward the entrance hall. "Double-time, men," one's voice echoed back to them. "The Empress Regent has ordered all available units to render aide to the sites of the explosions."

Issaria's heart broke for her battered people. Her aunt had done this before. Used *people* as cannon fodder. Treated innocent lives like pawns and less. Her collapse jerked Elon to a halt and he turned to find Issaria on her knees, tears streaming down her face. She hadn't wanted this to be real. Her aunt...her *family* had betrayed her, betrayed their people beyond a shadow of a doubt.

And yet...Issaria told herself there was no way Aunt Cate would sanction *explosions* in the center of the city. She needed the people's loyalty, she needed them to be on her side and a massacre like a detonation would cause so much devastation. Unless Hecate hoped the gain their favor with Issaria's death, avenging her with the trial or death of her killer.

"Hey, c'mon. You can't stop now. We have to go," Elon's said, trying to coax her from her stupor. "We have to get out of here and find help. The assassin—" Issaria's attention snapped to him at the mention of Blaze. "He offered sanctuary when this happened, you said he offered to help you. We're going to Hinhallow. Down in the store rooms, behind the tapestry at the back of the wine cellar, theres a tunnel. It leads out. It's a straight-shot from there."

"I can't *flee*, Elon. Espera...my people," she stammered.

"Issaria, I don't think you have a choice. She's going to kill you. If not tonight, she will try again. She'll kill anyone, *everyone* in her path the closer you get to—"

"To what, Elon?"

"The assassin was right. She was with Malek Wardlaw." He paused for a beat before adding, "I'm sorry, Princess."

His words struck like lightning. Malek was friend only unto himself and those who could elevate him. A foul, loathsome creature who'd somehow siphoned just enough power to earn him a name worth knowing, if only for the sake of knowing not to cross him.

It was all true. Her aunt had truly betrayed her. Had killed her parents and intended to kill her too.

All this time, she'd loved the woman who took everything from her. She cherished Aunt Cate, thanked the Cosmos that she was spared that night, that the two of them had made it through the storm together. She'd believed the lies that Daylight taken *everything* from her.

Issaria took a steadying breath and let Elon help her to her feet. Once she was standing, he took her hand and tucked a strand of her sleep-tangled hair behind her ear. "Can you keep up with me? We have to get to the kitchens for some supplies. We won't make it without them. I have a plan, but it's kind of crazy."

Issaria forced a smirk, her bravado masking the terror harrowing her spine. "Really now, Elon. What other kinds of plans do we have?"

After checking once more that the path across the intersection of hallways was clear of soldiers or palace staff, they took off at a wary sprint, darting between shadows and keeping close to the walls. At the end of the hall, across from where the regiment of soldiers had emerged, Elon and Issaria took the opposite doorway and descended down into palace's internal chambers.

Down on the subterranean level, they rounded a corner, and Elon stopped short. Issaria slammed into his back before peering around his left side to see what caused him to halt.

At the end of the hall, a broad cloaked figure stood, dagger drawn, gleaming in the moonlight. It was already slick with blood, ruby drops splattered to the hard-packed floor. Her hand flew to cover her mouth and stifled a gasp.

"Where do you think you're headed so late, Princess?" The cloaked figure asked, and Issaria shuddered to think that she recognized his voice. She had laughed and joked with him, and invited him to protect her after Aunt Cate and Commander Acontium had vouched for his upbringing. Pressed her on it. A talented, but unfortunate orphan boy who just needed a helping hand. Just like Elon. And maybe just like herself.

"I've been looking everywhere for you," Flynt taunted. "I said I wouldn't make it hurt but after you made me hunt you down...I kind of *want* to."

"Princess, I want you to run. Stick to the plan, and I will catch up when I'm done with this filth."

"Oh, Princess! My sweet, beloved—GAG. You two always did make me sick." Flynt snickered darkly. "You're so confident you can take me, *Captain?* I've been faking my fighting style for years. I don't think I'll even need my magic to take you down." He assumed wide fighting stance, his sword leveled at his shoulder. Issaria had never seen any of the soldiers in Espera start a sparring session like that. "You're a glorified farm boy. You'd be *nothing* if she weren't in love with you. I was born to hold a blade." He slashed his sword back in forth in a flashy pattern. "You, on the other hand, were born to shovel shit and be grateful for it."

"Excuse *you*," Issaria began, stepping forward to defend her friend, ignoring the fact that he just openly outed her most guarded secret.

"Issaria!" Elon grabbed her wrist. "What do you think you're doing? You have a plan to follow. I want to teach this piece of shit who he's messing with."

"Elon—"

"Princess." His voice was no longer a request, but a command. "Go."

She nodded once, then took off and resisted the urge to look back. The sound of alloy clashing on alloy chased her down the hall toward the kitchens.

The expansive hearths roared with wild, unkempt fires that charred the contents of cauldrons left abandoned on the flames. Issaria followed her instructions, located a satchel and began stuffing it with every manner of food she could find in the abandoned cavern of the kitchen. She loaded in at least a dozen apples into the bottom of the bag, which were joined by several loaves of soft fresh breads and some jellied pastries that had been left to cool on a wooden slab before she switched to ripping chunks of hard cheese straight from the wheel. When the weight of the bag was almost too much and she could no longer wedge stolen morsels into the spaces between foods, she cinched the bag closed and slung it over her shoulder. She was filling a second leather skin with water, her entire fist submerged into a wooden barrel of rainwater while the bladder bubbled when Elon entered the kitchen, blood on his blade, breathless.

"Elon! Are you—"

"He's dead." Elon announced. He snatched a rag caked with flour from a countertop and cleaned his sword before sheathing it on his hip and approaching her. "He's Malek's man through and through. I didn't even recognize the man I fought. Hecate put him in the Initiate Trials. Its funny how they like to talk when they think they're winning, but as soon as they lose the advantage, they start begging and pleading." Disgust dripped from his voice.

He eyed her loaded satchel on her back, and the full skin tied to one of the shoulder straps, bumping against her. "Good. You've gotten supplies." He took the second skin from her and corked it tight before tying it next to the first one. When he was done, he claimed a forgotten cloak from a chair by the hearth. The fabric, rough though it was, was warm from the fire as he wrapped it around her shoulders. "I'm not going to be able to go with you."

"What?" Issaria froze, feeling as though she was being betrayed a second time. "What are you talking about? Of course you're coming with me. I can't very well do this alone, you rock head," she protested, lightly punching him in the arm.

Elon's face remained strained as he clasped the cloak around her throat and pulled the hood up over her head. "You're going to be fine. Keep the moon to your back and you will be heading the right direction. You've got to survive and get help from Hinhallow."

"No, Elon, no. I'm not doing this," she said as she shook her head. "I'm not going without you. I can't. I...I won't make it." Her voice broke, tears burned the back of her eyes.

"Issaria," Elon's eyes met hers and she stared into their meadow-green depths as the first tear broke free from her lashes and ran down her cheek. "I have to stay here and maintain that you've been taken, kidnapped by someone. If you just vanish, she still wins. If you've been taken, if I tell them you were alive and they took you from me...

she won't be able to deny my claim without betraying that she's involved."

His plan made sense. She couldn't deny how clever it was. As always, it seemed Elon could not be out-strategized. It was throwing all the cards on the table, playing the ultimate risk, but it *could* work. But to make the plan work...

She swallowed. *It's kind of crazy.*

"Okay. I'll go to Hinhallow. I'll get help. For Espera. And for all those she's taken from us." Issaria felt her resolve strengthen. "I will not let Hecate win."

A solemn smile broke out across Elon's face. Firelight cast shadows dancing across the strong planes of his jaw, highlighting his hair like embers. "That's my girl," he said, voice tight as he reached out to adjust the too-large cloak around her shoulders even though it did not need to be adjusted.

Issaria told herself he was not just looking for an excuse to touch her one last time. They would not say goodbye. Goodbyes were for fools and forever. They were hopefully—*thankfully* neither, she thought.

"I'll see you to the tunnel and I'll cover your tracks, lay evidence for your kidnapping to keep you alive in more than just my word that I could not free you and...that I failed to save you." Even though it would be a lie, the shame Elon would feel, Issaria realized, would be very real.

For the first time since they met all those years ago, they were really, truly going to be separated. By thousands of miles, and count-less unknown obstacles...that was *if* she survived the trek.

The end of their time together loomed between them, a chasm of everything she would not say for fear it was not welcome in the way she wished despite his earnest vow of loyalty in his barracks when she knelt before him. Her throat tightened at the memory and she felt her own blush. Unable to hold his weighted stare, she looked to the rough carved crystal floor. Down in the servants' domain, where the palace staff carried out their duties, the efforts for detail and beauty had been minimal, even if the chambers were spacious. Here crystal clusters grew raw and wild, purple facets shifting in the firelight.

"Come," Elon said at last, his voice hoarse. "We shouldn't waste time incase Malek or Hecate goes looking for their assassin. I didn't hide Flynt very well," he confessed. "And Basl." He groaned. "I've also got that to contend with."

"The messenger boy?"

"I took the kill-order from him."

"Mythos above, is *everyone* corrupt?" Issaria exclaimed.

Elon took her hand, his fingers entwined with hers, and led her from the kitchens via a stairwell made of stone instead of crystal. Down into the darkness they went, until they reached a long hallway lined with dozens of doors.

"The cellars," Elon whispered into the dim lighting. Here the sconces were few and far between, casting deep shadows between the doors. Together they walked the corridor of heavy wooden doors and open alcoves to vast chambers packed with boxes, barrels and burlap sacks. They passed a chamber filled with shelves of pickled goods and preserves, and Elon led her to a wooden door cased with black alloy. He relinquished her hand to heave the door open, and close it behind them.

The chamber he'd taken her to had fewer sconces than the hallway they'd left behind, only one to her left, mounted next to the only door she could see, and one far at the end of the stone chamber, indicating an immensely large space filled with shelves of bottles of wine, mead, and ales. Hundreds, maybe thousands of bottles lined the shelves of such a vast chamber—but Elon strode past them all, and she had to jog to catch up. When he reached the back wall he led her down to the end of the last row. They reached the end of the aisle, and Issaria found that she stood before what must have been the oldest tapestry in the palace.

The rough fabric was more rope-like than spun. Issaria was surprised to identify that the massive wall hanging was painted, it seemed, instead of woven with dyed threads, making it more primitive than her more enlightened ancestors, but the depiction was unmistakable. The sheer size of it was impressive, as it hung at least half way up to the cavernous ceiling. It must have been immensely heavy, and she wondered only for a moment how it had been hung before the image upon it took her breath away.

A white-haired woman with glowing eyes, surrounded by a halo of purple high above what had to have been the Crystal Palace—a cluster of abstract of purple shapes that spiked out from the same point.

Issaria stared at it for what might have been a long time, or only a moment, she wasn't sure. Her wonder of who the woman was, who she held inside her, and why she was painted on such an archaic piece of art was interrupted when Elon lifted a corner and vanished behind it.

She lingered around the edge of the tapestry, gazing up at a face she thought should look familiar to her until Elon returned from behind the woven panel. "The way is clear for quite a length," he said. "I wish I could go further, but I must return before Hecate realizes something is amiss."

From his own waist he took the dagger, and he bent to fasten in around her hips. Her breath caught in her throat at the ghost of his hands on her, perhaps lingering a moment longer than necessary before he straightened and re-adjusted her hood. "You must use an alias until you find Blaze, but don't use anything that reminds you of home. Lie. Cheat. I know you're clever, and you've got to use it now. It is *essential* that you remain hidden since we don't know who we can truly trust. You'll think of something to explain the color of your eyes. Ration your supplies. Get to Hinhallow. Keep the moon over your shoulder, and when you cross the Timeline..." He paused to consider, then finished with, "You'll probably reach the Cyth a few days later."

A small, sad smile tugged on her lips as Elon listed out instructions in a last-ditch effort to help her survive the perilous and impossible journey before her.

He lifted the corner of the tapestry and she ducked beneath, savoring the sweet, rotten smell of the rope weave as she sidestepped the length of the wall until the rough stone gave way to a thin crevasse. She ducked inside and found herself overwhelmed by the rich, loamy scent of upturned earth, but the darkness of the space overwhelmed her other senses. She only knew Elon was beside her when the faint back glow from the last solarium sconce in the wine cellar was swallowed by the blackest black she'd ever experienced.

Even the night was not this black, and the scent, nay, the stench of earth gave her the sensation she was being buried alive. Her breathing hitched, and cold sweat prickled her brow. She felt Elon's fingers on her wrist.

Issaria lifted her hand to meet him, and his rough fingertips found her pulse, then slid between her own as if Elon had known exactly how his hand needed to curve to capture hers all along. At once she was grateful for the oppressive darkness, if only for the moment, to obscure the color staining her cheeks as she considered the expiration of shared time before her.

"Elon," Issaria whispered, a last moment to tell him—

She felt the warmth of his breath an instant before the gentle curve of his lips pressed tenderly against her own. In an instant her mind was rendered void of anything, everything except the gentle pressure of his hand on hers, the sensation of his lips, so satin soft but lined with the prickle of his beard, which she hadn't anticipated but found that she rather enjoyed.

Elon's other hand found her cheek, and his thumb tilted her head to his as his fingers entwined themselves in her hair. His desperation, his fear, desire, his *need* radiated through her. She didn't feel herself move, but the strong planes of his chest were beneath her fingertips and his restraint seemed to evaporate at her touch.

Hunger overtook him, and his featherlight kiss transformed, crashing down into her. His hand at the back of her head, her own wrapped around his neck, fingers weaving into his hair. Issaria's hood fell back as his arms wrapped around her, eclipsing her with his size as she arched into him.

Elon pulled back for a moment, just a moment, to whisper "Issa," into her mouth as her lips parted, and then his tongue met hers in heated anticipation.

The darkness held the secret of their forbidden embrace as Issaria allowed herself to share with Elon the only secret she still kept from him: the depth of her feelings. As they entwined, she imagined pouring every ounce of her wish to be with him forever and always into their kiss. She wasn't sure she would ever find the words or the opportunity to tell him just how beloved he was to her...no matter how forlorn their stars.

Elon's grip on her loosened, his hands fell from her hair and their kisses grew more light, desperate to claim one another's lips as much as they could before she was beyond his reach. Fat salty tears dribbled along the seams of her mouth, and Elon kissed her, tasting her sorrow. "Please don't cry, Issaria," he begged in a whisper. "If you cry, I don't know if I'll be able to let you go."

She wished she could see his face but was glad his last memory of her was not going to be her blotchy, tear-stained cheeks, but rather their passionate embrace. She sniffed only once before she managed to say, "I promise I'll come back to you."

"You can't," he said. "You can't come back until it's safe for you to return."

He was right.

This would be the last time she saw her city. She didn't even say good bye to her maids. Safaia, Isida...what would they believe had happened to her? *It's safer this way,* she told herself. If they did not know where she was, they could not be used against her. But Elon... she was deserting him in a precarious situation.

Elon pressed a glass ball into her hand. "Use the Lux or save it. Its up to you." His other hand brought hers to his lips, and he pressed a kiss against her knuckles. "I know I didn't get to swear to Bloodoath to you, but I swear to you, Issa, I swear on the Cosmos and all the magic in the world, I will find you again." He seemed to hold his breath for a moment before she heard his exhale. "When it is safe, I will make my way to Hinhallow."

Issaria nodded into the darkness, bracing herself for his final farewell when his whisper found her ear. "The name that Baelfor called you..." She froze, the heat from their kiss evaporating into the ink-thick dark. "Hecate knows who she is and knows that she is inside you." The information spilled from his lips in a hasty haze. "She wrote that you were awakening, and you had to be put down before the seal on the curse was broken."

"The name, Elon." She felt her head spinning, certain that if she could see anything beyond the black, her vision would be blurred. "The name...I can't remember. What is it? Who is she? Why is she talking to me?"

"Her name is Aurelia," Elon said. "The Mythos of Light lives again in you."

Issaria followed the tunnel of dirt and darkness for what was certain to have been hours, maybe days. At times the passage through the earth became so narrow, she had to stoop her shoulders or turn sideways to continue down the tunnel. She became painfully aware of the fact that she was still barefoot and wearing nothing more than a nightgown and an ill-fitting cloak.

The memory of Elon's lips on hers lingered like a half-believed daydream against the surge of acknowledgement for who's voice she heard calling to her from within her mana. Her ancestor was *alive* within her magic.

Aurelia.

She didn't let her mind linger on the name lest she summon her forth again. That was the last thing she needed right now. No, right now she needed to focus on getting out of this tunnel. The straps of the satchel bit into her shoulders beneath her cloak, but she would not slow to adjust it. She needed the stealth of mountain cats, the courage of the forest wolves. To survive this ordeal, she needed to be *more* than Imperial Princess Issaria Elysitao. She would rise like the sun and meet the challenge before her. She felt a fire burning in her chest, bright and eternal like the seed of a star.

She let the darkness obscure her presence, let it swallow her and any trace of her. Somehow, she found herself thinking of the story Blaze had chosen to share with her in the Baelforia.

Be afraid, but do it anyway.

Issaria breathed deeply, allowing the rich, wet scent of the soil to surround her. She was afraid. Her city was burning, people were dying. Her aunt had...ordered the destruction herself, had betrayed her most solemn oath to protect the people of Espera and all the cities of Ellorhys. Aunt Cate had betrayed them all, murdered her parents, and perhaps countless others in some self-serving quest to literally bring eternal night to the planet. To what end? Why?

It was madness.

This was all madness. Elon's plan was insane, even for them. Leaving him in Espera to wage a silent rebellion against Hecate went against all her instincts. If he was discovered, Issaria wasn't sure what her aunt would do, but she'd proved herself to be capable of despicable evils.

Her heart throbbed. Elon Sainthart was the best sort of man. If her father had been alive, perhaps she would have been able to persuade him to let them marry. Her father had a soft spot for his only daughter, and for his bloodsworn warrior as well. To join their houses...it may have pleased him greatly, given the sort of man Elon grew into.

To think of such happy endings warmed her heart but she knew it was naive to think of endings that would never be. She shook the thought from her head and focused on her right hand dragging along the side of the earthy tunnel, brushing against what she convinced herself to be knobby roots seeking deep, dark soil, and most definitely *not* bones. In her left, she gripped the Lux that Elon had gifted her, but she had not used it. She wouldn't, couldn't even.

At last, she stumbled out of the tunnel and into the warm embrace of the night. Crisp moonlit air washed away the claustrophobic feel of being swallowed by the earth and Issaria blinked like a moon-blind owl, drunk on silver light as she staggered forth. Arms spread, staring at the star-speckled sky, Issaria tripped on the uneven ground.

Sprawled on her hands and knees, she blinked until her vision cleared like mist burning off in the morning light. Beneath her palms she found an expanse of cold, shining crystal. For a moment, she wondered if she had wandered that infernal tunnel thinking she was going to die in there only to end up back at the palace. And then she lifted her gaze.

Issaria's mouth fell open.

It's kind of crazy.

That didn't even begin to cover it.

To get to Hinhallow, Elon intended for her to cross the Glass.

PART III
THE CRYSTAL SEA

12

CALIX

In Rosvia, the small Aresian town straddled on the edge of the Baelforia and the twilight-stuck Rilaan Mountains, Calix purchased a chocolate-colored mare from a farmer. After bartering for some supplies the disguised prince struck out from the Timeline, a strange hazy mix of dawn and twilight, neither day nor night that extended dozens of kilometers in either direction from where it bisected the land. Ares and the townships that fell within the city's realm were strangely blessed in that right. Their lands, favored by Baelfor himself in the old world, had fallen neither in day or night in the wake of the Eventide curse, and so it continued to flourish as it always had with bountiful harvests and plentiful livestock. A land of milk and honey in the face of what would become the worst drought in all of recorded time.

He had heard that the days of the Godsplague were as torturous as anyone had known. When humans were humans and magic, unless gifted from the Elementals before their extinction, apparently made them sick enough to die horrendous deaths: fevers that boiled your innards, drowning in your own blood, and worse. Anyone who lived through excruciating pain of the Godsplague gained anywhere from an ember to an inferno of elemental magic. Their children and their children's children inherited it as well, and now...everyone was a magician of one of the schools of magic: fire, water, air, lightning, stone, earth, flora, and fauna. From there, the possibilities were endless as to how a magician could find their talent.

Blessings from curses. He shook his head. From setting a plague upon the people to turn them into magicians equally, to possessing the body of their descendants, it seemed the Mythos catered only to their own desires.

Presently, the City of Ares found itself in a precarious political situation as a result of their so called blessing. Foolish King Fraxinus found his resources and aid split between two fearsome adversaries. His only daughter, Princess Shairi, was kept in Hinhallow, left to play lady-in-waiting to Calix's younger sister, Princess Bexalynn. Ares also made monthly relief shipments to the White City, something tacked onto the provisions of Shairi's wardenship after the drought hit Hinhallow. However the good Terran King satisfied Hecate, Calix was certain it was an arrangement that Hecate would indulge only until it no longer served her interests, much like King Akintunde often spoke of himself.

The horse he purchased was not as sure-footed as his Arietes, and probably worth far fewer Metals than Calix paid for her, but the mare plodded along well enough for him, and he would be damned if he was going to spend another two weeks, maybe more with the seas this time of year, on a Mythos-forsaken boat when the Razor would cut the journey in half. The Razor was a narrow bridlepath that snaked first through the Rilaan Mountains bordering the northern edge of the enclave of Ares; then down along the bank of the Cyth River that cut the Glass off from the rest of Ellorhys; and finally into the lower farmland of Hinhallow.

Once Calix rode through the northern most parts of the Baelforia, he emerged from the twilight of the Timeline into day, sunshine breaking across the horizon like a fresh dawn. Golden light beamed down though fat white clouds, casting shadows and brilliant patches of sunlight across the path before him. The trail dipped down from the winding path between the bases of the hills, and down to the riverbank—or what had been the riverbank before the Evernight.

Calix looked out across the mighty river. Once at least a kilometer and a half wide and full of rapids, eddies and even a few waterfalls as the Cyth's power continued to slice into the Glass, carving new, deeper gorges as time carried on. Now the river's edge was at least a hundred and fifty meters below the bridlepath, the river's elevation evaporated.

On the other side, his yellow eyes roamed over the wasteland of the Glass, shimmering and glinting like a handful of amethyst crystals. Calix closed one eye and reached out his blackened hand so that it blocked out the river and it almost looked, from the right angle, as if he was cupping the Glass in his—

Calix dropped his hand and peered into the purple horizon, trying to discern the white shape among the clouds. He blinked, rubbed his fingers into his eyelids and peered across the Glass again. If he hadn't just seen Aurelia and Baelfor in the forest, and then watched the Ethereal Lady turn into some ragged princess, he wouldn't have believed himself. Calix waited there, staring at the Glass for too long, he knew, but he couldn't tear his eyes away.

He was certain he'd seen...a white bird-like *thing* fly into the clouds.

The memory of Baelfor in the forest, glowing and molting the seasons like a phoenix in perpetual rebirth flashed across his mind. If the Terran Mythos was back, lumbering through his woods as some colossal rock-and-forest creature, Calix wasn't so sure he could say he *didn't* see something otherworldly wing into the sky.

Every time he thought of what to tell his father, his thoughts turned to Issaria. He wondered if he should have told her who was living inside her. Aurelia. The white-haired woman was the incarnation of the first Imperial, the mortal Mythos of Light, gifted with primordial magic from Vera Caelum, from Dovenia and Chronos themselves. Calix thought of what he knew of Issaria. It wasn't much, as she was always kept in Espera, and he wondered for a moment if her parents knew what lived inside her, if they kept her hidden from the other cities to protect her identity. After the Evernight was unleashed, she was spoken about as harshly as the Witch Hecate herself.

She didn't seem evil to him. Even if he didn't know that the Mythos of Light slept inside her.

He thought of her scraped and bloodied face. The poor thing must have had a tough time in the forest before he'd come along. Hopefully a healer could see to her injuries. She was fierce, more so than he'd been led to believe, and not at all in the way he thought she would be. The sensation of her finger jabbed into his chest still lingered in the forefront of his memory and it brought a smile to his face.

He was glad the Cosmos intervened and stopped him from completing his quest. It would have been a shame to take such a vibrant creature from the world. And he would have. For the crown, for his kingdom, he would have ended her. Snuck into that purple monolith and done away with her, a blade to the throat, something to implicate cowards, not crowns, had a hand in her demise.

At the thought of another quest, Calix swallowed his admiration for Princess Issaria's fire, his thoughts turning to Aurelia's task for him.

An *impossible* quest, he thought to himself.

The temple she spoke of was legend, something from the creation stories of the First Men, the magic-less ancestors of the Magicians. No Magician had ever laid eyes on the Vera Caelum, the sky spring. It was said to float freely over the planet, spilling magic over the its island edges like waterfalls while the Elemental Mythos carved out the world, sowed the forests and valleys, and filled the rivers and seas. Atop the lush paradise, a temple housed a throne room with seven thrones overlooking a pool of stars. As the story goes, Dovenia and Chronos never set foot on the world they created but instead watched from those thrones, holding council with the Elemental Mythos as they worked the land, sea, and skies; and the pool of stars was the source of all their cosmic power, a spring of magic they shared with the world they created.

He wondered if he should have told Issaria more, or if he'd told her enough. He recalled the heartbreak on her face as she realized the truth of her parent's deaths. Calix had no idea she never knew the truth. The realization felt foolish, but it made sense, and he wondered how many Hollowvanians, if his father had ever considered she might've been innocent all along.

Once the Evernight was upon them, Espera was cut off from the rest of Ellorhys. The cities didn't know what had truly happened for a long while. And then the refugees began to arrive. A trickle at first, and then they poured into the Daylight Cities like a torrential stream, all trying to escape Hecate…and all bearing news of the assassination of the Imperial Emperor and Empress.

The princess was as good as brainwashed by her own blood, and from the sounds of it, the reeducation didn't go so well if the pretty princess had gone rogue in the Baelforia.

With Aurelia's words in his heart, Calix continued on the bridlepath toward Hinhallow.

IT ONLY TOOK A WEEK TO MAKE THE RETURN JOURNEY TO HINHALLOW along the Razor on horseback, as he had predicted. Well, Calix had estimated a week but…he wasn't entirely sure anymore. It was faster than the ship, of that he was certain. Away from civilization, it became increasingly difficult to tell the hours of the day, though most magicians barely regarded time anymore. He slept when he was tired, taking shelter in a tent or under whatever foliage he could find, and ate when he was hungry, taking from his supplies. His horse ate and slept as she pleased and the trip had been fairly easy.

Glad to have cut his time in half if only to get out of the sun, he was still trying to find the words to tell his father what happened when he arrived at the border of the farmlands, and again he could see the glinting domes of the White City in the distance.

The ride through the farmlands took less time than he thought and soon he was funneling into Hinhallow beneath the massive arching gate of white granite stones along with the local traffic. Farmers brought in their harvests from the fields in baskets, wagons, and stacked in bundles as high as his own waist on their backs. Visiting caravans verified their credentials and paid dues with the City Guard before entering the city to barter their wares. The steady flow of foot-traffic kept Calix moving his mare though the throngs of people. He passed through side-by-side with a cabbage merchant who seemed to be struggling with a wheel on his cart.

Hinhallow was bustling with life as he rode his dusty mare through the streets, ducking wooden beams and signs as he navigated the crowds. The scents of the lower levels of the city wrapped around him, and he resisted the urge to cough as he rode up the cobblestone streets. Houses of wooden beams and squared roofs rose up precari-ously, showing taverns and inns for travelers for blocks. Stoked fires churned smoke into the blue sky, bidding warm meals and welcome for those who were weary enough to stop in the slums. Up the sloped city streets he rode, and slowly the crowds around him thinned. First the peasants and filth of the city's population filtered out into alleys and back streets. Then the merchants took their wares to the mills or artisans who would buy their labors from them. In the upper rings of the city, he rode alongside strolling ladies who giggled as he passed even though he was certain they had no idea their prince was beneath all that dust and black clothing. The aristocrats of Hinhallow dwelled on the upper rings of the cliffside overlooking the bay and lower levels of the city. Here the buildings were no longer crafted of timber and clay but were built by masons with stone.

At the castle gates, he cast a glance over his shoulder, thinking again of the princess and her fated path before her. A path, he real-ized, that would bring her to him. The thought sent something stir-ring within him, like churning the coals of a dimming fire. She hadn't known who he was, hadn't an inkling of a thought, but she trusted him. She might have been beautiful, but she was a damned lucky fool.

He tugged on the reins of his horse and brought her to a halt at the gate as he pulled back his hood for the first time since the Razor.

"Prince Calix, you've returned!" A soldier scrambled to salute as he realized the grubby man who rode up to the gate was in fact the Prince.

"I have. And I've got a new order for all the men who take rotation on the palace gates."

Another soldier came to stand in the doorway to the granite gate-house. "I'll make a bulletin of it, Sire. It will be known to all by the end of the day."

"Someday, a girl with black hair will come to the gate, and she will ask for Blaze. Bring her to me."

The guard arched an eyebrow at him. "Blaze, Sire?"

He considered for a moment what they must think of him. Calix knew he was well known for his reputation in the competition circuit, and for some reason many associated that with having bedded many women, but truthfully, he'd only had a few encounters. And none as of late due to the great number of solitary *quests* his father continued to volunteer him for. He wasn't even permitted to take Raif or Alander as backup. "She doesn't know who I am. I would like to keep it that way until…until I have a chance to explain."

Grinning, the soldiers nodded. "Of course, Prince Calix. We understand. She must be a beautiful girl to have turned your favor."

He was surprised to find that he agreed. Her fierce spirit was enough to ignite his curiosity, but she did have…an allure to her. "Quite," Calix said dismissively. "However, she is also clever. I'd like this little fox to come willingly." He didn't wait for them to reply as he kicked his mare into a trot and headed toward the palace. Behind him, he heard their laughter, and the stories they exchanged of conquests of their own.

13
ELON

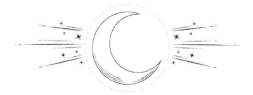

Elon hadn't seen Basl in the five mights that had passed since he'd left him unconscious when he'd helped Issaria escape the Empress Regent. He hadn't shown back up to the palace. Even Hecate seemed to be searching for Basl and had asked after the boy on two separate occasions that Elon had been present for. He couldn't tell if she was just goading him, showing she knows he took the scroll from Basl, or if she genuinely thought the boy absent from his post for unrelated reasons. The latter seemed unlikely.

The aftermath of the night was still being sorted through. More explosions were triggered. Fires still burned, black smoke churned up into the night, blotting out the stars, the moon. Teams of magicians were dispatched in waves but there wasn't enough water magi to answer the call for aid, and Espera had no allies in the wake of the Eventide.

Elon was stressed, to say the least. After a vigorous spar against a willing soldier, when he *still* needed to work off his energy, he found himself returning to the place it all started.

The stables.

Sweet hay mingled with the warm, earthy scent of the animals calmed him. It reminded him of...simpler times. As a boy, when his parents and sister were still alive, he loved to tend their plow horses after a day on the field. Those beasts had been at least eighteen hands high, menacingly tall. All shaggy beards and hooves, they looked like wild stallions compared to the lean, well-muscled bodies of the cavalry horses and even his own stallion. The village fire took *everything* from him in moments. Elon could still hear his sister's screams as he returned home and found their cabin ablaze.

After the Larkham fire he was an orphan with only the clothes on his back. By The Homing, a tradition going back to the era of Sister Queens and the days of the Godsplague, Elon and a handful of others from his village who had no family to claim them became wards of the Crown, and were brought to the capitol to live and serve in the palace or find a path of their choosing. To his knowledge, many of the palace staff in the old days had been brought in by the ancient tradition and remained on, grateful and loyal to the Elysitao's for bringing them into the palace.

Now, perhaps he was the only one left.

Elon stopped in front of his horse's stall and clicked his tongue against his teeth to summon the creature in question. The ornery male was another inheritance from Soren Sainthart. Elon was certain he would never name a horse, especially a soldier's *warhorse*, Dandelion. He wrinkled his nose at the thought. But alas, Dandelion it was, and the coal-colored horse refused to respond to anything else. Elon clicked his tongue again but the horse ignored him.

"What if I brought you a carrot?" The horse still remained head-down in the stall. "Dandelion," he said at last, and the beast nickered, lifted his head, and shook his mane.

Elon took the horses muzzle in his hands and gave him a good pet. "Yeah, you like that don't you, you stubborn old—" Dandelion nudged him in the chest with his snout. "All right, here you go, grump." He pulled the carrot out of his back pocket and offered it to his steed on an open palm.

Dandelion lipped at the carrot and chomped away as Elon he pulled the latch on the stall and stepped inside with the horse. He took a brush from the post just outside the stable and began to groom his horse. Small clouds of silver dust puffed off Dandelion's ebony coat with each stroke of the brush. As Elon worked, his thoughts drifted to his worries.

Maybe Hecate disposed of Basl for failing to deliver the spelled scroll to Flynt Petramut and Elon didn't even have to worry about the kid. Elon scoffed as stepped to the side, having left a shiny patch of fur on Dandelion's shoulder and began brushing his flank.

That was absurd. Of course he would worry about the kid. Not knowing what to do, Elon had turned to the only person he knew he could trust. Rhori Galeryder called in Xenviera Lightizner, and *she* in turn called on Roane Wetherwood, and before he knew it, a Mythos-forsaken rebellion had formed among the would-have-been Imperial Guard.

"We swore to protect her, Captain," Xenviera had hissed as she seized his collar. The fury in her eyes raged and electricity crackled in the air around them. "We thought she was dead. How could you keep this from us?"

"Xen," Rhori had said, laying a hand on her shoulder. "Flynt was the one she sent. Elon had to kill him when they ran into each other."

"That's why we haven't seen him?" Roane asked. "Traitorous bastard."

"I get it." Xenviera released Elon's collar and stepped back, looking away as the storm in her eyes dimmed. "Didn't know who to trust. But you can, you know. Trust us."

"Now let's find us a little rat." Roane clenched his fist and shards of stone hardened like dragon's scales.

Elon walked to Dandelion's front, gave him a pat on the forehead as he went to his other side, and began brushing anew. They *all* felt just betrayed as he had. Hecate had out-played them with a long game, planting him amongst them early on. Flynt had been one of more than a dozen Initiates who passed the written exams, surprisingly enough, and then continued to excel in weapons and mana manipulations. Elon had always believed him to be one of the team, a little rough around the edges but perhaps like Elon himself, he came from humble beginnings and he could be smoothed out with proper coaching and the right opportunity. Elon had been wrong, but he was also lucky that Flynt was the only plant among them.

As mad as he was that Princess Issaria had gone out into the Baelforia that day, it seemed it truly was for the best. Fated, even, as she learned invaluable information at a critical time. Elon hated to think what would have happened if he hadn't been there to intercept Basl and the scroll.

And then in his haste to get to Issaria, he left an unconscious and compromised messenger alone. A foolish, *stupid* mistake.

The worst kind of tactical blunder.

It had taken *hours* for Safaia to find Elon in Issaria's room and sound the alarm of her abduction. Cosmos above, he must have been Mythos-touched if Hecate hadn't sent another minion along to investigate how her little assassination attempt had gone. She had been *that* confident her plot wouldn't fail. Of course, Basl wasn't hanging around waiting for him when Elon got back after trashing Issa's room and staging the kidnapping. It was as close to a disaster as possible without Basl having gone *straight to the Empress Regent* upon waking. Instead, he seemed to have vanished off the face of Ellorhys.

Dandelion's coat gleamed like black velvet in the glow of the stable's lanterns. Elon returned the brush to its hook and stepped out of the stall, taking with him the half-full water bucket. He filled it from a fountain against the far wall, returned the bucket to its place and latched the stall closed. Elon might not have been closer to sorting out his issues, but Dandelion was content, muzzle-first in a bucket of oats. Elon had a pitchfork of fresh hay for his ungrateful beast when he heard the hurried footsteps on the hard-packed earth of the stables.

"Elon! Sainthart." Rhori was out of breath. "I've been looking *every-where* for you!" Rhori called out, a frantic note in his tenor as he skidded to a halt.

Elon hefted the hay over the barrier and Dandelion gave a grateful whinny. He leaned the pitchfork against the wall and turned to his friend. "What is it?"

Rhori was marred with scratches on his wrists, and even one on his neck. "Xen got him. The messenger. He was—"

Elon shook his head, silencing his friend. "Not here." He held his friend's stare. "Take me there right now. We have to end this."

RHORI TOOK ELON DOWN TO THE DOCKS. THE CHILL NIGHT AIR WAS thick with silver fog, ocean waves moaned like widows as they rolled beneath the crescent moon. They both had worn nondescript cloaks as they meandered among the fishermen and merchants, but Elon was certain everyone could hear his heart thundering in his chest. He still hadn't decided what to do with Basl. He wasn't certain if *anything* was off the table when it concerned Issaria's safety.

The fog swallowed them as they passed by docked boats in varying stages of loading or unloading cargo. A few were empty. Toward the end of the row, more and more boats were left moored and unattended. Rhori led him to a wooden shed built up against the backside of a fish cleaning house.

None of the docks nearby had any moored boats. The ocean waves rolled in, wave after wave of roaring tidewater hammering the harbor wall. Salt hissed in the wind, stinging cheeks and forcing the men to squint against it. Needle-point gusts howling in time with the tide. Both sea and sky seemed willing to aid their cause. Elon could barely hear his own heartbeat, which vexed him so only moments before.

Rhori rapped on the door and said, "Xen it's me. I got the captain."

There was a series of clicks and the metallic rasp of a bolt being slid, and then the door swung open a fraction. "About time," Xenviera said as her face appeared in the crack of the door. She pushed it all the way open to allow them both inside before closing the door swiftly behind them.

A single lantern hung askew from a nail on the only post in the small storage space. Alloy blades of varying lengths and serrations hung on the walls of the shed. An intimidating backdrop, the fish-cleaning utensils glinted with sinister intent in the faint lantern glow. In the center of the space with a burlap sack over his head, and tied to a chair, Elon hoped, was Basl the messenger.

"Where's the last one?" Elon asked, careful not to use Roane's name in front of the captive.

"Keeping watch. Making sure we're not...disturbed," Xenviera replied with a grim smile on her face. Her dark eyes glinted like jet in the low lighting, and Elon had to remind himself only *part* of this was an act. Roane was making sure Hecate didn't trap them here.

"Excellent," Elon reeled. "Where did you find him?"

"I followed him from his father's estate toward the docks. Had a stash of Metals and a sack full of belongings," Rhori said as he leaned against the door, acting as a secondary lookout, likely creating a barrier of wind as an invisible shield outside as well. He was a diligent second like that.

"Meant to skip out on a boat, eh?"

At this, Basl's breath quickened, a rapid succession of short gasps. The burlap sack molded against the squat shape of his nose.

"Likely. His father, Chancellor of Vox and Vita, supplied him with the funds to escape, knowing the moment his son reappears in court it will mean his quiet removal," Xenviera affirmed as she pulled on her silex gloves with a *snap!* and summoned a crackling dagger of white-hot lightning with only a roll of her wrist. The bolt sizzled the air and she gripped it, moving toward the chair and just *walked past* the kid. Electricity slung between the blade and it's wielder, snapping the air with hisses and pops. Basl cringed and started screaming into his gag, rocking back in his chair to distance himself from her.

Xenviera hoisted herself up upon the wooden counter behind Basl, and crossed her legs, using the back of his chair as a footrest. She preened, admiring the lightning she'd harnessed from the air pressures, a grin on her face like one Elon had never seen. "Kid's terrified of me. No idea why. All *I* did was stand there while this one," she said with smug satisfaction as she jerked a thumb over her shoulder. "And the *other* one tackled him to the ground."

Basl was whimpering, and Elon wanted to laugh knowing the little dagger was probably the smallest of armaments Xenviera could summon. "Shall we have a chat, gentlemen?" When Elon nodded, she pulled the hood off to reveal Basl Koellewyn, gagged and near hysterics.

Basl's bovine-brown eyes darted back and forth as he took in Elon, raven-haired Xenviera and her lighting-blade, and Rhori Galeryder posted-up by the door—the only exit in the small shed. His eyes widened as they focus on the blades against the wall behind them. He shook his head as tears leaked from his eyes, dampening the gag that held back his panicked cries and snot bubbles popped from his nose.

"Now, now, Basl. Why would you be so scared to see us?" Elon asked in the same menacingly calm voice he'd used on the boy in his chambers the first time he'd had him tied to a chair.

"Usually, Captain, that means he's guilty," Rhori said conversationally.

"As if that wasn't indicated by the attempting to flee on a boat," Xenviera said. "Just think, Basl. What would have happened to your father if the Empress Regent got word of your departure instead of little old us?"

Basl's rapid and haggard breaths continue but he stopped squirming and stilled in his seat.

"Easy, there guys. I'm *sure* that's not the case…right Basl?" Elon asked, his eyes fierce and hard.

Basl shook his head, then nodded, then shook his head again. Confused, he whimpered again and made a few muffled sounds that might have been words if his tongue wasn't jammed back to his molars by the charcoal-colored sleeves of Rhori's military coat.

"What's that? You want to tell us everything?" Xenviera asked as she cupped a hand to her ear. "That's fabulous Basl!" She barely touched her lighting-blade to the knot on the gag and it ignited, searing off in embers as it fell into Basl's lap.

"I swear I didn't tell anyone you took my letter, Captain Sainthart," Basl immediately began. "I didn't even tell my father. He has no idea the Empress Regent calls me into those meetings. I don't like the feelings I get when I think about the time I spend in that room with the Empress Regent. I don't remember things clearly, and it's frightening, and I think it would put him in danger if I told him why I want to leave. He's suspicious, but I think he'd be on your side. He hates the Eventide, but he's served the city for so long, he won't leave! A lot of magicians would be on your side! Not everyone here likes the way things are being handled! They all go to my house to complain to my dad and hope that as chancellor he can do something, and now that the princess has been kidnapped—"

"See, Xen? Even this idiot believes it," Rhori muttered.

"Slow down, Basl. Slow down," Elon coached, and the messenger paused, breathing deeply, nostrils flaring with the effort. "Now, why would you say something like *'you think a lot of people would be on our side,'*? What side is it you think we're on?"

Basl flicked his eyes between the three of them then said, "Whatever side doesn't want that witch to take the crown from the Princess?"

Xenviera snatched the burlap bag and stuffed it back over Basl's head. "Hey! What the—I was *participating!*" Basl cried.

"Shut up!" Xenviera shouted as she herded Elon and Rhori into the farthest corner. "*Obice*, Rhori," she barked. "Now."

Rhori nodded and his eyes flashed silver, like a trick of the light, before he said, "It's done. The kid can't hear a thing, and no one can hear us."

"What is it, Xen?" Elon asked, his nose wrinkled in a half-snarl at stopping the interrogation when it was going so well.

"The kid has a point, Elon."

"Are you guys still here? Hello?" Basl shouted from behind them, startling the trio.

"And what point would that be?" Elon carried on, ignoring the fidgety messenger.

"A lot of people *would* be on our side. Especially if they knew the truth," Xenviera said, setting her indigo eyes on Elon's with a frightening light behind them. "We could really do something here. Something that *matters.*"

"You're talking about a full scale rebellion?" Rhori asked, but his voice held more wonder than question.

Xenviera nodded and Elon glanced between the two of them. The idea had merit. They needed a phase two to his half-baked plan to get Issaria out. He had already been thinking about it. Hecate wouldn't stop just because Issaria was off the playing-field. Something had to come next to keep her in check, or at least occupied, and there were definitely those among them who didn't want to see Hecate with the crown. He ran a hand through his hair and scratched his head.

"It could work, Elon. I already know where we can start to recruit."

"HELP! HELP ME PLEASE!" Basl crowed, making them jump half out of their skins with surprise before cackling with laughter. Basl rocked back and forth in his chair, believing himself to be alone in the shed.

"I was waiting for that," Rhori managed through his chuckles. "They always try that when they think they're alone."

Shaking his head, Elon returned his attention to the matter at hand. "You both think a rebellion should be the next move?"

"All *three* of us think it should be the next move," Xenviera said.

"Roane will agree?"

Rhori and Xenviera nodded. "He already suggested a rebellion when he thought the princess had been taken. Thought this was all Hecate's fault regardless."

"Liara would be in," Rhori said. "I would be too, for the record."

"Safaia and the other girls in Issaria's household would also want to help her in any way they could," Xenviera added. "I know a few soldiers who share our loyalty as well."

Elon was silent as he looked between his friends and then back to the captive in the chair. He couldn't deny the idea was better than sitting around and waiting on whatever aide Issaria was going to summon for them. In the back of his mind, a dark little thought bubbled up from the mire. If she failed, Espera would still have a functioning force to defend the citizens since it was clear Hecate would not consider their safety.

But Issaria would not fail. Elon knew she would get help. She would make it.

"HELP! HELP ME! I'M OVER HERE!" Basl continued to cry out, causing further awkward chuckles to come from Rhori and Xenviera.

"What about him?" Elon asked at last. "I agree with you both. You're right about the rebellion. We should, *absolutely* try to expand our ideals. There are like-minded magicians in the city that would fight for their rightful Empress when she returns. We could...we could muster that force. Be ready when Issaria gets back with reinforcements. But that still leaves him," Elon reasoned, pointing to the kid. "What about Basl? He's still...a liability."

"Hecate will want him dead after he failed her," Xenviera said. "He knows too much. About her and about us, Captain. We can't risk it as much as she can't."

Rhori nodded. "He was probably trying to escape her, not us, based on what he's said about allegiances."

"Can we use him? Like a plant?"

"It's a good idea, Xen, but he said before he doesn't remember what happens in those meetings. They must warp his mind with black magic," Elon replied. "If anything...we would discover when she's hosting her meetings. Listen in a different way. Maybe they'll use him to deliver more scrolls and we can intercept again."

Rhori shook his head. "No. Hecate will be after him for certain. She'd likely use him again as a messenger as a way to bait us into taking the scroll and outing ourselves. We can't use him, and neither can she. He's expendable on both sides."

Elon shook his head. "Except the side where he's a kid who is in over his head, and he's scared." He paused and sucked in a breath before he said, "We're going to let him get on a boat. But we pick the boat. It's the only choice. He *has* to leave, or he will die, by Hecate's order or our own need to protect knowledge of the rebellion, of *us*, from slipping into Hecate's hands."

The three exchanged solemn glances. None of them wanted to lay hands on a child, no matter how it would save them from discovery.

"He can stay with my folks. Maybe when we're more established he can actually join the rebellion he doesn't know he started," Rhori volunteered. "He can help out on the farm, or maybe my dad will teach him to fish the lake."

"It's decided then," Elon agreed after a long silence. He turned back to Basl, who now squirmed awkwardly in the chair as he tried to figure out how to untie himself or slip the knots. Elon stepped out of the protective boundary of the *obice* and felt his ears pop as the air pressure returned to normal. He took the burlap sack off of Basl's head again.

"You guys are... here," Basl said as he blinked into the light, voice hoarse from screaming.

"Indeed. The whole time, in fact," Elon replied. "We've decided your fate."

Basl swallowed, sweat breaking out across his matted brow. "Please don't kill me. I just wanted to go to Ares or maybe even Sorair...just away from *her*."

"How about you head to Del and stay with my parents for a spell?" Rhori offered nonchalantly.

Basl blinked at him. "You...you mean it?"

Elon nodded. "You're right about a rebellion. But you know too much, and Hecate likely wants you dead. For your own safety, we're going to get you on a boat to Del. That doesn't mean *we* won't hesitate to kill you if we see you're not acting in accord with *our* plans either, but we've agreed that you could be valuable to us later."

Xenviera leaned in again and burned the ropes binding Basl to the chair, freeing the boy. Her gaze narrowed on the nervous boy and she whispered in a deadly tone, "Do not make me hunt you down, Basl Koellewyn. I will ensure that all the heartbreak in the world finds its way to you before you draw your last breath, *grateful* for the release death-bringer Zephyrus grants you when I'm finished."

Basl gulped and shook his head, "Yes ma'am. I mean, no, Miss Lightizner. What I mean to say is—" The brown-haired boy shook his head as he gulped again. "I won't disappoint you. I promise." He skittered around Xen and headed toward Rhori, the decidedly safer bet. The storm magician continued to glare at him as she followed in his wake like a shark.

Rhori rolled his eyes and unlocked the door, allowing Basl to duck out underneath his arm. "Easy on the kid, Xen. Going to scare him off women all together."

"Just making sure he remembers to whom he owes his allegiance," she said as she followed Basl out of the shed with a flick of her high-ponytail.

"You're sure about this, Rhori?"

His friend leveled his cobalt gaze and smirked. "I was about to ask you the same thing, *Commander.* Leading a rebellion, standing up for the people, for the *world?* It's a far cry from Captain of the Imperial Guard."

"It's kind of crazy, isn't it?"

Issaria's voice flickered like an ember in his heart. *Really now, Elon. What other kinds of plans do we have?*

But what other *choice* did he have? He was only trying to protect the princess when he sent her to Hinhallow. He hadn't planned a *next,* there hadn't been time. Next was surviving to see her again, and that wasn't going to cut it. Raising an army to fight against Hecate along-side her seemed the righteous course of action. "I don't know if I'll ever be ready for what lies ahead, Rhori, but I'm not going to sit around while Issaria risks her life for us. That's not what a *Defendier* should do. If I can't protect her...then I will do my best to protect her city."

"All right then," Rhori said as he clasped him on the shoulder. "We've got an eccentric, one-eyed Fire Magi to talk to. He knows *all* the rebels."

14

CALIX

As he untacked his weary mare in the stables, Prince Calix realized he was no closer to finding the words to say to his father than he was when he saw the strange bird-thing over the Glass. All he knew was he was going to have to tell him *something* about the quest, or else his father was going to incinerate him until he was nothing but ashes.

When Calix was finished brushing off the mare and leaving her in the best stall of her life with more than enough oats and hay for three horses, Calix headed for the front of the palace, knowing that at this time of day most of his family would be occupied in scheduled lessons or meetings. His mother kept herself and his younger siblings busy with tasks that would enhance their skills as prince and princess, and his father would be enclosed with one council or another.

Up the sweeping stairs to the grand entrance of the white fortress, Calix nodded to the soldiers who opened the heavy wooden and alloy doors to allow him entry. The doors closed behind him and he strode across the white marble floors through the fat columns of carved alabaster, flourishing cornices giving way to arching ceilings that displayed ornate glass-tile mosaics. Each alcove of the ceiling displayed a different colorful votive of the Creation of the Continents, the most ancient story of Ellorhys. Between each pillar stood a soldier at attention, inclining their head slightly as he passed.

Calix was halfway up the stairs when he heard his mother's voice and he felt himself drawing to a stop.

"And Bexalynn, you'll have to be sure to dance with the Chancellor's son at the— Calix! Oh, my sweet boy, you've returned much sooner than your father expected!" On the landing above him, golden Queen Emmaleigh had finally spotted him, frozen like a rabbit in the middle of the stairs. On his mother's arm, his teenage sister Princess Bexalynn grinned and looked over her shoulder at her lady-in-waiting, Princess Shairi of Ares. All three ladies wore lavish gowns far too extravagant for a mundane day in the castle, but Calix withheld his inquisitions.

"We were *just* discussing your coronation ball! Princess Bexalynn, Lady Shairi, and I were on our way to take dance lessons for the occasion!" his mother prattled on as she descended the stairs toward him, dragging the others in tow.

Over-eager Shairi, who's crimson flush and fluttering eyelashes gave away her intentions, as always. The princess floated in his sister's wake like her shadow, ready to attend at her beck at call. A humiliating position for her—lady-in-waiting to a teenage princess younger than herself. It nearly screamed that she would be a maid her whole life if King Akintunde had anything to say about it.

While he pitied her position in the Ballentine court, Calix was *well* aware of how the princess desired him. He dismissed it as the yearnings of a young girl, Shairi had been living in the palace since she was nine. Of course, she developed a crush on him. He was the *only* eligible man she ever interacted with other than baby brother, and Darres hardly counted as a match at the tender age of five. He'd had ample opportunity to initiate a courtship with her and while the brunette was lovely, he just didn't see Shairi as more than another sister. She and Bexalynn were incorrigible about the possibility of a match, though. While Shairi at least had the grace to keep to idle flirtations, Bexalynn found a way to slip it into almost every conversation she had with Calix.

He fixed his gaze on his mother's misty blue eyes to avoid Bexalynn and Shairi's tittering aspirations. "Father speaks of the coronation already? I'd thought he would have waited until my return."

"You know how Father is," his sister, Bexalynn interjected, drawing his attention to her. "He's already stirring up excitement about the announcement. Half the kingdom will know before you've even got the crown on your head!" His sister was a younger, mirror image of his mother. Her shining yellow hair was pulled up and styled much like the queen's tawny golden locks. Both the princess and the queen wore golden circlets tucked into the spirals of their up-dos. Diamonds and rubies glittered in the metal.

"Boasting already, is he?" Calix mused, enticing his sister to tell him more. Only thirteen years old, Princess Bexalynn was the middle child of the Ballentine family and as the only sister, he felt a duty to protect her, even if she was a brat most of the time. In addition to being the only princess on the continent who could literally have *whatever* she wanted, his sister had a particular talent for rooting out all sorts of information.

Bexalynn nodded, detached herself from their mother's elbow, and stepped forward. "He's saying he's going to throw the biggest celebration the continent has ever seen. He wants to show Hinhallow's might in the transition of leadership," she said knowingly.

"Well, Father is a very smart man, and a better king. I'm sure he only speaks what he means to say," Calix said.

"Speaking of your father," the Queen interjected, "I'm sure you're on your way to see him. He should be in his study with a few advisors." She linked arms again with Bexalynn, withdrawing the princess to her side like a little dove against its mother's wing. "Lady Shairi, come along. We mustn't be late for dance lessons!"

Chestnut curls tumbled over her shoulder as Princess Shairi sank into a low curtsey. Calix averted his eyes from the ample cleavage spilling over the front of her indigo bodice. "As always, it is a pleasure to see you, Prince Calix," she said sweetly, as her emerald eyes flicked up to meet his. "I hope at your coronation you'll do me the honor of trying out one of these new dances I'll learn with the princess and

Queen Emmaleigh?" She lingered, waiting for his answer as his sister and mother reached the bottom of the stairs.

He gritted his teeth as his mother turned, expectant. "It would be my pleasure," Calix conceded, lest the princess get herself in trouble with the queen. He might not have designs for her, but he wasn't cruel. She played a dangerous game, testing his mother's patience for a few half-hearted words from him.

"I shall dream of it until we dance, Prince," she said, her voice sweeter, more inviting than it had been in her request. Her freckled face flushed and she smiled before racing down the stairs with the skirts of her dress gathered in her hands to keep herself from tripping.

Calix sighed as he watched the trio of ladies disappeared down one of the hallways that extended from the grand entrance and into the castle. He had hoped for a shower, again, but he supposed he would prefer to bear the weight of his father's anger sooner rather than later. Calix began the long trudge up the stairs toward his father's study.

THE CRIMSON-CLAD GUARDS OUTSIDE KING AKINTUNDE'S STUDY reached to open the doors as he approached. He held out a hand before him, and they held their position, hands on the handles. He slowed and came to a stop before them.

"Your Highness?" The guard, a man he knew to be called Elkadhir, looked him over with concern, his large forehead wrinkled as he lifted his brows.

"It will be a difficult conversation. I just wanted a moment," Calix confessed.

"Whatever it is, the king is wise and just," Elkhadir said with confidence.

With a bracing breath, he gave a curt nod and said, "Open them."

The guards opened the doors and Calix entered his father's study. The room resembled a long, white hall of marble pillars, at the end of which sat great King Akintunde behind a black obsidian desk in a throne of ivory tusks harvested from ancient grass mammoths of the

Ascalith. Before the red desert was a windy basin of sand, it was a lush valley home to gigantic, tusked creatures with thick leather hides called mammoths. Long extinct, it was thought that their tusks held their earth magic in the marrow.

Three advisors stood between Calix and his father, so he took time to observe the walls set back beyond the rows of columns as he approached. King Akintunde's personal study was a veritable library of some of the rarest and perhaps most dangerous literature in Ellorhys. Solarium sconces glowed between vast shelves of tomes and scrolls. A table near a tall, arching window held a globe of the planet, and a stack of books.

When he was halfway between the door and the king, he said, "Father, my apologies for interrupting your meeting—"

"Calix? So soon?"

His father's questioning tone set his gait off-kilter, and he stumbled mid-stride as the advisors turned and parted so his father's gaze could fall upon him. He caught his balance and sank into a kneeling bow. "I come bearing urgent news of the Evernight. I seek a private audience with you at once, Father."

"Councilors, we'll finish this another time. I'll send for you." King Akintunde dismissed the men.

They departed, but Calix remained in his deferential bowed state until the guards had closed the doors behind them and he and his father were alone in his chambers.

"Rise, my son. Tell my what news you bring that is so imperative that I have dismissed the councilors of the refugee committee? Surely you could not have done the deed so soon."

Calix stood and met his father's stormy gaze. Grey streaked his black beard making him look like a thunderhead. His tan face was weathered with age, time and experiences Calix could only dream of shouldering. In failure, he ultimately felt small before this great Warlord of the West. His long hair was pulled to one side, exposing the tattooed side of his scalp. He loved to show his crown, tattooed into the side of his head among the bold lines and whorls that traced down his spine and around his neck.

Because you'd have to take his head to take the crown from him.

"I did not kill Princess Issaria, or the Evernight Witch."

His father's face contorted in anger, and veins bulged in his forehead and in the cording of his neck beneath his beard. His cheeks were crimson as he said, "Do tell me why you have failed a quest that would secure you the crown and my blessing to take my *country*," His father's calm voice was emphasized not by volume, no, but only in disappointment.

Calix took a deep breath. "Honestly, Father...it's going to sound crazy, but the Mythos told me not to. I was given another path to follow. One that brings the princess to our gates as an ally against the Evernight Witch," he spouted half-truths, hoping to fill in the rest of the story as he expounded on his journey.

King Akintunde said nothing. His orange-yellow eyes, like molten steel at the forge felt just as hot upon him. The heavy weight of his gaze was more than Calix could bear.

"I was in the Baelforia, walking to Espera when I saw a...a bright light. And I approached it, and I swear to you Father, on my life as your son, on the Cosmos, on all that is good in Ellorhys...I saw Baelfor. He was..." Calix swallowed and thought fast. "He was sent to intercept me. He was weak. New even."

"New? Baelfor is as old as the planet itself. Boy, Baelfor made the very castle you stand in!"

"Not anymore, Father." Calix tried to gather his thoughts into a coherent story that his father would believe. "He was new, forming. He had awakened just to come speak with me, awakened before his time and he told me that I could not harm the Princess of the Celestial City."

"Could not...that girl is as evil and corrupt as they come! Her coronation is upon us in a month's time, and mark my words, boy, all my spies tell me the witch has her coached to wage war. They want to conquer us all, cast us all into an infernal night!" Akintunde's fear cast spittle from his lips in vehement rage.

Calix shook his head and made his lying yellow eyes meet his father's gaze and remain steady as he said, "Baelfor said that the Imperial Princess and I share a cosmic fate, and that soon she would learn the truth behind the Evernight, and it would turn her against the witch. She will seek our help, the last allies her parents knew, and we are beckoned by the Mythos to answer her call."

His father remained silent, his eyes narrowed as he contemplated his son's words, supposedly at the bidding of the Mythos. Long-dead Mythos. Calix swallowed hard, feeling his throat bobble like gravel against itself. His father's gnarled hands, thick and scarred, folded before him, hiding his disbelieving scowl.

"We will deal with the Princess of the Evernight when and *if*," King Akintunde put a heavy skepticism behind the word, and after a lengthy pause he continued, "*if* she arrives asking for help. In the meantime...we will carry on as planned. I am disappointed, Calix. I had hoped to be conquering Espera and righting the celestial balance of our world would be the mark and legacy of your reign. What should I do with you now?"

"I am at your disposal. I have failed your command, and while the quest linking me and the Imperial Princess lies on the horizon, I will redeem myself with whatever you command, Father."

King Akintunde lowered his gaze, looking over his knuckles at the spread of documents on his desk. "I have already begun planning your coronation ball. I have no choice but to continue lest your embarrassment become my shame. However...if I cannot seize one part the continent, perhaps I can utilize you to lay claim to another." The king's voice was no more than a whisper but his rumination set Calix into a cold sweat. "Ares, as you know, still thrives despite the current environment of the world."

"Of course," Calix replied out of expectance.

"You know that your mother is the cousin of the king of Ares? That idiot Fraxinus only managed to get the throne because your whip of a mother was only a young girl when the last king died, or I'm sure she would have wiled her way to the crown."

Calix felt his throat closing. He had to proceed with caution. He felt his vision being reduced to a pin-hole and focused on the receding hairline of his father's thinning mane.

He hadn't seen it before, but the ink in the king's tattoos had faded with exposure to the sun, and his bronzed skin was weathered. He was nearing his two hundred and eightieth birthday. Even the strongest magicians only lived a decade or two past three hundred. Akintunde was nearing the end of his life, and perhaps, Calix thought for the first time, he felt his age like a noose around his country, his kingdom. The only true love his father had ever known.

"You will enter a courtship with the Lady Shairi."

"Father, pl—" Calix protested. Anything but that.

"Boy, I'll not hear it. You have no choice. You said you would serve me, and this is how you shall do it." The finality in his father's voice made Calix grit his teeth.

Hands clenched into fists he stared at the polished marble floor and said, "Yes, your Highness. I will court the Aresian Princess at your command. May I ask to what end this courtship will serve?"

His father chuckled then, and a chill went down Calix's spine. "To what end? To marriage, of course! And to many babies after that! May you only have sons!" And then he guffawed, a full bodied, rumbling laugh. "The girl is already begging your mother to ask me, and ask she has. For years, I've neglected the idea thinking you'd make a wise match on your own, but no more. I will orchestrate the future of our kingdom as I have always done, and the path you will walk be the path I have constructed for you."

It took all his strength to keep his spine straight, to keep his lips closed. Protests bubbled up from within him, and while he raged, eager to deny the Warlord of the West...Not now. Not when the crown and a kingdom full of people relying in him wavered in the balance. Rooted to the spot, all Calix could do was nod and say, "Of course, your Highness. You are wise and I am blessed to have your thoughtful guidance."

King Akintunde snorted at that. "Be gone with you. I will summon you when I wish to see you again. When I do, you had better have many things to tell me about our *dear* Princess Shairi."

"Of course," Calix said as he turned on heel and strode from the King's study.

He did not stop walking until he was far from the king's chambers and rounding the eastern pavilions. Flowering gardens, tended to and kept alive in the constant sunlight by dedicated gardeners, bloomed in abundance in the courtyard. The pungent aroma of blossoms and pollen floated in the air. The cavernous expanse of the library welcomed him with a dark, cooling embrace. To protect the ancient tomes within the archives of the First City of Men, the drapes were drawn, and solarium sconces, producing light without heat, illuminated the wide oak shelves and volumes.

Deep within the halls of the library, Calix began to scan the shelves for any scrolls or texts that may hold the most ancient stories of the past. His father may not believe in his meeting with the Mythos, but Calix knew what he had been bid to do. When Aurelia came to him as the Imperial Princess, he hoped to have some answers about the Vera Caelum.

15

ELON

He had not allowed himself to look in the direction of the Glass since he sent Issaria through the tunnel in the wall of the storage cellars more than two weeks ago. He could not let himself look in her direction for fear Hecate would see his wish for her safety and swift journey in his eyes, the loss on his face. He dared not give himself the chance to betray their plan.

Not when it was working.

Elon found himself often in this hallway, staring at the city, pock marked by black scars where the explosions had taken place. There had been seven of them. It was overkill, even for Hecate. A thousand were dead. Probably more. They still weren't sure. Reports of the missing just kept climbing in numbers and the rubble was often too dangerous to sift through until proper teams of magicians arrived. Some of the explosion sites had been near the slums, and Elon knew firsthand that sometimes a small building held a lot of bodies on a cold, moonlight night.

Movement caught the corner of his eye and he looked down the corridor to see a palace maid, cloth on her shoulder and bucket of water in hand, enter from beyond the double doors. The guards stationed at the end of the hall—the ones that hadn't held this position yesterday when he was here for more than an hour—didn't break their attention from their silent duty.

Elon watched from where he stood at the far end of the hall in the center of a wide viewing window as the maid got down on her hands and knees and began to polish the floor, dunking the rag into the bucket and scrubbing in circles, crawling forward in slow inches. At that rate, it would take her a good hour or more to polish the floor. Elon sighed heavily, frustrated that his pensive time had been interrupted not once, but twice now with the maid. He turned his attention back to the city and waited as she approached on her knees, pausing only to drag her sloshing bucket forward on the crystal floor.

The guards remained at their posts and Elon's suspicions were confirmed.

He was definitely being watched.

He stayed where he was, gazing thoughtfully out over his ruined city. Hecate was a parasite upon Espera. Upon Ellorhys, really. And now she'd taken from him the one person he had left in the world.

He refused to wonder if Issaria was alive. Of course she was. She had the Mythos of *light* within her. Aurelia was more than just the first Imperial Empress, she was the bringer of balance to the world. Her radiance and goodness were the foundations of the Dynasties. Had her sister not murdered her, Aurelia would probably still be alive.

No, Issaria was *definitely* alive. Elon only wondered when he would be able to follow her.

For now, his charade had to continue. New to the game though he was, he was not alone in his defiance. Others were ready to stand beside him. Beside her. They had sought him out after tales of his ordeal came to light.

The maid was at his feet, sloshing puddles on his boots.

"I am so sorry—Oh! Captain Sainthart! Apologies. I—" she stammered, her honey eyes locking on his as she knelt before him, auburn hair spilling over her shoulder in waves.

"It's all right. No more harm done than a walk in a rain shower," he said dismissively as he side-stepped her and turned his back to the guards, as if to remain and keep his watch over the city while she scrubbed. "We have to find a better way of meeting, Safaia," Elon whispered as he leaned down to rub his thumb on the dampened toe of his boot.

She waited until he straightened and resumed his lonely watch over the city and she too had turned to polish at an angle where the sentries could not see her lips. "You're being followed. You'll have to shake your tail, but we can meet as planned. I'll have them gathered. Go to the Amber Rose and make yourself comfortable. We'll find you when we're ready."

Safaia turned and rang out her rag, dipping it again in the murky water within her bucket. Again, it splashed over the side and onto his boots.

Elon stepped back, aghast at the maid's mistake. "Come now, girl! You're far too clumsy for this!"

"I'm so sorry," she cried, making a show of her fear of him.

"I'll be speaking with the Staff Master about you!" he exclaimed, though there was no such position within the household staff. For show, Elon kicked over her bucket, the water a murky wave that flooded the remaining unwashed portion of the hall. "At least now it won't take you *an hour* to wash the rest of the hallway!"

Safaia actually looked affronted at his harassment and Elon immediately felt as if he'd gone too far, but the corner of her mouth ticked up in a smirk as she threw her hands up over her face and pretended to weep. Shaking his head, he turned around and stomped down the hallway, storming past the guards without looking at them. As if their presence was no disturbance to his routine. Perhaps he even expected them to be there. Perhaps he believed the Palace Guard to be increasing checkpoints within the palace for enhanced security, which would have been a good call for Acontium to make in the wake of the very publicly known *abduction of the Imperial Princess*.

But no such order had been issued.

In fact, Elon was forced to acknowledge as he walked aimlessly through the palace that Commander Acontium hadn't made any efforts to recover the princess at all. Despite Hecate's very public mourning and declarations of profound sorrow at her niece's disappearance, no more riders were being sent out.

His trap had worked perfectly. Hecate stumbled into it and had no idea it had even sprung. After helping Issaria get out, Elon went back to where he'd hidden Flynt-the-traitorous-assassin in a less traversed hallway, tied inside the curtain, and disposed of the body with the help of a palace chef who was always fond of Issaria; as a child she snuck into the kitchens and stole his honey-custard pastries, as many as she could carry in her dress, held like a smock to contain them all. He believed Flynt to have been incinerated in one of the many kitchen hearths, but he wasn't entirely sure what old fire magi had done with the assassin.

He'd also gone back to Issaria's room and staged a struggle. Her bed was already haphazard and he tipped over her favorite chaise and broke a pedestal bearing a solarium geode. The geode rolled until it came to its open crevice, then wobbled into a steady place beside the empty hearth. The fire within had gone out, and the charred logs were no more than lumps of charcoal in a pile of ash. Closer to the entrance to her suite, Elon staged more upended furniture, a Rhunish rug askew on the floor among scattered game pieces. And the finishing touch? He knocked himself out, right there in her quarters to frame the whole thing.

Safaia found him, and he felt terrible for her fear at the blood that leaked from the gash on his temple. She believed every word he told her about the fight against a group of unknown assailants. Overpowered, they took her—they took the princess! Word of her kidnapping spread like the fires from the explosions Hecate had set off that night. The damage to Hecate's plans just about matched the damage done to Espera, he mused.

Elon stopped in the middle of the hall.

He had been wandering, he thought, but his feet seemed to know his destination better than his own mind did.

He was standing in Princess Issaria's chambers.

The mess he'd made staging her kidnapping had long been cleaned, probably by Safaia, Isida, and Daphnica themselves, homage to their missing mistress. They would probably maintain her quarters until she got back, just to keep up appearances that they hoped and expected her return. It was a good ruse.

They were all performing well.

One false move and it all fell apart.

Elon sighed, turned from her sitting room and exited the princess's chambers without stepping further than the receiving room. He didn't need to mourn her. He knew she was alive out there, somewhere on the Glass. She was much stronger than anyone gave her credit for.

And Aurelia is inside her, a small voice inside his head reminded him.

On his way back through the palace, Elon found himself entering a hall to find a pair of guards standing sentry at the opposite end of the hall. He'd been distracted by thought, but he hadn't been so oblivious as to miss walking past two guards, was he? As he approached, he realized they were the same guards as before.

They weren't very stealthy, or very well staffed in their espionage venture, were they? Elon decided that he too, wished to gain some information on them. As he neared them he put on a sad smile. The look of a man barely holding it together.

"I just keep ending up back here, boys," he said, really laying into the regret and self-pity. "I let them...I let them take her."

The guards exchanged uneasy looks before the one on the right offered him a sympathetic shrug. "I mean, I heard there were a whole squad of them, and you tried to fight them all yourself?"

Elon gave an ambivalent shrug. "All I can think of is that I failed her." He put a hand up to his eyes and rubbed, pretending to hold back phantom tears. "I remember her screaming my name and I just couldn't...I couldn't get to her." He shook his head again and coughed, as if trying to cover up his emotions.

The guards looked on, their discomfort obvious.

"I'm sorry, guys. I, uh...I need a drink. More than one. Got any recommendations?"

"I like a tavern on the north side of Espera called the Rook and Raven," the second guard on the left, said.

"That's too far, Terek. Besides, the best tavern in the city is the Barking Clover, and everyone knows it," the first guard retorted.

"The Barking Clover, eh?" Elon mused, considering the suggestion. "Ah, but I remember this sweet thing last time I was at the Amber Rose. I haven't seen her in a while, but..." He let his voice trail off for a moment as if the thought of her had just occurred to him. "I might need a little more than a drink to forget the ghosts that keep me awake at night, if you know what I mean," he added as he gave the second guard a parting clasp on his armored shoulder. He pushed through the doors and almost ready to let go of the door when he said, "Maybe I'll see you boys there after your shift, yeah?" The guards leaned into the open door way, as he let the door fall out of his grasp. "Think about it, at least!" he said desperately as the door closed between them.

Elon continued his dejected trudge down the hall, and was not at all surprised when he heard the doors in a hallway behind him open.

16

ELON

The Amber Rose met its name in the hazy amber glow of candle-laden chandeliers that hung from the rafters, but the tavern Safaia had instructed him to was no rose. The lingering smell of sweat and fish on the bodies of the men packed in after a long night's work was overwhelming. In fact, it was so near to the docks and the market, that the entire patronage of the ale house seemed to be fisherman or merchants of some sort, which was no problem in itself...save for the stench. Though among the working men wasting their Metals on weak ale, Elon spied a series of working girls batting their eyelashes each time they made eye contact with a man. The Amber Rose was a haven for debauchery, it seemed.

He lifted his half-empty flagon of ale and downed what remained. He wiped his mouth on the back of his hand and put his mug back on the table. Eyeing the crowd as if he was looking for a barmaid to get him a refill, Elon placed a stack of bronze Metals on the table as he marked the two guards who had been tailing him in the palace. Little rude they chose to hide in the corner and watch him get himself belligerently drunk, he thought. After all, they had accepted his invitation!

A blonde barmaid came over, swiped the Metals into a pocket on her apron, and replaced his empty mug with a full one. She had tried flirting with him when he'd first sat down, but he'd only grunted at her, and she had been short with him since. Probably not the best move when trying to remain inconspicuous, but he didn't want anyone else getting too close to him tonight. Elon took a hearty swig, keeping an eye on the men in the corner. This was his third ale, and while he wasn't a lightweight, he also wasn't trying to lose his senses while two of Hecate's men stalked him all over palace and city. In case watching was the mildest of their orders, he needed to make sure he kept his wits about him, lest he find himself having to battle them both. One unknown assailant wasn't easy when you weren't sure what type of mana they were going to launch at you. Would they be a typical armament magi, creating weapons from their given element? Or a beastmaester, summoning a corporeal creature to attack from behind while he was engaged in a physical brawl?

Elon took another sip of his ale.

Elon wondered if he was too early. Or too late. Did his mark miss him? Or worse, was his mark jeopardized, and this was all a trap lain by Hecate to eliminate him? Without him propagating that Issaria was kidnapped, she could even say that Elon himself had disposed of her.

He forced himself to remain relaxed and leisurely at his table in the back of the Amber Rose even as his heart thundered in his chest. Hecate was much more experienced at this intrigue thing; she was going to see right through him, Cosmos above, she already had considering the way she'd clearly sent a pair of oafs to tail him.

"You've been here a while, soldier," a velvet voice said from his left, drawing Elon's gaze from the rest of the room. "I sure hope you're waiting on me," said the woman. Her ample cleavage very nearly spilling over her corset drew his eye more than her sultry smile and vivid honey-colored eyes. "And if you're not waiting on me...maybe I can help you spend the time while you wait for someone else," she said as she leaned in and planted her lips on his scruffy cheek—putting his face between her and the men Hecate sent. "Safaia and the others are upstairs. Let's make this good. You brought friends."

Elon let a lazy smile ease onto his face as he took another swig from his mug. "Don't worry. I've been playing with them for hours," he whispered as he leaned into her neck.

"She said you were different, but I didn't realize she meant daft," the woman said as she settled herself in his lap and boldly settled his free hand on her hip. Elon arched an eyebrow at her, knowing his new friends would think him a flirt. "In that case, I'd say we're both lucky. I'm free for the next *several* hours…if you can pay the price," she continued their charade, no room for error in their show.

"Pay?" Elon laughed louder than he would have naturally, but it worked. His false bravado had his friends standing to leave. Lazy, he thought, Acontium will not be pleased they were so easily deceived. "Woman, I work in the palace. I can pay your fee and then some."

"Then let us make use of your hefty wages, soldier. I have a room upstairs."

Elon let his gaze flick to the door as the men who watched him headed outside, pipes in hand as the door swung closed behind them. "Well, that was—"

The redhead smashed her mouth against his and Elon almost resisted at the force of the kiss when he saw the third man at the bar—staring at them over the rim of his mug with keen eyes. The guards he invited *had indeed* accepted his invitation…and then invited at least one more friend of their own.

He leaned into the startling kiss and tangled his fingers in her red curls. Eyes closed, the memory of Issa's kiss in the passage assaulted him. How soft she'd been, the silken touch of her lips against his. He pulled away and met brothel girl's honey eyes, his own heavy-lidded and full of intention. "That room you spoke of is upstairs, yes?"

"It is," she said sweetly, her cheeks flushed and her breast heaving after their kiss—a flattering trick for soldiers wishing for the helpless damsel instead of the illicit lady of the night—as she slid off of his lap and took his hand, helping him rise.

He stumbled over his own boots and leaned heavily on his contact, letting her struggle to support his weight and pretend him drunker than he was. Together they staggered through the crowded tavern, jostled between groups of rowdy fishermen. At the bottom of the stairs, Elon caught the toe of his boot on the tread of the stair, making a show of falling down—much to his redheaded companion's embarrassment. He eyed the place at the bar where this third friend had been, but no longer. The place was vacant, only an empty flagon left as proof that he'd been there.

Elon wasn't so foolish as to believe the man had left the tavern. No, he would watch, and wait. And see how long it took Elon to return from tumbling the tavern wench. Perhaps if he was very thorough, he would follow and try to confirm their illicit acts for himself.

He allowed the woman to help him to his feet, and he stood, swaying in place for a moment as if to regain his balance. Many eyes watched, but none seemed interested in him beyond the act of drunken buffoon. Together, they took the stairs to a dark and narrow hallway lined with doors. Muffled moans escaped from behind those doors as they continued down the hall in a stumbling zig-zag, the woman bearing his weight and the burden of their act the entire way. "Almost there. The one on the left," she mumbled, groaning slightly at his weight. "This is for calling you daft, isn't it?"

Elon fought to keep the smirk off his face. "You *said* to make it good."

He felt her stiffen before she slipped out from underneath his arm, and keying into the door while Elon toppled over, catching his balance last minute before following her inside the darkened room.

He heard the lock click into place before the lights came on from various clusters of solarium situated in groups around the room. Elon straightened as the magicians in the room stood, fists clasped over their hearts.

"Commander, you made it." The brunette maid who scrubbed the palace hall, Safaia, smiled as her honey-colored eyes fell upon the busty redhead beside him. "And I see you met my sister, Maiyra," she added. Her smile slid into a grimace and the infamous Maiyra rolled her eyes as she elbowed past her.

"I didn't do anything to him," Maiyra said as she settled herself in front of a vanity and began brushing her wavy locks, the solarium crystals casting golden threads throughout as she stared at herself in the mirror. "He *was* followed though. Heavily. At least five men by my count."

"Five?" Elon exclaimed.

Maiyra stared at him through her reflection in the mirror, her honey-eyes void of surprise, as if she'd known he'd miscounted his tails. "The two obvious ones, of course. I knew you saw them—idiot couldn't stop glancing at them," she said, glancing around the room. Elon felt himself flush at her words. "Then there was the ugly one by the door; he waited a right long time for *that* seat. He was to stop your escape, last resort and all. There was the broody-looking fellow at the bar who had just about as much to drink as you did. I'm sure he knows you're not that drunk. And then there was a fisherman at the next table over who hasn't said a word to his companions since you sat next to them. Not sure if he was a watcher or not, but better safe than sorry," she finished with a shrug. "You really do need to be more covert for these meetings. We're all risking quite a lot to be here."

"That's enough Maiyra," Safaia said with a tone of finality. "You wouldn't know *half* the things you do if it weren't for the winds!" Safaia looked to Elon then added, "She's a Whisperer. The winds translate languages and pass secrets to her." She looked back to Maiyra, rolled her eyes and spread her hands wide. "We're *all* risking a lot here."

Elon looked around the room at their rag-tag group.

Other than himself and the Cardinalè sisters Safaia and Maiyra, Elon met the wary eyes of at least a dozen other individuals who now thanks to Maiyra, thought him an incompetent leader for their rebellion. Among them were the other maids from the princess's personal household, Isida and Daphnica, as well as a smattering of palace staff including Rhori's laundress Liara. Rounding off the group were a few soldiers including the remaining members of the would-have-been Imperial Guard, Rhori, Xenviera, and Roane, as well as a few others he recognized from the ranks of the Imperial Guards for the late Emperor and Empress, Gilben Hamm and a fellow called Yaxin. Issaria's tutor, Magi Caltac Kholozzo was seated near the hearth. It seemed their loyalty as well as his ran toward the Elysitao bloodline of

Imperials, and Elon found his chest swelling with pride. Perhaps they really could do this.

They could overthrow Hecate.

"Is there any word of the princess?" Xenviera asked from her station near the door. She was no doubt listening for footsteps in the hallway beyond.

"None yet," Elon replied as he settled on the bed.

Safaia sat down next to him and shook her head. "The Empress Regent is furious that she has to keep expending resources. Her letter carrier likes my turn-overs, and I trade them for insight on the Empress' mood so that I may prepare her favorites when she is in the most need of them." She rolled her eyes before continuing, "Daxios requested that I make her favorites more often since she's been in such a foul mood. All her letters are to pull back the riders she dispatched to find the princess in the first place." She turned to Elon. "She's going to call off the search soon. If Issaria doesn't make it across—"

"She'll make it," Magi Caltac said from where he sat by the hearth, hands folded into the sleeves of his white Magistrate's robe. He kept staring at the solarium in the hearth, the dancing light casting fire-like shadows across the valleys of his face. "Issaria is a smart and resourceful girl unlike any I've instructed before. She will make it across the Glass. She must."

Elon nodded and stood back up, taking to pacing the room. "He's right. Princess Issaria is going to make it to Hinhallow and she will bring word of Hecate's betrayal. When she does, we will know. Until then we must prepare the rebellion as much as we can. Gilben," he said, addressing the black-haired commander of the Archers. "Where do we stand with numbers?"

"Near about two thousand right now. New recruits are coming every day. The rumors of Hecate's involvement in the assassination on the emperor and empress are spreading faster than we thought."

"And we're certain of their loyalty, Captain Hamm?" Safaia asked from her seat behind Elon.

"Vetting them myself," the tall man said from where he leaned against the wall. Gilben had been on Empress Umbriel's Guard and was fiercely loyal to the Imperial family, even going so far as to look in on Elon after Soren's death. The man never tried to replace Soren as Elon's father, but his care and attention were noted after the massacre. "We're thinking we may have to hide the troops in the moorlands as we increase the ranks," he added, crossing his arms over his chest.

"Outside the city?" Elon weighed the option. Hiding two thousand rebels in the city was one thing. Hiding ten thousand and training them under the Hecate *and* Galen's noses? "When the time comes, we will move them to the moorlands. Send a rider to scout for locations that will house ten thousand."

"Ten thousand?" Rhori said from his place near the window. He peered out the side of the blinds, into the moonlight street below. "Aren't we being optimistic, Sainthart? Most of these recruits are farmers and fisherman who've gotten tired of the Eventide. Training them is going to take more time than we've got. The witch already has an established army. As soon as she's gotten a whiff of us she's going to wipe us off the map!"

Elon averted his friend's eyes. Rhori was right. They were heavily outmatched. The magicians in the Imperial Army would follow Hecate unless they realized that she'd been betraying them all along. Their rumors were working, bringing recruits to the rebellion's cause, but not fast enough. Rumors only held so much weight when Imperial Propaganda was on every street corner claiming the princess to be a martyr to the Eventide cause—slain by the Daylight heathens just as her parents before her. Fear was a powerful motivator when there was no idol to stand against it.

"She's not just the princess," he whispered, afraid of what desperation they might see in his admission.

Rhori scoffed. "We know she's the love of your life or what-have—
"

"Rhori!" Liara scolded from beside him.

"We *all* love her," Safaia said in Elon's defense, her face red as she did so.

"Sainthart speaks the truth!" Magi Caltac announced loudly, trying to amplify his voice over the rising clamor of argument that had erupted in the small room.

"Quiet! Hush up!" Xenviera hissed from her post at the door.

Silence fell over them as the pony-tailed warrior held a finger to her lips, her ear pressed against the wooden door. Dark eyes wide, she pointed at Maiyra, who scampered from her seat at the vanity to the bed, sliding the frame against the floor as Safaia bounced off of the mattress.

"Ohhhhh, yes!" Maiyra cried out passionately, and the authenticity of her cry made Elon's heart rate quicken. "Yes!" she cried out again and snagged his sleeve, eyes frantic. "Just like that!"

Face flushed, Elon jostled the bed frame and groaned as loudly as he was able, trying not to meet Rhori's eyes as he stifled his laughter in the corner. Liara rolled her eyes, looking unamused by his mirthful reaction. Elon looked from Liara to Safaia, who had retreated to where Isida and Daphnica, Issaria's maids, had gathered near the writing desk. She kept her back to him as he upheld the charade of drunken soldier entertaining a whore...or by the overly expressed moans of pleasure Maiyra continued to bleat from the sheets as he continued to grind the bed frame across the floor, the whore was ensuring she earned her tip and the drunk soldier was doing a mild job of entertaining her.

Elon and Maiyra met each other's eyes and she smirked. This was definitely to evade suspicion, but Elon suspected that it was also payback for pretending to be drunk and making her bear his weight.

He looked back to Rhori, who had tears rolling down his cherry cheeks as he swallowed his laughter. Everyone else in the room was also holding an amused smile on their face and Elon looked over his shoulder.

Xenviera leaned against the door, a smirk on her lips, arms crossed over her chest. Elon stopped shaking the bed frame. "Oh, no. Don't stop on my account. The watcher's been gone for a good minute or so though." Her dark eyes twinkled in the light from the solarium crystals.

Elon righted himself and straightened his tunic. "You could have given a signal or something," he muttered as he sank onto the edge of the bed.

"Oh but you were so *enthusiastic*," Maiyra cooed from where she lay tangled in the sheets before erupting into a fit of giggles that rippled throughout the room.

"This isn't a game!" Elon nearly shouted. Silence fell over the group and Elon shook his head. "This is treason. The Empress knows that I helped Issaria. She can't turn against me yet, not without implicating herself, but she's working on that, I'm sure. She's going to kill me if she can find a way to do it, and the first step is by proving to the public that Issaria is without a doubt dead. She tried to plant Flynt among us, and it almost worked. He betrayed us, and tried to kill her before I helped her escape. Now we have to wait and trust in Issaria." He took a deep breath and said it again: "She's not just the Princess..." Elon lifted his emerald eyes from the splintered floorboards to meet Magi Caltac's golden eye. "You know what she is?"

"I've had suspicions for some time now," the old magistrate said, adjusting his eyepatch. "But only recently was I able to confirm my theories. Unfortunately, I am not the only one who was watching the princess for signs, and when she finally displayed them, the release of power was so strong I doubt I was the only one who felt it for what it was."

"Signs of what?" Safaia asked from where she stood behind Isida and Daphnica. "What release of power?"

"That she has broken the Saros Cycle, a bloodcurse on her magic that will eclipse her soul." The Magi seemed to bear the weight of his words on his hunched shoulders.

"The what?" Xenviera asked from the doorway.

"It is for all intents and purposes," Magi Caltac explained, "a way to come back to life after one is murdered by black magic. It's the sinister origin of the much more gentle *Sanguinem Defendier* blood-oath Elon would have taken, which only would have allowed Issaria to use Elon's lifeforce as her own if she were injured. The Saros

Curse takes years for the legacy to come to fruition in a descendant, but it awakens the might of old mana with the vibrance of new mana."

"But Blood Magic is forbidden," Maiyra said confidently. "The Black Arts require covens and there haven't been covens since the War of the Cities—"

"There have always been," Magi Caltac interrupted, "and will *always be* covens among us, child. We are magicians, and forbid it or not, Blood Magic is powerful. Those that seek power so hungrily will not heed the laws of morality," Magi Caltac replied. "I always thought that the Empress Regent was a dark sorceress, but I never had the proof until she killed Helios and Umbriel."

"You knew of this plot?" Elon asked, feeling a fool for not having seen the signs all along.

Wizened Caltac nodded and turned his face back toward the hearth. "I have known the Empress Regent was not strong enough on her own to enact an event like the Eventide. I dared to hope she did not gain power from the deaths of the Imperial Emperor and Empress, but it appears my trust was misplaced. After I realized my mistake, I thought I would train the princess to be able to resist her." The magistrate sighed and folded his hands in his lap once again. "Issaria is strong of mind and of mana, but the power within her is… unpredictable. I fear it is my own fault that her powers were betrayed so unexpectedly. I pushed her, in our last lesson, but there was… something else about her that day."

"Is that why she was so strange that evening?" Safaia asked.

Magistrate Caltac looked from the hearth to Elon, his solitary eye bearing the weight of truth down upon him. "Despite what Xenviera believes, Blood Magic does not require a coven if one is calling upon *ancestral* bloodlines. Issaria seemed to awaken, in our lesson. She was unable to control the tempest of power that emerged, as is usual with her wild talent, but it came to me in that moment. The Saros Cycle wasn't just a lock on her magic, it was a lock on her soul. Awakening the power within her also awakened the magician it belonged to," the old magician continued on.

"Can we stop being cryptic here?" Xenviera retorted from the door. "Just say it already."

"When Obsidia slaughtered her sister for all the power of balance, she was the one who enacted the curse and set it upon the bloodline. The same blood flows in our dear princess as did in the first Queens of Ellorhys," Magi Caltac finished.

Safaia's hands flew to her mouth as her hallowed whisper permeated the room, "Aurelia."

"Well, that sounds wonderfully mystical and powerful," Xenviera said, "but if that were true then how come Obsidia didn't just curse the bloodline right back when Helios and Umbriel united against her?"

Magi Caltac shrugged. "The Black Arts are beyond even my knowledge. I know *of* them, not about them."

"What does that mean for Issaria? Is she just...like a body for this dead relative? Does she have a choice?"

Xenviera's honest concern silenced the room. Magistrate Caltac and Elon exchanged glances before Elon shook his head. "We're not really sure. I sent Issaria across the Glass before we really figured out what was happening to her."

"And now we're not even sure if she's alive," Maiyra said sarcastically from the bed.

"She's alive, child. Send your winds to seek the truth if you must," Magi Caltac said with resolution. "She will make herself known when the time is right. Issaria is the vessel for the first Primordial. She did not cross the Glass alone. I do not believe that Aurelia would wait some three hundred years to have her vessel snuffed out before she's had the chance to truly awaken."

The room fell silent for a beat and Elon mused aloud, "She was always so afraid of using her magic. She said it was wild, and dangerous, and I..." He swallowed, knowing the truth of his dedication to her. "I thought her weak because of it." He couldn't hide the shame in his voice. "All along she..."

"All along, Issaria had access to the most ancient and powerful of all the magics," Caltac finished for him. "She still may not realize what's happening to her, and that may be even more precarious." Elon looked up to meet the Magistrate's eye. "Hecate may not be the only one hunting her. There are other forces at work in the realm. I've felt the echoes of their power, seen the migrations change abruptly, the change of the tides out of sync with the moon—I don't know what else is out there, Hecate keeps me on a tight leash and ensures that I know my place as a tutor *only*."

His bitterness leached into his tone as he continued, "The world is changing, Hecate made sure of that, and we live at the heart of the Eventide. Issaria will need an army when she returns, and if she can't make it back to us before the realm revolts, we may need an army regardless. Her power alone may not be enough to turn the tides. Those with black hearts have been aligning themselves with Hecate for years. I've seen them come and go, and I know her to be as corrupt as the blackest of magic. If this is to be the battle Issaria fights when she claims her true heritage, we *will* ensure that righteousness prevails." The old man's voice wavered proudly as he met the gaze of each magician in the room. "I will not forsake my promises. And that girl *will* be our Empress and triumph over the evils of this world."

His hope permeated the room. The Imperial Guard, still fresh from their own promises to pledge themselves to Princess Issaria exchanged glances. Already their ranks had been penetrated by the enemy. Flynt had somehow...Elon shook the thought from his head. The army they had within these incredibly thin walls—he could hear *real* moaning from the other rooms—was more powerful than at least a dozen units of Hecate's forces. Each one of them was a talented Magician, highly ranked and rigorously tested in their own right. It seemed he was not alone in his thinking, as he met the determined eyes of each member of their new army.

"Well, then. It seems we have some work to do," Elon said, a smirk sliding onto his face. "Let's go make some mischief for the *Empress*, shall we?"

Equally sinister smiles met his own, and Elon was the first to sneak out of the room, a satisfied patron happy to have spent his coin with a pretty girl.

17
ISSARIA

Twelve nights she walked. She slept little, unable to find comfort beneath foreign skies.

Jewel-drenched with more stars than Issaria had ever seen, the sky overhead shifted into constellations she'd never gazed upon before. Over her right shoulder, almost on the horizon, the Vitalief, held aloft by Tarlix, pointed her home. She feared the next time she looked for its guidance, she would find the amaranthine glass had swallowed it behind her.

Her water supply was gone, her food diminished near to nothing. A few crumbling chunks of cheese, and an apple was all that remained of her stash from the kitchens. The cloak was stuffed into the bottom of the satchel.

The Glass itself shivered with reflected moonlight. A razor-sharp wasteland of refracted purple light that shifted and glistened like a mirror. At times the frozen dunes of glass were as tall, perhaps taller than the spires of the palace in Espera, and so thick no light shone through to the other side. Monstrous waves cast her in chilled shadows where the temperature of the night chattered her bones and reminded her that her nightgown was barely a covering now, shredded by her many falls and stained brown with blood from her scabbed knees, and blistered feet.

The Glass was no ocean. It wasn't even a desert, as it had been before the comet's heat changed it. It was an endless labyrinth in the moonlight, but it was worse in the dark, when the clouds blotted out the moon and rendered her blind, stumbling recklessly through the dark.

Once, on a cloudy night it rained for a few minutes before the ocean winds pushed the storm inland, leaving her even more thirsty and shivering in its chilled wake.

Nervous sweat beaded across her skin like dew as she tried to keep herself from walking in circles. She fixed her gaze on a single point as far in one direction as she could see and walked toward it. When Issaria arrived at that point, she oriented herself in the valley between crests, selected a new point in the distance in what she hoped was the right direction, and kept walking.

Every now and then, a ridge, a shift in the planes of the crystal, caught her toes and sent her to her knees. Pain shot through her bones like lightning, leaving a criss-cross of lacerations in their wake. Sometimes the wind ripped across the Glass, carrying with it the scent of stale salt air from the Lanzauve Sea in the west. But mostly the air was stagnant with darkness, and silence crept into Issaria's head like ghosts crawling in through her ears.

Her pace dragged as the nights blurred. Time...didn't exist anymore. She wasn't even really sure if had been twelve nights. Maybe it had been fifteen. Maybe it was only two and she was a foolish girl to think she could survive this unholy expanse. Maybe she was to die out here and damn her city to eternal night. She knew she was foolish then, to think for an instant that Hecate would hesitate to complete her curse and unleash the Eventide on Ellorhys. Her stomach rolled to think that it was not just her people whose fates rested on her shoulders, but perhaps the whole of Ellorhys.

The idea was enough to keep her trudging onward even when her food was gone.

When sleep did manage to find her, Issaria curled beneath the thickest crystal wave she could find and pulled the cloak tight around her body. She hoped to look like a lump of glass to anything that may pose her a threat. To combat the cold, she tried to sleep in the light of the moon, but more often lately it was tucked low on what she hoped the southern horizon behind her. As it became easier and easier for sleep to take her, she began to wonder if she would wake up at all.

In her heart she prayed to the Cosmos. Hoped with all her might to Ethereal Dovenia, divine creator of all, and her consorts—Essos, the cupbearer of all magic, and Chronos, the lord of Time—that the moon fading behind her meant that she was nearing the Timeline and would soon see Daylight. Issaria would have asked the Elemental Mythos but they had shown her no favor thus far, and she dare not evoke their gaze now for fear it would be vengeful instead.

On what might have been the eighteenth night or the eighth, she uncurled herself from her cloak, grateful that sleep had claimed her for a time and that she was able to ignore the sharp pain in her belly. As she adjusted her cloak around her, Issaria repeated her mantra in her head.

Be afraid, but do it anyway.

She stretched out the cramps in her muscles from the hard glass and rubbed her eyes as she took in the warm amber glow that bled vermillion into indigo from beyond the endless peaks of purple glass.

Issaria's chest clenched and she held a hand to her trembling lips.

She was seeing the twilight stain of the Timeline for the first time.

Exhausted, Issaria dropped her hands to her sides, tilted her face back to the sky and let tears of relief trickle into her matted hairline. She was closer now. She could see it. She would not disappoint Elon. He was right, this *was* crazy. But this was something she could survive. She knew that now.

A low, long horn blasted through the night, and she snapped from her internal soliloquy as frightened eyes raked the area for the source of the distinctive bleat.

Behind her, nearly half an hour's trudge back in the direction she'd come was a line of wagons and riders on horseback. Silver moonlight gilded their slick black hoods in a convincing replica of the moonlight's reflection on the Glass. If she hadn't heard the horn herself, she might have thought them a mirage. Even the wagons were dark in color as if to camouflage the caravan against the Glass.

Issaria's heart swelled at her luck. She would not have seen the trade route, nor would the magicians who manned the wagons or mounted more than two dozen steeds have seen her had she not awoken. They could have passed in the dark and she would have been none the wiser. She was close to the Timeline, yes, she reminded herself, but she recalled the map of Ellorhys in her mind. The Timeline fell far from the border of the Glass. There were still miles, perhaps weeks of travel between her and the promised sanctuary of Hinhallow.

A pair of riders dispatched from the long line of travelers nudged their dark steeds into hastened trot and she realized they were not horses, but camels. The trumpet blared again in a swift triplicate, sounding sweet to her desperate ears. Issaria's lips cracked and crusted with fresh blood as she smiled at their swift approach. A half hour's walk for her weary, dehydrated self was nothing for strong, well cared for steeds and their broad, shadowed riders.

The riders near and the princess's smile faltered.

Hope sank in her stomach like a stone.

These men were merchants, no doubt, but not of silks and wares.

As they drew closer, it became apparent that the men approaching looked at her with greed in their hungry eyes. Sly smirks graced tanned faces hidden by the shade of shiny black hoods. Beneath, it appeared they were shirtless. Taut muscles were hidden beneath thick chains of gold and gems draped from their corded necks.

It was forbidden to forge with gold, as it was saved for the minting of Metals, the currency of Ellorhys. Old blood families may still have gold jewelry from the times before the War of the Cities and the Godsplague, but those old blood monarchs would not be stupid enough to traverse the Glass. But for criminals, thieves, and slavers who held no regard for the laws of her Imperial Ancestors that forbade such infractions on the basic rights of all magicians, crossing the Glass with illegal cargo to avoid detection would be brilliant.

Issaria sank to her knees.

She was about to be captured and she had no energy left to fight them or try to escape. She was thin, weak from days without food. Defeat drained the color from her face as she extended a hand toward them.

"Girl, what manner of demon chased you out here?" one called as he dismounted, still a short distance away.

"A pretty one, she is. Would ya look at them curves? After we clean her up, I'll wager Jallah will be thrilled we spotted her," the other said, close on his comrade's heels.

Dizziness overwhelmed her senses. Her vision swam with spots.

"Woah there!" Issaria felt strong arms catch her as her eyes closed and gravity claimed her.

SHE HEARD THE WHISPERS IN HER SLEEP. ISSARIA KNEW SHE WAS NOT alone. The stench of unwashed bodies clogged her nose and tainted her mouth.

"Is she a noble? Sethik said she was probably a noble because her nightgown is silk."

"Noble or not, she reeks." Someone nudged her calf with the sharp crescent of her nail.

"We all reek, Rhaminta."

"She's so frail, it's as if I can see her bones."

It took all Issaria's restraint to keep her eyes from flickering beneath her closed lids and betraying the fact that she had awoken. Issaria knew she had only moments to think, to find a way out of this mess. She fought to keep her breathing steady as she tried to discern details about her captive environment.

"Zhaniel said she had a fine dagger on her hip when they recovered her."

"I bet that's not all he tried to find on her hip."

"Hush! He might hear you!" another whispered harshly.

"I heard that other girl from Roark's wagon—the real pretty one? She was crying after he brought her back from...the washroom."

"We don't talk about that, Asmy," an older voice said with authority.

The conversation immediately stopped. So there was someone in charge here.

"Where do you suppose she came from?"

"Forget where she came from, where was she going?" an eager voice replied. "What would drive her mad enough to walk across the crystal? It's suicide!"

Issaria was surrounded by women, she thought, or hoped. The gentle lurch and steady rhythm of the wheels clicking in the Glass placed her in one of the purple painted wagons she'd seen before fainting. It was unclear if one of the riders was in the wagon with them or how much time had passed.

"Well, I think she's brave. She must have some amazing story to tell when she wakes."

"Brave," the older voice snorted with disdain. "Brave is just another word for stupid. Now tilt her head back and give the fool a sip of water." Someone obeyed, their fingertips gentle and Issaria kept her jaw slack. Her lips parted with gravity, as they would if she were still unconscious.

Issaria intended to let it trickle down her throat slowly. She meant to remain still, and buy herself more time before she had to explain and likely endanger herself. But the moment sweet, cold drops wet her sand-dry mouth, she was gulping it down, her hands reaching to hold the skin and crush the remainder of its contents into her starved belly.

"Easy, girl, you'll make yourself sick." The old woman's voice held no kindness in her tone, just the truth of the warning.

Issaria nodded as water dribbled down her chin in rivulets, aware of the ache that had begun to form beneath her ribs. With an idea in mind, the princess opened her eyes, and blinked bleary-eyed into the gloom of the caravan carriage. "Where am I?" she asked, her throat tight around the words, her voice hoarse.

"Jallah Coppernolle has claimed ownership on you," a black-haired girl murmured by way of an explanation, although the name she uttered sparked no recognition in Issaria's memory. "He owns us all."

The sorrow in her voice weighed heavily in Issaria's stomach. She trembled as she pushed herself to her knees and leaned against one of the wagon's walls. Her eyes adjusted to the dim lighting. She had been right about being within one of the wooden wagons. Issaria was also correct about being with women, perhaps just shy of a dozen in total, in varied colors and shapes. Thankfully the interior of the of the wagon was absent of any men who might belong to the master of this slave caravan, but less lucky, it was also void of any windows. The only door opened at the back of the slightly sizable rectangle. She didn't need to ask to know that it was locked.

"We wish we could tell you where for certain," a blonde-haired girl probably no more than fourteen or fifteen, barely a woman at all really, said with a shrug. "But we do know where we're going," she said as if they had some dream destination instead of some blasphemous black market to be sold like cattle. "Hinhallow."

Issaria schooled her features into shock and awe. "You're pleased to be sold?" The girl's face fell and Issaria looked from her naive, amber gaze to the other eyes she could make out in the hazy shadows. Some met her distraught gaze, but others would not or could not meet her eye.

It was a long while before someone broke the silence that had fallen over them, but it was the old woman she'd heard who spoke from the farthest corner of the carriage. "Name yourself, girl. Your eyes...they are telling."

"My name is Kyria, but often I am called Kai. I dance for a traveling troupe," Issaria lied smoothly as she jutted her chin out at the statement. Mentally she chanted her new identity over and over so that she would respond when addressed, but said without skipping a beat, "My eyes are fun, yes? It is a dye meant to imitate the Imperial violet. Harvested from the petals of violetta flowers. The craftsmagician in Espera said it was brand new," she boasted.

"The color is false?" A raven-haired woman with a thick braid draped over her shoulder leaned forward, dark eyes narrowed as she peered deep into Issaria's gaze.

"It is temporary, though I'm not certain how long it will last. I confess, I am perhaps the one of first to use the beautician's drops," she said, dropping her lashes for a mildly embarrassed effect. "I'm sure other ladies purchased her wares. I do not know how their experiences have fared. I was in the Celestial City on the first eve of the crescent moon, and still the dye lasts." She looked between the women, hesitation on her lips. "How long have I wandered the Glass since the attack on Espera?"

"Espera has been attacked?" the elderly lady echoed from where she sat in the shadow of the other women.

"Kidalma, Jallah favors you. How long has Kai been wandering the Glass?"

"Nearly a full moon cycle. The dark moon rises the eve after next."

Three weeks. Issaria felt her nausea return. She had wandered the glass for nearly a month, and she had not even crossed the Timeline. She would have died had this caravan not found her. The truth of the life debt settled in her stomach, souring the water she'd gulped so thirstily.

"Are you going to faint again?" the blonde asked.

"Such a weak spirited thing," Kidalma–the elderly lady Issaria realized–spat. "Answer me, girl. You said Espera was attacked?"

"It was," she said with a bob of her head. "I was there with my troupe for a performance for the Evernight Witch," she explained, stealing snippets of Daylight slang from her conversation with Blaze to earn their trust. "I was…taken with the captain of the guard when he was roused by his men to tend fires in the city. I waited in his bed for his return until…" Purposefully, she let her voice trail off.

"What happened next!" one of the younger girls in the cart asked, eager to learn more about Kai.

"Was the guard handsome?" a redhead dusted with freckles asked from her left.

The brunette beside her with emerald eyes, identical to those of the girl next to her, gave the redhead a light punch as she giggled, "You would ask that, Cizabet."

"Out with it, girl!" Kidalma urged, her voice breaking above the clamor of the rest. She leaned forward enough for Issaria to know that her thick braid was silver and her pale blue eyes were set deep into her weathered face. They seemed to see right through her murky lies.

"I heard the attack was ordered by the Evernight Witch herself. That she attacked her own subjects in order to murder the princess and throw suspicion from herself." If she was to pretend to be someone else, she could at least lend aid to her own cause and spread the truth of her aunt's betrayal across Ellorhys.

A hush fell over the women in the caravan's wagon. One by one, the eyes of the captives turned to the elder Kidalma, whom one of them had identified as the Caravan Master's favored slave.

"What?" Issaria asked after a moment of the silver woman staring at her with disbelieving eyes.

With a movement she did not see in the gloom, Kidalma rapped her gnarled knuckles on the side of the carriage. At once the wagon jolted to a stop, swaying the women inside like reeds in the wind.

A series of metal clanks and the harsh grind of a gear proceeded the door at the back of the wagon opening outward. Blinding sunlight poured in through the open casement. The brightness of it rendered Issaria sightless, and she threw an arm up to shield her eyes.

"Jallah will want to speak with her. She speaks treason against the Evernight Witch," Kidalma said from the back of wagon. "Take her."

Issaria was powerless as strong hands seized her wrist and opposite forearm, and in one swift motion, hauled her from the confines of the wooden cage.

18
ISSARIA

Oppressive light beat down on Issaria as the slavers hauled her from the wagon. Slack-jawed, her eyes burned as she blinked awestruck into sunlight and saw blue sky with bulging white clouds lazing on the horizon for the first time in nearly a decade. Hazy heat radiated off of the shimmering violet and amaranthine waves of glass that rose up like broken shards around the multicolor caravan. Camels, instead of horses, with colorful woven saddles bore bare-chested men and large mounds of leather parcels— possibly the men's personal belongings, she thought, her hungry eyes taking in as much detail as she could while the men dragged her along the long line of carriages. Jallah Coppernolle's troupe of slavers was *much* bigger than Issaria had anticipated.

Escape might prove difficult, if not impossible.

The carriage that held Jallah was gilded with gold and painted so deep a purple it might have well been black, but the wood was old and split from the persistent heat. Windows were mere cuts in the wood blocked off by rough-spun curtains the color of cream. The men who held her leaned one such the window, and after a few minutes of murmuring, the carriage door opened. Rough hands thrust Issaria inside, and she crumpled to the floor of the carriage without a sound.

The door closed behind her and familiar darkness enveloped her senses. Her eyes strained from the sudden lack of brilliant light.

"Would you like some water?"

Issaria shifted her weight and brought herself to her knees, nodding but wary of the man before her. Jallah was *handsome,* in a terrifying kind of way. A broad, golden-skinned man with a waxed mustache the color of rust, his broad nose defined his square face and his nostrils flared, as if he could scent her like a hound would to pursue its quarry. The left side of his head was shaved bald, and bisecting scars crisscrossed his skull. The right had reddish-brown hair swooped deftly to the opposite side of his head and tucked behind his ear.

"Here, settle yourself. The convoy will be on its way and you'll want to be sitting." Jallah Coppernolle's voice was rough and slurred. His scarred hands knew no discretion as he grabbed Issaria by her arms and seated her on the plush bench opposite himself. "You're the one we scraped off the Glass?" He guffawed, deep bellowing laughter. "You're tiny! You've got to be crazy! Aha, but aren't we all." He shook his head and fixed his dark eyes on hers. "I'm surprised you made it this far, truth be told. By the look of you, you wouldn't have reached Timeline before your bones needed to rest. That's a good day's ride off, longer if you're walking. A few days beyond that and you'd have reached the edge of the Glass."

At that rate, she would have died before even seeing the Timeline. She would never have made it. Another two, three days wandering between canyon walls of glass would have found her dead in a gorge.

Crimson-faced, Issaria heard him and acknowledged the defeat in her own quest, but her eyes darted to the platter on the bench beside him. Her stomach ached at the sight of the polished alloy tray laden with fruits—strawberries and green grapes, glistening orange wedges and halved melons mingled with crumbling blocks of cheeses. A pair of gem encrusted goblets stood sentry beside a crystal decanter of what could only be a red wine, the sweet burn of alcohol permeated the air along with the sea-salt sweat glistening on her own skin. Beside the decanter was an alloy pitcher. Jallah followed her hungry gaze with his own and smiled, showing his white teeth like a predator revealing his fangs. He poured himself a goblet from the alloy pitcher —*water*—and sipped it. The carriage groaned as it jolted forward. As promised, the convoy, as he called it, was on its way again, and Issaria wasn't sure if she should be more fearful of their destination...or of the man before her. "Would you like some water...?"

He was asking, she knew, but by the lingering question in his tone and the fact that he had yet to move for the second goblet, Issaria knew he was looking for a name before she was allowed to partake in his refreshments. She swallowed again, her throat and tongue gritty with thirst and recited what she'd told the women, the mantra in her head. "My name is Kyria. I dance with a traveling troupe. We were in Espera when the city was ransacked by the Evernight Witch as she attempted to assassinate the princess."

Wide-eyed, Jallah stared at her, seeming to assess her and her story. Issaria wondered if she shouldn't have shortened it quite so much, but she was prepared for more interrogation. Finally, after several minutes of silence between them, Issaria's eyes flicking between Jallah and the pitcher of water all the while, he shook his head once and let out a whistle as he reached for the second goblet. "That is one farfetched story, Kyria—"

"Kai," Issaria interrupted and Jallah looked up, pausing to pour her water. "Please call me Kai. Everyone does. Only my mother calls me by my given name," she elaborated, giving depth to her identity with small details. Elon's constant pestering when they were children would pay off at last if this thin facade worked.

The lie seemed to do the trick. Jallah poured the water and handed her a cup. Her lips stung when the water touched them and her mouth felt like dirt trying too hard to swallow the rain, but when the water reached her empty belly, it was suddenly sweet. Not enough and too much. She gulped it down and handed the cup back to him. "More. Please," she croaked.

"Aha! That's a girl." He poured another goblet and put it in her hand, watching with beady eyes as she guzzled from the cup. "Now tell me exactly what happened that made you mad enough to walk across the Glass," he requested as he filled her cup a third time. She looked quizzically at the pitcher, knowing full well it should be empty. "There is an Aquathyst forged into the interior of the pitcher. It will always replenish itself. Useful for crossing the Glass," he said with a wink and cheery smile. "Please, drink your fill, Kai. You have walked nearly half the southern continent. Quite the distance for an Esperian! How long has it been since you've seen the sun?"

"Actually, I'm from Ares. My troupe traveled to Espera to audition for Princess Issaria's upcoming coronation. We were one of many invited to showcase our skills." Issaria sipped from her goblet, making this third last despite Jallah's generosity. "I was with the captain of the princess's guard—Elon Sainthart—when the attacks began."

"On Espera? That can't be so. Not a soul is crazy enough to attack them. The Evernight Witch would annihilate anyone stupid enough to oppose her." He scoffed at her tale, but leaned forward, elbow on his knee. "That dark sorceress...she *anchored the moon.* Changed the whole cosmos forsaken planet with one curse. No one—*no one* is stupid enough to oppose her. Tell me why you think this to be true."

"You would think so," she mused, leaning forward to match Jallah's eagerness, "but I was in the Captain's bed when he received his orders to go help the city extinguish the fires. He ran out to attend the city, and I remained in bed for his return. It had been a while when I heard footsteps outside and heard the Witch herself order the assassination of the princess now that the guards were all distracted."

"Kill the princess? Why?"

Issaria shrugged and took another sip. "I can't pretend to know the Witch's mind, but I would assume to take the crown for real. No princess, no coronation. She becomes the Imperial Empress instead of a regent. It isn't really a stretch to think that she'd attack her own people if she'd kill her own blood."

Jallah nodded and moved the platter to his lap before gesturing with an open hand that she may eat as well. Issaria leaned forward and selected the fattest, reddest strawberry on the plate and wedged the whole thing in her mouth, cheeks puffed out as she bit off the berry, leaving the green crown in her hand. He chuckled at the juice dripping down her chin and offered a crimson cloth napkin from his own pocket as he said, "The motive makes sense, I suppose. And what happened to the lovely princess? Was she able to escape? Do you know?"

She wiped her mouth as she chewed and swallowed the berry, savoring the bright taste of sweet sunshine on her tongue before she replied, "I've no idea. I hope that the captain was able to help her escape. I do believe his intentions to protect her are true. As for myself, as soon as I heard that treason? I dressed and stole away through the same secret passage that the captain snuck me in through." She shook her head and took a deep breath before choosing a branch of plump green grapes from the tray and pulling them into her lap for snacking while she wove her origin story. "Once I was out, I saw the fires, the smoke. I knew I couldn't go into the city, so I went the opposite direction."

"Across the Glass?"

Issaria nodded. "You don't know the horror I saw in the Celestial City, Lord Coppernolle."

He chuckled. "Lord Coppernolle," he said before his amused chortle turned into a belly rumbling laugh. "Oh my sweet, you've a thing or two to learn. Your behavior betrays you. I would have to be *blind* to not believe that you are, in fact, the run away princess."

She forced herself to gasp. "Me? No, sir! I assure you, I am no princess."

"No princess, eh? Perhaps you could enlighten me as to how you manage to have Imperial Irises but you're *not* the princess?"

"My eyes? What are—Oh!" Issaria feigned her realization. "Oh, my eyes! I'd forgotten!" she exclaimed, even letting herself giggle. "Oh my, my good sir. My eyes are fake."

"Fake?"

"I visited a beautician in Espera when we arrived, and one of the treatments I selected was an herbal dye that tinted my blue eyes to look violet like the Imperials!"

"A dye," Jallah repeated, his flat tone conveying disbelief in her explanation.

She forced herself to remain light, and casual. As if this were the simplest of things. "Oh, yes. It was quite new you see, and with our impending audition and myself being the lead, I wanted to stand out to the Empress Regent." Issaria shrugged. "In retrospect, now that I know she wishes the princess dead, I regret the choice. I've no idea when it will wear off. She said a full moon cycle so I suppose I still have a few weeks…" She shook her head and popped a grape into her mouth. She chewed and swallowed before she added, "Walking across the Glass for weeks…one forgets such trivial things."

Jallah was silent and rolled his auburn mustache between his finger and thumb. Issaria ate another three grapes from her small branch before he asked his next question. "And you crossed the Glass….why again? If Ares is home and all that grand story of yours is true, then why did you cross the Glass? Ares is just east of Espera."

"Like I said, *sir* Coppernolle," she spat, putting and emphasis on his downgraded moniker, "you have no idea the destruction I saw. The smell. The smoke." She looked at her hands in her lap and rolled a fat pale grape between her thumb and forefinger. "The screams," she whispered, allowing her true sorrow at what her aunt did to the city seep into Kai's story. "I've never seen anything like it. I honestly didn't know if anyone would survive, and with the knowledge I carried…I thought that if I could bring the truth to Hinhallow, if I could get to—"

"If you could get to Hinhallow maybe you could see the fat old King and tell him what you know, and he would reward you by letting you marry his handsome young son?" Jallah interjected with his own distorted view of what Kyria would be doing walking an insane distance for no reason that would benefit herself.

Issaria fought her disgust at the man before her. Helping others was such a foreign concept to him that he was inventing some insane extortion plot in which little dancer Kai puts herself on the western throne. It was repulsive.

"I…well I hadn't thought *quite* that far," she stammered, hoping to appeal to this creature's innate greed. "But when you put it like that it would be nice. Yes, I would feel as though I deserved *some* sort of reward," she finished.

"And would you mind tellin' me where it was that you got such a fine dagger?" He brandished the blade that Elon gave her from beneath his thigh. "It's such a fine piece of work. I think I'd like to get me one myself!"

"It was a token from the captain I mentioned. He was quite taken with me," Issaria said sweetly as she cocked her head to the side. "It's yours if you wish to have it...for a price," she said with a coy smile.

He bellowed with laughter. "Aye, for a price? Kai, my dear, if that's who you claim to be, your price is that I haven't killed you yet. Be glad about that!" He wiped a false tear from the crinkled skin around his dark eyes. "At least you'll be going where you were headed. You can spread your truth all you like. I've got no love for the Evernight Witch."

Her face fell. "What?"

"Kai, my dove, you're going to make me very rich," he mused, and popped a grape into his mouth. "When we stop tonight, I'll have Kidalma clean you up, and we will see what I'm really dealing with here. You'll dance for my men at the fires so you better hope that part of your story isn't also a lie, *Princess*," Jallah sneered, and Issaria felt the noose closing around her throat. "If you're as good as you say, I'll let you dance for your auction in Hinhallow and maybe you'll get to meet that fat old king after all, or maybe you'll end up with a mistress in a brothel." He shrugged carelessly as he chose a cube of cheese and ate half before making a face and putting the rest back on the platter. "Only Metal can decide that now."

Issaria felt her stomach churn as the realization of her predicament set in.

This man intended to sell her. He'd sat here and listened to her lies and whether or not he believed them, whether or not he thought her to be the Imperial Princess or some dancer from Ares, it mattered not. She was no longer a princess. She was no longer a person to him.

She was a slave.

The realization must have been written on her slackened face because when Issaria looked up to meet Jallah's eye, he was grinning. His white teeth gleamed beneath his mustache, as he offered her the platter of remaining fruit and rejected cheeses. "I see no one told you what I call myself." When she did not take the tray of fruit, he placed it back on the bench beside himself and turned back to her, his smile feral. "I am Jallah Coppernolle. I am the Merchant of Men, and no matter who you are? You now belong to me until I say otherwise." His hand shot out from his knee and seized the goblet in her hand. He threw it to the carriage floor and grabbed her wrist. "You don't want to know what else they call me, *princess,* so I suggest you make yourself useful." In a fluid motion with his free hand, he whipped the door of the carriage open and wrenched her out into the heat. Issaria saw the crisp blue sky and a strange bird-shaped cloud flap into the brilliant light of the sun, blinding her as she struck the Glass and all the world went black.

ISSARIA'S HEAD WAS CRADLED IN SOMETHING SOFT AND WET, AND SHE could hear the gentle breathing of several bodies around her. Without opening her eyes, she knew she was in the carriage of women again. The gentle sway of the wagon and the rhythmic clacking of the wheels on the varied planes of glass told her they were steadily on the move. Her head ached, and she trembled to think that Jallah could be so drastically violent even as he feigned comfort and safety at their initial meeting.

She clenched her teeth. If only she could summon her magic without bringing Aurelia to the surface. If only she wasn't a failure of a magician. Hot tears stung the back of her eyes and threatened to leak out of her clenched lids. It took all her strength to control her breathing and stifle her tears. She would not let herself be weak. Not yet. Not now.

Issaria may have lied about herself, but she did bring the truth with her from Espera. The city did burn for her. Her aunt really did try to have her killed. *Just like Mother and Father,* she reminded herself, and her resolve hardened like metal quenched at the forge.

She had a mission to accomplish, and she could not be afraid now. She would let Jallah bring her to Hinhallow, and she would find a way to free herself or get herself into the palace. It mattered not now how she accomplished the deed. Her people burned and died, and worse while her aunt sat upon the throne, free to do whatever it is she wanted this entire time. Issaria owed it to the people, the innocent in her beautiful home, to get them help—no matter how that happened.

Issaria would turn the tide against her aunt and she would vanquish the darkness she had brought upon Ellorhys.

19

ISSARIA

Wake up, girl!" The old woman's voice jolted Issaria awake as the carriage jostled to a stop, rocking back and forth ever so slightly as the caravan settled.

The women in the carriage were all crouched and bracing themselves on the walls and ceiling as metal scraped on metal. Their breathing was heavy, and they were all silent, wary eyes on the door at the back of the wagon.

"What's happening?" she asked in a whisper, not knowing why she was suddenly afraid.

"Making camp," someone behind her whispered in reply.

The wagon door opened, and sunlight poured into the gloom of the carriage. The first woman jumped out, then paused as an alloy collar and chain was locked around her throat. Issaria watched as one by one, the women in the cart all clambered out of the wagon and accepted their collar without complaint before shuffling off out of view, their chains rattling on the glass behind them.

Finally, only Issaria and the old lady, Kidalma, remained in the cart. Issaria looked to the silver woman and shook her head. "I won't wear that."

"You'll do what you're told, girl," the woman growled as she grabbed Issaria's wrist and hauled her from the wagon with surprising strength for one so old.

"Get your hands off of me!" Issaria protested, struggling in the woman's firm grip as a sandy haired man approached her with a collar. His green eyes bore down on her and she froze in his gaze.

The woman held up a hand and the man stopped. "Not for this one Sethik. She's too weak as it is; I've got to hold her up so she can keep her balance."

At Kidalma's word Sethik returned the collar to a peg on the side of the cart. "Then she is your charge for the duration of the stay, Kidalma," he said and let them pass.

Wide-eyed, Issaria looked to the woman who still held her arm with a vice-like grasp as she dragged her through the establishing campsite. In the sunlight, Issaria could finally see why this woman was the leader of the group. A thick, jagged white scar slashed across the darkly tanned and wrinkled skin of her throat like a lace choker Issaria had worn to a ball in Espera. The strange comparison made her look away from the garish mark, almost embarrassed that she'd looked at it.

"You will not run. If you do, he will catch you, and he will do the same to you. I was lucky and managed to survive. Others have not been so fortunate, and often he is not kind enough to use a blade. Do not be foolish girl. You're already in over your pretty little head."

Issaria nodded and kept silent as the pair wandered between men sparking fires with a snap of their fingers and others erecting temporary structures. Yurts if she wasn't mistaken—small collapsible homes meant to be transported with a migrant lifestyle. Around the camp, like little rattling ghosts, woman shuffled, bringing bedrolls to the slavers who chained them in intervals around the campsite. And Issaria realized for the first time that hers was not the only wagon of stolen women in the slaver's caravan.

"Why does no one use their magic to escape?"

Kidalma didn't even look at her as she replied, "Is my scar not evidence enough to convince you not to attempt such a thing, girl?"

"Surely someone has tried?"

"Many have. These women are the daughters of farmers and herdsmen. Their mana is not that of the warrior." She scoffed, her gravelly voice mocking her again in the next breath. "City girls never understand that."

Issaria held her breath for a moment then asked in a soft whisper, "And if there was someone among you who did have the mana of a warrior?"

Kidalma paused, and for an instant, her grip on Issaria loosened.

"Then perhaps I wouldn't be the only lucky one."

Issaria followed Kidalma through the camp as fires were established and cauldrons were heaved onto the coals. Across the camp, the ocean lapped quietly in an empty bay. "The caravan often beats the ships back from Ares since they stop in Sorair to barter goods. Then they usually drink and fuck themselves stupid with their shares before skipping port to meet us." She snorted. "They should be here in a few days to take us to the White City," the old woman explained as she stopped next to a newly erected yurt. She selected two leather sacks from a pile and thrust one into Issaria's hands. "We make camp until they come. While here, you work to prove your skills. Women with no skills make no Metals, and you now know what Jallah thinks of things that do not make him Metals."

The old woman led Issaria to the shore, where the shallow waters reflected iridescent refractions of sunlight across violet waves that lapped the glass. Kneeling, she sank her leather sack into the sea and looked to Issaria as bubbles streamed out of her sack as it filled. Copying Kidalma, Issaria kneeled and filled her own sack with ocean water.

"Bring it to one of the cauldrons and fill the pot. Go back and do it again. Do not fill the same cauldron twice." The instructions Kidalma gave were simple, but she gave no explanation as she heaved her sack out of the water and hauled it over her shoulder. "When you're sure every pot has been filled, come find me where we got these skins for your next task."

Issaria did not reply but focused on the weight of her oversized water-bladder on her back. The contents jiggled and sloshed as she took weary steps back to the growing campsite. At least a dozen fires were sparking to life on the shimmering glass. Yurts were adorned with multi-color sunshades, triangular cloth strung taught between tents, making a patchwork of shaded areas across their camp.

The sun beat down, and heat radiated up from the Glass in waves as Issaria made her way to the first fire near the shore. She set the leather skin filled with water beside her selected fire and stood for a moment to inspect the camp.

"Gonna have to go quicker than that, girl," a slaver said from where he said next to the fire, making Issaria jump. He sat cross legged, stringing a bow, and Issaria resisted the urge to glare at him as he lazed about while she worked. She lifted the skin again to empty its contents into the cauldron. As steam billowed up from the scalding iron, she glanced about the camp and noted that *all* the men were sitting, resting, or completing idle projects while the women, chained and collared to their respective wagons around the camp, rattled between campsites tending fires, filling cauldrons and emptying bowls of chopped vegetables into the boiling pots.

"Still not going to go faster, eh? I'll have to tell Jallah you're no good with the chores. Less places for you to go when you can't do chores," the blond man continued, eyeing her as he rolled the bowstring between his fingers, globs of beeswax smoothing the string. He would have been handsome if it wasn't for the loathsome tone in his reprimand.

"I can do chores," Issaria retorted as she threw the empty leather over her back. "I'm just not as strong after crossing the Glass."

"Oh, you're *that* one, eh?" The slaver rolled his eyes and returned his focus to his bowstring. "It's a shame you're off limits. I was thinking of taking you to my yurt tonight. At least then I could tell Jallah that you're worth the whore's fee he would put on a girl who can't do chores."

Issaria snorted and shook her head. "I wouldn't lie with you if you were the last man alive."

Brown eyes snapped up to meet hers and an icy wind rushed past him, chilling her to the core as it seemed to draw talons down the length of her exposed leg. The blonde man replied with no hint of warmth in his voice, "It wasn't going to be an invitation, slave."

A chill shot down her spine and she turned on heel, making the return trip to the beach with her empty leather much faster than she had with Kidalma. With the storm magi's threat looming over her, Issaria focused on her task and knelt at the water's edge to fill her leather. She would have to be careful here. She wasn't anymore safe as Kai than she was as Issaria, and Kai's identity was about as flimsy as her nightgown at this point.

After a few treks between the shore and the campsite, when Issaria was certain the cauldrons were all filled, she went to meet Kidalma, as instructed. The old woman waited at the yurt in the center of the camp. Besides Issaria, she was the only woman not chained to a wagon by a collar. She was also the only one not working. Her eyes— sky blue—found Issaria as she approached and immediately began digging through a pile of linens in front of her. "You need to change. You attract the wrong kind of attention," Kidalma said as she thrust a wad of cloth at her. "Go change in the gorges. Relieve yourself out there too. Tell the guards I've given my word you'll return." She met Issaria's eye and added, "That means they will kill me if you do not return."

Issaria shook her head. "I'm not going anywhere, Kidalma." She held the old woman's gaze for a moment, wondering if the depth she saw there was what Aunt Cate's gaze lacked all these years. Blue eyes. So similar, and yet, so different.

With that thought, she turned away and sought the edges of camp where slavers were stationed at intervals to prevent run-aways, or, she imagined, anyone from sneaking up on the camp unexpected. At the border, she recognized the guard she was approaching. "Um… Kidlama told me…to tell you that she gives her word that I will return. I just want to change…and…relieve my bowels," she said, looking away.

Sethik, the man who had refrained from collaring her before, nodded as she walked past him. "She likes to do that for you, huh? Vouch for you, I mean. Why is that?"

Issaria didn't stop walking but shrugged. "I just thought she was nice to every newly enslaved girl who didn't want to be enslaved."

The slaver didn't say anything to that, and so she walked around the corner of a glass dune—a sheer peak of opaque purple glass that rose like a kite or a pyramid, nearly impossible to climb or pass, and at its thickest, too dark to see through. When she was certain she was away from prying eyes, Issaria stripped out of her nightgown, and stepped into the new linen clothes Kidalma had given her. It wasn't much, she had to admit, but it was much better than the remains of her nightclothes.

The pale top was short-sleeved, and in her opinion, a bit too short all round. It exposed a great deal of her stomach—which was very pale due to life in the night: having it exposed to the sun seemed like a very bad idea. The skirt fit just right in the waist, and fell to her knees in the front, her ankles in the back. It was actually two *different* patterns, a sort of up-and-down, black-and-white triangle pattern on the front half while the back was a soft grey that reminded her of her chiton dresses back in Espera.

Issaria took a deep breath and held it for a long while before releasing it as she counted to ten. It didn't matter what the skirt looked like. It didn't matter if the top didn't fit. Issaria was not here. Kai was. Kai was used to this; Kai was *fine* with this.

When she opened her eyes, Kai was ready. She had to get to Hinhallow, and once there, she had to get to the palace, even if that meant being sold as a kitchen slave or...were there such things as kitchen slaves? Issaria shook her head. Cosmos above, she was in Tarlix's Fire now.

She had to get to the palace. That was crucial to her plan...as loose of a plan as it was. She hoped Jallah's itinerary for Kai would back up her prospects for an exclusive sale. Once inside the Palace, she could find Blaze, and he could vouch for her and set her free. Then *somehow* they could march an army to Espera and take it back from Aunt Cate!

She took another deep breath. This wasn't some fantasy plot, *Princess*, she thought to herself, the memory of the blond slaver threatening her fresh in her mind. This was real, and so much harder than she was making it out to be.

And she really *did* have to go to the bathroom.

After she was done relieving herself, she returned to the mouth of the crystalline gorge and back to Sethik, who was still facing the camp.

"And you *did* return," Sethik said mockingly as she passed him by.

"Kidalma gave her word to you, but I gave my word to her."

"Thought I was gonna have to go fetch you."

Kai turned like a viper and met his mossy-green eyes. "Fetch me? Like I'm some pet?"

Sethik glared and shook his head as he said, "Keep that tone and you'll find yourself collared like one regardless of what the old woman said about it."

Kai backed down, but shook her head, her tone meek in the face of a collar. "But really, Sethik, where would I go that you would not find me quickly? I am *weak* after my journey. You slavers are many in numbers—many more than I had ever guessed."

His verdant eyes widened as he saw, perhaps, the truth in her words, in her eyes. He didn't have anything to say after that, so Kai headed back to where she'd left Kidalma in the central yurt of the expansive campsite.

"You'll have to be collared before the ships come!" Sethik called from his post behind her. "No hard feelings!"

Kai raised a hand up over her head to let him know she heard him and continued on her way.

2 0

ISSARIA

At the very edge of the slave camp, a tent much larger than the rest had been built. From where she stood at the central yurt handing out cooking rations with Kidalma, Kai could tell the massive tent was three-times as tall and at least ten times as wide as all the colorful little yurts that had popped up across the crystal bay Jallah had hidden them all away in. Kidalma caught her eyeing the men bringing loads of firewood into the large yurt, while others climbed ladders on the outsides and laid pelts or ornately woven blankets across the reed skeleton and frame. Other teams of men followed behind with a second set of ladders, adorning finished panels with large animal skulls. Issaria could identify a stag, an elephant, and a ram before she turned her gaze away and found the old woman's pale eyes on her.

"The ship will dock tonight. Jallah always has a feast when the whole crew comes together," she explained.

"And *everyone* can fit in there?"

The old woman snorted. "Everyone who matters." When Kai didn't reply she added, "The women will stay out here and tend the fires while the crew gets a feast and a show."

"You'd think they'd get tired of the same show," she mused aloud as one of the girls from her own transport wagon approached their yurt.

The raven-haired girl wore a long braid down her back, and as she came out from beneath a yellow linen cloth strung up like a sunshade between two nearby yurts, her copper skin glistened in the sunlight. As she neared, Kai could see that red welts had formed under the collar on the tops of her shoulders and on her collarbone where it bumped.

"I know you, don't I?" Kai asked, trying a smile. Some of the other girls had been wary of her smiles.

"So this is where they've got you?" she asked as she adjusted her collar, keeping the chain in front of her so she could hold it as she walked.

Kai shrugged and jerked a thumb toward Kidalma, who was packing a wicker basket with the same ingredients she was giving every slavegirl that approached. One onion, maybe moldy, three carrots, no matter what size. Proportions may vary. Two potatoes—same rules apply as to the carrots. One leek, a head of cabbage, and a little paper package wrapped with twine that Kai thought smelled an awful lot like roasted pig.

"She's got me helping until I can get some strength back," she said.

The girl nodded, dark eyes flicking toward the back of the hut where silver-haired Kidalma was emerging with her rations and very nearly threw the basket at Kai. She was getting used to the old woman's approach though, and she knew now to bend her knees *and* her elbows, both to brace for the weight of the basket but also the gravity of Kidalma's throw, which seemed to vary on how annoyed she was with the particular slavegirl who was picking up the baskets. Kai took the basket from the old lady and handed it, much more gently, to the girl.

"You really crossed the Glass because of some crazy rebellion in the south?" She adjusted her grip on the basket, and using her hip as a crutch, she adjusted her collar chain to fall on the opposite side of her body. When she straightened again, Kai was impressed to see that the girl holding her chain in one hand as she balanced her basket of supplies between her hand and her hip.

She was very experienced walking with one of those collars. The realization broke Issaria's heart.

"I did," Kai replied.

"Huh. That's something crazy, isn't it?" she said, with a bemused smiled on her face.

Almost like she didn't believe she'd done so, even after the slave caravan had *scraped her off the Glass*, as Jallah had so kindly put it. Kai had to laugh at that skeptical look, which just made the girl look at her like she really was crazy. She shook her head and said, "Everyone keeps saying that. At the time...with what was happening, and what I know? I swear, it didn't seem that crazy."

From behind, Kidalma clicked her tongue. "Girl, you better get back to that fire before Zhaniel finds a reason to lay hands on you."

Her dark eyes widened for a moment and she looked back to Kai with an apologetic glance before turning away. She took a few steps with her basket then glanced over her shoulder and said, "My name's Rhaminta. I'll get you a bedroll over by our wagon's fire. A good one, too. With actual padding."

Kai watched as raven-haired Rhaminta disappeared back under the yellow awning between the yurts, following her chain back the way she'd come. She could feel Kidalma's hard glare on her back, but Kai kept her eyes on the slave-girl's retreating back.

"Zhaniel likes to hurt the girls?" Issaria asked, her voice a hollow whisper from Kai's lips.

"He really only gets one in a bunch but...the girls he picks don't do well on the market when he's through with them," the old woman confessed with horror in her voice.

Kai glanced into the shadows of the yurt and saw the old woman sitting on an upturned bucket. Sunlight slashed a deep shadow into the back of the hut where piles of potatoes and onions were heaped against the far wall. Loose hairs fell like webs of spun starlight from her bun. Pale blue eyes held a distant gaze as trembling fingertips found her scarred throat. She suddenly looked so frail in the dim light and in an instant Kai understood the woman's reluctance to rebel.

She'd had the fight taken out of her in the worst way.

Issaria took a hesitant step into the yurt and kicked a potato.

Kidalma looked up and scowled at her. "You stay away from that man. He is *dangerous.*" She swallowed hard and without breaking her hold on Issaria's gaze added, "And he's not the only one of his breed."

Issaria wasn't sure who was more outraged: herself or the persona of Kai. She opened her mouth to say something to the woman, anything to comfort her broken soul, but a shadow loomed over them from behind and Kai turned from the moment of honesty with the crone to find Jallah himself at the door of the yurt.

"I thought I'd find you with the old hag!" Jallah announced as if proud of himself for his guess. He narrowed his eyes at them. "What's this? No collar? Explain yourself."

"Bah!" Kidalma exclaimed, interrupting Kai's stammering as she pushed herself off her knees and came to the doorway. She rattled a broom handle between Kai's ankles as she came forward from the back of the yurt. "This little doe can barely keep her own feet under her, Master Jallah. I doubt she'd be of much use with the weight of the chain."

He seemed to consider her words, then nodded as he said, "So be it. But she gets a collar after the show. Can't have my big dancer sneaking off once I've secured the interest of the King of Hinhallow." He waggled his eyebrows at her as he selected a small wheel of cheese —whole—from the stack on the table to her left. He made no attempt to hide it as he snuck it into a pouch on his belt.

Issaria wasn't sure if it was the truth or just something to challenge the story she'd fed him. Either way, Kai wasn't intimidated. "The show, Master?" Kai asked, imitating the way Kidalma had deflected to him.

"I told you, you're going to show me what you're worth tonight, little dancer! And if you're lucky I'll send a falcon to the king and confirm that I do *indeed* have something worth his time and his Metals when we reach port." Jallah looked at Kai expectantly, as if she should balk at the proposal.

She let an easy smile spread across her face. "You do at least have a drum for me to keep rhythm with, yes?"

Jallah's sly smile grew sinister as he flipped his coppery hair, exposing the gruesome scars that marred his head. "Many of the lads play something or other. Keeps the nights fun while we travel."

Kai gritted her teeth and hid it with a grin of her own. "*Great*. Then I should be all set. May I have some more water before the show? I'm rather parched still."

"Kidalma," he said without breaking eye contact with her, "see to it that *Kai* has a full meal before she is allowed into the tent. I don't want her...getting dizzy and tripping up."

Jallah's dark eyes conveyed the truth: He didn't believe a word she'd said. He was convinced she would fail this trial.

"Of course, Master."

Jallah turned about and pulled his black hood up as he sauntered around the camp, shaking hands and clasping shoulders of the men he employed. His voice boomed out as he made his rounds, and soon, even though she could hear him still, Kai was certain she wouldn't see Jallah Coppernolle again until her great performance was underway.

"He thinks you lie about your trade," Kidalma said as she shoved a hunk of stale bread and a steaming bowl of stew from one of the cauldrons around the campsite at her.

"I get the feeling it's a good thing I'm not," she said as she dunked the wedge of loaf into her broth, letting it soak up the flavor of the vegetables before stuffing it into her mouth.

DRUNK LAUGHTER AND RAUCOUS CONVERSATION BILLOWED OUT OF THE large yurt like shadows spilling off of a fire's light. The hour was late, even if the sun was high. Issaria was dazed by the constant presence of the sun, and blistering heat oppressed her senses at every turn. Even in the shade she dabbed gently at her face with the back of her hand, sticky with sweat and red from the heat.

The ship Jallah had spoken of arrived hours ago, and the caravan had gotten themselves fat and happy in the shade of their social hall while the slaves of the camp sat, inching into the shadows cast by meager sunshades, hoping for scraps of their master's meals. Inside that tent it was dark save for the large fire at the center. Heat and smoke funneled naturally though a circular hole in the center of the roof panels leaving the rest of the yurt clear of smoke and filled wall to wall with men.

Through the throngs of men stumbling around between conversations, Kai could see a group of five sitting together on a woven reed mat near the fire.

Her merry band of musicians.

Each held a different instrument and tended to it before their performance; testing notes on a flute, another tuned strings, and one man sat with a trio of drums bound together with twine in his lap. He rolled his wrists and tested patterns on the leather skins stretched across the barrels of his drums. Each sounded out a hollow note, slowly becoming a rhythmic tat-a-tattatat-tattat-tat-a that felt a little too much like Kai's heartbeat in her throat as she peeked into the tent from a side entrance Kidalma and Sethik had brought her to.

She pulled her face back from the amber glow of the fire and looked back to her companions. Kidalma's weathered face seemed dark, even as the sun beat down on them from above. Stark shadows crisscrossed the campground behind the old woman, and Kai could see the huddled silhouettes of the slavegirls, never too far from their wagon.

Kidalma grumbled and then closed the space between Issaria and herself. "Cosmos watch over the path you take, child." The old woman stood before her, contempt on her face, a sour smile on her wizened features. She drew a symbol on Kai's forehead with her thumb, and Issaria tried to remember the shape of it. "Your lies will get you in trouble someday. That's in the stars, it is. " Kidalma turned away from her and hobbled back through the campfires.

219

In the yurt behind her, the rhythm of the drums had steadied into a quick and melodic beat. A sitar kept time with its hypnotic song as a flute trilled a demanding pace.

Kai took a deep breath and bounced on the balls of her feet. Beside her, Sethik looked her up and down, emerald eyes roving her with more friendliness than before. "Kidalma doesn't act like that with anyone and *everyone* knows she's got some sort of...*black magic*," he hissed, drawing Kai's attention from the fire. "Jallah's wrong about you, isn't he?" he asked, and the thoughtfulness in his voice made Issaria look out at him from behind Kai's facade.

Maybe the shimmering rattle of the tambourine called to Kai's free spirit, or maybe Issaria was feeling particularly reckless, but she looked at Sethik and held his gaze.

"But what if, Sethik, what if he's not wrong at all?" she asked.

His eyes widened, and that was the moment she chose to rip aside the linen panel of the wall that held her back from the music.

Kai launched herself into the yurt and felt the melody spiral around her like smoke on the wind. It pulsed and wove its way around her; she could feel it in the air, taste the harmonies on her tongue. Black hair whipped about her, storm-wild. Her feet found the drums and she leapt, surprising a group of slavers near the door through which she'd come. The sitar's languorous tune harnessed her hips and she glided sideways, deeper into the yurt, pulled this-way and that by the music.

Cautious applause gathered upon the slaver's hands like tentative butterflies as Kai moved about the space. She found Jallah near the center and made a point to ignore him as she lavished her attentions on a slaver nearby, ensuring her *master* saw the longing on his employ's face as she dipped back into a fast-paced swirl of hips and skin.

Arching backwards, Kai rolled from one tantalizing pose to the next, skirt displaying her toned legs like a flower in bloom, pistons quivering in the breeze. While these weren't the steps Aunt Cate had had her instructed on, and her dance masters would probably blush to see her provocative flair, Issaria found that music, unlike politics and hierarchies, was raw and real and *genuine*. Dancing was almost as intricate as the warrior's stances Elon went through in sword-training. The only difference to her was that she used her body—the pale expanse of her stomach, a small smirk with a bold sashay, a collarbone glistening with sweat. *She* was the weapon.

And she would teach them not to underestimate her.

The final refrain was upon her. Her bones could feel the change in the music, it in the way the air seemed charged with energy. Her muscles tingled as she turned about, surrendered entirely to the harmony. She could almost feel the mana in her just beneath the surface, as if kindly asking to come out and see what all the *joy* was about. It crackled inside her as she stroked the desire to set it free, to let the power know what it was that brought her such unbridled passion—

Kai's eyes snapped open. Slammed back into her body, she was still whirling about like a flower petal cast on the breeze.

She would *not* let her out. Not even for a dance.

With a flourish of her hands, she leaned back into a final pose as the last notes of the song held out across a silent gathering.

Breast heaving with the effort, Kai righted herself and sent nervous hands about flattening the wild tangle of her black hair. She felt beads of sweat trail down her spine as she turned and met Jallah's furrowed brow. She looked between him, with his arms crossed over his chest and a few faces among the men.

"Well?"

After a long moment, Jallah's scowl broke into a grin. "Kai, my sweet, I'll forever thank the Cosmos for the day we scraped your skinny hide off the Glass!" A cacophony of applause, led by Jallah, erupted from within the yurt as the mustachioed Merchant of Men crossed the tent. "Get me a damn falcon! I've a king to bribe!"

Relief flooded through her, and Kai smiled, knowing she'd won her first battle. Somehow, this plan was working. Kai could be the hero Issaria was not.

Her smile turned into a grin and she spun, looking for Kidalma's silver hair in the crowd. The crone would probably be upset that she'd danced as she had, as it would definitely draw the wrong sort of attention, but Kai also had Issaria's problems to worry about, and securing a benefactor in the palace was crucial. The king, though she did remember hearing was a crass sort of man, would probably not come to a slave market himself. Making herself as desirable as possible to whomever the king sent was going to be her next hurdle in getting to Blaze, whomever he was. Probably some Magistrate or Councilor—or some master assassin from a secret guild which was how Akintunde contracted him to kill her in the first place.

She shook the thought from her head and turned to leave the yurt, intent on finding Kidalma and telling her of her success.

"And where do you think you're going?" Jallah's voice was unmistakable.

Kai looked over her shoulder, innocent enough. "I was going back to Kidalma. I thought I had been dismissed." She shrugged and pointed toward the flaps. "You know, performance over? Back to work?"

Jallah laughed his thunderous guffaw, hands on his crimson belt. "I like your work ethic, but you're an asset now, Kai. Pretty little thing like you? Can't have you wandering off now, can I?" He snapped his fingers and she heard the rattle of chains being dragged across the varied facets of the Glass. "By the way, before I draft my enticement to His Highness in the west..." Something about his tone, getting slimier than it had before, drew her gaze from the alloy collar that Kyrel brought forth to meet Jallah's dark eyes. "You *are* a virgin, aren't you? He's been looking for a special present for some time now and I'll be damned if I didn't at least try to haggle—oh! Look at that blush!" He clicked his tongue against his teeth, scolding her. "I knew that story about the soldier was just another lie among many!"

Jallah's grin didn't waver the entire time he secured the heavy, scratchy, alloy collar around her throat. It balanced awkwardly on her collarbone, digging into the thin skin, pinching it between the cold metal and bone. When the fitting was complete, her master looped a chain through a stud at the back of her new necklace, and the weight of it pulled the collar back against her throat, choking her until Kai adjusted the weight again, mimicking what she'd seen Rhaminta do earlier.

Jallah chuckled as he watched her struggle to master the chain and collar. She fell twice, skidding knees across sharp planes of glass, gashing her flesh. "Easy on the product, Kai, my princess! If you damage the goods I'll have to dock your cut of the sale!"

Confused by the prospect, Kai looked over her shoulder at Coppernolle, who met her glance with more raucous laughter. "Look at her! She thought I was going to *pay* her when I *sell her*!"

Jallah's hysterics was joined by the laughter of the slavers around him, each one looking at her with amusement, lust, and greed. A moment ago, she'd felt the magic. She'd enjoyed her place in the madness of the moment. But now she was nothing but a joke—a *thing* to them.

Kai staggered from the yurt and pushed through the side panel she'd so eagerly entered through earlier and nearly colliding with Sethik.

Of all the looks she'd gotten from the men inside, the one he gave her hurt the most.

It was a look of pity, and with his emerald eyes, the expression looked all too much like Elon. She didn't want him seeing her like this.

21

SHAIRI

Princess Bexalynn's golden hair was soft and tame as Shairi passed the bone-toothed comb through it for the exact one-hundredth time that evening. She was amazed she did so without breaking her molars from gritting her teeth. In the mirror, Shairi made eye contact with Princess Bexalynn, and they maintained their placid expressions, but she could see by the blush rising upon the apples of the princess's cheeks that she was ready to burst. Usually, Shairi was dismissed by this time, as Queen Emmaleigh loved brushing Bexalynn's hair.

But today, Queen Emmaleigh took residence on the green velvet chaise by the solarium hearth. She sat straight-backed and proper, not lounged out and giggling like the girls would have been if she were not present. Their hibiscus tea had gone cold on the table between them.

The queen kept her frigid blue eyes on them as she waited for the news to settle.

Shairi and Calix were going to be married. She'd almost swooned at the announcement, but the sour look on the Queen's face made her hold her tongue until she was certain what her reaction was *supposed* to be. Queen Emmaleigh looked as though she had sucked on a lemon.

For all her apparent want of this exact situation, this wasn't how she'd planned it. It wasn't how Shairi wished to win Calix's heart either, if she was being truthful with herself. Calix was ordered. The queen had said it just so; *ordered* to court her.

Her. A princess of Ares—Cosmos, she was *the* princess of Ares. Did that matter for nothing? Had her city lost all it's respect since she'd been kept behind the walls of the White City? She'd spent years trying to get Calix's affections to fall upon her, all while waiting beck-and-call on this little brat. Shairi looked to Bexalynn and let a sad smile cross her face. It wasn't that she didn't like Bexalynn. Quite the opposite, actually. The girl was sharp as a dagger and ready to use whatever skills she possessed to carve her way in the courts, as Shairi had shown her was possible. The two were probably more alike than even her mother knew. But Shairi loathed being a handmaiden. Some of her skills, she wasn't going to share with anyone, and secrets were much harder to keep when there was a little blonde busybody asking questions all the time.

Shairi raised her green eyes to meet Queen Emmaleigh's indeterminable blues in the mirror's reflection as she continued to brush Bexalynn's brassy curls.

"Auntie," she began, letting the endearment for the queen seep into her voice like sugar. "I know this isn't what we planned...not really. But I *am* happy." She swallowed hard and nodded. "I know he doesn't love me now, but...he can grow to love me in time, I think." She gestured to herself. "I am not so unseemly, and I have a great many skills! I will be a devoted wife and queen for Prince Calix and for Hinhallow."

Shairi knew they were thinking of her courtly qualities. Her ability to spy, lingering in corners with uninteresting companions to listen intently to the gossip of the court or her ability to make young Magistrates very willing to crawl into Akintunde's pocket at the opportune juncture. Yes, Shairi had proven herself *very* useful to the Crown, and this was her reward. Married off to Calix as a punishment for his failure to secure Espera as part of the citadel's dominance.

But Shairi was thinking of the secret set of skills she had with her magic as an herbalist–in particular, her ability to resist the toxins of most poisonous flora. Terran power ran deep within her veins and like Queen Emmaleigh, she was a bloom that had her thorns. She could be the queen Hinhallow needed. The ruthless sort that would ensure Calix's dominance expanded without so much as a peep from opposing monarchs. She would do it.

She would do anything for him.

"That's quite enough," she quipped, and Shairi immediately put the brush upon the vanity, next to several pots of makeup and fine horse-hair appliqué brushes for each of them. She stepped aside with hands clasped behind her back. "You have been a marvelous handmaiden to the Princess these long years, Lady Shairi."

"Thank you, my Queen, but you are too kind. I have only done as I thought an elder sister should, and Bex—" She glanced away at her familiarity with a modicum of embarrassment, then continued, "Princess Bexalynn has been a darling charge." She dipped into a low curtsey, not meeting the queen's eyes. "I have been blessed with my station in your household."

"I *can't believe* you're marrying my brother!" Bex clearly couldn't contain herself anymore. She bounced off of her plush vanity bench and over to her mother, then back to Shairi where she pulled her out of her curtsey. "Mother, she shouldn't be brushing my hair any longer! Shairi is going to be a queen!" Bexalynn looked as though she were going to scream from the sheer excitement of it all. She looked at her mother, blue eyes wide. "Tell her about the pavilion, oh please, Mother! Tell her now, I can't stand it any longer!"

Shairi had to smile, at least a little, after that. Bexalynn was right, in way. She was going to get everything she came here for. She was going to marry Prince Calix Ballentine. Handsome, strong, a marvel in the colosseum with his flaming weapons—and oh how *beautiful* his eyes were when filled with those flames. Her heart quickened at the memory of his most recent competition. He'd dominated the brackets with ease, felling enemies with his flaming scimitars. She even found his fever-blackened hands appealing and often thought of what it would feel like to have his charred hands upon her.

"Shairi?"

"I'm sorry, I was thinking about the, uhm...wedding," she replied, avoiding eye contact and thoroughly blushed.

Queen Emmaleigh rolled her eyes. "Shairi, dear niece, don't let your heart get ahead of your mind," she said, tapping her temple. "We must always outwit and play the long game, for men are too impatient to reap the larger reward for want of the here and now."

Both girls nodded dutifully.

"Yes, Mother."

"Yes, Queen Emmaleigh."

"Good. Now, off with you Shairi. Bexalynn is right. With your betrothal to my son I would have you take a place in the household yourself." She smiled, and it almost reached her eyes. "I've had the West Pavilion made up for you, with a full staff, until the wedding, and then you and Calix can make other arrangements." The West Pavilion. It was nearest to Calix's rooms and was mostly reserved for guests of the highest caliber. "I will not have you looking as though you were *beneath* him in anyway."

But that was what she was. That was what she always was. The disgraced *ward* of the king. Insurance that her father would send relief supplies to Hinhallow. Ares was already in the King's grasp, and marriage was hardly necessary. Though perhaps the marriage would also sever ties between Ares and Espera. Cosmos knew her father wanted to get out of *that* little dilemma for a while. He'd been banking on her marriage to Calix to secure the armies for a revolt against the Evernight.

Yes. This arrangement would do just fine. Love or not, Shairi would get everything she came here for and more, in time.

SHAIRI HAD ALL OF HER BELONGINGS MOVED FROM PRINCESS BEXALYNN'S suites down to the West Pavilion and by mid-morning, she was already set up in the gorgeous rooms. The sitting room, ringed with ornately carved alabaster pillars, was open to the western gardens. Beyond beds of colorful flowers, gnarled citrus and olive trees reaching jeweled leaves to the bright sky, the white stone wall divided the White Castle from the Lanzauve Sea crashing against the cliffs below. Her breath caught in her throat as she opened the doors to her new bedroom, a spacious pavilion house with a window and balcony overlooking those very cliffs and the endless horizon of the Lanzauve to the West.

And last, but not least, she'd personally brought her flowers over to the pavilion, least some fool touch their toxic petals and fall prone in the halls, exposing her talent for what it truly was. There was a small sitting area near the balcony, and thanks to Queen Emmaleigh, she suspected, it had been converted into a glass atrium, a greenhouse for her collection. While Bexalynn didn't know what talent Shairi actually had for the flowers, Shairi was fairly certain that the queen did.

She entrenched her many pots and planters in the bright sunlight room, and soon it looked as though the Baelforia were spreading to her balcony. She looked upon their vibrantly painted petals with pride. Many of these flowers were rare, and rarer still were the poisons and antidotes she could cultivate from them.

Sighing happily at the sight of her babies flourishing in the sun, she thought about how to explain them to Calix, should he ever ask about her hobby and why he could not touch a single one.

"Are they to your liking, Princess? The rooms?"

Calix's voice made her jump and she turned, hand to her breast.

"Oh! Prince Calix, you startled me!" Shairi pretended to regain her composure, running fingers through her hair and patting down the pleats in her yellow dress. "The rooms are beautiful, as to be expected of the West Pavilion." Not willing to let him get too close to her little garden she retreated from the greenhouse across the bedroom and closed the doors behind her, separating them into the sitting room.

Calix leaned against the doorframe, looking amused with his blackened arms crossed over his broad chest. Shairi felt her blush turn genuine and she forced herself to meet his yellow gaze. She had closed the bedroom off to protect him from any airborne pollens that she would be immune to, but from his perspective, she imagined closing off the bedroom insinuated a proper setting between the betrothed. "I...I would not have anyone passing think that we are indecent," she stammered in explanation.

"Nor would I." He pushed himself off the doorframe and walked into the sitting room, looking over the plain-but-pretty garden flowers that had been placed in vases around the room and the solarium geodes in the hearth as if everything had to be up to his standards.

He was silent for so long that Shairi tried again to initiate a conversation with him. "Is there...something that brings you to my door, Prince Calix?"

He paused in his inspection of the room and looked back at her from where he perused a tall shelf of books and scrolls that was built into the wall near the writing desk. "I'm sure this won't come as a shock to you, but I would speak to you of our...arrangement."

"Arrangement." Her voice was flat. That was not how she wished him to see this. He could have used any other word: betrothal, engagement, *future* even.

"I realize it has been thrust upon us both, and I wished to clear the air regarding it," he said.

"Clear the air," she repeated, very much wishing one of those pollen spores found its way down his pompous—

"I did not wish to trap you. This was not my idea, nor do I believe it was yours," he continued. "After all, I look upon you as a sister to Bexalynn and myself, and indeed, you must see me as a brother after all these years."

She felt her throat close upon itself. He knew. He must know that she loved him. It was plain as the nose on her face and yet...Shairi could feel her heart shattering in her chest.

He would find a way out.

"If I may interject, Prince Calix," she interrupted, and he looked upon her, yellow eyes wide. "I would not have you misconstrue what it is that I think we have here."

Confusion twisted on his handsome face. "And...what would that be?"

"I thought us to have an arrangement of documents and duty."

"Documents...and duty?" He repeated, and Shairi found that she very much liked having him look at her with such astonishment, even if this farce was a twisted dagger in her heart.

"Well, yes, of course. It is clear that you have no romantic designs on me, or you would have bedded me along with all the rest." The prince's jaw fell open, perhaps at her crass admission of her feelings toward him, or perhaps at the fact that she very nearly admitted to wanting him to bed her. "And by that look I'd say you knew how I desired you all along." She smiled and turned away from him, walking instead toward the hearth, staring hard into the solarium geodes and their shifting lights within iridescent yellow-orange crystals. So much like the prince's eyes. "I've no need to disguise our relationship with lies to each other about what it is we will have. We will have to lie enough to the people that one would think lies would get tiresome, yes?" She looked at him over her shoulder, as if to check that he was still following along.

"Princess," he started.

"Shairi. Please, my *love*, call me by my name. After all, I am to be your prize, your queen, am I not? Let us at least be familiar. We are, after all, like brother and sister, as you say."

He blinked a few times before nodding. "I...suppose you are right." He looked at her sideways and shook his head. "This is very strange, Shairi. I had expected...something different of you."

She shrugged and turned back to the hearth. "Perhaps, Calix, it is that you have not known me all along."

"It would seem that way indeed."

"Would that it were, if you'll excuse me, I do have some duties to attend to. I must appoint a replacement handmaiden for your sister, and perhaps a few others to attend her in my stead." She crossed the room and lingered at the doorway, a stunned prince still standing in her sitting chambers. "Perhaps...we shall dine together soon? I would like to hear about your recent expeditions! You have been gone from the palace too long as of late."

Calix perked up at the idea. "I'll send for you this evening and we can dine in private. Perhaps I can get to know the Shairi that has been hidden behind my sister all these years." His smile was one that she had longed to see directed at her, but she found it irritating in the moment. Beautiful though he was, Calix was perhaps, very dense if this ruse was working so easily.

She shook her head, "No, I think I would dine with you in the hall, where the court can see that we are strongly united." It only took him a moment to consider the political impact it would make. At least she hoped that was what made him nod in agreement. "Wonderful. I am most excited for the escort to arrive." She said as she turned and left him alone in the West Pavilion.

IT DIDN'T TAKE SHAIRI LONG TO LOSE HERSELF IN THE CASTLE'S HEDGE-gardens and fall to her knees between two rows of perfectly manicured rosebush walls. Tears clouded her vision and sobs caught in her throat like a frog's croak in the summer as she pounded on the brittle lawn with her fists. Calix did not love her and now she had to pretend in order to see him look at her the way she'd always dreamed. Her shoulders shook from her cries, and eventually, they subsided into a series of wet sniffles.

The lie hurt, but his dismissal—she shook her head. He had come to her chambers looking to release them both from their arrange-ment. It was in his tone, his disinterest. She'd turned the political alliance upon him as a last resort. Shairi was not the queen he chose, and the best she could do for him would be to be a strong and smart alliance.

That was how Emmaleigh had ensnared Akintunde all those years ago, after all. Beautiful though the queen was, she had told the girls that Akintunde would have married some Rhunish Princess for the trade agreement when Emmaleigh had shown him what a fierce magician she was and what that could do for the expansion of Hinhallow. Similarly to his father, that front seemed to pique Calix's interest in her, and perhaps if she could keep it going, it would build over time into love. Or a kind of love that would be a required devotion to a queen who has borne him many sons and daughters.

Yes. She steadied her chin and wiped her tears with the back of her hand.

She would not let this trip her up. She was Shairi Chrysanthos, Crown Princess of Ares, and she could *still* have it all. In time. She just had to play the long game, like Queen Emmaleigh had taught her. She was about to rise from where she had fallen among the flowered hedges, when the footsteps and murmured voices held her in place like a rabbit afraid of the hound. She'd not done anything wrong, but the thought of anyone seeing her so disheveled was truly unbecoming.

"Jallah claims to have a great beauty in his chains that meets the criteria you'd set forth, my Liege."

Shairi knew that voice. It belonged to Magistrate Kobzik, a very strong fire magi with the gift of Sight. He could see the future in the flames, or so it was said. The man was so firmly rooted in Akintunde's pocket, she wondered if his visions of the grand design for Hinhallow's future were fabricated. She admitted to thinking that seers and oracles were hoaxes. As a girl, she'd been told by a festival oracle that she would marry a dark prince who was to be heir of all of Ellorhys. Continental domination aside, Calix was no dark prince, and Ellorhys was far from a united continent.

"That buzzard," King Akintunde replied. "He always says that. What is his claim now?"

King Akintunde was taking a private council in the gardens. On her hands and knees, she crawled back down the path, trying to separate herself from them without being seen. She halted not a few paces away. There were guards, Kingsmen, stationed around this stretch of garden in intervals. She was trapped.

"Well, first he says that he's got a virgin dancer that would be just perfect for the prince's coronation."

Shairi froze. They were talking about Calix.

"Dancers *are* very entertaining," the king mused. "I've got a few of them in my own seraglio. Eliandra and Sylvassa were dancers, and they've always been some of my favorite girls."

Shairi did not like the satisfied purr that crept into the king's voice. It was known that the king had his dalliances, and while it was by no means forbidden, the queen had long since secured the realm with the prince and his siblings making whatever the King did with other women of less consequence to her reputation. It was a wonder King Akintunde didn't have any other children from other women. Granted, she wouldn't have put it past her Aunt to have crafted an... antidote to pregnancy should the occasion arise.

"Should the prince not wait to assemble a seraglio until he has sired an heir?"

King Akintunde's laughter bellowed from within him. "Kobzik, you did not see my son's face when I told him the Aresian girl was to be his bride. That boy will find no pleasure with that golden tart. No more than I did with his mother at first." He laughed some more and sighed. "No, she will make a fine queen. Obedient and pretty enough. Besides, queens are for whelping heirs. Calix will need somewhere to vent his frustrations, as I do."

"Very well, sire," Kobzik said flatly. "I shall make arrangements for Rohit to view the wares when they arrive in port."

"You said first, Kobzik? What else has the Maggot Man got to waste my time with?"

"He says the dancer he wants to sell you was recently in Espera. On the night the refugees spoke of. The fires and the abduction."

"So it's true then. Someone was fool enough to steal the princess away from the Evernight Witch!" Akintunde bellowed, obviously nonplussed that the Imperial Princess was apparently missing.

"Not so, Sire. Jallah wrote that the dancer claims she was with a soldier the night it happened and that she herself heard the Witch call for an assassination."

There was silence for a moment, and Shairi felt her breath stop in her chest for fear they knew she was near, eavesdropping.

"Has she said anything about that niece of hers since?"

"No, my King. She had not been recovered as of this time."

"An assassination," King Akintunde said. He mulled it over, repeating choice terms as he grumbled to himself. "Recovered...pah! That old witch. She's a crafty one. Did away with the Helios and Umbriel, may they find peace in the Cosmos, and now she's gone and rid herself of the girl now that she's become a liability. I'll have to contend with her sooner or later. I'd though Calix could do the job but that forsaken Mythos— "

"A liability, your Eminence?" Shairi could hear the hunger in Kobzik's voice. "Whatever do you mean? I thought the Evernight Witch and the Imperial Princess were...comrades in their quest for the continents? Is that not what the Celestial Alliance believes?"

There was some shuffling of robes, and a few grunted murmurs that Shairi could not hear. They had stepped several paces away.

"Cosmos above, the Mythos *spoke* to the prince? This is—Why this is monumental! It changes everything the Celestial Alliance has spoken of! We have to contact the Temple—"

"Don't be daft!" Akintunde cut off the magistrate's excited babble. "The return of the Mythos could upset the very balance of society. Those brutes have been gone for over five hundred years. What do you think they could possibly want in the wake of their return?" There was a long silence and Shairi could imagine Kobzik's narrow, weasel-like face contorting in confusion. He never had been bright; but his dense replies made even rocks look smart. "Their cities! The very kingdoms they created!" Akintunde bellowed at last and Shairi wondered if this was indeed a private council or just a walk in the gardens for all the secrecy the king managed with his uproarious tone. In a lower, more reserved voice, the king asked, "Cosmos above, Kobzik, one would think you weren't just feigning ignorance so as to not reveal your accursed future paths. For Mythos sake, man, give me something!"

"The Imperial Princess is not yet dead but neither has she awoken," Kobzik said, but his voice was gravelly, as if he'd swallowed the earth and spoke with it caught in his throat. "The Cycle has been broken again. Within the battle begins."

"A vision," King Akintunde said, his voice filled with wonder. "Quick! Fetch a scribe and a scholar! He's having a vision without the flames!"

Many sets of feet thundered off to find what Akintunde wanted. Almost as soon as the flurries of footsteps faded into echo, Kobzik's grave voice spoke again, "Entwined are fates of the Stars and Flame, but shadowed Dark the path be tread with arcane evils rooted deep. Thrice defied death's decree, twice of the earth and once at sea. Dark seeks the Light to extinguish She."

At once there was gasping, and a hacking cough.

"Kobzik!" Akintunde's voice was full of concern and Shairi dared to pry back a branch so she could see through the bushes. "Magi!"

In the adjacent garden path, great King Akintunde was on his knees beside his oracle advisor, looking around expectantly for his requested aides. "Where is the damn scribe? We've nearly missed the whole prophecy!"

Prone, on his knees and bent backwards toward the sky, the grotesque and unnatural position of Magistrate Kobzik's body was enough to churn Shairi's already anxious stomach in roiling waves of nausea.

"She comes this way!" gasped Magi Kobzik. He shook violently, mouth frothing as he toppled onto his side.

From a corridor on the other side of the garden, a line of soldiers escorted an older man with a greying beard and ink stains on his face into the gardens at a hustle. "I'm here, sire!" The inky-man said as he descended into the garden, a pad and quill before him as he trampled the flowerbeds in his quest to get to the king.

"And so the garden spider finds its prey," Kobzik managed to whisper, and Shairi felt cold.

Kobzik was sprawled on his side, looking past the King's crouching form, directly at Shairi peeking through the garden hedge. Their eyes met, emerald green and darkest brown. She knew in that moment the prophecy he spoke of was not for the king's ears, but for hers.

King Akintunde was talking rapidly with the scholar while the

235

guards were helping a very stunned and confused Magistrate Kobzik to his feet. A healer hovered nearby to inspect him. With all the commotion in the garden, it was easy for Shairi to slip away.

She dashed back to her rooms at the West Pavilion, repeating the phrases over and over. Reluctance shadowed her thankfulness to find Calix had vacated her chambers, but the words would not stop forming on her lips until she had a quill in her hand and the verses on the page.

The Imperial Princess is not yet dead but neither has she awoken.

The Cycle has broken. Within the battle begins anew.
Entwined are fates of the Stars and Flame, but shadowed Dark the path be tread with arcane evils rooted deep.
Thrice defied death's decree, twice of the earth and on the sea.
Dark seeks the Light to extinguish She.
She comes this way!
And so the garden spider finds its prey.

22

ISSARIA

Sleeping with the collar was impossible. Issaria tossed from side to side, which only rattled her chain, and that made the other slavegirls groan and curse her. The fires were burned down to embers, but it didn't matter because it was *broad daylight* and everyone except Issaria seemed to be asleep! She repressed a deep sigh and gathered as much of her chain in her hands as possible before rolling onto her knees and crawling toward the carriage.

It seemed like an awful lot of effort to go through to remain silent for people that she was going to be sold alongside soon. What did it matter if they hated her? She was as much a slave as they were and they weren't *nearly* as considerate as she was.

When she reached the wagon's five-spoked wheel, she stood and with one hand, straightened her skirt, then her collar so that walking would be easier. The sun was still as high in the cerulean sky as it was when she'd filled the cauldrons with water from the sea. It was at least five times as hot. She shaded her eyes against the harsh glare of the sun as she looked out across the camp for a space where she could stretch her legs. A few wagons away she saw Sethik, leaned against the wagon talking in low tones with another slaver.

Confident that he would vouch for her as Kidalma had, she headed out from the camp, letting a little of her chain fall behind her with each step. She rounded her wagon, and was nearing the perimeter of the camp, where she'd seen Sethik on guard duty before, and only stumbled once! Feeling like she was getting the hang of this collar thing, she smiled to herself.

"Now, I don't suppose you think you're going to escape," a cool voice said from behind her.

Kai froze. She had to be Kai, and not Issaria, because Issaria was terrified at what this man insinuated he was capable of. Kai, Issaria reasoned, was well-accustomed to men getting possessive of her and had the temperament to handle this. She looked over her shoulder and found the blond slaver from her first day leaning against her wagon.

Zhaniel.

"Don't give me that look, slave," he said, kicking off the wagon and closing the distance between them in a few easy strides. He seemed to consider her, his brown eyes lingering as he took her chains from her arms with one hand. With the other he caressed her jawline down to her collar, where he fingered the space between her throat at the alloy.

Kai jerked away but Zhaniel held her chain and a wicked grin crossed his face as he yanked her forward then up abruptly. Kai gagged and her hands went to the collar, frantic to create space for herself to breathe. "That little dance you did earlier," he hissed, his dark eyes glinting with glee as Kai struggled to keep her toes on the Glass. "It was real nice to see those pretty shapes you can make your-self into while you was prancing around, showing off that little body of yours." He leaned in and she felt the heat from his breath on her shoulder where her top fell loose around her neck. "Got me and few of the fellas all riled up good and ready, didn't ya?" His mouth brushed the base of her throat as she gasped for breath, choking on her slave collar. "You might be off limits now that Jallah's got a buyer for you, and you're a bit pale for my tastes, but I'm not picky." He eased her down from his manmade noose as he spoke but didn't free her from his control.

He pressed her backside against him and Kai felt his physical need against her back. She struggled against him, but his breathing increased and he held her tighter. She could feel his smile in his ragged breaths, and Kai realized he liked the fight. The struggle excited him.

"I woulda given that to you after a show like that. Shown you a real good time. But I guess I'll have to give it to one of your friends."

She forced herself to still and after a moment he pushed her away from him, her chains falling to the ground around her like shattering glass.

"I'll make sure I get me a screamer so you can hear what I would have done for you." Zhaniel turned and left her on the Glass, alone on the outskirts of camp.

Kai shook from the encounter. Inside, Issaria was weeping, and even deeper down, she was struggling to contain the surge of power threatening to spill from within her. It was curious about her dancing, but it was *furious* about Zhaniel's violation. Trembling, she found that she didn't want to go back to the slave camp. She was a fool to think she'd had power there, and despite who or what was dwelling inside her magic, Issaria knew she couldn't fight to keep control of the primordial magic long enough to make it do anything she wanted, let alone keep it from destroying everything and perhaps everyone.

She continued out the way she'd intended to go and lingered when she'd found a private place behind a dune of glass to relieve herself. Kai then trudged back toward the caravan, letting her chain clatter against the glass as she moved, no longer concerned for the sleep of her fellows when there were nightmares afoot. Closer to the caravan, she saw another man leaning against the wagon as she approached.

Sethik leaned with his arms crossed over his chest, his hood up, protecting himself from the sun with its deep shadows. "I wanted to check on you after I saw Zhaniel leave from this direction." Kai nodded as she neared, and the concern on Sethik's face was clear. "Did he do anything to you?"

She shook her head. "Not really. Threatened me a little and..."

"Look, Kai. There are rules in Jallah's crew. Zhaniel toes just about

239

every one of them. If he did something to defy Jallah and I knew, and *didn't* say anything? I'd be just as guilty."

"I'm off limits because Jallah says so, but it's okay if he takes another girl in my place?" Kai asked, her accusation hot like a brand on her tongue.

Sethik stepped back. "I didn't mean—what I meant was—"

A sob strangled Kai's throat as a girl's startled cry pierced the quiet camp and she stumbled in the direction it came from.

"Woah there," Sethik said as he caught her around the waist with one arm and picked her up. The girl's protests were clear, ringing out across the empty Glass like a wolf's lone lament. Kai kicked against him, but his grip didn't tighten or loosen. "Kai. Kai, hear me out. You *can't* stop him. He's just—"

"He's a monster!" Kai's voice was gravelly as her thrashing slowed.

"He is," Sethik agreed. "He's worse than that because even if you stop him tonight, he's going to do it again as soon as you leave." His words washed over her and she stopped fighting. He put her down and shook his head. "I'm really sorry. I...I don't like it either but I don't make the rules. Jallah has to give the beasts...something or else they'll succumb to more devious desires."

"That sounds rather rehearsed, Sethik."

He grimaced. "I didn't say I liked the reasoning either."

Beyond Sethik, Issaria's eyes tracked Zhaniel's movements as he staggered out from the bulk of the slumbering caravan, dragging a slavegirl by her long, black braid.

"No." Sethik looked confused as she met his emerald eyes. "I'm not going let him get away with this."

She looked only once at the slaver with familiar eyes, before she burst into a sprint toward Rhaminta and Zhaniel, chain clangorously clattering across the Glass as she ran. She fell deep inside herself, brushing up against that power. The power that yearned to be free.

Ahead, Zhaniel shoved Rhaminta ahead of him. She fell to her knees and scrambled forward on all fours.

"Don't you *touch* her!" Issaria screamed as she launched herself into the air.

She collided with Zhaniel as she felt a surge of power crackle through her veins. The sheer momentum of her tackle took them both to the ground, and she threw the first fist at his face. Her knuckles screamed in protest as her fist cracked off his jaw. Wind ripped around her, gripped her with phantom hands and wrenched her back from Zhaniel. Issaria gritted her teeth.

She wasn't going to be that easy to get rid of.

With a fistful of his hair, and a leg hooked around his, she *made* him come with her as his magic tossed them both. Her bones cracked against the Glass as they toppled over one another in a blur of kicking and jabbing elbows. Stars erupted from behind Issaria's eyes, a hefty fist connected with her temple as they grappled. Issaria's throaty war-cry left her hoarse, but she swung again and connected with his nose with a satisfying crunch. He didn't even flinch as he gripped her arms and wrenched her off him.

Zhaniel launched her away as if she were nothing.

Issaria tumbled down a slight incline in the planes of the crystal-ized dunes. Her leash reached its length. The generous length of alloy chain given to the slavegirls so they could navigate the camp had come to a tangled end, and her collar choked her to a halt.

Zhaniel coughed. "You bitch! I'm going make you—"

"That's enough!" Jallah's voice silenced Zhaniel's vulgar threats.

Jallah surveyed the scene.

Rhaminta, blouse torn open and tears running down her face as she cowered between the camp and Zhaniel. Issaria—Kai sported a few good wounds, but the blond slaver suffered a clearly broken nose, courtesy of Issaria's fist, which throbbed in agony as she congratu-lated herself on a getting in at least one good shot.

And that left Zhaniel. He stood in stoic silence, awaiting the judge-ment of Jallah Coppernolle.

Dazed, Issaria struggled to her feet. She wasn't sure if she'd broken anything in her hand, but her face definitely felt the power of his hit. Her left eye was stuck shut and when she withdrew her hand, her fingers were sticky with blood. She looked around, wobbling in place as Rhaminta edged away from Zhaniel and closer to Jallah and Issaria. From behind Jallah, Sethik watched the proceedings.

He'd gone for Jallah when Kai attacked Zhaniel.

"You damaged my property, Zhaniel," Jallah growled.

He hesitated for a moment, but then replied, "I wouldn't have hurt her if she didn't attack me."

The slave master did not reply. He looked placidly between his slaver and his slavegirl. "You mean to tell me," he started, "that a chained and collared *girl* got the best of you?" Zhaniel looked at his feet. "Sethik, get these girls to Kidalma. See to it that the dancer is fixed up right. We need her face to turn that profit."

Sethik swept forward and seized Rhaminta and Issaria by the wrists, towing them back toward the camp. Issaria looked over her shoulder at Jallah and Zhaniel as he asked, "What are you going to do to me, Jallah?" The slaver's voice wavered between goading and genuine self-preservation.

Issaria glanced at Sethik, then to Rhaminta, whose brown eyes were wide, her terror still written on her face.

A strange buzzing sound seemed to leak out of the vast expanse of Glass behind them until it was a loud, steady droning that pierced the sky. "What is that noise?" Issaria asked, looking around.

"Don't look back," Sethik said with a shake of his head.

Behind them, anguished cries echoed out over the Glass. Issaria jerked her head toward the screams but Sethik tightened his grip on her wrist.

She met his eyes instead.

"Don't look," Sethik commanded. "You don't want to look."

The haunted echo in his eyes made her listen this time.

EARLY MORNING WAS QUIET IN THE SLAVE CAMP. EVEN AFTER ZHANIEL'S tortured screams stopped, the camp was slow to rise in the wake of Jallah Coppernolle's wrath.

Zhaniel never came back to camp.

Embers grew cold and bodies burrowed deeper into their bedrolls, while those lucky enough to claim a yurt the day before were left to sleep well into the day. Inside the central yurt where she'd taken instruction from Kidalma, Issaria, the old woman herself, and Rhaminta dealt with the events in varying ways.

Kidalma applied ointments to Issaria's face, murmuring words and radiating little bursts of light like fireflies in a summer meadow. Issaria sat on an upturned tin bucket trying not to flinch as the old woman worked, and Rhaminta had cried herself to sleep in a blanket behind a barrel of cabbage heads. Again, the old woman squeezed a wet cloth over Issaria's upturned face and said, "Hold still," as she winced at the water on her tender flesh.

"Be a bit gentler, would you?" Issaria hissed as she held out a hand to stop the woman from rubbing the wound again.

"You go to auction in a few days. Your face is a mess!" She turned away, shoving her medical supplies across the make-shift table. "You are a stupid girl."

Issaria rolled her eyes as she rose from the bucket. "Thanks for trying to help," she said as she turned toward the door.

"You are stupid, *stupid* girl," Kidalma said again. Issaria felt the woman's wrinkled hand on her own. "But you are brave." She looked back and found Kidalma's pale eyes glittering with unshed tears. "Come, child. Sit with me a while. I believe we were meant to meet, and the stars...they wish for me to show you the path they've chosen for you."

The silver-haired crone led Issaria back into the yurt and paused only to hang a violet linen cloth from the door frame to give them privacy. It was thin, and with the brilliant sunlight outside, the inside of the yurt took on a distinct purple hue. Issaria lingered in the violet light as Kidalma set to work quickly and quietly, flipping over a wooden crate that had once held onions, unrolling two woven mats. If it were not for the heat of the sun and Kidalma's overbearing presence, if Issaria closed her eyes she could almost pretend that the purple light was coming from the Crystal Palace. She could be in her rooms with Safaia and Isida, laughing about something Elon had done to upset her again—the big oaf never could get the right words out—but she would have told them about the kiss—

The striking of a match, the sizzle and smolder, snapped her eyes open and she looked around the yurt. The brilliant purple aura dimmed as Kidalma put the match to the lantern, igniting an amber glow from above their heads, then to a bundle of dried herbs that she smudged into a smoldering stick. She left that in a small ceramic bowl in the center of their make-shift table. With Rhaminta's soft snores in the background, Issaria sat cross-legged on a woven reed mat across from Kidalma, who spread a colorful variety of square sheets across the box.

"Choose a silk."

Issaria looked hesitantly across the thin squares of fabric. They were stiff, starched until they held their rigid form like parchment, but Issaria could see the fibers in each pretty square. "And the...stars? They told you to show me these fabric samples?"

"They did not," Kidalma said flatly. "Do you know what I am, child?"

Issaria shook her head.

"Humph. I thought not. Not many stick around long enough to know, and those that do, well they tend to leave an old woman alone," she said with a shrug. "I'm an Oracle. My mana allows me to connect with the threads of the universe and see the most likely path for a person."

Issaria listened to Kidalma speak, but her eyes were drawn to the squares of fabric.

"While each fate can be changed at any time, such is the gift of free will, I can help the most likely one make itself known."

Each square was different. Blue, yellow, green stripes, purple flowers, one that looked like ripples on water, and another that looked like sunlight through the treetops. One seemed to glow a pale purple light, and Issaria reached a hand toward it.

"Is that the one you wish to work with?" Issaria could hear the smile in Kidalma's voice. "That's a good one. Okay, now I select mine," she said as she reached out and pulled a nondescript yellow one from the stack, then shuffled the rest off to the side. "Now, for this to work, I'm going to need you to clear your mind."

Issaria arched an eyebrow at her. "I just got my face beaten in and only the Cosmos knows what happened to the ingrate who did it and you want me to clear my mind?"

Kidalma stared at her. "Must you make everything so difficult?" Issaria shrugged and the old woman rolled her eyes. "If it will help, I can instruct you. Close your eyes."

Issaria did so.

"Breathe deep," Kidalma said.

She took a deep breath. Smoke from the bundle of herbs still smoldering on the table between them filled her nostrils. The charred, floral aroma clouded her mind and she felt herself falling inward as she released it.

Rhaminta's snores faded into the distance and only Kidalma's voice seemed to reach that place deep inside her.

The place where Issaria heard *her* voice.

A part of her wanted so badly to open the door, it seemed so easy now. Like touching a pond and watching the ripples cascade endlessly.

"Think of what you hope to attain."

The Esperian crown flashed in her mind, shining atop her head. But it wasn't the crown, it had never been about the crown. No, those crystals forged in molten ore…it wasn't about the crown. It was what it represented, that it gave her responsibility for the wellbeing of her people. With the crown upon her head she could free them—free them *all* from her Aunt's Eventide. Balance restored to the realm.

Peace across Ellorhys once more.

"Think of your heart swelling with joy and love."

Elon's arms wrapped around her, his lips against her own, darkness crushing around them as they finally let themselves feel.

"Think of the things that haunt you, the hard truths that are your very essence—your *geheime harte*."

Though she'd never heard the arcane words before, she knew.

A dark night, and bloodied halls made Issaria's breath quicken.

The sword her aunt brandished in front of the entire palace that night had been bloodied. She dared to mourn them, dared to speak their names while their blood was still warm on her blade? Hecate *held her* while she sobbed, and she had been their murderer all along. The hurt ran deep with her betrayal, the endless lies she'd been told over the years. Lies she *stupidly* believed.

But that night she'd *seen* the blood.

Had she only dared to wonder, if only for a moment…

…had she? Dared to wonder?

"Open your eyes," Kidalma said, and Issaria did as she was commanded, meeting Kidalma's eyes—so much like Hecate's but warmer, kinder in a way her aunt's had never been. "Steady yourself, Kai. And think of your path. Choose your destiny, and fold your square as I do mine."

Issaria set her hands on her square as Kidalma had. At her touch, the illumination rippled out from her fingertips in crimson rings, cascading one by one, larger, and larger, and larger until—the square was *red*. She made to pull her hands from the square but Kidalma put a hand over hers, clicking her tongue she said, "Ah, ah, ah. Now you've started, you can't stop. Red is good. Red is passion, the color of the heart of the world, unyielding and fierce. It is a good color for you, I should think."

The old woman held her gaze until she was sure Issaria understood. Then she nodded and placed her fingertips back on her square and said, "Watch closely now. I'll try to go slow, but once the stars take me…I can't make promises for stars, you know."

Confused but enchanted by the scent of the herbs on the stale air and the smoke lingered in a haze about them, Issaria watched as the old woman's fingers pressed and folded her yellow square in half, and in half again. Keeping a close eye on Kidalma's deft fingers, Issaria folded and unfolded her square. She pinched where Kidalma pinched, creased where she creased. Once, and only once did she look up to see Kidalma's face. The old woman's eyes had gone dark. Not black, but within them, she saw the reflection an endless, starry night. Gasping at the sight, Issaria refocused on her folding.

Faster and fast they folded, their squares of fabric taking on definitive forms. Smoke lazed about in ringlets on the tabletop. The folded shapes swirled through the floral mist like phantoms.

Each movement seemed direct and intentional, but as Issaria realized she was running out of fabric to fold, Kidalma had ceased her crafting.

Before her, lain sideways across Kidalma's palm was a yellow folded statuette of a dancing girl. Issaria looked closely at the girl's face and found little pinches in the starched silk to make a nose, and little indents for her eyes. She would have sworn to the Mythos *and* the Cosmos that she was looking at a little paper version of herself.

Grinning, she looked to her own figure, expecting to see a little dancer girl of her own.

But what Issaria held up to the Oracle was not a dancing girl.

"I don't understand? I mimicked your folds exactly!" Issaria looked from her own statuette to meet Kidlama's stare. "How did you…"

The old woman shook her head. "I didn't do anything. This was all you. Your path is determined by your own choices," Kidalma said again. "Mine, as the outlet, always ends up being the thing about the magician that brought us together for the path to be read."

She squinted at her folded companion in her hand. "But I don't understand. What does it even mean?"

Kidalma shrugged. "Who knows?" She extinguished the bundle of herbs by smothering it into the bottom of the bowl without ceremony and began clearing the table. All the mysticism of the moment gone as she cleared the upturned crate and returned it to its place. "Not me. Not you. Maybe they do," she said, as she jerked her head toward the sky. "The moment is in the future."

She seemed to consider this for a moment before she shrugged and continued on her path of cleaning, putting her little yellow dancing girl in a large jar with at least a hundred other folded creations in an assortment of colors. "Or it can be, if you take the *right path*. What I *can* tell you, is that when you reach *the* moment—" She jabbed with her hand at the little red figure in her palm. "When you reach *that* moment? You better be ready for something big. Life changing." She looked at it again and smiled. "And it will probably be red."

"Big? How can you tell?" Issaria asked, holding up her palm again. "It's so… *little*." She rubbed it gently with the tip of her finger. "And… kind of cute?"

"I don't make the rules," Kidalma said as she ripped the violet blanket off the door frame, letting sunlight blast its way into the yurt, shaking all thoughts of magic and starry-eyed old women from Issaria's head. "Now get out of my hut and get some sleep. Tell Sethik that I said you're not to be disturbed on account of your messed-up face!" She ushered Issaria toward the door. "Take your little cow and go!"

"Cow?" Issaria held up her little folded friend again and looked closer at his features. Two long, straight horns emerged from the sides of his squared head. A large, powerful back and thick haunches were posed as if the steer were running. Or charging. Issaria shrugged as she gently collapsed the folded animal and flattened him out so that she could refold him later. No matter what happened, she was keeping this. "I thought he looked a little more like a buffalo…or a bull?" she mused aloud as Kidalma tried to shove her out the door.

"Cow. Buffalo. It is not for me to say. The stars don't ask for me to interpret their signs, they just want the outlet *through* me." Kidalma turned her back on Issaria and pretended to sweep the floor of her yurt as she retreated. She paused for a moment, looking pensive, then turned to Issaria in the doorway, just over her shoulder. "Maybe it is a bull. Bullheaded as you are!" She snorted at her own gibe and fell into giggles.

"Thanks for the cow, Kidalma," Issaria replied as she rolled her eyes and retreated into the camp.

Behind her in the yurt, the old woman seemed lost in her own laughter. Issaria could still hear Kidalma across the camp at her wagon where she crawled into one of two empty bedrolls. Rhaminta had stayed in Kidalma's yurt, and Issaria fell asleep with a small silk cow folded into the palm of her hand.

2 3

ELON

It's been nearly a full moon since we've seen her, Sainthart," Empress Regent Hecate challenged as she fixed her glacial gaze upon him. "We've got to admit at some point that she's not coming back." Her voice carried out across the empty throne room, echoing off the far corners to taunt him: *not coming. Not coming back.*

"All due respect, Empress Regent," Elon started, "but I just can't believe that. Princess Issaria is still alive out there." He held her heavy stare, refusing to buckle before her.

She considered him from her seat on the Imperial throne, he imagined, as one might consider an annoying insect before them. The throne, a hulking high-backed chair carved from the ore of the meteor that ushered the Sister Queens to Ellorhys, was supposed to be where the Imperial Emperor or Empress sat. It sickened him to see this sycophant sitting where Issaria should be.

"Be that as it may, you two never *did* complete the *Sanguinem Defendier* ritual, did you?" Elon held his tongue and the Empress Regent simpered at him as she leaned her head in her hand — bored. "So your innate *belief* that my niece is alive is nothing but fool's hope. No truth lies within your claim."

He couldn't help himself. "One would almost think you *want* her to be gone, Empress Regent," he growled out.

She at least had the wherewithal to look affronted, even if it was blatantly faked, as confirmed by the sneer on Commander Acontium's face. A shocked hand to her heart, mouth agape, she stammered, "Captain Sainthart. I *assure* you that there is no one more upset than I at the prospect of Issaria having been taken from us, at such a *young age* no less." Hecate barely fought to keep the smirk from her face. "But rest assured when I say that the princess is gone, if not already, then soon. Nearly a month without word from the Daylight Cities? No ransom? No threats?" She clicked her tongue against her teeth. "No, Captain. I have mourned her absence, and it seems my heart will never stop mourning. Princess Issaria is likely dead. I cannot carry on any longer under the guise that she may return to us. *Espera* cannot continue on hoping for something that may not happen. Not after... the first time."

Elon gritted his teeth and ran a gloved hand through his copper hair, pulling it back from his face as he rounded on the Empress Regent again. He was running out of options and this battle wasn't one he anticipated losing quite so soon. He'd hoped for a little more time before he played these cards.

"Not yet. I beg of you," he said, letting the true loss and sorrow ring through his voice, "Hecate. You...you know what she means to me." What it would take for him to admit it, even to her when they *both* knew they were playing a dangerous game together. "Please, *please* don't take my hope from me. Not yet." Her face softened, if only for the small part of her that cared for Issaria once, if ever. "Send one more cadre of riders to the cities to search for her. Send *me*. I'll not fail her again. Just one more attempt to find her. If she's out there, I'll get her back. I'd never forgive myself if we just...stopped trying to bring her home."

Hecate was silent as she pondered his plea, no doubt calculating how yet another delay would affect her designs for the crown. She'd tried twice already to announce the loss of the princess. Both times Elon and the Chancellors present motioned to keep the hope of

Issaria's safety alive, if only for the time being. It was too early to claim she could not have survived, not without word or a body to support the official passing of the throne. No, without proof, it would look as though Hecate *herself* had usurped her niece. And they couldn't have *that*, now could they?

How close the Chancellors had come to the truth when they cautioned Hecate's hand at the announcement. At the time, Elon wondered if some of them had come to that conclusion on their own and realized what conspiracy they had unearthed. But no one pointed a finger, and Hecate sent out a teams of riders and trackers to hunt her down instead.

They all returned without so much as a scent trail between them. Not a single one of them had headed toward the Glass, though. Hecate was convinced that Issaria was hiding somewhere in the Baelforia after her last adventure. Elon wasn't about to correct their egregious errors, but all the soldiers roaming aimlessly in the wood was making it difficult to conceal the rebel encampments as they gathered their ranks.

This time, Elon alone challenged her decision. Not only for himself, but because the rebellion needed to believe that they could outlast Hecate. This was the hardest part. Waiting and preparing. The longer Issaria remained off the map, the longer Hecate had to wait to lay claim to the Imperial Crown. Until she had the crown, there would be no invasion into Daylight, although reason to attack had grown stronger since the kidnapping was attributed to them. Restless Esperians were ready to take blood for all the wrongdoings against them.

"Very well. I will send riders out one last time," Hecate agreed at last. "But not you, Sainthart. I require you here."

He didn't like the way she said that, as if keeping him in Espera was as much to her benefit as it was to his. "But I would be of better use searching for Issa—Princess Issaria, wouldn't you think?"

Hecate shook her head, her black hair catching indigo highlights in the solarium glow. "Nonsense. You keep *my* hope alive." Her wicked smile grew and Elon took an involuntary step backwards. "If Issaria *were* to return, I've no doubt in my mind who she would want to see first."

And it was then that Elon realized, safe or not, if Issaria got the chance to come back to Espera, she would come. For him, and for her friends. The memory of her parents. For her city. He'd sent her away, but like a butterfly in migration, she would always return to the place she from whence she originated.

Hecate had baited the trap. All she really had to do was wait.

"Do stay close, Captain Sainthart."

Elon fought the chill that chased him from the throne room and managed to keep his steps steady until the large double doors closed behind him.

As was becoming habit for poor, broken hearted Captain Sainthart, he trudged through the lamp-lit Esperian streets with his hands in his pockets on his way to visit his new favorite girl at the Amber Rose. Shoulders slumped against a non-existent wind, hood pulled far over his face, Elon all but reeked of despair and loneliness. Maybe it was overkill, but good ol' Ersol and Terek, his *favorite* of the soldiers assigned to tail him night in and night out, were merely a block behind him and had not taken care to hide themselves this evening. He'd have seen them four blocks ago even if he hadn't known they were there.

He'd hardly settled himself at his usual spot at the bar when Maiyra, very curves-forward, leaned on the bar beside him. "Hey, stranger. Didn't think you'd be coming to see me so soon after the last time?" she asked without asking. This meeting wasn't arranged. He was lucky she was even lingering around the tavern that evening.

"Maybe I missed your particular talents," he said without looking up from the mug that the bartender, Laurent, slid in front of him as she'd arrived.

Maiyra didn't hide her scowl as she tucked her fiery hair behind her ear. "I don't *actually* take clients, as you know," she hissed. "So I hope you're talking about my *other* skillset."

Elon nodded into his mug, taking several hearty gulps before setting it back down. "How about you and I go for a moonlit stroll? What do you say, Maiyra?"

He left twelve copper Metals for Laurent, the extra because he was most certainly going to be stiffed by Ersol and Terek who were settling into a booth against the far wall, when Elon and Maiyra left through the front door. They vanished back into the city before the soldiers could hurry back outside, leaving Laurent shouting behind them about their unpaid tab.

AT LEAST THIS TIME ELON DIDN'T NEED TO APPROACH TO KNOW WHAT dark magic shrouded that room. Maiyra's skills as a Whisperer were such that she could use her storm magic to capture the words said between parties and bring back the sound of it so that she could hear it again and again. It was as good as being in the room with them, and even better, it was virtually invisible. No one could *see* the sound waves, or the airwaves that trapped them and returned them to Maiyra's waiting ear. The downside was that she had to be relatively close to retrieve the sound before time and distance distorted it, like grains of sand caught against a violinist's bow stings.

And 'relatively close' it turned out meant lurking in the same stairwell he'd abducted Basl from, just out of sight of the pair of guards posted outside the council chamber doors. A new addition since the last time he'd snooped on these stairs, likely *because* of his actions that night. Which might have been even more suspicious than Elon just walking straight up to the doors and asking if they planned to kill him any time soon or just play with their food like a cat with a mouse.

Maiyra, on the other hand, seemed perfectly at ease sleuthing through the Crystal Palace. She sat on the stair below him, elbows propped on one behind her. She leaned her head back as far as it would go and watched as he eased the door open and a sliver of light cut across the darkened stairwell. "Don't need the door open," she commented.

"Not doing it for you," he murmured as he took a visual on the two guards.

They stood at attention, if not somewhat sloppy in the tilt of their pikes and casual lean-against-the-wall posture. Their faces were obscured by their helmets and the shifting glow of the solarium geodes outside the chamber doors.

"It's starting," Maiyra whispered, though nothing had changed in the hall to give them any indication of events occurring behind the closed doors. "Magistrate Sabien is calling for them to be seated. His voice is very distinct, full of austerity," she continued narrating the winds.

Elon kept the doorway slightly ajar, then settled on the stair beside her and withdrew a notepad. He would take notes in alchemic short-hand, and had assigned the council members elemental sigils on a cypher in his pocket for decoding later. Charcoal nib sharp, he began to scribble symbols and runes as Maiyra chronicled the meeting for him.

"'The people are growing restless.' That's Koellewyn. What's his first name? Edvard?"

"Edlaire," Elon replied. "Chancellor of Vox and Vita." The voice and life of the people; he was a voted representative on behalf of the citizens of Espera. *Basl's father.* He would be a key player in influencing the rebellion as the rightful Esperian Army once all was said and done.

"Oh I like him," Maiyra said with a grin. "Said that the princess is the rightful heir and we simply cannot crown a new line of Imperials until it is without a doubt that she is gone."

Elon recalled Basl's pleas, claiming his father would have been an ally. He smirked to himself. The kid was right. He would send a contact to Edlaire immediately. And eventually, they could send Basl to the encampments to join the rebellion and reunite with his father. A happy ending for the family.

"Magistrate Sabien says Hecate has been Empress Regent for so long, surely she can stand to wait a while longer. Hecate says it's not about the crown." Maiyra scoffed and Elon shot her a glare then glanced back through the opening.

The guards were oblivious to the conversation being transported before their eyes. Stolen snippets and phrases drifted under the doors like motes of dust caught in an errant breeze.

"Hecate says she worries for the heart of the people. 'Without strong leadership, they could fall prey to one of our Daylight enemies.'" Maiyra rolled her eyes as she whispered, "Full of hot air, isn't she? They actually buy this garbage?"

"Politics is a game of smiles and lies," Elon commented as he continued to notate the meeting like a scribe taking minutes.

"I'll say. She says that it breaks her heart to think of calling off the search for the princess." Elon could tell she was quoting the Empress Regent directly when she put on a funny accent and said, "If she's out there, we will find her. I've issued another cadre of riders to the cities. I'd never forgive myself if we just stopped trying to bring her home.'" Elon snapped his head up at that. "What?" Maiyra asked, her voice her own again.

"I said that. Earlier today. Those are *my* words." Rage didn't begin to cover it. That evil *bitch* was using his feelings for Issaria to manipulate the council into doing her bidding. Into believing her filth and *lies.*

"You really love her, huh?" Maiyra mused.

"Of course I do," he spat as the nib of his charcoal snapped. Blank faced at his admission, Elon stared at the useless charcoal wedge poised above the page. "Of course I do," he repeated in a whisper.

Maiyra kicked her feet back and forth idly as she said, "Seems to me that you know it's all for nothing."

Elon looked up and met Maiyra's honey eyes, glowing gold in the slanted light from the doorway. She obviously didn't know what she was talking about. The feelings he and Issaria shared, the memory of her folded into his arms for the first, and last time…Maiyra knew *none* of it. No one did. "What do you mean?"

"Sainthart. Elon," she said as she laid a hand on his knee. "You know what she is. Who she is. Even if she cares for you the same way...she's bound to duty eventually, isn't she?"

Yes. No. Perhaps. But if she *were* Imperial Empress...who could tell her no? He felt a fool, thinking that all he had to do was wait for her to be crowned and then...and then what? He would have *still* been her sworn sword. Her protector of the most sacred order. And he would *still* not be able to love her as he wished. Nothing would have changed other than more titles and duties between them.

No matter how high he climbed, he would always just be a stable boy shoveling hay while she was...

Out of reach.

"Just...relay the meeting, Maiyra."

"We haven't missed much. Just her usual gambits. Acontium will ready the riders and outfit them himself, yada yada. Chancellor Jadzya claims the monthly shipments from Ares are delayed by the negotiations with Hinhallow following a marriage proposal between their princess and the prince, blah blah blah. Hecate's not thrilled about that last bit." Maiyra pitched her voice in the absurd accent that Elon supposed *sort of* sounded like the Empress Regent. "'Can't have Fraxinus allying himself with that Warlord. Bound to bring that conqueror to our doorstep if we allow the union. Akintunde would like nothing more than to get his grubby hands on my crown.'" Maiyra pitched her eyebrows up at her own voice as the words tumbled out. "Getting a bit daring with that verbiage, isn't she?"

Elon didn't reply as he withdrew a small blade and shaved a new nib from the charcoal wedge, replaced the blade into a flap at the front of his notebook, and resumed his sigil-and-rune notes.

"Chancellor Elizer?" she asked.

"Coin and Crown." Maiyra stared blankly at his identification. "Taxes and Charitable Donations in the name of the Crown."

"Oh. Makes sense then. He says taxes this year were light from the outer cities. Larkham the most, Hokaan and Del as well. Entire families abandoned homes, and farms, many leaving their belongings behind. His officers reported back with over sixty-two percent losses."

Ouch. That had to hurt, Hecate, Elon taunted silently. Not to mention that the rebellion had sent riders to the villages recruiting able-bodied fighters for their ranks. Anyone who wanted to fight was gathering in the Baelforia north of Larkham and they were learning to hone their skills for battle, in many cases, for the first time. It was a rag-tag bunch, but they were fiercely adamant that the rightful heir would return, and when she did, they'd be ready to help her. He let himself feel a smidge of pride for the small digs they were taking at Hecate's empire of darkness.

"Oh, wait," Maiyra said, sitting straight and looking into the darkness of the stairwell. She cocked her head to the side, listening. "Something's happening." As if it would help her hear better, she tucked her fiery hair behind her ear.

"Are we caught?" Elon looked back at the guards. One yawned, but nothing appeared amiss.

"No, hold on. This is…tricky." She held her hands in front of her, bending and weaving them through the air. Around her hands, blades of white light began to slice the air, slipstreaming around her fingers like a river around rocks. Maiyra gasped. The river of light around her hands flickered from existence but lingered like an afterimage on his eyelids as her hands flew to cover her mouth. "Cosmos above, Elon."

"What is it?" he hissed, eyes wide as he grasped her shoulders.

"She pulled him aside with Acontium. I secluded their conversation from the rest of the chatter." Her honey eyes were so wide, he could see the whites all around her iris.

"Maiyra. What. Is. It."

She brought a hand to his ear, and he felt the pulse of her mana just before the soft silver glow that had streamed around her fingers like a river lit upon his cheek. And then he heard Hecate's voice like a whisper against the shell of his ear.

"…Hinhallow. It's the only place we haven't checked. Be thorough."

Followed by another voice he recognized though the change in pitch from Hecate's sultry elegant speech to gruff and grim made him start. "Am I ever anything but? It shall be done, of course, Commander

Acontium. No need for threats," Malek Wardlaw said, probably to something Acontium had done with his hands.

"I want to be clear, Malek," Hecate said sternly, "if you find her, be quick, but be *certain*. I can't have her coming back and ruining everything again. I've waited too long."

"And of my...appointment?"

"Yes, yes. Upon your return we shall discuss your appointment to Master of the Guild of Shadows and Bone." Hecate didn't sound as though she were very invested in whatever scheme that was, but the next words out of her mouth must have been to convince a skeptical Malek because even Elon believed it when she said with a voice full of sugar, "We will orchestrate it together, Malek, dear. I need my *best* assassin in the highest of authorities, and where better than the guild of assassins? Just kill the princess first. Prove to me that you've earned the title."

Elon's met Maiyra's in the dark. "Can we keep that?"

Maiyra shook her head. "Only for a little while. The more I replay it, the more it looses its constitution."

He stuffed his notebook in the pocket of his jacket and grabbed Maiyra's hand, tugging her down the stairwell after him. "We don't need to hear anymore."

They'd gone nearly to the bottom in silence when Maiyra ripped her wrist from his grasp. "Elon, what are we gonna do? That guy is going to go find her!"

He shook his head and clenched his hands at his sides. "What can we do, Maiyra? He's a month behind, just like us. We have no idea where she is, only where she's headed, and that's one step ahead of them as long as we keep it secret." He hung his head. "I can't help her with this one, Maiyra. If I went there searching for her Wardlaw would just follow me straight to her. She's...she's better off on her own. We just have to trust her and build the rebellion while there's still time."

Maiyra was silent as she took the remaining steps between them and wrapped her arms around him, his forehead coming to rest on her shoulder amidst her strawberry-colored hair. "We have to remember she's not alone. She has us. And she has *her*."

When Elon walked Maiyra through the palace gates amid crude remarks about Elon's bedding techniques, he was thrilled to see a stupefied Terek and Ersol blundering up the road from Espera, wondering how Elon and the redhead from the Amber Rose ended up back at the palace, of all places. He even spared them a little wave just as he turned back up the road and tucked his hands into his pockets, the picture of aloofness.

PART IV
ON THE HORIZON

24

ISSARIA

I f Issaria thought the slave wagon had been cramped quarters, it was nothing compared to the belly of Jallah's slave ships. Knees tucked against her chin, she sat side-by-side, chained at the wrist and ankle, with the other women from the caravan. Not just her wagon, but all the wagons.

It was not lost on Issaria that Kidalma was not among them. One girl down on the end, the young one Issaria had seen when she had first awoken among them, had thrown up, sickened by the sway of the sea. The cabin was filled to the brim with the sour smell and Issaria—no, she had to be Kai again. Kai...for a little bit longer—tucked her nose into the collar of her shirt, smelling her none-too-ripe body odor and finding it preferable to vomit.

She couldn't be sure how long they were at sea. Long enough to fall asleep, slumped against the beautiful chestnut-haired Eiren, who leaned against Kai in turn, the pair supporting each other throughout their slumber.

Eiren nudged her in the morning when the ship above them was waking. Footsteps on the panels above their heads, the shifting dust and dirt raining down upon the girls. "I think we're about to make port," she whispered when Kai blinked herself awake.

"Where?"

Eiren's blue eyes were unwavering in the slanted beams of light that managed to siphon through the floor and illuminate the freckles smattered across the bridge of her nose. "Hinhallow," she said gravely.

The girls were shuffled from their filthy hold, many covered in excrement and other things, and herded off the boat and down the gangplank in their shambling line. From the docks, Sethik, Curwin, Roark, and Kyrel—Jallah's generals, as Kai had begun to think of them —escorted the chained ladies through the narrow streets and into a blue tent just beyond the shipping thoroughfare.

Assembled in a canvas tent somewhere on the edge of the bazaar, each girl was doing her best to look angry and worthless. Thalia had even gone so far as to give herself a blistering black eye while they were on the ship so that she would look like she was worth too much trouble. She was holding out for a position on a farm, like home, she'd said.

Jallah Coppernolle, Merchant of Men, entered from the same flap they had been herded through like cattle and went to stand at the back of the tent, drawing all their attention with him as he moved. Kai didn't hold back her glare as Kidalma followed close behind. Sethik and Roark took up posts at the doors, but the others lingered around the outside of the tent, shadows prowling the canvas like a pack of wolves.

Jallah considered them, meeting each girl's gaze with his dark, unfeeling eyes. "Girls, I'm going to sell you for quite the profit," he explained, his dark eyes roaming over them with greed. "But *some* of you are going to be very lucky." He paced the length of the tent, then reached a hand up to twirl the end of his mustache before saying, "I wrote to the king. I told him I've a very special set of girls this time. I've been gathering you beauties up, you see, because the *prince* is getting coronated in a week's time." He kept his back to them, the scarred side of his skull tilted in their direction as his words sank in, and a few girls started whispering.

"So he's going to buy *her*?" a brunette named Jhenna, asked, jerking her chains in Kai's direction.

Jallah pivoted and met Jhenna's hazel eyes. His lips drew into a thin line beneath his mustache. "Jealousy is an ugly thing," he said before walking down the chain-line until he reached Kai. He reached out and stroked her knotted hair, his scarred knuckles lingering too long on her cheek. She jerked away, and he gave her a wicked smile. "You should all be thanking our *dear* Kai. Her talent sparked the idea and now, if he likes what he sees, the king himself may purchase a select few of you to join Kai as a gift for the prince from his esteemed Majesty."

His eyes lingered on Kai's. She forced herself to hold his repulsive gaze, but was near trembling when he clapped his hands together and turned away, searching the tent for—"Kidalma!" Jallah took a leather pouch from the pocket of his duster and tossed it to the old woman. "Clean them up. There's a stable across the street. See if they'll let us use their well to rinse them off."

And with that, he left the tent, leaving Kidalma and his men to ensure they were cleaned. In a barn. With the cattle.

Issaria's face burned with shame as Kyrel, apparently a water magician among Coppernolle's slavers, used the stable's well to drench them each in a wave of icy water. Her alloy collar had rubbed her neck raw, and her scabs were bleeding again. She hoped this crazy, *stupid* plan of hers was going to work, or Espera was lost for good.

HOURS LATER, EACH AND EVERY ONE OF THEM WAS AT LEAST REASONABLY clean, if not a little damp and shivering in fresh outfits. Each girl wore a simple linen shift that left very little to the imagination where their wet hair fell against their bodies. They were free of their chain-line for the first time in weeks, but now they each had their original collars and a pair of manacles. Kidalma and the generals had paraded them into the tent again, but this time, Kai noted some differences. There were *refreshments* on a table against the opposite side of the canvas tent. At least a dozen goblets and multiple decanters of wine.

Kai's stomach sank as she realized what was about to happen. She looked around in panic, trying one last time to escape this.

She found Kidlama's clear-blue stare upon her. The old woman's leathered skin creased around her frown. Kidalma held Issaria's stare as she reached into her own skirt pocket and withdrew the tiny folded dancer. At the recognition of the memento, Issaria subtly brought her bound wrists to the side of her skirt and patted her leg. There *was* something there. She wanted to touch it, to make sure it really was her little paper cow, but Issaria snapped her gaze back to Kidalma instead. With a subtle shift of her silver hair, she nodded in confirmation before turning and leaving through the same flaps they'd entered through without a second glance.

Just as Jallah Coppernolle arrived with the rest of his horde.

Jallah came back to give them a final once-over. After Roark and Sethik lined them up along the far length of the tent, Jallah prowled the line. His dark eyes roved over their bodies hungrily as he paced back and forth before selecting his first girl. Cizabet, a pretty redhead with mossy eyes and long, willowy legs. Asmy, her younger sister who did not share her fair coloring, made to grab for Cizabet, to hold her back as Jallah yanked her forward, but the other girls in line restrained her. A wise move by the flicker of fire Kai glimpsed at Roark's fingertips.

Every inch of Cizabet shook as Jallah circled her, a vulture over carrion. He took her face in his hand and leaned in close, tilting her face as if to get a better look. Like she didn't just spend weeks traveling with him, waiting on him and his men hand and foot. He dropped his hand to her breast and gave a squeeze, bringing Cizabet to tears, her green eyes shimmering with her shame.

Issaria felt it then. A tap, deep inside her. Her anger had summoned it to the surface, and it wanted—

She closed her eyes and took a deep breath, bringing herself inward to that door. But it wasn't a door. It was a…it was a pond with a shimmering, iridescent surface. And she could see herself in it.

"Kai, are you okay?" Eiren whispered.

Kai opened her eyes and found the brunette looking at her, blue

266

eyes wide with alarm. Kai nodded, though it took some effort to make herself do so. She could still feel the tapping, see the ripples on the pond's surface. Each time they passed she could see...someone looking out at her from between the ripples. "I'm okay," she managed, and though she doubted Eiren bought it, it silenced her questions.

Cizabet had returned to the line and was shaking in Asmy's arms. The small brunette cradling the tall redhead seemed strange, and then Kai remembered it was Jallah they were dealing with. Cruelty was his specialty.

Each girl he yanked out of the line followed suit. He grabbed chins, jerking faces left and right; he made girls open their mouths, while he peeled back their gums and looked at their teeth. Rough hands gripped breasts and backsides. Tears rolled silently down cheeks while girls found anywhere else to look. He took his time going down the line, selecting girls at random. The longer it took, the more firmly Kai held her chin, scowl plastered on her face. Behind her in the line, Eiren shrank, whimpering at his approach.

When Jallah reached her, nearly three-fourths through the girls, he stopped and looked into her eyes. A small, knowing smile beneath his waxed mustache. "I see your eyes are still the most interesting shade of purple," he baited.

"Are they? I haven't seen my reflection in weeks. I do hope that beautician's drops weren't *permanent*."

"It would be a great offense to the Imperial family."

She wouldn't be goaded. Not by this slime. "Whatever's left of them after the Witch has her way."

Jallah's smile grew and for the first time, Issaria could see the hints of chestnut and gold in his cruel eyes. "I've seen enough," he declared, not taking his eyes off of her. "Bring them in."

Someone behind her gasped, and girls started moving around her. Chains rattled, and the girls broke into panicked whispers, but she held Jallah's stare. "This is going to be so much fun," he said so quietly, she wasn't sure she heard him. But she definitely heard him hiss, *"Princess,"* as he turned away from her and started toward the tent flaps.

Sethik and Roark peeled back the flaps of the tent and a drove of men entered, escorted by Curwin, Kyrel, and at least a dozen of Jallah's slavers. A perimeter was formed and the men shuffled about. Jallah wandered among them, shaking hands and pointing vaguely at random girls, directing their attention, Kai realized. The girls remained in their staggered line, still reeling from their examination. Jallah wandered closer, his hand on the shoulder of a tall dark-skinned man with brilliant cobalt eyes as he guided him toward Kai.

Jallah gestured down the line with an open hand. "Feel free to give them a preliminary inspection, Rohit. I know the king would want you to examine the wares since you're taking the five for such a *bargain*. They've all got their teeth, no addictions," he leaned in close to Rohit as he added, "But we can discuss means of control a little later, should the need arise." Jallah's crudeness never failed to amaze her. As they parted Jallah's black eyes met Kai's. "This one," he said, jerking his thumb in Kai's direction, "She's the one I wrote about initially."

"She looks like a drowned rat," said Rohit. He was a dark-skinned man with a long, thin nose that accentuated his distasteful expression in such a way, that Kai was certain he would always look upon her with that sneer. "What happened to her face? And she smells faintly, too."

"Maybe if I wasn't a *slave*, I'd smell like roses," she quipped, unable to keep her tongue.

Jallah laughed off Kai's remark. "Vicious little thing. But talented. She had my whole caravan in a frenzy after her show. Her face will heal. Its much better than it was a few days ago. I had to make a lesson out of one of my own to keep her pure for you. He...laid hands on her."

Rohit seemed a little *too* pleased to hear she'd been roughed up by one of Jallah's men. "And she's so pale. Doesn't she ever see the sun?"

"She's from Espera," Jallah said.

"Ares," Kai corrected. "I'm from Ares, though this pig caught me after I left Espera."

Rohit slapped her across the face.

It happened so fast, Kai was in shock. Her head snapped to one side, her cheek stinging as a welt began to form. "You'll mind your tongue in the White Palace, *slave.*"

She tasted copper and flicked her tongue out to test her busted lip. Issaria's glare deepened as Eiren drew her back. She brought a trembling hand to cup her cheek.

Jallah didn't even flinch, he just plowed on, "I've heard the brave prince would enjoy taming a wild creature or two, isn't that right?"

"I suppose Prince Calix might enjoy a spirited gift," Rohit replied, his blue eyes regarding her with disdain. "And if not, I'm sure the king would find her face pleasing. He is always looking for something *new* for his seraglio." He broke his gaze away and looked back to Jallah as he said, "And you said she's an entertainer? It would be most advantageous if that were true."

"Oh she can dance," Roark said thickly from his post by the door, jabbing Sethik in the side with his elbow.

"It's what made her worth so much Metal," Jallah said. "Five hundred golds for her."

Sethik, at least, had the decency to look ashamed when he met Kai's eyes.

"I'll pay double for her," said a voice from behind. "Triple, if you must."

Jallah and the heavy robed merchants that were admiring the other girls, fell silent. From the tent flap, just behind Sethik and Roark, a cloaked-figure stood gilded in sunlight. Jallah straightened and hooked his thumbs into the emerald zoster around his hips. "Come again, friend? That offer sounded a might generous for someone who hasn't even seen the wares yet."

The hooded figure remained on the threshold. Not in or out, but intruding and uninvited. Roark and Sethik each had a hand on their weapons, eyes darting between Jallah and the stranger. Kai's face remained stony as she looked between the two men who would hoped to own her, but inside, Issaria was bleating in panic. The hooded figure had a low voice that made the hair on the back of her neck stand on end despite the oppressive heat of Hinhallow. She was certain she'd heard it before but couldn't place to whom it belonged.

Ice shot down her spine at the thought that Aunt Cate may have sent mercenaries to hunt her down.

Kai peered at the figure, hoping to place a sigil or a face, but the man remained obscured beneath his hood. A thousand gold Metals was a small fortune. Too much for a single consort.

"I saw you unload them from the docks. The one you speak of now —black hair, pale skin. I'll buy her. Name your price."

Jallah's dark eyes were hooded in shadow. "She's promised to the king."

Kai's mouth went dry. It wasn't a refusal. Jallah was bargaining.

"My Master has been searching for one like her. I would not return empty handed." He made to enter the tent further, but Sethik stayed him with a hand on his shoulder. The man shook him off and looked back to Jallah. "Name your price."

After a long while Jallah said, "No deal, friend. Your Metal would not be worth the wrath of King Akintunde. I made him a promise. Were I to turn him away, he would be sure I never did business in this port again." He gave the figure a winning smile before adding a conde-scending, "You understand, *friend.*"

The figure stood there a moment too long. Kai couldn't tell where he was looking, but she could feel his eyes on her. Eyes that knew she was no Aresian dancer. She repressed a shudder as he turned on his heel and left without another word. The atmosphere in the tent was never pleasant, but it was somehow lighter after he left.

Until the bidding started.

Cyara, a dark-skinned girl from Nazarovo, deep in the Hollo-vanian territories, was first. So close to home and now she was here. She sold fast and was dragged from the tent by her new master. Issaria would never forget the look in her silver-blue eyes as she gave them all one last glance.

Iryna was next. Several men wanted to own her, and for obvious reason. She was easily the bustiest of them all, and still held a tiny hourglass figure. She had told them as much on the ship. Kai rolled her eyes as Iryna cast her a smug smile before flipping her damp hair over her shoulder and sauntering out on her owner's arm, his other hand on the leather leash he'd affixed to her collar.

The hardest to watch was Keely—the youngest of them. The man who paid for her made it known that her age was his preference. "Younger, next time," he said as he handed Jallah his metals and affixed a rope to the collar around Keely's neck. She tried to be brave, Kai could see it in the way she stuck out her chin, but no one could unsee the bald tears rolling down her face as her new master reined her in tight, fisted her tangle of blonde curls, and gave it a hearty whiff. "I'm going to treat you real nice, Felisa."

"M-my name is Keely," she stammered.

The man licked his lips before growling out, "Not anymore."

Issaria's heart broke. She wanted to throw up, sick from the injustice of it. But Kai was impervious to the horror she stood bearing witness to, and like Keely, she kept her chin up, her glare razor sharp. She'd crossed the Glass. She'd survived. And she was getting into that palace, and Cosmos be damned, she was going to free her city and stop atrocities like this. Her fury writhed inside her. Molten rage.

The girls went, one by one, and Jallah collected the Metals for each one. The more girls were sold, the larger his smile grew. And then Rohit stepped up and handed Jallah Coppernolle a fat pouch made of crimson velvet. It clinked, and Jallah's hand dropped slightly under the weight.

Jallah looked down the line of remaining women and met Kai's glare. His grin turned wicked and he blew her a goodbye kiss.

"You'll find it all there. And then some, to alleviate your pain for turning the other party away," Rohit said as he turned his attention to the line of girls. "King Akintunde greatly appreciates your loyalty to his crown…and to his delicacies." He strode down the line and began, "I'll take this one," he said pointing to a blonde in the group Kai hadn't interacted with. "And this one," he continued on, pointing to Rhaminta, who looked neither relieved nor disgusted but hesitant. She looked back to the blonde and gave her a nod; they were going together. They both stepped forward, and Jallah leashed them with braided ropes as white as sea-foam in moonlight.

"The redhead—"

"NO!" Asmy cried out, clinging to Cizabet, who'd already gone through so much. "You can't take my sister from me!"

Rohit gave her a shriveling glare and sniffed. "I can, and I will. You're too plain. Ruddy hair, watery eyes," he explained. His blue eyes were nothing but cruel malice as he failed to mask his disgust with them. Kai could hardly believe she'd thought them beautiful. "While your sister is quite interesting to look at with her russet hair and that lovely skin, so pale and freckled."

As he spoke, Curwin and Kyrel took a few steps toward us from their posts around the tent. Unsure if they intended to protect the girls or the patrons, Asmy shrank a little, but remained holding onto her sister's shoulders. Cizabet was collapsed around Asmy's neck, sobbing, "I love you, be brave. I love you, don't forget me. I love you."

"Please," Asmy begged. "Please don't take her away."

"Release the king's property, slave," he demanded, leaving his threat unfinished. *Or you'll lose more than just your sister.*

Curwin made it to them first and began to pry Cizabet from her sister. He didn't look happy to do so, but he gritted his teeth and wrenched them apart. Kyrel stepped in and held Asmy back as she began to thrash. She pounded her fists on Kyrel's chest, clawed and raged—and almost in irony, beneath their feet, like spring coming early, green shoots of grass accompanied by puffs of white clover heads pushed through the hard-packed earth with a shimmer of Terran magic. Asmy's heartbreak in that moment, whatever control she'd had on her power was shattered as her life, whatever was left of it now, was torn before her eyes.

Issaria understood then, what Kidalma had said about their powers, and being unable to fight back against their enslavement. If that was the best she could do—grow some pretty flowers—Issaria shuddered to think even *touching* her own power would do to Curwin, to Rohit and Kyrel. She looked at Kyrel again.

Beneath his mop of mahogany hair, his eyes were clenched. And he didn't hurt Asmy, in fact, Issaria looked closer and saw what perhaps no one else did in that moment. He was hugging her to keep her from her Cizabet. To protect her from what would undoubtedly happen if she further disrupted Jallah's auction.

Cizabet was limp as Rohit shoved her toward Jallah. How he kept a blank face as he wrenched *families* apart for profit...Issaria saw red. And then she heard the voice.

You can stop this.

It was like thunder clapping in her head.

"I'll find you again," Asmy shouted as she snarled and shoved against Kyrel's thick arms. "I promise, Ciz. I promise!"

We can end *this.*

"This little viper, of course—"

Issaria's mind went white as Rohit pointed at her. She knew it was what she wanted. To get to Blaze. For Elon and Rhori, for Safaia, Isida and Daphnica, for Magistrate Caltac— for *all* of Espera.

She *would* do this. She wouldn't fight it.

"And this one should be the last," Rohit said as he gestured vaguely to Eiren, still shrinking behind Kai, who hadn't flinched when she was chosen. "Get them in my carriage. I've spent too much time wallowing." He didn't look back to see if his orders were carried out as he left the tent.

If Jallah understood that he'd been insulted, he didn't betray it as he produced similar white ropes for Kai and Eiren and affixed them to their collars. Sethik and Roark led them unceremoniously from the tent and escorted them to a square black carriage that was neither ornate enough to have come from the palace, nor dingy enough to be from the market. Rohit was already perched on the coachman's seat, reins in hand for a team of four brown horses. Their tails swished back and forth, shooing flies as they shifted uncomfortably in the heat.

"Come now, get them in. I haven't got all day," Rohit said.

Sethik rolled his eyes as he turned his back on the King's lackey. He opened the carriage door and ushered the girls in one at a time. Each pair of manacles fell away at the turn of a key before each one stepped into the carriage and scooted close to the girl before her, trying to make room for all five of them in a carriage only reasonably meant for four, until they were all crammed into the seating compartment. Issaria settled in last, practically sitting on Rhaminta's lap.

"Don't cause too much trouble," Sethik said to them, but his verdant gaze was locked on Kai. "Merry meet."

Then the door snicked shut and they were on their way, carriage rolling across the cobblestones. Kai pressed her face to the window and looked back at the canvas tent. It looked so much like every other makeshift waypoint on the docks in Hinhallow. Hard to tell that lives were changed there only moments ago. That lives were still being changed. There were at least a dozen girls left when they'd been purchased. She wondered what would happen to the rest of them. To Thalia who'd broken her nose to look like too much trouble for a brothel or a bed. She sighed and watched the city change as the carriage clattered along.

The tent was well out of view when Issaria realized that, for all his teasing, Jallah didn't even have a final quip for her. In the end, all he'd ever cared about was the money.

They were rolling through the upper rings of the township when Cizabet, still sniffling in the corner and staring blankly out the window, said, "The flowers Asmy summoned are the same ones that grow in a field by our farmhouse in Snovic in the summers."

A hush grew over the girls, who had been tittering excitedly about what the palace would be like.

"When we were girls we would pick the clovers. As many as we could carry in our aprons." Cizabet smiled, for a second, at the memory. "We would sit for hours on the hilltop behind Snovic overlooking the village and the Almystrov and make crowns from the flowers." She was silent for a moment before adding, "Asmy made the best ones all braided together and they lasted for days. It was years before we figured out it was her talent, but I think she knew all along. She just liked making the good things last. Even in our last moments, she was still trying to make something good for me."

"They won't be your last moments, Cizabet," said Eiren, as she put a hand on her knee in condolence. "You'll see her again. She said so. She's going to fight to come get you."

Cizabet didn't blink as she continued to stare out the window but replied, "I'd be foolish to hope for that, and we both know it. I don't know what I expected to happen—that we would be sold together to a little old couple who would treat us like their daughters?" She scoffed. "I'm not that foolish, and neither is Asmy."

25

ISSARIA

The carriage arrived at the White Palace, aptly named for its white stone walls and massive spires that speared the sky with shining gold domes. Rohit wasted no time in hastening the girls across the yard, leading them by the length of their ropes like wayward sheep. They were deep within the palace when Rohit brought them back into the daylight. They had exited the keep of the White Palace, and into the inner gardens.

A pond with fat orange and white koi fish that swam lazily beneath lily pads was surrounded by a series of large pagodas. They coexisted, separate but sharing the same space by way of a grid of interlocking paths. In the garden, soft white sand wove between blue and purple hydrangea bushes and tall skinny trees with jade leaves. Around the buildings, arching alabaster porticos drooped with fat, purple wisteria blooms that battled golden star-shaped honeysuckle climbing the columns.

If it weren't her new prison, it would be beautiful, but all Kai saw was a pretty cage—and a mouth to the lion's den.

Across the garden courtyard, a spire of the White Palace rose up, and at its base, a door at which there was not one, but two guards in crimson livery, chatting idly with each other. Someone important lived in that tower and she was willing to bet it was her new master. Of course he'd want to be close to his new toys. Her stomach roiled with the thought.

Rohit continued to lead them toward one of the buildings when a tall blond man exited the tower in question, and when he spotted their little troupe, he made in their direction. Kai looked from Rohit to the approaching man, wondering if *this* was Prince Calix Ballentine.

Kai cast a glance at the other girls and could tell from their curious expressions that they were wondering the same thing. Rhaminta caught her eye, quirked a dark eyebrow, and gave Kai a devilish smirk as she looked back to the prince with appraising eyes. Issaria turned her attention back to the blond as he cut across the garden path.

He wasn't bad to look at. Tall, definitely the warrior-type if she had to judge by his physique. He'd fit right in with Elon and the others on the Imperial Guard. His dark eyes were pools of honey as he stepped into the harsh sunlight. Bronzed skin was taut across the exposed slice of chest where his indigo tunic was open. His hair was long enough that it brushed the tops of his broad shoulders.

"You're late," he said to Rohit as he mounted the stairs two at a time.

"There was a commotion. I was delayed."

"Not my problem." He held out his hand, palm up and waiting. "King Akintunde sent me to relieve you. He requests your presence in the Blue Room."

Rohit hesitated, his fists clenching on their ropes. "And what of them?"

"Another problem I wish weren't mine, but it is. I'm getting them settled. The king wants to see them when he's done with you."

Rohit pursed his lips before handing over the rope leashes. "Very well, Evanoff. See them to their pavilion," he said, then retreated quickly back the way they came. Issaria was sure that as soon as he was out of sight of the girls he would be running to wherever the Blue Room was.

She was yanked forward by her collar. "Ungh! Watch it!"

Their new blond escort glanced over his shoulder. "Eyes forward, Miss, and it wouldn't have happened."

Forced to keep pace with the rest of the girls, Kai glared at Evanoff. "It wouldn't have happened if I wasn't forced to wear this collar."

He cast her a sidelong glance as they turned toward a white building with a copper roof supported by thick dark oak beams. "You were the commotion, weren't you?"

Behind them, the girls giggled, and Rhaminta flat out snorted. Kai cut her a withering glare at the betrayal before turning back to their caretaker. "With good reason." She paused, considering if it was worth the risk. This man clearly wasn't the prince but...he was part of the palace staff. Perhaps... "I'm looking for someone, actually. They work here in the palace."

"No one can help your situation, girlie," he said flatly.

"I don't need help," she snapped. Indeed, she was exactly where she wanted to be, if not in the exact manner she intended.

"For what it's worth, I would take this collar off of you if I could. None of the king's girls have collars. Rohit's a little slime ball. Even Calix doesn't like him."

Issaria's attention piqued at mention of the prince. "You know him?"

Evanoff shrugged. "I might. I know a lot of people in the palace. Benefit of being a Kingsguard," he said with a wink.

Maybe this Evanoff knew Blaze too, if he knew the prince. She just had to find Blaze and then he could—what *could* he do? What place did an assassin have in the court of fire? Something, hopefully. Otherwise this was more of a disaster than she wanted to consider.

"His name is Blaze and—"

This time Evanoff snorted. "That's a stupid name."

"That's what I said," she sighed. "It's an alias."

"How can you look for someone if you don't even know their name?"

She rolled her eyes. "I was going to describe him to you, rock head."

And for a moment, Issaria was back in Espera, teasing Elon or Rhori about something in the shadow of the Crystal Palace. Her heart ached and she bit down on her tears as they continued to walk.

They reached the pavilion and he opened the dark wood double doors. Eiren couldn't hold back a shocked gasp as they stood in the doorway to their room—no, a suite of rooms, complete with a common sitting area full of plush chaises and lounge chairs, bookcases and musical instruments and even an easel waited in the wings. A hearth housed glowing solarium geodes and white alabaster columns carved in scrolling filagree like lace ringed the room. Flowers spilled from vases on every tabletop, and in the dining room, the table was full of food, apples and venison, cranberry and walnut glazed ham, and tiers of tortes and cakes, little biscuits, and a steaming kettle of tea.

Cylise, the blonde who's name Kai hadn't known before, gave a great sigh as she took the first steps into the room. Her bare feet, still caked with dirt and dust, fell upon the soft white carpet that extended around the sitting area. She looked back over her shoulder at the girls still lingering in the doorway. "Oh, I think I'm gonna like it here, girls."

Eiren giggled and entered the room next, going as far as to sit on a fat turquoise pouf. She actually groaned. That was all it took for the other girls to push their way in and start touching and eating and laughing—a reward for all they'd endured. To end up here. In a damn palace. Kai lingered in the doorway with Evanoff. He still held her leash in his hand, half-forgotten as he'd let everyone else slip through his fingers as they walked past him. But that wasn't what held her in place.

This was the first time most of these girls had seen such finery. Guilt filled her mouth with a sour taste. Issaria grew up with this, was returning to it like a lost child and she realized how much she didn't belong with these girls, finding life as a palace concubine to be a gift from the Cosmos.

And how badly she wanted to. How easy it would be to be Kai. To be here, with these girls, living like sisters in these beautiful rooms.

Rhaminta squealed, "Have you *seen* the bedrooms? They're divine!" And the girls each raced to claim a bedroom.

Kai looked to Evanoff. "There were circumstances surrounding our meeting that made names dangerous. He's got black hair and golden eyes. And his hands…they're really black."

Evanoff's eyes flashed but he shrugged in that nonchalant way he had. "Maybe if he gave you a fake name, this Blaze fellow doesn't want you to know who he really is."

Issaria narrowed her eyes at him. "Then why would he tell me where to find him? He said I could ask for him at the palace."

He shrugged again. If he was going to say more, they would never know.

Eiren ran back into the common area beckoned to Kai with frantic hands. "Kai, you have got to see this. There's a steaming bathing pool in the back that's just for us! C'mon, there are flowers in it. It's huge!"

"Now that *is* something. Solarium hot springs for the concubines. Even the soldiers don't have that," Evanoff scoffed. Then he was standing at attention, ramrod-straight and saluting. "Your Majesty."

Issaria turned in the doorway and had to tilt her head to meet the eye of the King of Hinhallow.

Akintunde Ballantine.

He loomed over her like a mountain. His broad shoulders blotted out the sun. Similar to Jallah, the king also wore his hair shaved to his scalp on one side of his head, and the remaining locks of tousled silver and black were styled over the opposite side of his skull. Unlike the ugly scars that had bisected Coppernolle's scalp, King Akintunde's flesh was decorated in the sharp, precise lines of black tattoos. Bold, black lines and smooth spirals crawled down the back of his neck where more black bands wrapped around his thick neck above and below his collarbone. His beard was kept close to his chiseled face, dark and streaked with silver like a storm cloud. His hazel eyes glinted with gold as he looked down on her.

"Oh, I like this one," he said as she met his stare. "Excellent eyes. How *did* you do that? No! Don't tell me. I enjoy the mystique." He turned to Rohit, dwarfed by the king's presence, and said, "Tell me the others look like her."

"I selected a variety," he said scooting past the King's elbow to enter the pavilion. "Girls! Your presence, *immediately!*" he called shrilly. "The king wishes to view his purchases!"

Footsteps sounded on the floors as they all came running from inspecting various areas of the pavilion house. Eiren was already there, on her knees and eyes on the floor. Cylise and Rhaminta came in from different bedrooms immediately off the hall, and Cizabet arrived last, but it was her who made the king grin again. Upon seeing Eiren in subjective posture, they all in turn sank to their knees and kept bent heads before him.

It took Issaria a moment to realize that she, too, should be kneeling before him. She'd never knelt before a monarch before; that was one of the first things her father had taught her. *Even as a child, you are* Imperial. *We are of the very Cosmos themselves. You bow to no one, my little star.*

In that moment, it was decided. It was still too risky to be Issaria. This king had no affiliation to her, had not been the one to promise her safety. She could *only* reveal herself to Blaze. Anything else could end her life before Blaze even knew she was here.

Kai sank to a curtsey and held the position until he grunted and they all looked up to meet his assessing gaze.

"You may rise."

When they were all standing before him, Kai scampered down the stairs and joined the girls before King Akintunde descended. Much like Jallah had done, he walked back and forth before them as he looked each girl over, nodding eagerly.

"Well done, Rohit. Well done indeed." He reached out and fingered the rope and collar on Rhaminta's caramel throat before twirling one of her sable curls between his fingers. "Which one is the dancer? Step forward."

Heads swiveled in Kai's direction. Even if she hadn't wanted to reveal herself, the group's reaction to the question betrayed her. Kai stepped forward, jutting her chin out. "I am, your Majesty."

The King chuckled, and Kai's breath stilled in her chest. Had she offended him? She'd heard of how ruthless the Warlord of the West was.

"Oh yes, I like her a lot." He stood in front of her again and considered. His hazel eyes lingered on her breasts, on the curve of her hips. Kai flushed at his heavy gaze. At last he said, "My son will be crowned as my heir in a week. I have made certain promises of entertainment to my court. You will be it. Jallah has written me extensively about your abilities, and I am most excited to see your performance."

"I'm grateful, and honored, Sire," Kai lied.

"You are *all* to be a gift to him from me. He's got a girl to marry but…a man needs release and to satisfy his needs." As if he had to justify his purchase of five young women from a man who called himself the Merchant of Men. "After the vows and the ceremony and the tedious bit, before the festivities begin, I want to have you dance like you did for Jallah. All of you. Show him what a woman can be."

"Sire," Cylise peeped, and the king's head swiveled to land his amber eyes upon hers. "Beg pardon, for the interruption, my King, but only Kai can dance."

Rhaminta scoffed. "I can dance. Maybe not as good as Miss twirls-and-hips over there, but I can dance."

The king arched an eyebrow and looked back at Kai. The unasked question hung in the air. Would she teach them—*could* she teach them a routine and have them dance at the coronation in a week?

Issaria weighed her options. The king—the very person she wanted to speak with, to plead with for soldiers and aid for her city—was right here. Standing a meter away. This would delay her, if she committed to it. But Eiren's azure eyes were wide, and Rhaminta had crossed her arms over her chest in a challenge to just *try* and upstage her.

They deserved this. They could be happy here, in the luxury and safety of the palace. It was something she could give these girls who had already lost so much. Cizabet seemed to sense Kai's deliberation and offered a timid, "I'd be willing to learn if…you'd be willing to teach me."

"Well, what do you say then, Kai?" The King askcd as he stroked his beard with a broad hand.

She would only be delayed a week. Her city was strong, and they had Elon looking after them for her. She had to trust him, like he trusted that she would get her and get the help they so desperately needed. Elon wouldn't tell Issa to turn her back on the people of Ellorhys now, not when they were suffering too. It was only a week. And when she was certain they were safe and secure here in the palace, Kai would tell them who she really was.

"I'll do it."

26

ISSARIA

By midweek the girls weren't terrible. They weren't good, but considering they'd only spent the first afternoon in the palace working on the basic positions…they were definitely *not* terrible.

They had pushed all the sitting room furniture aside and rolled up the white fluffy rug that they had all luxuriated over and made a dance studio. The dining room table, which had never been as full as that first night, now served as the barre, where they now stretched after a rigorous session in which Kai corrected feet, hips, and hands. Lunch was arriving soon, and they were famished. Even Kai's voice hurt from shouting the tempo; *one-two-threefour, one-two-threefour.*

Rhaminta, as promised, was a natural at the basics, but the king didn't want ballerinas, and she had a hard time losing control. Letting go of her lessons went against her muscle memory. No one was more frustrated with it than she.

It only made her work harder.

Cizabet had also taken to it with abandon. Kai was impressed with the excitement with which she embraced her natural talent when they heard her cry herself to sleep at night. But Issaria remembered the words she'd said in the carriage, and she knew that smiling, laughing, *dancing* in the face of her heartbreak, was what Asmy would have wanted for her sister. What she *herself* would be doing...wherever she'd ended up. They hoped.

But Asmy knew where her sister was. And that was something. Even if Cizabet didn't believe it herself.

Eiren was the worst of them, all legs and no rhythm. It took Kai almost a day and a half to get her to stop dancing off beat, and on the third day, she was no closer to being presentable than when they'd started. Kai wasn't quite sure what to do about that.

And finally, there was Cylise, the blonde Kai hadn't known. Her hazel eyes glinted with copper flecks in the sunshine and her lithe, tanned body looked wonderful as she posed in long *arabesques,* but she struggled with moving from pose to pose without falling apart between.

Kai's head was throbbing when Rhaminta climbed the small stair set to the large double doors and said over her shoulder, "It smells like sweat in here. I'm going to open the doors for a little."

"Is that a good idea?" Cylise said, almost reading Kai's mind.

"Rhaminta, the king himself said for us to stay hidden until after the coronation," Eiren cautioned as she turned from where she was braiding her long, chestnut brown hair against the back porch doors, already thrown wide against the stench.

"It's only for a little bit," Rhaminta parried as she reached the doors and opened one, then the other. She stood in the doorway and spread her arms wide. "Besides, lunch will be here in a little. We can shut them again after we eat."

As one, each head in the room swiveled to Kai, as if asking her approval on the matter. It was happening more and more as they spent time together, dancing, talking, and laughing as they splashed each other in the lagoon-like bath house tiled behind the pavilion. Somehow, they'd elected Kai their leader. Deep down, Issaria felt proud that somehow, even as a slavegirl, she was a leader among them. Her father and mother would have been proud. Elon would have made sure to tell her so.

She swallowed the thought as she shrugged. "Just until after lunch.

Then we can shut them again and get back to practicing. The coronation is only a few days away and we have a lot of work to do."

Rhaminta, rolled her eyes as she returned to the barre and propped her leg up. "We worked enough this morning. When are you going to tell us about your mysterious *Blaze?*"

Kai felt her face redden as she crossed her arms over her chest. "He's nothing. No one."

"Didn't seem that way when you were talking with that Evanoff guy. Black hair, golden eyes?" Rhaminta teased. Dark brown eyes glittered with mischief as she added, "Those black hands sounded sexy. Is he a handsome fellow?"

"Oh that's right!" Cylise chirped. "Is he your lover?"

"My lover? No!" Kai exclaimed, waving her hands as if to shoo away the idea. "Absolutely not. He's just...someone I know. And he works here in the palace."

"And *who* exactly, are all of you?" a disdainful female voice quipped from behind them and Kai felt as though molten alloy had been dribbled down her spine.

They were supposed to remain hidden. The king made that much perfectly clear.

Kai shot a murderous glare at Rhaminta for opening the doors. "We're guests of the king," she said, giving no further explanation as she turned to face the woman in the doorway.

The brown-haired woman put her hands on her hips as if to say, *Is that so?* "And what are you doing in the West Pavilion?" Her pretty face furrowed in rage as her eyes darted from girl to girl.

"We're practicing for the coronation by request of the king himself." Kai replied as she lifted her chin as she met the other woman's emerald gaze. "Perhaps it is we who should be asking who *you* are."

Next to her, Eiren bit back a nervous giggle as the woman sized Kai up with a heated glare.

The brunette took three haughty steps into their pavilion, stopped at the top of the stairs and stared down the steps at Kai and the other girls. She was dressed elegantly in a silk peach-colored dress threaded heavily with gold. It featured a high, tight collar of lace that framed the woman's long throat. Her dark brown hair was piled on her head in curls and braids, and it was clear she'd spent some time on her makeup as well. "*I* am the prince's fiancé. *Princess* Shairi Chrysanthos of Ares." She looked them over again, her green eyes roaming their sweat-sheen shine in every shade of moonlight and earth between them before falling on the collar around their necks. "And as such, you will address me with respect," she spat, "slave."

Their leashes had been removed, but the alloy collars remained in place as symbols of their servitude until their presence in the palace was made public.

Though her face burned with the embarrassment at facing down yet another monarch with a slave collar around her neck, Kai held her ground. She felt the other girls shrink back at the princess's declaration and obvious hatred for them, but she arched an eyebrow and smirked. "Oh, then I suppose we really should be introduced properly," Kai said as she stepped forward and took the stairs to meet the Aresian Princess at eye level. "I'm called Kai. Your prince's new consort." She let her bite find its mark before she continued. "King Akintunde bought me special, just for the Crown Prince, he said." She gestured behind her at the other girls as Shairi's green eyes ignited from within. "We all are. Isn't that right, girls?"

"Actually, Kai, the king said that he wanted us as gifts for the Prince," Eiren corrected, finding her voice.

"*You're* the one who's supposed to show him what a woman can be, Kai," Rhaminta said as if she didn't even want to contend with Kai for the pleasure.

"You're lying," Shairi hissed.

"Are we? It's strange that we've been here for days and we've only just now seen you," Kai mused. "We've been busy you see, preparing for the moment the king unveils us."

"At the coronation," Cizabet chimed in.

"So you can see if Kai is lying then," Cylise finished with a satisfied *hmph.*

"Calix isn't a heathen like his—" She caught herself and said, "like *some men,"* instead. "He doesn't seek the company of concubines."

"We prefer to be called consorts," Rhaminta snapped. "Or courtesans, at the very least."

"Ladies!" a shrill voice sounded from behind them. In the doorway, two women from the kitchen they'd come to know as Marni, the head cook, and Aleida, one of her assistants, had come bearing trays of sandwiches and fruits for the girls. "The king told you to stay out of sight!"

"Aw, I'm sorry Marni," Rhaminta said. "It was just so hot in here, and I didn't want you fussing with the door when your hands are full." She swooped up the stairs with Cylise on her heels. Rhaminta took Marni's tray and gave the plump brunette a warm smile.

Cylise took Aleida's tray and the short blonde shied back from touching Cylise's hands. If she saw the motion, Cylise pretended not to notice as she brought it down to the table, no longer used as a barre while the girls ate.

"It won't happen again," Kai said as she gestured out the door for all the ladies to exit. "I promise. I'll shut the doors right now, even." This seemed to satisfy the cook, as Marni waved them off as she turned to go. "We'll have the trays and plates done when you come back. See you soon," Kai said, then looked pointedly at the princess and gave her a radiant smile. "Though I suppose I'll see the prince before I see you, Princess."

Princess Shairi's face paled as she realized the implication of Kai's words. The prince would be seeing Kai, and maybe the other girls, any time he wasn't warming Shairi's bed. And that thought would haunt her.

Kai didn't relish the idea of bedding the prince, or being cruel to Shairi, who for all she knew was truly in love with him. Kai could have had just broken her heart. But these girls had gone through too much to be looked down on now. And not by some princess who'd never known the fear they had, the danger and abuse. While they were in this palace together, Kai was going to protect them.

✳ ✦ ✳

THE DAY OF THE CORONATION, NO LESS THAN TWO DOZEN DRESS BOXES were delivered to the pavilion with a handwritten note that said, *For the true gems of the gala. Do not disappoint. King Akin.*

Within were swaths of dresses and skirts in sheer silk and gauze. Peach, russet orange, emerald greens and turquoise blues. Each box was feathers and jewels and fabric shimmering in golden sunlight.

The girls went wild at the sight of such finery.

All of it. For them.

Cizabet seized the fox mask, bejeweled with citrine and quartz. It would do well against her plait of fire-orange hair. "Oh, give me the orange one; I want to be the fox!"

"What's this pink thing?" Cylise asked, picking up a mask that looked to be carved of pink scales.

"This one looks like a swan!" Eiren called, hoisting a white feathered mask with a gilded point above the brow like a beak.

"That's not a swan! It's a unicorn! Anyone can see that!" Rhaminta laughed as she swiped it from Eiren. "This little filigree part is a horn! See how it sparkles? Beaks don't sparkle!"

"Neither do foxes but look at me!" Cizabet called as she turned her face into the sunlight and set the gemstones on her fox mask agleam like a blaze of autumnal fury.

Kai picked up the closest item as the girls claimed dresses and began to strip, trying them on right there. It was a mask made of dark shimmering feathers of emerald and turquoise, and indigo blue. Peacock feathers were elegantly molded across the mask and flared out from the ends, over where one's hair would be beneath it.

Rhaminta plucked it right out of her fingers. "I'll be the peacock, if you don't mind. Unlike you, *I'm* actually from Ares." The Aresian flag bore the peacock as it's sigil, violet on a field of turquoise.

"I'm from Ares," Kai replied too quickly and tried not to wince at her amateur mistake.

"Uh-huh," was all Rhaminta said as she quirked a dark eyebrow at her and gave her an expectant look.

"I did travel with my troupe a lot though, so I can see how you'd think I'm not from there. I guess the road was always my home?" She tried not to make it sound like a question but Kai wasn't sure how much of Kai they were buying anymore.

The more the girls were together, the more they talked about home and their lives on farms and in fishing villages. Cizabet was in love with a woodsman in her village. Cylise's mother had expected her home from the market the night Jallah took her. Rhaminta was even an equestrian dancer back in Ares, the city Kai had blurted out as her hometown.

At the time, she'd just kept on chewing her sandwich. Slowly waiting for the conversation to dip past Ares and sail straight on to whatever equestrian dancing was—some sort of rhythmic horseback riding, Rhaminta tried to explain. *"You'd have to see it to get it. You can't just imagine the magic. You have to be there and see it with the horses and music,"* she'd said, but the girls pressed and Rhaminta had given Kai a sidelong glance before launching into a detailed explanation of equestrian dancing.

By the look on Rhaminta's face in the moment, Kai was pretty sure her luck had run out in one way or another. "I really am a dancer. Sort of," she offered with a shrug. Aunt Hecate had been adamant about Issaria being proficient in the arts and all things lady-like. Dance lessons were among one of the first things she had her learn as a way to enforce discipline and keep her from running wild. Calling herself a dancer was true enough.

"If you're not ready to trust us, after everything you've done for us, after what you did for *me,* and again after you—" Rhaminta cut herself off, and Kai looked up. Her dark brown eyes were glistening with unshed tears. She sniffed hard, and the other girls in the room fell quiet amid their elated displays of bejeweled tops that hugged their breasts and little more, the matching hip-bustled skirts that shimmered when they moved as Kai had instructed for these past few days.

"After you stayed with us when you could have told them who you are."

The girls all looked between Kai and Rhaminta.

"What do you mean, Mint?" Cizabet asked as Rhaminta cast her amber eyes to Kai. "Who does she think you are?"

Kai looked between Rhaminta, on the verge of tears and the other expectant stares. "Well, I…" She looked down at her hands where the peacock mask had been moment before—where her Kai mask had been only a breath before. "I might be no one, now," she said as quiet as she could.

"Don't say that!" Rhaminta hissed, and the tears that clung like diamonds to her dark lashes plunged down her bronzed cheeks. "You said she tried to kill you." Issaria clenched her eyes against it, but her voice was whisper soft as Rhaminta pressed, "That's why you crossed the Glass. It was because she tried to kill you and now you're here looking for someone who can help you."

"We can…talk about that after the coronation."

"As you wish, *Princess*." She let the word fall between them, and Issaria's eyes snapped open to meet Cizabet's mossy stare from behind Rhaminta's looming form.

"Mint, are you saying Kai is…is…" Cizabet couldn't seem to bring herself to finish her thought. Her eyes were locked on Issaria's, examining the deep hue of them. Perhaps recalling the way Kai never really met anyone's eyes.

Rhaminta thrust the unicorn mask into Issaria's waiting hands. "Try this one. White looks good on you and I think the white skirt Eiren kicked aside had some purplish accents— to match your eyes." Issaria snapped her attention from Cizabet to Mint and met her dark eyes, still rife with tears. Fabric shuffled and the skirts in question were passed up from hand to hand until they reached Rhaminta, but still she did not look away. "We could help you, you know. We want to."

The words resonated, and Issaria glanced around the room. Besides Mint, only Eiren seemed unaffected by the sudden revelation, even if nothing had really been said. She met Eiren's steady blue eyes. The brunette nodded and said, "You spoke in your sleep on the ship. Nightmares about being caught by *Cate*."

Issaria felt her heart snap in two. They'd known all along who she was. And they helped her keep her secret.

"Why now?" she asked in a whisper. "Why do you need to know now?"

"Because tonight things change. You become Kai for real if you go out there and...you don't really know what's going to happen after that."

"None of us do," Eiren added.

"He could be cruel, like Zhaniel," Mint said, a shudder coursing down her spine at the memory of almost being taken by him. She looked to Issaria and said, "We won't be there to stop him."

"He owns you now, Kai. He has the right to do whatever he wants," Cylise said. "That's what being a slave is. What being here in the pavilion means. This is the prince's seraglio—just like the king's."

"You let him own you," Mint whispered. "For *us.*"

Quiet befell them again. Only the rustle of fabric and the occasional clink of gemstones could be heard against the dull buzz of insects in the garden beyond.

"He already keeps one princess—Shairi. We met her the other day. That's when I knew for sure who you were. I could see it in you when you stood next to her," she said in a rush. "Don't let him keep you too. Ares is in Hinhallow's grasp because Fraxinus' daughter is *here.*" Mint clutched Issaria's shoulder. "You're scared of Cate? Cate should be scared of Akintunde. He's set up a dynasty to conquer her."

"And now I'm here."

"Cosmos above," Cizabet gasped, her hand flying to cover her mouth. "She's the—"

Issaria took a deep breath before letting it out and saying, "If Akintunde can help me get my city back, then it's *me* Cate should be scared of."

"Is that the plan?" Eiren asked. "To ask him for help?"

"Not exactly," Issaria confessed.

"It's the Blaze-fellow, isn't it?" Rhaminta asked again.

Kai nodded. "It is. I met him when I was...home," she said, choosing her words very carefully. "He told me enough of the truth that...that I realized I was in very real danger. And I had been for some time. So when it happened I had help getting out."

They all stood, half-in, half-out of their dresses and stockings, masks askew.

"After the coronation we will have free rein of the Pavilion. We can go out to the gardens and probably other places too. We can ask magicians other than that admittedly-rather handsome Evanoff oaf about Blaze." Rhaminta took Issaria's hands in hers. "We're sure to find him with all of us looking."

Issaria looked from Mint to Eiren, who said, "You still have help," which brought hot tears to her eyes.

She clenched her eyes as the tears spilled over and whispered, "Thank you, thank you." Mint wrapped her arms around her shoulders, allowing Issaria to put her face into her friend's stomach as she cried.

Then she felt a second set of arms and a third, and then a fourth as Cylise completed their little huddle.

Finally Eiren said from somewhere in the tangle of their limbs, "I'm all for this mushy-sister stuff, but we do have a party to get ready for, and I, for one, want to bathe."

Cizabet giggled and their cluster dismantled, each girl dispersing to claim the pieces of her costume from the piles on the floor before retreating to ready themselves.

The last to let go was Mint. She looked down at Issaria, still seated on a chaise in the sitting area, and brushed back her bangs from her eyes. "I'm going to make you look like the true terror that *both* monarchs should fear. May I braid your hair?"

She only nodded in reply.

And so, Issaria helped Rhaminta gather items for both the swan costume—"Unicorn!" She was corrected over and over—and then helped her destroy an unclaimed brassiere to harvest the smokey quartz and shimmering pearls from its embroidery for use in the braids Mint envisioned for her.

When they were through, Rhaminta sectioned out Issaria's hair and wove thick braids and thin, threaded through with the stolen gemstones before being knotted on the opposite side of her head with a feather-and-gilt barrette that scooped her mass of braids and tumbling curls into a cascade of starlit sky. The swan mask was affixed firmly to her head, the black ribbon wound tight between braids.

When she was finished, Mint gave her a mirror and said, "I wore braids like this when I did my equestrian dancing. My gran told me that they're special, passed down from when her people were still tribesmen in the Rilaan's peaks and we were a warrior people."

Issaria reached up a hand and touched the braids, tight to the side of her head in intertwining loops of raven-black hair. "A fierce look, indeed," she replied, not missing the message behind such an updo.

War was inevitable, and Issaria was no longer just a scared little girl running for her life. After this—whatever the coronation led to— she was going to fight to get back what was hers.

"Aren't you ready yet?" Rohit's unmistakable snivel sounded from the sitting area. "I've come to remove your collars before the show."

"Finally," Issaria grumbled as she and Mint returned to the sitting room to find Rohit and Evanoff, who bore some sinister looking tool in his hand.

One by one he clipped their collars off with the scissor-like tool, and handed the broken halves to Rohit, who disposed of them in a burlap sack. Evanoff let himself look over the girls as they arrived in various stages of dress and undress, but none as fiercely as he did Kai.

"Somehow, you look like more trouble now than you did when you got here," Evanoff quipped as he positioned the sharp blade just below her ear.

Issaria leaned her head as far away from the blades as possible as they crimped down and pinched right through the thick alloy. When her collar was in pieces and she could rub the welts that had formed on her collarbone and shoulders, she looked him over once before shrugging. "I *suppose* you look like one of the Kingsguard. Your hair looks a mess, but you look better than you have. Though I've no idea why you're playing locksmith to us *slaves*."

Her retort on his somewhat less than standard appearance of military grey made him scoff and when they were all collar-free, Evanoff took the sack of collars, his tool, and left without looking back.

Rohit looked the girls over. "The coronation is beginning shortly. Everyone is assembling in the grand hall, where you will perform. The colored smoke will be your entrance." He narrowed his intensely blue eyes at Kai and sneered, "For your sake I hope you're all prepared."

Issaria glared daggers at the king's lackey. "Remember this moment, Rohit," Kai said softly. "I know I will."

"What is that supposed to mean, slavegirl?" He asked vehemently. "Is that a threat?"

Issaria turned her voice syrup-sweet. "Of course not, Rohit. I just want you to know that I'll always remember how kind you were in *obtaining* us from Jallah's care."

Rohit tucked his hands into the sleeves of his robes. "Mind your place, slave." He looked over her head to the rest of the girls. "I'll be back in an hour to deliver you for your performance. Do be ready."

And then he left them.

"Do be ready," Cylise mimicked in a high pitched, nasally voice.

"Ugh, I hate him," Cizabet groaned in agreement.

Rhaminta's gaze lingered on the doors through which Rohit had left. She sighed before turning back to them. "Let's finish up. We're running out of time and I haven't even started my *own* hair."

"Whose fault is that," Issaria replied coyly.

Mint cast her a smug smile before retreating to work on herself. "Get dressed, *Princess*. Your handsome prince awaits your seductive dance!" She taunted from down the hall.

The girls broke out into giggles from their various rooms, and Issaria gathered several white-and-purple items from the piles to assemble a suitable outfit for their dance.

When Rohit returned, in an hour exactly, all the girls were dressed in scantily clad masquerade, silk scarfs clutched in their hands. Alloy bracelets, bangles, and anklets tinkled on wrists and ankles. Gems sparkled across low-riding waists and the curve of breasts. Ribbons and lace gathered skirts in semi-transparent layers.

Each girl was as perfect as she was going to get. They knew enough, she told herself. They knew enough to survive one song. One dance.

Rohit met Issaria's eyes and asked, "Are you ready?"

She gave a sharp nod. "We are."

27

CALIX

Calix stood behind the heavy crimson curtains, peeking out at the growing crowd in the hall. His father really had pulled out all the stops for the occasion and spared no expense. The glittering chandeliers were lit with hundreds of solarium crystals, casting the hall in a warm, buttery glow. The alabaster pillars that ensconced the hall were wreathed in garlands of crimson and gold silks braided with burgundy flowers and yellow sprigs of buds. The floral accents continued on banquet tables laden with roasted pig, and goat, plated whole with open mouths spewing flowers and berries. Plates of cheeses, fruits and roasted vegetables were piled high among towers of pastries and cakes on tiered stands of gold and onyx. A myriad of musicians gathered in a domed alcove built into the hall, each tuning their instruments and creating a cacophony of competing sounds that echoed out amongst the murmuring voices of the magicians assembled.

He could pick out his mother and father among their council. Commander Jaried, Captain Tochka and Major Silfa were ever at their side, both for protection and because the five were old friends in their alliance to protect Hinhallow. Magi Kobzic, his father's advisor was there as well, and standing just off to the side was his aide Rohit.

They were joined by the diplomats from Rhunmesc and Ares: white-haired Magistrate Nicora Firstfrost and Magistrate Zaledria Sirechi, whom Calix knew was an old friend of his mother's growing up in Ares. They seemed amicable enough as they chatted, gesturing idly with their hands. His father laughed, holding his belly as he guffawed.

Calix took a steadying breath. At least his father was happy today. That was one indication this was going well. The crushing pressure in his chest made him feel otherwise, but he swallowed hard and tried to calm his thundering heart.

His gaze slid across the hall to fall on his betrothed. Her chocolate hair was braided and piled on her head, a crown of red roses woven in amongst sparkling clips and loose curls. It still unsettled him to call her that. *Betrothed.* It didn't feel right. Her strategic breakdown of their union and her aloof demeanor forced him to realize that maybe it really was he who resented the idea of marrying for alliance. He scowled, thinking momentarily of wild black curls and the brazen fire in those violet eyes as she poked him in the chest.

Calix shook his head and looked again upon his soon-to-be-bride. Shairi truly was a vision in Hinhallow colors. The crimson and lace of her corseted gown left him wondering how far she would go to indenture herself to him, to the crown he was about to receive. He swallowed hard, watching her emerald eyes glitter in the light of the solarium chandeliers as Zakarian made her laugh with whatever witty comment had spilled from his lips before he too joined in genuine, shoulder-shaking laughter. Zak was the only one of Calix's personal guards officially labeled "off-duty" for the coronation, though both of them knew it was a ruse and he was guarding the princess with his life.

Coronations always attracted some sort of chaos.

From Zakarian who was on princess-duty, Calix found other trustworthy faces posted around the hall. Raif and Khodri were on either side of the dais behind which he was watching the assembly, his most trusted closest at hand. As if sensing his gaze, Raif turned his head to the side, and gave him a grin and a thumbs up. With his blond hair pulled back in a spiky, short ponytail and he almost looked neat;

Calix was almost certain his mother had insisted Raif pull his hair back for the ceremony. Orig was by the balcony, watching the stairs up from the gardens. Alander and Jephte were in the back of the hall monitoring those still arriving.

He raked his gaze across the hall once more before pulling himself back from the curtains and retreating to the small antechamber where he was to ready himself. He'd been ready for hours now, it seemed. But it was almost time.

The musicians quieted. The voices hushed.

He gave himself a final once-over in the tall mirror leaning against the wall. His white tunic was open at the collar, bearing the golden column of his throat. His pants were black and tucked into his boots, polished for the occasion. For ornamentation more than necessity, he also had a sword belted to his hip. A symbol of his role as a warrior for his kingdom. He couldn't very well bring his scimitars, all flame and fury, to a holy ceremony...though he had suggested it.

The people ought to know who was going to be their king.

His gaze fell upon his blackened hands in his reflection. The only blight upon him. He clenched his fists and watched the fissures in his flesh glow with molten heat before he released the pressure. No King of Hinhallow before had such an obvious flaw. His father, even roped with as many battle scars as he has, was never marked by his own power the way Calix was. He wondered how hard he would have to compensate for it, this magic eating him alive. Perhaps marrying early into his reign would not be such a bad idea. He could produce heirs early for when he was eventually consumed by the *Fervis*. It was a singularly morbid thought that he wished immediately he hadn't pondered.

At last, he met his own gaze. His yellow eyes hid behind a fringe of unruly black hair. He took a steadying breath and gave his reflection a convincing grin when his mother, sister and younger brother hurried behind the curtain.

Queen Emmaleigh held his younger brother, Prince Darres, in her arms, his little golden crown sitting crooked on his blond head of curls. Though he was nearing the age when he would start weapons training with a master, he was still very much a child to his mother, and even to Calix. His magic had not yet awakened and while he and Bexalynn had both been children of Tarlix, Queen Emmaleigh was still holding on to the frail hope that the last of her children would be of Baelfor's Blessing. Behind his mother, his sister fell into a chair and leaned back. "I'm exhausted already," she sighed before propping herself back up and pouring a cup of rose tea from a silver samovar. "Can I eat any of the cakes yet, Mother?"

"You shouldn't ask questions you already know the answer to." The queen's reply was clipped as she looked Calix over and passed Darres off to Bexalynn, who struggled to balance the boy and her tea before opting to hold the young prince instead.

"Come now, my love. Your father is almost ready to present you." Emmaleigh fussed with Calix's hair, his sleeves and the scabbard on his hip. "Do you remember your oaths?"

"Of course I do, Mother."

She paused, her hands lingering on his shoulders as she met his eyes. "I know you do, my darling boy. I am *so* proud of you. Of the man you've become. Your father is as well. He has known he would crown you from your first breath," she whispered. "You will make a fine King." She pulled his head down and kissed her son's bowed brow. "I believe you can be the king that *all* of Ellorhys needs, not just Hinhallow."

And from the solemn look on her face, the way her eyes seemed to settle into the sadness that was being loved by Akintunde, he knew she was telling the truth.

Beyond the curtain, Magistrate Kobzic announced his father, and he could feel the anticipation of the gathered mounting as King Akintunde's voice boomed. "Today is a day I have dreamed of for far longer than any of the grand achievements I have bestowed upon Ellorhys in the name of Hinhallow." His voice seemed to reverberate as he carried on, regaling the hall with tales of Calix's emerging fire magic as a youth. The court tittered with mirthful laughter as King Akintunde reminisced about the time Calix burned the stables to the ground when his fires first awakened. Pride spilled into his father's voice as he recalled Calix's first conquests, and Calix felt himself shrinking in the shadow that was King Akintunde Ballentine.

Won tourneys and completed quests paled in comparison to the conquests of his father's reign.

His mother had already stepped up to the part in the curtain, Prince Darres standing by her side, his little hand held firmly in her own as he pressed his face through the curtain. When King Akintunde announced her name, Queen Emmaleigh looked over her shoulder at her son and smiled at him. "Just remember to breathe. The rest will come naturally," she said as her last bit of advice before she stepped through the curtain to deafening applause.

"She's right you know." Bexalynn stepped up beside him, gloved hands smoothing pleats in her champagne colored gown. Her blonde hair was left long and curling down her back, and a silver tiara of pearls lay across her temple. "You were born for this."

"Is that so? Now that I'm to be crowned, all the wisdom of the stars has befallen my little sister?" he teased her.

"I don't know about all that, now," she snorted. "I wouldn't be Father's pick for heir. He's going to sell me off to the highest bidder for alliance if he gets his way." She looked up and met his gaze and the severity of her tone struck him much like Shairi's candor over their engagement had. "See to it that when he does sell me, I'll at least be comfortable, if not happy."

With that, she stepped out from behind the curtain to more applause, polite if not more reserved. The young princess was not as exposed to the court as Calix had been by her age.

Alone behind the heavy crimson curtain, Calix readied himself, running over the lines of his oath in his head.

"It is with great pleasure that I, King Akintunde Ballantine the first of my name, crown my firstborn son, Calix Ballantine, as your Crown Prince of Hinhallow!" Calix stepped out from behind the curtain. He had not thought it possible, but the celebratory cries grew louder. His heart ached with the swell of pride he felt for his people. The love they felt for him, his family all seated in their identical golden thrones upon the dais. All but two were empty.

The king's and the crown prince's.

"My son! Kneel and recite your oath of fealty to the Kingdom and our People! Claim your crown, your birthright as sure as Tarlix's flame in your soul." King Akintunde stood out on the front of the dais, before the assembly of magicians. Hundreds of eyes fell upon Calix as he made for his father's side.

Before the crowd, Calix knelt and spread his arms, bearing not just his body to the kingdom but his blackened hands as well. His weakness and his might. King Akintunde draped a sash of gold and crimson silks across his shoulders as he tilted his head back to drink of his father's cup. Red wine splashed into his mouth and he gulped it down before setting his eyes on the courtiers. "I swear my people before me, my kingdom's honor above mine, and justice above all. I swear the sword and bow, and the sweat of my brow to uphold the integrity of my kingdom. I shall give my last breath before surrender and my last loaf before I let my people starve. I, Calix Ballantine, do so vow upon the blood in my veins and the breath in my soul!"

Silence prevailed as King Akintunde took a golden crown, studded with solarium and onyx and laid it upon Calix's obstinate black hair. Under the weight of the crown, it finally stayed flat. Calix rose from his knees as his father bellowed, "I give you your Crown Prince! Calix Ballantine!" The musicians struck up the vivacious ballad of Hinhallow and the people cheered. Hats and flowers were thrown high, some caught in the silk that draped across the ceiling beneath chandeliers.

Calix grinned as he surveyed the joy on his people's faces. Shairi and Zakarian were very near the front of the assembly and he did his best to avoid meeting his betrothed's heated stare. While the negotiations were underway, their engagement had not been made public knowledge. Though he wished he could withdraw from the arrangement entirely, his father was still king until he drew his last breath. His orders remained and Calix was a man of his word. He would not forsake his vow.

This crowning was a turning point, he knew. He would be the one to ride into battle in his father's stead now. He was the one the kingdom would look to for a vision of the future. He looked out across the gathered crowd and saw the people he would change the world for. Weakness or no, loveless marriage or not, he would be the king *they* deserved.

He looked back at his mother, sister, and brother still seated on their thrones behind him and Akintunde. The thin patience on his mother's golden face made him look back to his father. The ceremony it seemed, was not quite over.

The cheers died down, and King Akintunde's jolly face was flushed red with wine. "I would like to give my son a present now. His mother, Queen Emmaleigh told me I should make a gift of a fine horse or a sword, and I would have, easily, had an old friend not dropped by with a gift that I would have liked for myself!" He gave a hearty laugh, his shoulders shaking with his own amusement and whether or not they knew what the king was speaking of, courtiers joined him in his laughter. "Calix, my son! My heir!" Right then, Calix met his father's eye, and witnessed the pride there, swimming behind his familiar hazel eyes. "My gift to you."

King Akintunde threw his hand out with a flourish as colored smoke poured onto the dance floor like a fog, clearing a large portion of the courtiers as they pushed back from the expanding plumes of iridescent mist. The music shifted from vibrant trills and happy strings to the decadent thrum of drums.

From within the colored clouds four lithe, scantily clad women emerged, arms raised above their heads and silks drawn tight between their slender hands. Each was unique from the others, and they all wore masks of varying creatures: a red-haired girl wore a fox mask of jewels that shimmered, a small blonde wore pinks and had a mask of shimmering scales, a girl with black curls wore a feathered peacock mask, turquoise and purple shifting jewel-like colors in the light as they pranced around the space that was clearing for them in the center of the hall. Their hips gyrated in time with the drums as hypnotic strings wailed a melody that hushed the crowd.

Calix felt his mouth go dry. He looked to his father, a little bewildered at the audacity of his gift and the presentation if it. He knew of his father's voracious...appetite when it came to women, but he never thought it would be something he was expected to inherit.

If his father sensed his concerns, he ignored them well. His eyes fell hungrily upon the dancers until he seemed to feel his son's eyes upon him. Calix schooled his features into that of amusement as the king turned his attention to him. He wrapped an arm around his son's shoulder in a way that Calix would have treasured, if they were not enjoying camaraderie at the expense of slave girls.

"I know you weren't thrilled about the Aresian girl. I wouldn't be either," his father said, doing nothing to mask the volume of his voice. "With beauties like these at your disposal, you should find the arrangement more suitable, even if the princess isn't to your tastes."

"I truly don't know what to say, Father."

King Akintunde grinned in a way that revealed a darker, predatory side that Calix usually associated with battle. "I'm sure you'll have something to say after a night with that one," he said pointing to the dancers still twisting and leaping, showing their long limbs and arched backs, seductive and gyrating in time with the music's erratic pace. "That's the one I wanted you to tame. She caused quite a bit of trouble for the merchant on her way here. I've heard she's quite the little liar, too." His father gave him a smile that turned his stomach. "The ones with the filthy mouths are always the most fun."

Calix followed his father's gesture to the center of the dancers and he realized they were pretty, but they were there for her. Support in the show. A petite woman with a mane of black braids had emerged from somewhere he hadn't seen. Sheer skirts of white and lilac swayed around her as she moved like a phantom through the colored smoke that had settled into mist across the dance floor. Her white feathered mask bore a gold crown-like point like in the center and even with most of her face obscured, Calix would have had to have been blind to not know she was beautiful beneath it.

She writhed against the music, her movements solid and sure. There was something *demanding* about the way she threw herself into the melody, as if she could take from the music what it would not yield. Her feet commanded rhythm like a tribal chant within her bones. She threw her head back, and while Calix knew she was a slave, he couldn't take his eyes from the curve of her throat, ringed with a faint pink scar just above her collarbone. He couldn't not take notice of the way her supple mouth was curved in a smile of unbridled ecstasy as she rolled her hips, her arms. She spun and dark eyes, obscured by her white feathered mask, found his across the hall.

His breathing hitched.

Her step faltered, and her smile flickered as she stumbled.

Calix was already moving down the dais as she went to her knees, her lilac skirts askew around her pale legs.

He knelt beside her, offering his hand to help her stand. "Are you all right?"

Her mouth hung open a little as she put her hand in his. "*You,*" she breathed as he helped her to her feet.

She jerked away as a heavy hand landed on his shoulder, his father joined laughing in that manic way of his when he was showing off. "No need to charm her, son. She's bought and paid for." He flicked his hand, and a pair of guards arrived. "Take this one to the prince's chambers," he said none too quietly.

The dancer's head whipped from side to the as the guards seized her arms from behind. "What? No! Get your hands off me!" But she was already being dragged through the crowd, many of the party-goers and courtiers snickering as she thrashed in the guard's grips. The other dancers had stilled on the floor, the music forgotten. The blonde held her hands over her mouth. The dark-haired peacock wrung her hands tight around the violet silk in her hands as the girl was man-handled through the crowd, her protestations clear.

"Father," Calix objected as the girl's panicked shouts bleated out over the crowd now. "This isn't necessary. Your...generosity knows no bounds. However, I..." he struggled to find words to stop this without insulting both father and liege.

"Is she not beautiful?" King Akintunde asked baldly.

Calix bit his tongue, then said, "She is. Of course she is, but—"

"They all are. If that one is not to your liking, select another. They are for your pleasure." King Akintunde waved him off. "If not that one, then your soon-to-be bride. There's nothing quite like owning a woman and a kingdom, Calix. You'll soon find wisdom in those words." He narrowed his eyes. "Go enjoy your crowning, Calix. Yesterday you were a prince. Tomorrow you may be a king. Drink. Fuck."

Get out of my sight before you embarrass us both.

The king had made himself clear.

Calix separated himself from his father, and he was immediately swept up by Councillors and Magistrates alike, all congratulating him on his newly minted title. He cast a cursory glance around the hall between handshakes and praise. The other dancers had been removed from the hall, returned to wherever they were being kept. His mother had sequestered herself off to the side with an array of courtiers, probably having given his brother off to a maid before the presentation. She looked furious and pursed her lips as she met his stare before looking back to her attendees. Nearby, Bexalynn had found herself a suitor and was walking her date to the dance floor. Raif was within reach, leaning against a pillar next to Zakarian, who still stood near...Shairi.

Her emerald eyes smoldered with fury even as a placid smile was plastered on her face. The look alone was enough to cool his heated blood from the dancing girl. It was clear that like his mother, Princess Shairi wasn't pleased with his father's present. She held his gaze just long enough to ensure he understood her revulsion, then turned on her heel and stalked from the hall. Zakarian met his eyes and shrugged before following after her, still on orders to protect her.

He would have to clear that up with her before it got out of hand.

Calix started after her and was at once swarmed with courtiers wishing him well and inquiring as to his plans for the future of the kingdom. He fielded the questions, deferring to the age-old, "My father's groundwork has been well laid for generations of expansion and growth for Hinhallow," and "Long may he reign, his wisdom will guide my hand in matters of state in years to come," as well as the classic, "I have already learned so much, and I know there is a wealth more to learn still."

Each time he separated himself from one throng of courtiers, he found himself pressed into another fold with another matter to discuss. The drought. The crops. Refugees pouring into the capitol by the hundreds. Another hand to shake. The Magistrate. The Councilor. Courtier after courtier after courtier. He nodded when he was supposed to, smiled so hard that his cheeks were sore, and laughed at all the right places.

A headache was winding its way up the back of his skull when Raif stepped to his side and blocked the next assailing wave of courtiers with a well-timed scowl. Slowly, the guard extracted him from the hall and escorted him up the dais toward the antechamber behind the crimson curtain.

"Thank you," Calix mumbled as the pair stepped into the antechamber.

Raif crossed his arms over his chest and shook his head. "I could see the tension in your jaw. Your smiles were starting to look psychotic," he said.

"I'm going to have to get better at that. The politicking," Calix confessed to his friend.

Dark eyes seemed amused at the idea of Calix schmoozing the Magistrates of the other courts to assuage his own means to an end. "You're going to have to get better at juggling your women, too. Shairi was livid when your father brought out the dancers."

Calix paled. He'd almost forgotten about that.

"She'll be okay, Calix. It's not like she's not used to you rejecting her, right?" Raif said dismissively. Of all the members of his guard, Raif probably knew the best how far he'd gone to make his dismissal of the princess clear, even when his teenage hormones would have had him act otherwise. "And besides, you said she was...what was the word you used? *Calculating* about your engagement? Maybe she won't care that you've got a whole pavilion of women waiting to sleep with you."

"A pavilion?"

"Yeah, your father placed the girls in the West Pavilion," he said as he jerked his thumb over his shoulder in what was most certainly not the direction of the West Pavilion. "Told them they could go anywhere in that wing of the palace."

Calix closed his eyes and leaned against the wall, his head throbbing. "Shairi is being housed in the West Pavilion."

Raif let out a low whistle. "That's tough luck, man," he said, shaking his head. "Though, you might've known that if you'd visited her since your lovely dinner date." Calix shot him a glare that made him raise his hands in surrender. "You can always move her?"

"I visited her. Once," he said without much conviction. "She was just moved into the pavilion, if I move her again it would send the wrong message. I can't believe my father didn't—no, he thought of it."

Calix groaned. This was typical of his father. Making decisions on everyone's behalf. All the quests across the kingdom, the assignment to *assassinate* the Imperial family...he took a deep breath. "The girls... they're not going to stay. We'll find them work elsewhere in the palace." Calix rested his head in his hands. "I don't want them."

"Not even the wild one that's in your chambers right now?" He could hear the grin in Raif's voice. Calix lifted his head and met his friend's clear eyes. "She's a spitfire. I do *not* want to be the one to untie her."

"Untie?"

"She almost got loose in the hall. Gave one of the king's soldiers a black eye with a solid elbow before they got her in ropes."

He groaned again. Now there was a girl tied up in his room, a crown weighing on his head, and an impossible mission from a goddess lingering on the horizon. "Wonderful. Just wonderful."

"Not how it was supposed to go, my Prince?" Raif asked, amusement lilting his voice.

Calix shook his head. "Not at all, Raif. Not at all."

28

ISSARIA

Issaria grunted as her knees slammed into the marble floor, taking the brunt of her fall as she managed to roll herself off of the prince's bed. Her gag, one of the guard's cravats, kept the noise muffled. They'd grown weary of her screaming, of the obscenities she threatened to unleash upon them if they didn't let her go and talk to the prince. Her mask—her *infernal* mask, held its place across her eyes and upper portion of her face. It remained firmly affixed to her head even as she struggled against the ropes that bound her to the dark oak of the prince's four-poster bed. Of course it didn't come off. They'd secured it so it would outlast their performance.

The brocade bedcovers were a mess; she'd thrashed and kicked and squirmed until she'd been able to somersault off the foot of the bed. Now her wrists twisted above her head and the ropes were so tight that her fingers had turned into fat little sausages from the pressure.

She whimpered but turned the noise into a growl. She had to keep the fire, or she was going to lose it. She could already feel the tapping from the other side of the door deep inside her. She ignored the internal summons by remaining furious.

Blaze...there was no Blaze. Prince Calix was Blaze, and Blaze wasn't real. He wasn't really an assassin—well maybe he was. She had no idea what the prince's skillset was after years of isolation in the Eventide. Issaria felt stupid, and naive and betrayed. A sea of emotions churned inside her as she tried to recall meeting the liar in the Baelforia. He'd mocked her, clearly had a dislike for her, but by the time they parted, she had felt as though Blaze could have been an ally. A friend, even, after he spared her life. He could have easily completed his assignment and instead he had walked her home. Something she hated to admit she'd desperately needed.

And now come to find out he was the sort of man who kept girls as pets and had them tied to his bed like an animal.

How was this even the same *planet?*

She glared at the door across the room, daring him to enter and face her, though she was at a loss as to what she would even say. Issaria wasn't entirely sure how much of this was her fault. She *had* allowed herself to be sold to the king, wanted it, even, as it got her inside the palace and closer to Blaze. She'd gotten lost with the girls. Lost sight of her mission.

After the loss of her home, Issaria wanted to *be* Kai, if only for a few days while she'd been with the girls. Knowing now that they knew who she was...they were certainly going to be worried about her absence from the pavilion.

She should have—could have sent word to the king and revealed who she was days ago, but she didn't. Caring for the girls, teaching them to dance, helping ensure their secure future within the palace was something she wanted to do. Something she had to do.

And now Issaria had to get out of this mess.

With some great effort, she grunted and pulled at her hands. The ropes were knotted tight. One separate knot for each wrist. Her fingers were already numb from the pressure of pulling against the bindings. A little more couldn't hurt *that* bad, she reasoned. Her thumb was going to pop out of the socket with the pressure, and she was just fine with that if it would free her. Preparing for the burst of pain that was sure to accompany it, Issaria parted her lips, allowed the revolting gag into her mouth and forced it between her teeth.

She might be okay with popping her thumb out of the socket, but she needed her tongue in one piece. She took a deep breath, clenched the gag between her teeth

And then the bedroom door opened, and *Crown Prince Calix* strode in.

Blaze.

Issaria froze as the doors closed behind him. She had been so focused on the ropes, on preparing for the pain of dislocating her thumb to escape that she hadn't heard him approach. And seeing him now…she still wasn't quite sure how this was going to go.

He was just as tan as she remembered from the Baelforia—over a month ago now, but it felt and seemed like a lifetime. Bronze skin glinted in the glow from the solarium geode hearth. Black hair fell into his eyes as he walked into his room, still crowned in gold and gems. He did not look at her as he shrugged out of the sash of Hollowvanian colors and laid it almost reverently across a table near a dark bookcase she hadn't deigned to notice before. The crown followed suit, and only then did he turn to her.

Face unreadable, he surveyed her, his arms crossed over his chest, black hands mostly obscured. His golden eyes roved across her contorted limbs, the mess of a bed, and lastly, the ropes cutting into her wrists and turning her hands purple.

"Well, that can't be a comfortable position," he said after a while.

He closed the distance between them and deftly hoisted her up from the floor, the ropes around her wrists loosening almost immediately after the tension had been alleviated. Calix placed her on the bed facing away from him with her knees firmly beneath her, as he worked at the knots at her wrists. His fingers fumbled the rope a few times, and then he said, "There we go. They did *not* mess around with these knots, huh? I heard you put up quite the fight."

He gave her an apologetic smile as the ropes fell free from one wrist, and then the other. She pulled her arms out from behind her, rubbing at her raw skin, trying to circulate the flow of blood into her fingers again. Slowly, the sensation of electricity roiled beneath her skin as her nerves came back to life, and a small part of Issaria wondered if storm magic felt like that.

She turned around as she massaged her wrists. He stood at the end of the bed, and reached for her gag, then paused. "May I?" His blackened hands held still, inches from her face, waiting to touch her until she nodded. He smelled faintly of citrus and bonfire, and his charred fingers were surprisingly soft as they accidentally brushed her cheek.

"I am sorry about all this. My father…" He gave a rueful chuckle then shook his head. "My father and his *displays*. He has his expectations for how he thinks I should act." His discomfort was clear. "I'm not going to hurt you." The gag pulled at her mouth ever-so-slightly as he untied the knot that had migrated from the back of her head during her struggle.

Issaria wasn't sure what she was expecting, but this was not quite it. He pulled the cravat from between her lips and chucked it away from them. She wiped clumsily at the drool that had smeared across her face beneath the gag as he eyed the mask, still affixed to her face. "What are you even supposed to be?"

"A swan," she rasped out, her voice raw from screaming.

"A swan." He leaned in, and she leaned back keeping the same amount of space between them. But he didn't meet her eye. He only examined the feathered mask with intense scrutiny. "I've got to admit, I'm not seeing it."

She could hardly believe this was happening. This was not the conversation they were supposed to be having. She should be screaming at him, furious and frightened. Instead she said, "Mint said the gold part was a unicorn horn, not a beak."

"Mint?"

"The peacock."

"Ah, yes, the peacock. Mint, " he said with far too much familiarity for someone who'd never even met her. "Well, I do commend your performance. It really was…lively." Prince Calix's eyes found hers but he looked away as he said, "I'm not going to hurt you but I am going to ask that you stay the night. Expectations and all." He wouldn't meet her eye and she realized he was as ashamed of this predicament as she was. "I'll sleep elsewhere. Please, take the bed, enjoy the room. I daresay I've slept worse places than my lounge. If I can get you anything by way of refreshment—"

"You don't recognize me at all, do you?" she asked, her voice no more than a whisper.

Calix leaned back from her. She reached trembling fingers up to the black ribbon that wove into her braids to keep the mask on. He looked her over again as she fought to pull the ribbons free from her hair. "I'm ashamed to say, Miss, that I don't?" His voice held a question, as if he didn't quite believe himself—or maybe it was her he didn't believe.

"I told you Blaze was a stupid alias," she said quietly as the bow unraveled and her feathered mask dropped away, bouncing off the bed once before clattering to the floor.

"You—" Calix stumbled back as if she had burned him. He backed away from her until he was up against the mantle. "You can't be here." His voice was hollow. "Not like this."

Issaria grimaced. "If it helps, I wish I weren't."

Prince Calix looked as though he'd seen a ghost. Almost as fast as it happened, he snapped his head to the door. "RAIF!" he bellowed, then looked back to her. "How did you even *get* here? Why does my father think you're a—"

The bedroom door burst open and a blond-haired man hurtled in from beyond. He wielded an arc of pure fire like a bow, a bolt of flame notched on some invisible string, drawn tight and ready to shoot. His wild eyes roamed the room for danger before landing on her, still perched on the bed in her costume.

It took Issaria all of one moment to realize that his was yet another familiar face. Evanoff. The irony did not escape her.

He looked to Calix, backed against the mantle before lowering his weapon and chuckled. "C'mon man. I know she's feisty but—"

"Raif, she's the Esperian Princess."

The blond man's head snapped back to hers, eyes searching her face, though for what she wasn't sure.

"Hello, *Raif*," Issaria said letting the recognition of who she was settle in. "I thought you said there was no one in the palace that met my description?"

Raif's bow extinguished itself in a plume of white smoke that he waved off before putting his fingers through his hair. "Actually, I didn't answer you at all." Issaria opened her mouth to protest but found that...he was right. "I just said Blaze was a stupid name," he continued, "which it is." He looked flatly at Prince Calix.

"You tried to reach me?" Calix asked, looking to Issaria for a heartbeat before turning his heavy gaze on Raif. "And you didn't tell me she was here?"

She looked away. "Just the once. When I first arrived a few days—"

"A week ago," Raif corrected, "and to be fair, Prince Calix, I didn't know who she was, or I obviously would have told you. Or killed her on the spot. Speaking of, is there a reason we haven't? She's a witch. She's probably here to kill *you,* now that you've been named the heir."

"She's no witch," was all Calix gave by way of explanation.

Issaria wasn't about to waste his good graces, so she rode Raif's coattails. "To be fair, Prince Calix, I haven't had much contact outside the pavilion and the other girls. Different servants bring our meals and we were under strict orders not to speak to anyone."

Calix observed her for a moment, then looked to Raif, seeming to weigh the scene before him. He cast her a flickering glance of molten yellow and asked, "Who else knows you're here?"

"Your absolutely *lovely* bride-to-be has crossed my path," Issaria said, but shrugged it off. "She thinks I'm the dancer. I *was* the dancer when I met her," she emphasized. "I...I didn't know you were Blaze but I bet Princess Shairi knows I was looking for you or someone who looks like you." She looked pointedly at the prince. "We might not be on the best of terms. I *might* have emphasized the fact that your father bought me just for you." She didn't bother to mask the revulsion on her face.

He grimaced. "That's unfortunate but would explain a bit. And the girls, as you call them?

"They're my friends," Issaria said.

"They're problematic," the prince finished at the same time.

314

They exchanged perplexed looks before she replied, "They're *prob lematic?*"

At the same time, he said, "They're your friends?" Issaria opened her mouth to protest but he waved her down. "Wait, wait, they're your friends? In what capacity? Because they're only problematic in that I don't want or need them. I was going to set them free, help them get jobs elsewhere in the palace, whatever they needed."

Issaria sat back on her heels. "You were?"

"I'm not my father. I told Raif before I even came in here that I didn't want any of you."

"He did," Raif confirmed from where he remained rooted in place.

"Well...I know they might take the offer. Cizabet especially. She was separated from her sister at the auction." He gave her a horrified look that made her say, "I was a slave, Prince Calix. That's what it took for me to get here."

She touched the scars on her neck and steeled herself. Everything she'd done, everything she went through was to get here. To find Blaze and tell him what happened after they parted ways in the Baelforia that day. "I let myself be sold into slavery so I could come find you and tell you that she attacked the city. *My* people, Prince Calix."

"Her own people?" Raif asked, half in awe, half in shock.

"We've heard reports of some sort of disturbance from some refugees," Prince Calix admitted.

"It was a distraction to get the Imperial Guard into the city so she could murder me. You were right. I...I grew too curious I suppose or...maybe she never meant for me to live this whole time. I don't know," she stumbled over her words, thoughts that she'd had across the Glass spilling from her lips in a landslide of explanation. "Elon helped me escape, and I crossed the Glass. I swam the crystal sea and I was picked up by Jallah Coppernolle and—He's a *slaver.*" She looked between Raif and the prince incredulously. "Did you know that? There are *slaves* in Ellorhys!" She touched her throat again. "*I* was a slave. I don't know if Jallah knew who I was but I kept my identity a secret no matter what he implied he knew. He scared me a little,"

Issaria confessed, a little dazed as the memory of Sethik's command surfaced in her mind.

Don't look. You don't want to look.

She wasn't sure exactly what Jallah Coppernolle's magic was. She'd never seen him use it except that one time and all she could really hear was that insect-like drone and Zhaniel's screams. He hadn't needed to use magic to keep his caravan in line. There had been no argument. Jallah's word had been law and his power lay in not resorting to it. Not needing to. He'd had complete control over them.

"When I found out that I could be sold to the palace," she said at last as she continued, "I leaned harder into the persona I'd given."

Calix couldn't seem to help himself. He smirked at her and asked, "And what alias did you use this time? The Issamarya one?"

"At least it's better than Blaze," Raif muttered under his breath.

Issaria scoffed. "No, I couldn't use that one or any other one I'd ever used." Elon's words echoed in her heart. *Don't use anything that reminds you of home.*

"Wait, hold on," Raif said where he stood. "You're a princess—the *Imperial* Princess, mind you." At this he cast Calix another meaningful look before adding, "And you're familiar with aliases? Why are we so casual about this again?"

Prince Calix didn't look away from Issaria as he replied, "I've met her before."

"I was taught to be cautious even before my parents were assassinated. You know, by my Aunt Hecate who tried to kill me about a moon ago," she replied, voice dripping with annoyance before she looked back to Prince Calix. "Kyria. They knew me as Kai and I said I was a dancer. It was the only thing I was confident I could do to back myself up." She shrugged.

"A princess certainly shouldn't know how to dance like that," Raif mused. "How do we know she's telling the truth?"

Prince Calix seemed to debate his options. He looked between Issaria and his friend, then sighed. "I told my father that when he sent me to assassinate the Evernight Witch and her little protégé I met Baelfor in his wood and he told me not to kill her."

Raif was silent for a moment before he shouted, "And *when* were you going to tell the captain of your Kingsguard that you were out gallivanting around in the woods with *Mythos* on some super secret quest for the Alliance?"

Issaria bit her lip as she watched the exchange. She stifled giggles as the Crown Prince was scolded by his guard like she had been by Elon.

Calix only shrugged. "When it was no longer 'super-secret.' Besides, I didn't exactly tell the truth when I got back." Finally he met Issaria's eyes and she saw some shadow of regret in their molten cores. "It wasn't Baelfor who told me to be your ally. It was Aurelia. I should have told you then, but I guess maybe I still didn't trust you."

Silence fell between them, and Issaria broke her gaze away from the golden stare of the prince to lose herself in the shifting light of the solarium geodes in the hearth behind him.

Even Raif didn't make a comment.

Issaria's heart thundered in her ears like the roar of an ocean swell crashing upon rocks.

She'd known, of course. Elon had told her. She'd even heard her voice, calling to her from the other side of that reservoir inside her. She may have even seen her face when she was in the market with Jallah. And if she was being truthful with herself...she'd been hearing that voice for a long while now.

She'd heard it when she'd been in Magi Caltac's annex when she tried to heal the rabbit for Abihail.

She'd heard it the night Aunt Cate murdered her parents.

And it had promised vengeance.

"I know," she said at last. "She's been there for a long time." When no one said anything, she lifted her gaze from the hearth behind the Prince and said, "I think she's why I can't use my magic without it... absolutely backfiring. It's not mine. It never was. She told me as much the first time I heard her."

"Does she speak to you?"

Issaria looked away. "Not exactly. More like...I can hear her in my head."

"She did call you her vessel."

"So, Aurelia is going to swoop in, smite the Evernight Witch and then what? Poof? We all live happily ever after and Ellorhys goes back to normal?" Raif's sarcastic questions were baiting, but valid.

What *was* going to happen? She had only planned on finding Blaze. And now she found a prince in his palace and...

"Aurelia told me that we're going to have to bring her to the Vera Caelum," he said more to Raif than to her.

"Yes, of course. Let's just pop on over to the old Temple of Life and see what's next on this incredibly nonsensical quest." Raif's sarcasm was punishing, but Issaria could understand where his frustrations were coming from.

She'd been piecing it together on her own, like assembling a shattered kaleidoscope in the dark. But suddenly, she could see the colors. Visions flashed before her eyes like the flicker of a candle's flame in the wind.

The red sands of the Ascalith surrounded a lush oasis deep within its dunes. She saw the path she must take, her footsteps solitary across the crest of the dune. The sun beat down on her, casting a long shadow to her right, but it wasn't oppressive and grating like the Day she'd come to know.

Bring me to the celestial spring, the voice inside her mana said.

Sparkling rivers of starlight bounded down haphazard plateaus that looked like they had been precariously stacked one on top of the other until they touched the sky itself. Below, the water met the lagoons that pooled like puddles at the base of the towering plateaus.

Bring me to Vera Caelum, she whispered from just behind her heart.

Above, waterfalls fell from a floating island in the sky. White roots dangled beneath it, trailing idly across the tops of the red stone plateaus.

A radiant glow emanated from whatever was on the top-side of that floating island. It looked like starlight, or moonlight. Maybe even sunlight. Whatever it was it was calling to her.

Return once again to the stars and sleep.

But she could feel the vision pulling away. She held out a hand to grab it, to pull it back. "Wait!"

Prince Calix and Raif were staring at her, bewildered expressions on their faces.

Issaria bit her lip as she dropped her hand into her lap. "I...saw something. Just now. In my mind?" She couldn't meet their eyes. It had been hard enough talking about...whatever this was with Elon, someone she trusted beyond anyone in the whole of Ellorhys. Someone she *loved.*

Now she just sounded crazy.

"I think she can hear us. Talking about her."

Calix stepped toward her for the first time since he'd backed himself against the mantle. One step. "She can hear us? Right now?"

Issaria tilted her head to the side and stared the floor, eyebrows furrowed in concentration. If she were quiet enough, could she hear the Mythos of Light inside her? Silence answered her thoughts but she shrugged and nodded once. "I think so. She just showed me the spring."

"What, like a map?" Raif asked.

At that she rolled her eyes and shook her head. "No, rock head. She showed me a vision. It was before my eyes just now. I could see the Ascalith's sands, and an oasis. I think I know how to get there...if we get close."

"You think?" Raif repeated. "Or you know?"

"It's a gut feeling," Issaria replied. She shifted her attention to the prince. "Well, Mr. Assassin." She pushed herself off the bed, coming to stand between the prince and his guard. She felt both their eyes rove her very *exposed* body, and she tried not to flinch into hiding herself as she maintained a hand-on-her-hip confident pose that she definitely did not feel at that moment. "If your offer to meet the Celestial Alliance still stands, I think now would be a good time."

"With how drunk the king is bound to be at this hour, I think not," Raif said.

Prince Calix sighed and ran a blackened hand through his equally dark hair, pushing it out of his face. "I agree with Raif. My father, and the members of the Alliance, are all bound to be too drunk to make sense of all this in the moment." He looked down at her, and she realized again how very *tall* he was. "You'll meet the council. Of course you will. But let's... first, let me speak with my father and try to explain to him how exactly he ended up purchasing the Imperial Princess."

"Then you can work on explaining why you *lied* to him and need to leave with her on some quest. But that second one you might have to explain to your *fiancée* first." Raif threw his hands in the air. "This one Calix? This one is *all* on you." He turned and headed back through the doors toward the prince's suites. "May the Cosmos favor you on your mythical journey!" he called over his shoulder as he left them in the bedroom.

Calix stared after him, seeming to expect this reaction. "I'll see you back to the Pavilion."

"I thought you wanted me to stay?" she asked baldly. "Expectations and all." She couldn't keep the smirk off her face as he snapped his head back in her direction, golden eyes wide at her suggestion. She quirked an eyebrow at him and jerked her head toward the rumpled bed.

He laughed. The deep chortle churned embers in her stomach. "That was before I knew the Imperial Princess was in my bed," he said. "I'm fairly certain propriety's sake will be on my side when your identity comes to light."

"It's just down the stairs and through the garden, right?" Issaria turned and started toward the door herself. "I made it across the Glass. Stairs should be easy."

A heavy cloak *fwumped* around her shoulders. The prince kept pace by her side.

"I'll escort you."

"And the cloak?"

Bronzed cheeks flushed as he held the doors for her and looked sternly ahead as he guided her down the hall. "Propriety's sake," he murmured.

ISSARIA

Raif lounged on a couch before the hearth with an arm over his eyes. "Do shut the doors on your way out," he called after them.

"He seems comfortable," Issaria commented.

The prince smiled. "He's an old friend. I didn't have many, not real ones anyway, growing up. He was the only one who didn't let me win." The memory warmed the prince's voice and he continued on as they walked down the stairs. "He's definitely an acquired taste, but he means well."

Issaria nodded along as she thought of Rhori and his flirtations with anything that so much as looked his way and understood what Calix meant. Definitely an acquired taste, but Rhori was as loyal to her as she assumed Raif must be to Hinhallow. To the crown, and to Calix.

"And you," he said. "You really crossed the Glass?"

Issaria nodded once. "Jallah picked me up somewhere in the middle, I guess. I could see the Timeline bleeding over the horizon. I don't think I would have made it though, if he hadn't scraped me off the Glass." She couldn't keep the bitter tone from her voice as she recalled the slaver's words.

"No? From what I've heard, you're a fighter now."

Issaria chuckled. That was true. When she'd met him last, she'd called herself useless. It was funny. She didn't *feel* useless now. She hadn't changed all that much, but she wasn't sure the girl in the Baelforia and the girl on the Glass were even the same. Maybe she'd always been a fighter. She'd forgotten though. Forgotten how to stare down a challenge and walk away feeling taller. "Someone once told me that life is not about being fearless, but having the courage to overcome our limitations."

Calix was silent for a moment. "Be afraid. But then–"

"You must do it anyway," she finished.

They emerged from the tower at the base, and walked past the two guards stationed outside the doors. "Renford. Bhanu," Calix greeted them with a nod of his head.

"Your Highness!" they said, clasping fists over their hearts. Their rigid postures slackened as their eyes fell upon Issaria. "Milady."

Calix didn't miss a beat. "This one is allowed to see me anytime she wishes. Make it known. My tower is open to her at any time, for any reason."

"Yes, sire!" they replied without question.

When they had gotten out of earshot and into the garden, Issaria said, "Are you sure that was wise?"

Calix shrugged as he dipped his shoulder sideways to avoid hitting a low branch of a lemon tree as they walked. "Right now, they think you're Kai, right? As far as they know, I've just had a delightful time with you, and now I want more."

"Wonderful." Issaria's voice fell flat. She should have known her reputation would be tarnished by pretending to be a whore. For *letting* herself be sold as one. There might be no coming back from this.

"We'll clear it up once…" He sighed. "Once I can explain this to my father."

White gravel crunched underfoot as they meandered the garden path toward the fishpond. Sunlight lit down upon the lily pads and lotus flowers. Orange and white scales flashed brilliant in the rays that sifted through the water.

"It would probably be best," Calix said, "at least until we can figure out how to officially announce your presence here in Hinhallow, that your identity remain as secret as possible."

She stopped walking. "What do you mean?"

He looked at her over his shoulder before turning around. "I only mean to say that this is a precarious situation."

"You don't have to tell *me* that." She fought to keep the scowl off her face.

"Princess, your aunt has been spreading the news that you're dead."

"I'm *dead?* No, that can't be." Issaria's thoughts began to circle, picking up pace like a cyclone would collect debris. "I'm supposed to be kidnapped. Taken by...*whomever* in the attack on the city. Elon promised—" Her heart stopped in her chest. "He stayed behind for nothing. He was supposed to make sure the people thought I was taken. That was the only reason he sent me across the Glass. If I'm dead then he's—he's—"

"So you see," Prince Calix interrupted her downward spiral. "Announcing that you are not only alive and well but that you're also a ward of an opposing kingdom could start the war sooner than any of us anticipated. Hinhallow isn't ready to take on the Evernight Witch. Not yet. There are too many refugees and not enough to feed them all." His love for his kingdom swelled in his chest, in his voice. He stood taller, spoke with more vigor. "Not enough to protect them or keep them here while we wage war for who knows how long."

It would have been quite the sting to admit such weakness to the princess of an opposing kingdom.

"Am I even..." Her voice was weak, no more than a whisper. "Is Espera even my city anymore?" She couldn't voice the question that had been on the tip of her tongue. Not yet. It was too soon, perhaps too real for her to ask. If Elon was dead, and she was dead by rumor then...

"Of *course.*" He was before her in an instant. "Of course, Espera is still your city. The world will know you're alive. You can take the throne back from her. Take it all back from her."

Eclipsed in his shadow, she had to tip her head all the way back to look up at him. Tears blurred her vision as she croaked, "She sent my *friend* to kill me, Calix. He came to do it, too."

His embrace crushed her against him. Folded against him, the press of his arms a heavy weight around her back, her body shuddered around a sob. Tears stung as her breath caught in her throat and she let herself fall off that precipice.

Face buried in his chest, she cried.

She cried for the people who'd burned in her beautiful city at her aunt's order. She cried for her parents, murdered at Hecate's hand. She cried for herself. For the assassination attempt and for the way she *ran away* across the Glass. Again, for Elon being left behind, a tear for every wish for their future she'd ever had. Tears for his kiss and all the ones they would never share.

Tears for Rhaminta who'd almost been *raped.*

More tears for all the girls Issaria knew had suffered before, and would suffer after. Everything her parents had stood for, all the good in Ellorhys that had been drained away by the Eventide. She had been so sheltered, so naive, and now it had cost her the *most precious thing.*

Everything was just so wrong and she hadn't even thought about what it meant to have her ancestral deity inside her mana.

"It's okay, Issa," Prince Calix murmured as he held her, his breath mussing her hair as he continued to console her. "It's going to be okay. You made it." A steady hand stroked up and down her back as she shook with grief. "You crossed the Glass, and you escaped *another* assassin," he said. The smirk in his voice made her hiccup. "You're not alone, Princess Issaria. You have an ally in me, and with me, Hinhallow."

She took another deep, shuddering breath before stepping out of the protective circle of the prince's arms. She wiped her face with the back of her hand and sniffed. "I'm okay," she repeated his words. "I'm okay," she said again, with more conviction this time.

When she met the Prince's yellow eyes and said, "I'm going to be okay," he only replied, "I know."

Not willing to make a bigger scene, Calix deposited her at the bridge that crossed over the pond in the center of the garden. Across the bridge was the marble walkway that connected the Pavilion house where she was staying with the other girls to the other pagoda structures situated throughout the garden.

"I'll make an official document about the other girls when this is settled, but let them know they can either stay or go. I'll happily give whomever chooses to leave Metal and rations to get them wherever they're headed."

Issaria smiled at him. "I will. Thank you. They'll appreciate that."

"No one deserves to be a slave, Princess Issaria," he said as he turned back the way they came. "I'll come for you tomorrow, after I've had a chance to speak with my father when he's not celebrating."

Indeed, even out in the Western Pavilion, if she listened behind the cicadas and the leaves in the breeze, she could hear the revelry pouring out of the palace where the party for the Crown Prince was still raging on. "See you tomorrow, *Blaze*," she called out after him, a smirk on her lips as his retreating figure visibly cringed then raised a hand in a final farewell before the garden swallowed him on his way back to the tower.

Issaria turned her back on the prince and headed across the wooden bridge to her pavilion house. She had *so* much to tell them. Cizabet would never believe that she could just...go find Asmy. Just like that.

She was about to open the doors when a shadowed figure stepped around the corner.

She stepped back, ready to run—

But it was only Princess Shairi.

Her beautiful chocolate-colored hair was unbound from her updo. Red roses were missing petals and her curls had lost their bounce. Red-rimmed eyes looked upon her with a hatred Issaria didn't feel entirely undeserving of. Shairi was clearly out of sorts thinking the prince was taken with Issaria. It certainly hadn't helped that he'd tried to assist her when she'd fallen during the performance.

Issaria had been unnaturally cruel to the Princess when she'd faced her before. It had been out of a fierce desire to protect the girls and whatever honor they had left regardless of their station in the palace, but now it felt wrong.

"You were right," Issaria said.

"I am? About what?"

"Your Prince Calix isn't a heathen."

Something like relief broke across the princess's face. "I am... grateful," she stammered, before she turned down a path toward another pavilion house and stepped back out into the sunshine where she paused, her face upturned toward the sky. "I shall...see you around the pavilion then," Shairi said over her shoulder.

"Indeed you shall, Princess," Issaria replied as she watched her continue on and retreat into a pavilion house across the flower-laden portico. Maybe she and the princess could be unlikely friends, the way she'd become with the girls. The thought brought a small smile to Issaria's face in the wake of such atrocious thoughts of home.

Turning her heart again from that swallowing darkness of loss, Issaria went inside to tell the girls about their freedom.

3 0

CALIX

Calix stirred sometime early in the morning with his face buried in the intoxicating scent that lingered on his bedlinen. His fists curled into his sheets as he slit his eyes open and peered into the shade-drawn haze of his bedchamber. Across the room, his new crown glinted in the solitary beam of dust-mote clouded sunshine.

Yesterday, he'd been crowned heir. Hours later he'd found his entire kingdom on the precipice of a war he never wanted. He *wanted* to close his eyes and pretend it was just a nightmare, but the scent of her remained in his bed, all around him. He could still feel her in his arms as she broke down in the garden.

She will wear the guise of another as I wear her face as my own.

Aurelia had said as much but Issaria arriving as a concubine was not exactly what he'd anticipated. He sighed before he pushed himself out of bed and went to his bathing chamber to ready for the day. In the hall between the various rooms of his suite, he smelled the sausages that accompanied whatever breakfast Marni had prepared for them today. Calix's stomach growled at the sweet and peppery scent and he passed the bath on the way to the study where his meal would be waiting.

His meal wasn't alone. Raif had gone, probably to sleep until his next shift. Alander sat at the table, a plate piled full in front of him. "Sleep well?" he asked incredulously as his dark eyes focused on him from across the room.

Zakarian lounged on the same sofa where he'd last seen Raif with a book in his hand and an arm cushioned behind his head. His blue eyes flicked over to assess Calix, then returned to his book. "Princess Shairi is really upset with your father's *gift.*"

"She can stop being upset," Calix replied as he reached the table that had a very hearty buffet of still-steaming delicacies waiting for him. He stabbed a sausage link with a fork and took a bite, allowing himself to chew and swallow before he said, "Nothing happened. Nothing was ever going to happen, I was just going to let the poor girl sleep in my bed for appearances and then—" He had to take another steadying breath before he finished. "Zak, the girl that my father tied to my bed last night is the Imperial Princess."

Alander laughed around a mouthful of quiche and sat back in his chair as he swallowed. "So that's what Raif meant by, *'this is going to get exciting,'* eh?"

Zakarian held the prince's stare with unwavering blue eyes for a long while before he closed his book and sat up. He leaned forward, elbows on his knees and his hands calmly folded before him. "Does your father know about this?"

Calix shook his head. "I'm going to tell him shortly. I...I don't exactly know what he's going to do. Or say."

"He's not going to like it."

Calix took another bite, but found he was losing his appetite as he thought about it. "He wouldn't kill her, would he?" He asked the question but both he and Zak knew the answer.

He might.

Especially if King Akintunde thought it would solidify his crown's hold on Ellorhys.

"Would it be a bad thing if he did?" Alander asked.

"She has to make herself invaluable to him," Zakarian offered.

"She's—" Calix started then froze. Could he tell a secret that was not his? Alander and Zakarian were just as much a friend as Raif and loyal soldiers as well. But the more people knew she was here the more endangered she could become. Without an alliance secured, she really was just floating. A princess without a crown, without a *kingdom*. "She is not without her charms," he finished. "I want to help her."

"Help her with *what?*" Zakarian's cold eyes narrowed.

"Take back Espera from Hecate."

Alander raised his eyebrows and nodded, before tucking back into his breakfast. "That's going to be some task."

Zakarian was quiet. His eyes fell to the carpet, considering. "Your father does love war."

"Indeed he does. I'm going to bank on it." He returned his fork to the tabletop and turned to leave. "Tell no one else about her. I'm going to bathe and then find the king."

Calix was halfway to the bathroom when he heard Zak say, "Best not to bet all your Metals on one hand, Prince Calix."

CALIX STRODE TOWARD THE ROYAL SUITES IN THE HEART OF THE PALACE. His parents kept their personal rooms, and until he was old enough, his little brother would sleep close by in one of the rooms. Like himself, Bexalynn had her own personal suites in the Southern Wing of the palace. He passed by portraits of Ballantine kings of the past; Sunilda, the Queen of the Hunt, and Azathiel and Orianna, his grandfather and grandmother, holding a fat little baby boy—the baby who would become King Akintunde.

Calix rounded a corner and headed down the final length of hallway between himself and certain doom. Two guards were posted outside the ornately carved oak doors and nodded as he approached.

"Good Morning, Prince Calix," Elkhadir said with a smile.

"Is he awake?" he asked by way of greeting.

Elkhadir shook his head. "Your esteemed mother has risen with the young prince. She should be with him in the great hall, or perhaps the library for Prince Darres' lessons?"

Calix shook his head. "No, I must speak with the king immediately. I'll find Mother after."

The other guard, a dark, quiet man called Vasaan, leaned forward and opened the right door for him, gently closing it behind as he crossed into his parent's suites.

The murmur of voices leaked out from a door further down the hall. His father may not have risen yet, but he was not alone. Perhaps Kobzik had beaten him here. He tried not to groan at the idea of the fire-seer bringing news of Issaria to his father before he could.

Three doors down and on the right, the door opened and a pale, dark-haired woman emerged into the hall donning a very loose blue silk robe around her nakedness. She was still looking into the room she'd emerged from, and her wild hair shrouded her face. Calix froze.

Princess Issaria couldn't be *here*, with his Father, of all people.

She turned, and her blue eyes lit upon the prince and she blushed, pulling her robe tight around her body.

"Oh! Prince Calix!" She dipped her head in a bow as she fled past him with bare feet.

She was far too tall to be the Esperian princess, but that hair…He turned to look at her as she skittered down the hall behind him.

"Calix? So early?" His father's voice met his ears before his father, bare-chested and buttoning his elk-skin slacks, stepped into the hall. Horror must have shown on Calix's face as he turned back to meet his father's eyes from where he'd been staring after the consort. Clearly *not* the princess, but so close in appearance that it was uncanny.

King Akintunde chuckled and swiped a thick hand through his greying hair, brushing it off to the right side of his head to clearly display his tattooed scalp. "Vizenya has the look of the one you took to bed last night. Jallah wasn't lying when he said she was skilled," he probed, hungry eyes staring after the consort's form as she slipped through the doors and back to the King's Seraglio.

"That's actually what I need to speak with you about, Father."

"I don't care how pretty she is, son. You can't marry a whore," he said dismissively as he turned and headed further into the royal suites.

330

"I don't want to marry her," Calix said quickly as he followed behind.

"Then what could we possibly have to discuss about a slave? I care not what you do with her now."

King Akintunde swept into a spacious parlor adorned with stuffed animal heads— bear, mountain lion, wolf, and more—mounted as trophies above the mantle and around the room as if all the souls of the departed were watching them with glass eyes. Among the hunted heads, historic weapons were mounted amid little alloy plaques that titled the displays: 'King Banzul's halberd, still bloody from a battle with the Rhunish Prince Rhaizon in the Citadel Wars, year 2614,' and 'Princess Katenya's broadsword, in pieces, after the Battle of Black Sands, year 2792.'

Marni, the palace's cook, had been here as well. Trays of fruit, warm surrepan rolls and sausages scented the room sweetly with cinnamon and pepper. Calix waited until his father seated himself at the head of the table, surrepan in one hand, an empty goblet in the other. Calix stepped up, seized the carafe from the center of the table and poured an ample portion of red wine into his father's cup.

When the prince was certain the king was satisfied with both food and drink, he rested his blackened hands on the back of the chair to the right of his father. His chair. Where he should feel entitled to sit. At the right of the king. Calix's mouth felt dryer than the Ascalith itself.

"Father, forgive me," Calix began. "I lied to you when I said that I'd met Baelfor in the wood."

King Akintunde had stopped chewing his sweetbread. He'd thought his father angry before, when he'd confessed to failing at the assassination. But this—a face void of all emotion, just waiting for an explanation—this was the face of King Akintunde Ballantine that no enemy wished to see.

A face that would regret nothing.

"I went into the Baelforia expecting to hike through to Larkham, then take a horse to the capitol. It would have been easy...but I encountered a light. And when I approached, it was the Mythos

331

Baelfor, as I said, but he was speaking to a…" He left his voice trail off. How *much* truth should he tell? What would be crossing a line and get Issaria killed anyway? "An ethereal lady," he finished. "Everything I told you about the Terran Mythos was true, but I left out the Mythos woman. She was of the Cosmos in all ways, I was certain of that," he continued on. "White hair, glowing eyes, she was *floating* in the woods, Father. I swear to you, she spoke my name inside my own head, without ever opening her mouth."

His father took a measured sip from his cup. "And what, pray tell, did this *ethereal lady* say to you?" King Akintunde growled out evenly. His knuckles were white as he clutched his goblet.

"She told me that she'd summoned me there, just like she'd brought Baelfor, and…" He hesitated, only for a moment before making the choice and announcing, "The Imperial Princess was there as well."

As well. As in, also. Simultaneously. At the same time as himself and Aurelia. Definitely *not* a vessel.

"You found that little whelp in the woods and you *still* failed to eliminate her?" His father's orange-yellow eyes were molten as he met his son's stare.

"I didn't fail. I was commanded by the Mythos not to harm her, that much of what I said was true. And that she would one day seek us out as allies." Calix found that his voice grew stronger now that he'd decided to try to protect her in what little way he could. "The Mythos spoke and told us that we must go find the Vera Caelum but that we must not go without the other."

"And why is that?"

Calix shrugged. "She didn't say. But she made it very clear that when the princess came to Hinhallow for help, we were to give it." He took a steadying breath before he finished, "She's here. The Imperial Princess is the dancer you bought. She lied and let herself be traded as a slave to get into the palace safely."

King Akintunde was silent for a moment before he laughed uproariously. "That little hellcat told you she's the *Imperial Princess* and you bought it?" He continued to laugh, stopping only to slug back his wine and put his empty goblet down. "Jallah said she was a liar, but I didn't realize he meant she was *that* fantastical with her tales!"

Calix ground his teeth so hard his jaw ached. "Father, she's not a liar. I met her in the Baelforia that day. They are the same girl. I told her my name was Blaze; she arrived after I did, and neither I nor the Ethereal Lady told her who I truly was."

"I stood before her in the Pavilion when she arrived and she did not tell me her identity. Why? Why wait if obtaining help is so imperative to her?"

Calix hesitated then shook his head. "I would have to think she didn't know if she could trust you with her identity. She knows you as the possible assassin of her parents."

"Assassin?" he roared. King Akintunde's chair flew backward as he slammed his hands down on the table, searing the tabletop with his rage and flames. "She would DARE call *me* assassin?"

"She said no such thing, but I did speak with her in the woods and at the Ethereal Lady's request, we spoke of that night. The witch deceived her. Wove an intricate lie and kept the truth hidden from her for years," Calix pleaded the story to his father. Willed him to see the error in years of thinking. "I told her the truth, about the Bloodoath and how it could not have been an order given from their lips, from *your* lips."

His flames subsided, but the tabletop was charred through where the king's palms had been, leaving open holes to view the floor and table legs. His face was still contorted in offended rage, but he righted his chair and sank back into it. "I assume there's more to this tale?" He gestured with a smoking palm for Calix to continue.

"Hecate tried to have her killed, so she fled."

"The Witch is now spewing some filth about her being kidnapped and murdered, though you've heard as much from the reports?"

Calix nodded numbly. "She wants her dead. And with good reason. The Ethereal Lady led us to believe that the princess could reverse the Witch's curse. And that's when she told us to find the Vera Caelum."

He held his father's gaze as the silence wrapped around them. It permeated the roof of his mouth and made Calix feel as though sand were rushing out to sea beneath his feet. King Akintunde sighed and folded his hands on the table before him. His eyes darted back and forth between the holes he'd scorched into the tabletop, and his silver-streaked mane of black tumbled over his shoulder. He looked older then, older than he had in years. Calix did the math and put his father's age at nearly two-hundred and eighty—likely nearing the end of his life. And now his son and newly minted heir was bringing another war to their doorstep. If his father hadn't been dubbed 'the War Lord of the West,' he would almost call his posture defeated. Head hung, hands clasped together almost in prayer—

"You're certain she's the Imperial Princess?"

"I am."

"How many know of her presence here?"

"Myself, and Raif—I called him in to my chamber last night when I knew who she was." He thought about Shairi, who would be of no consequence, and of Alander and Zakarian. "Perhaps a few more, but I'm not certain. The numbers are very low. She has been kept isolated with the other girls, and she was very convincing with her alias."

At that, the king chuckled. Actually chuckled. "Convincing, indeed. Bring her before the Celestial Alliance," he commanded. "I'll summon them at once to the Blue Room and then we'll see what to make of this little mess."

Sunlight gilt the garden in golden drops of dew. A water magician must've been through the Western Pavilion recently, tending the gardens with their mana, keeping things alive when they should have long ago shriveled under the constant barrage of sunlight. A piercing shriek followed immediately by laughter, pealed through the garden from the pavilion house across the bridge. Through open doors, Calix spied Issaria as she chased another girl with black hair—the peacock...Mint, was it?—Across the room with a saffron-colored pillow brandished as a bludgeon.

"Rhaminta! I swear if you scare me with *another* frog..." her voice trailed off as she chased her friend through the house.

"You'll have to catch her first, Kai!" another girl called after them from where she sat sunken into a chaise with a pile of books at her feet.

A girl with red hair and brilliant green eyes sat up as he crested the bridge and brought her hand to her heart. She turned to let the girls know he was coming, then fixed her eyes upon him again and rose from her seat. There was something about the look on her face as he closed the distance between himself and the pavilion house that left him feeling guilty and unsettled, though he'd never seen the girl before last night.

"Good morning, ladies," he said as he tucked an arm before himself and bowed.

"Cosmos above," a blonde said breathily from the hallway before turning and sprinting into a nearby room and screaming, "Kai! *THE PRINCE IS HERE!*"

Calix looked between the place where the blonde had been to the redhead and brunette still before him. "I was under the impression that...*Kai* would have told you all the news?"

She'd called them her friends. He wanted to believe that they were, if only so she wasn't so entirely *alone*.

The redhead nodded eagerly, fresh tears springing up around her sorrow-swollen eyes. "It's true, then? It's really true?"

Calix smiled in a way he hoped wasn't condescending to her disbelief, or to her experiences that made her doubt. "Of course it is. Even before Kai came to my room, I never wanted to own anyone. Least of all take anyone from their family." He realized who this one must be.

She was separated from her sister at the auction.

"Cizabet, I take it?" The redhead nodded, and her face flushed. "I'll personally write to Jallah Coppernolle and find the location of your sister. I cannot begin to apologize enough for what you've endured." He looked around to see the rest of the dancers assembled, including Princess Issaria, who looked more warrior-queen than Aresian dancer with those braids in her hair. "For what you've *all* been through. Many things have changed since the Evernight came, and many more will change again when I am truly king. You're welcome to leave whenever you wish, and I will gladly supply you and give you Metals for your journey home—or wherever you would go."

"I'm staying with Kai," the brunette said, flashing blue eyes toward Issaria. "I'll do whatever she needs."

"I *at least* know what a handmaiden is supposed to do," said Mint with a smirk as she threw an arm across Issaria's shoulders. "So I'm going to have to stay. Anyway, no one else could tame her hair," she added as she plucked a curl and twirled it around her long brown finger.

Issaria's face had flushed scarlet and she looked between the girls, hands clutched to her chest. "You guys don't have to–"

"Where else are we gonna go?" the blonde asked from beside the princess. "Besides...I heard what you did for Mint at the camp. No one *ever* fought back. If I'm not going back to Sorair, I'm going to stay where it makes a difference."

"Asmy," Cizabet said, drawing all their attentions. "I have to find Asmy but once she's back...we could probably write home and let our parents know we're okay..." She looked over her shoulder at Issaria before nodding. "I don't think I'm ever going to see Snovic again, but I'm okay with it if you'll have us?"

"Oh Ciz..." she started, "Ciz you and Asmy should go home to your folks when you're together again. Isn't that what you want? I don't *need* handmaidens. Or any kind of maidens."

The redhead shrugged and looked back to Calix. "I've never met anyone like her so don't you let *anything* happen to her." Her emerald eyes flashed and Calix felt that sisterly protection.

"On my honor as the Crown Prince of Hinhallow," Calix replied as his eyes locked over Cizabet's head with Issaria's amethyst gaze. "Though I did come to summon you to the Blue Room. The Celestial Alliance is being assembled as we speak. King Akintunde will see you now."

Issaria stepped out from under Mint's arm and nodded as she approached him. Resolve masked her fear in the first step. The pain in her eyes reflected strength in the second. And by the third she was no more a dancer in a pavilion than he was a pauper in the streets. When she turned her face to him, a serene smile on her lips, he was looking at the Imperial Princess.

The Empress of their realm, whether she had a kingdom or not.

31

CALIX

There were mere moments before Princess Issaria would be in front of the people who despised her most in the whole of Ellorhys. Calix wasn't sure what was about to happen; he'd admitted as much as he escorted her to the Blue Room. He had sworn her protection though, and he meant it when he'd said it to Cizabet in the Western Pavilion, and before when he promised not to harm her in the Baelforia.

Whatever this was, it was bigger than all of them and the pieces were only just being assembled. The idea of being outwitted by fate, as it were, didn't settle well with him. Calix liked to have the advantage in a battle, and he couldn't help but feel like he was coming to the battlefield with no planned strategy or trained any men.

No guards were posted outside of the Blue Room as the pair approached, though Calix could hear the murmur of voices beyond the heavy doors.

He caught her by the elbow as she reached for the door. "Princess."

She looked up to meet his eyes, tilting her head back in a way that made his pulse skip a beat as she said, "Yes?"

"Whatever happens in there…we're going to the Ascalith."

She looked down for a moment before she nodded. "Yes, that *does* seem to be what she wants from me." She bit her lip, clearly wanting to say more.

"What is it?" She started to shake her head and he added, "If you don't tell me now, I can't help you once we're behind those doors. I'll try to help you where I can, but I have a responsibility to my own people as well. If there's something I should advocate for—"

"Espera. I have to liberate the city. Those people all think she's fit to be their Empress. Their *savior*." She couldn't keep the revulsion from her voice. "I want your father's army to march against my aunt. I want to be there as the ships breach the harbor. I want her to know it was me who brought them to the gates."

Calix was silent. He knew it would come to this eventually, either from his father's need to conquer, or just a need to protect Ellorhys from a more permanent night. "You're asking for a war, Princess."

Red-faced and eyes shining with tears, she looked up at him and he felt the air between them crackle with electricity. "I didn't ask for any of this, but I'll be happy to end it," she spat.

Calix nodded once to let her know he understood. And he did. Her family had been ripped apart, and for what? A need for power, to rule all? How tragic. And now her very birthright had been stripped away in yet *another* attack against the innocent. Another attack that sent more refugees fleeing to Hinhallow, taxing the city's stores and bringing more hardship to a kingdom already struggling.

Issaria was right. War was going to come regardless of the catalyst. If not now, then perhaps when Hecate was strong enough to unleash worse upon the realm. Maybe the witch was waiting to harvest Issaria's magic to enact her final conquest. The thought sickened him almost as much as the idea that she very well could have if Issaria hadn't taken that wild chance and crossed the Glass. If they were going to wage war, it may as well be with a valiant cause behind their banners as they marched upon the Celestial City.

"Are you ready, Princess?" he asked as he put a hand on the gilded door handle and offered her his elbow.

"No, but I'm going to have to do it anyway," she said. Without looking at him, she put a hand on his elbow and nodded. "Go ahead."

And Calix opened the doors.

The Blue Room was fuller than he'd ever seen it before. He felt her recoil next to him but he took the first few steps and she fell into place beside him. His Father and Mother—his mother was here?—sat side-by-side at the head of the long table.

"This is her?" His mother's question felt like jab as she scoffed and turned to Commander Valente, a sly smile on her face as she whispered something behind a gloved hand.

Kobzik sat to the king's immediate right and Commander Jaried Valente was on his mother's left. Down the table the members of the King's Council *and* the Celestial Alliance sat: Auric Alesio, Tochka Friegdan, Silfa Tilak, Nicora Firstfrost of Rhunmesc, Zalendria Sirechi from Ares—

"She certainly looks the part," Zalendria said from where she sat midway down the left side of the table.

"Just because she's pretty doesn't mean she's the princess," Magi Auric said from next to the Commander.

"She's not the first to claim to be royalty in the wake of a tragedy. The interregnum always summons the liars and thieves to see what they can make off with," Queen Emmaleigh said dismissively as she looked to her left, sizing up her husband's reaction.

And then Issaria slipped from his arm and advanced on an auburn-haired man with a mustache about midway down the table. The man sported a black eye that was swollen shut, and he seemed unaware of the princess's approach as he spoke amicably with an associate, judging by the similar vagrant attire. The associate saw her descent upon them first and sat up, rigid in his chair. Green eyes wide with shock as Issaria slammed her hands down on the table across from the strange pair.

"WHERE IS ASMY!?"

All conversation stopped. She had everyone's attention now. The man with the mustache smirked at the enraged woman before him and twirled his waxed mustache between his fingertips. "Pleasure to see you again, *Princess.*"

At that, King Akintunde scowled at the man. "Jallah, you knew?"

He shrugged. "Not at first. I had suspicions when her eyes never changed back to—oh what color were they supposed to be, Kai my dear?"

"Blue," Issaria growled out.

"Yes. There you have it." He made a wide gesture to the princess as if it absolved everything. "She said her eyes were blue and she'd been to see a beautician in Espera who *dyed her eyes.*" Jallah scoffed and put an apologetic hand to his chest, embarrassed by his blunder. "Again, I offer my deepest and most *sincere* apologies, your Excellency. I didn't realize how true my suspicions were until your men so *kindly* found me at the harbor this morning."

If Calix didn't know any better he'd push all in and wager the man knew very well what cargo he'd carried with him.

The blond associate, clearly Jallah's henchman of some sort, dropped his eyes to the table and Calix knew. Friend or foe, Jallah Coppernolle had taken Issaria in as a slave and he had *known* who she was. And still he degraded her so?

Calix's fist clenched at his side, embers stirring from his knuckles. He brought his hands behind his back, smothering the fissures cracking across his knuckles with his other hand. He held at attention while they spoke, rubbing his fist into his palm behind his back.

"Asmy," Issaria repeated. "Where is she? Who did you sell her to?"

Jallah seemed unperturbed. He examined his nails, and the back of his scarred hands before he looked back up at her. His dark eyes bored into hers and even from where he stood, Calix could feel the fire coming off of her. Even her hair seemed to shift as if being caught in a heated wind. He looked again. Her hair *was* moving as if she stood in the center of an inferno.

Calix glanced around the room, but no one else seemed to be looking at her. Everyone else was focused on Jallah, and what he would say next. The slaver didn't even realize he was bringing a dragon down upon himself.

"I'd have to check my ledger to be certain, Kai, dear. Are we still calling her Kai? Or is it well-known at this point that this is Issaria Elysitao?" he asked absently as he looked around the table at the

Councilors before settling his dark gaze back upon Issaria. "Which one was Asmy again? You know how expansive my inventory can be."

"MONSTER!" Issaria screamed at him. Calix launched himself across the room, his arms coming down around either side of her as blue-white flames rippled across her fingertips. Chairs scraped against the floor in varying shrieks and screams, but Calix wrenched her back from the table. "LET ME GO. He *sold* her! He sold us all!" She kicked and thrashed, but he held firm, cinders coming up from his blackened hands where she scratched.

"Issaria, please. This isn't helping," he murmured against her shoulder until she stilled beneath his grasp. Calix leveled at the slaver as he pulled her away. "You *will* provide the girl's location, Jallah."

"She behaves like a wild animal!" Queen Emmaleigh said from her place at the head of the table. "How are we to be sure she's the Imperial Princess? *I* heard she was dead. The Evernight Witch is in mourning."

"This *is* Issaria," Calix said as he relinquished his grip on the princess and let her step away from him. "Mother, I swear to you—"

"There was to be a marriage alliance between our families." Issaria's voice rang out clear across the chamber, and even Calix felt himself go still at her inflection. When she was certain everyone was listening to her, she continued, "I was young, and perhaps I wasn't supposed to know, but I overheard my parents speaking of the proposal nonetheless." She wouldn't look at him. He saw it in her jaw, clenched and poised like an adder ready to strike. Her vivid eyes were rooted on his father's unwavering orange stare. "King Akintunde, you wrote to Helios and Umbriel about a marriage alliance between your son and their daughter—between myself and Prince Calix."

He looked to his parents, and his mother's misty eyes met his only for a moment before flicking to the tabletop. It was enough to confirm what Issaria said was true. He'd never known. He glanced to the princess, her stare still locked on his father's, rivaling the king himself in iron-will. Calix fought to keep the smirk off his face as he reminded himself that it was a bargain of the past and had never even been a bargain at that. He put the thought from his mind.

342

"Are you satisfied," she asked, "King Akintunde? Queen Emmaleigh?"

His father grunted and sat down, running a hand through his hair. "It's her. Cosmos be damned, but it's her."

"What are we to do with her now?" Auric said from his place at the table. The Magistrate held the allegiance of no court. As part of the Magistrate's Guild, his role was to uphold the laws of magic itself and ensure the Dark Arts held no footing in the White City.

"It seems to me," King Akintunde began, silencing all debate about Issaria. "That you're a princess without a kingdom, without a crown. Perhaps once we spoke of alliances…but what now, little girl?"

"I am *still*—"

"Still a princess? Your aunt would have you killed as she did your parents before you." King Akintunde did not hold back as he berated her. "You have been under her thumb for nearly a decade. You want me to help you? You want me to believe you're not here to usurp my throne? You've not a century of life under your belt. You are a *child*."

"I—" Issaria stammered.

"Father—"

"Give her back to the Witch," Commander Valente said. "Perhaps they'll do us a favor and fight each other."

"And what if that's exactly what the Witch wants? To get her little protégé back?" Magi Nicora refuted. "Send her north."

"She can't go back, Hecate tried to kill her," Calix protested. "She'll try again."

"Fallen kingdom, a fallen princess," his mother chided.

"The south *has* fallen," Tochka Freigdan agreed. "Let the darkness take them!"

Calix rebuffed, "There is more at stake than just Espera. There are forces at play—"

"Forces? That's all this is about! The forces of nature being *desecrated*," Kobzik shrilled as he pointed a knobby finger at the princess.

"Please, my people need help." Issaria's voice drowned among the clamor. "I can't just abandon them to her."

"Abandon them? Rumor is that you're *dead*, dear," Jallah said.

"Help Espera? What of Hinhallow? We've too many refugees as it is!" Adeleke Sinclair joined the fray. "We're running incredibly low on rations and the farms haven't been able to produce enough to cover the taxes."

"If we're to give aid to a city it should be Rhunmesc!" Magi Nicora said. "The north is melting. The landslides and floods are devastating the smaller villages."

In the rising din of debate Calix and Issaria looked to one another. The Blue Room felt full enough to drown them all in the hate they carried.

It was then that a green-grey moth, maybe the size of his hand, fluttered in through the garden doors on the far side of the council chamber. The creature, though larger than the average moth, drew little attention from the bickering council as it fluttered aimlessly overhead. Winging itself at the chandelier, it clinked and tinkled among the crystals until it had drawn the irritated stares of everyone in the room.

"Oh, do get rid of it," Queen Emmaleigh said as she waved her hand at it. "Someone do something."

Almost at the queen's behest, the moth seemed to fix its attention and it swooped down from the solarium chandelier to flap silver-dusted wings in Issaria's face until alighting upon the crown of her head.

And then the Blue Room was pitched into darkness, save the chandelier glowing like a small sun above their heads. Screams could be heard issuing from other places in the palace, terrified as darkness overtook them all.

Queen Emmaleigh shrieked and pointed at the blue-glass dome. "What is it?"

Shadow writhed on the glass dome, looking like ripping ocean waves.

"I'll investigate," Calix said as he started across the chamber, his eyes fixed on the shadows shifting across the cupola. The sound of the ocean seemed to be rushing overhead. He pressed the door open and stepped out into the small garden area behind the council chamber. "It's…moths," he breathed.

Calix beheld hundreds and thousands of green-grey moths, just like the one on Princess Issaria's head. Thousands didn't cover it. The eclipse flew so thick and close together, they inked out the sun. Little bits of light managed to flicker through the dense tapestry of wings, dappling the ground in amber light. Over the white stone walls of the palace, over alabaster spires and stained-glass windows. Shouts and cheers from the city echoed from beyond the walls, but the sound of their joy was muffled by the roar of the moths fluttering and flapping overhead.

The councilors fanned out in the garden, trampling flowers and small bushes underfoot as they craned their neck to look at the seemingly endless river of luna moths.

"What does it mean?" Kobzic, of all magicians, asked, his eyes wide upon the wings glinting in the sky.

Calix looked over his shoulder as Issaria, moth still upon her hair, stepped outside. Fearful eyes looked up to see the thousands of insects migrating overhead.

"Where are they going?" she asked.

As if in response, the moth upon her head flapped his wings until he'd cleared her hair, circled a few times as he got his wings beneath him, then joined his comrades in the sky as they flew over Hinhallow.

Headed east, he realized. Toward the Ascalith.

He elbowed through the councillors, past his speechless father and his stupefied mother. A tall alder tree grew gnarled near the northeastern wall of the palace. Calix found his footholds quickly and scaled the tree until he could see over the wall.

"What do you see, Prince Calix?"

In the distance, a strange, towering figure lumbered across the horizon. Stretched out as far as he could see, the river of luna moths flowed toward the rugged silhouette with strange spires extending like antlers from its head. The moths seemed to come to rest on its form, the stream of wings fanning out in a dense cloud around it. "Mythos above," he said to himself as he tried to make sense of it.

Last time he'd seen Baelfor, the Terran Mythos had been large. But now he was *colossal*. Even from this distance, Calix knew the god towered over even the highest tower of the White Palace. A literal forest grew upon him. Green light gilded his rock-hewn limbs in mossy light, seeming to radiate from within the titan himself. The seasons had evened out across him in a shifting autumn fire of orange and red among golden leaves.

"What is it, Calix?" King Akintunde asked from beneath him at the base of the tree.

"It's Baelfor," he replied. "It's *Baelfor*, Father. He's right there for all the world to see. Just walking the countryside."

"Impossible!"

Calix began to climb down as he said, "Ask anyone in the streets if you don't believe me."

Indeed, the chants could be heard rising from the streets.

Baelfor! Baelfor!

Calix met Issaria's eye for only a moment before he gave her a quick nod. He was going to make their move. "He's here for her," he said as he pointed across the garden at the princess. "Why else would that one moth come into the chamber and land on her?" He looked to his father. "I know you said we shouldn't speak of it, but they're here. You can see the Mythos for yourself, Father. There's no going back now." Calix looked to the other councilors. "When you all sent me to the Evernight, I met Baelfor before I even got to Espera. And I met…" He looked to Issaria and held her gaze as he said, "I met Aurelia."

"Prince Calix, please." Issaria's face fell at the mention of the Mythos' name but the uproar from the councilors drowned her out again.

"Aurelia," Calix said loudly, bringing everyone back to an irritated silence, "brought Princess Issaria and myself together in the woods that day, and *that's* why I didn't complete my assignment." He paused, and when no one interrupted him he continued, "The Mythos told me that I couldn't hurt her, and that when she came to ask for our help, we were beholden to answer the call."

His lies registered on her face only in the fact that Princess Issaria shut her mouth, which had been open and ready to protest.

"Calix," King Akintunde's voice was low and held a warning he'd not heard since he was a boy testing his limits.

Calix turned toward him. "Father. King Akintunde. You made me your heir only hours ago. Now a Mythos walks the horizon and you want to argue with *fate*?" He looked to Kobzik. "I sound like a superstitious fool, but I see your advisor has nothing to say of the Mythos' presence after all these years? Did you not see them waking in your flames, Kobzik? Did you even know Baelfor had spoken to me?"

Kobzik paled. His nostrils flared, accentuating his hooked nose. "The Prophecy, Your Highness."

"What prophecy?" Calix asked, his question echoed on the faces of many councilors.

"Entwined are fates of the Stars and Flame..." Kobzik let his sentence trail but grabbed at King Akintunde's arm with scrambling fingers. "She comes this way!"

Disgusted with the Seer, his father shook off the old magician's knobby fingers and looked to his son. "What would you have me do," King Akintunde asked, "yield my armies to a nobody, a *nothing*, for nothing?" King Akintunde found Issaria on the other side of the garden. The King's molten eyes lingered and a snarl of a smile grew upon his face. "You wish to help her? To give aide to her city and free them?"

This was a trap.

He could feel it in his bones. Wary, he looked to Issaria for only a moment before he settled his gaze on his father. "Yes?"

"Then what?"

"Then...Princess Issaria will assume her proper place on the Imperial Throne, I suppose? She *is* the rightful Empress, even the Mythos have returned from the dead to give her their support." He bit his tongue before adding, "And I support her claim as well."

His words seemed to be the exact thing his father had wanted to hear. King Akintunde's orange-yellow eyes flickered with golden victory. His smile grew wicked, and Calix knew the trap had sprung. *He* was the trigger. His father was trapping *him*.

"We shall arrange a marriage."

"What? No!" Issaria's protest was immediate.

"Father, that's not necessa—" Calix joined in but felt himself wavering. Once there had been an offer between them. Perhaps he hadn't known about it, but now, knowing who she turned out to be...*Maybe.* Calix shook his head. Now was not the time. "There doesn't need to be a marriage in order to supply military aid."

"Akin, my love," Queen Emmaleigh said as she laid a hand on the King's wrist, "Calix is already promised to my niece. To *Ares*."

King Akintunde waved her off and looked down the table to the councilor from Ares, Magistrate Zalendria Sirechi, who sat stiff-backed at being addressed under the circumstances. "Negotiations with your liege lord have been frustrating. He stands to gain much from his daughter marrying my son, but all *I gain* is two-hundred thousand more mouths to feed and defend against Hecate."

Zalendria's mouth turned down in a frown as she turned her dark eyes upon King Akintunde. "King Fraxinus sends his apologies at the perceived frustrations, I am sure. However, Princess Shairi is his only daughter. Forgive him for being *overbearing* when it comes to her happiness."

"Nonsense. The girl has been pushing her agenda on my dear wife for years. Fraxinus and I know perfectly well why she's been in Hinhallow so long. Why he's practically *paid me* to keep her here, hoping she'd eventually tempt my boy to her bed on her own."

"Father—"

"Calix, you want to go to war for that girl?" King Akintunde pointed a vindictive finger across the crowded courtyard. "You want to give her our armies, the very *lives* of our countrymen? All to proclaim *her* the rightful Empress?" He shook his tattooed head, turning so that the assembled could see clearly the way the seemingly abstract whorls and bold lines on his scalp formed the image of a crowned flame. "To what end for Hinhallow? All that sacrifice for nothing? I'll not stand for it." Akintunde looked back to his son with a smolder of a challenge in his lantern-like eyes. "If Hinhallow is to support this bid for the Imperial Throne, it is because we will put our blood on that very seat. The southern continent will unite under the Imperial Crown once more." Triumphant in his reasoning, he looked back to Princess Issaria and grinned. "What say you, girl? I'll give you what you ask, if you marry my son. Your victory will truly become *our* victory."

Issaria's face was unreadable as the sea of moths overhead ebbed and thinned until only a few dozen stragglers remained, flitting in the breeze on their way east. The sun blazed down on the garden again and her black hair shimmered with silver wing-dust, a thousand stars in the long-forgotten night sky as she lifted her head and brought her violet gaze to meet the King's. Jaw set, she nodded once. "I am undecided."

"Undecide—" King Akintunde bellowed. "Do not test me, *girl*. This is my final offer—"

"Your final offer before what?" Princess Issaria's eyes shimmered, but it wasn't tears Calix saw behind her hateful stare. "Before you take my crown? Before you slay my parents?" She stalked across the garden toward the old king with each statement from her lips. "Your last offer before you set explosives on innocent people, or before you set assassins on me?" She whipped an accusatory finger across the garden at Jallah Coppernolle, still in witness to these discussions of crowns and titles for some Cosmos-unknown reason. "Before you turn me back into a slave and let that *filth* sell me to someone else?" Dry laughter echoed hollow from within her before Issaria shook her head. "No, King Akintunde, with all due respect, you do not get to offer me anything. I have endured enough cosmos-forsaken *shit*. I am *still* the Imperial Princess, and I have been chosen by the Mythos for some task that I have *no idea* how to complete and no one has asked me for my input on any of this! If it is on my throne that you wish for *your* kin to sit, then it is I who will make the choice if I am to join my house or not."

She stared up at the king, barely half his height, defiance written all over her posture as she held her own against the Warlord of the

West. Never in all his days had Calix seen anyone speak to his father like that. Impressed, and a little ashamed that it had never been himself, he held his tongue while the king wrestled with such impudence.

"You will give me an answer in three days time, *Princess*," King Akintunde growled. "Get out of my sight until you've had ample time to provide me with the correct answer."

Princess Issaria held the king's glare as she stepped back. "With pleasure." She didn't look at Calix as she left the garden and exited the council chamber through the doors at the front of the Blue Room.

"You'd dare insult me, my *home,* by abandoning negotiations for that *beast* of a girl?" Queen Emmaleigh's hurt was not well-timed or disguised.

King Akintunde didn't even look at her. "Don't ever question me, Emma," his father said quietly. The king's weighted stare was on his son. Eyes alight with the glow of conquest, as if he hadn't just been talked down to by a *child,* as he'd been so keen to point out. "I'd give up quite a bit to see Ballentine blood on the Imperial Throne."

3 2

ELON

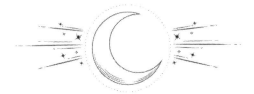

I t's blather, of course," Chancellor Koellewyn said for the umpteenth time that meeting, "But, there are rumors in the bazaar yesternight that Naia swam the Southern Seas beneath a fleet of fishing boats! The fishermen can't stop talking about the experience. Quite a tale."

"Unfounded," Hecate drawled, half ignoring Edlaire, as she had for all the prior presentations by the Chancellors of Espera.

They crowded the throne room to bring forth problems or developments that were thought to be of prime concern to the crown. Today, it seemed, Hecate had no mind for the machinations of the city as she'd met each proposal and report with the same enthusiasm. She plucked and preened at her shimmering bronze and wine-colored gown, as she issued the Chancellors to resolve the matters as they saw fit before dismissing them back to their place in the hall. Peeved when they should have been placated.

Mention of the water Mythos, however, had piqued Elon's interest. Issaria had seen Baelfor, spoken with him, just before this had all started. He scoured anything and everything to do with her for some semblance of a plan, for what to do once their insane phase one was complete. She was heading to Hinhallow to find Blaze and get the king's help with fighting Hecate. Elon was building an army to support her claim upon her return.

Maybe Baelfor wasn't the only one who'd come back. "How did the fishermen know it was truly Naia, and not a whale or shark? Sea creatures of great size *have* been seen before," Elon asked dubiously, knowing his interest in the subject would not be lost on Hecate or Commander Valente.

Edlaire wrung his hands together as if the question caused him great discomfort. His beady black eyes darted between Elon and the Empress Regent, as if questioning his place to answer. Hecate waved him on with her hand before examining her nails like a flaw just caught her eye, though Elon was certain she was listening intently now that he'd pried further.

"Well, there were more than one who saw her, and they all say the same thing."

"And what are they saying, Chancellor Koellewyn?" Commander Acontium questioned from where he stood just behind Hecate's chair.

"They say they could see the mana that held her form within the sea. She was glowing with blue runes from *deep* beneath the ships."

"So a blue glow is all it takes to become a Mythos these days?" Hecate asked skeptically. "Galen, can't *you* harness a blue light through your water magic?" She'd turned her face toward her fox-haired general and smiled at him expectantly.

Galen Acontium held out a gauntleted hand palm up. The hexagonal aquathyst in his palm twinkled as it caught the light, then one by one, wobbling globes of water rose out of the gem, each issuing a slight blue radiance to them. They joined together, and the aura began to glow. "It would seem I can, your Imperial Grace," he replied. Thin-lipped and unamused by his own trick, Commander Acontium clenched his fist and the blue light blinked out. The water-orb splattered apart when it hit the floor.

Everyone knew that water magic gave off a faint blue light. They weren't learning anything new and the Chancellor just seemed like he'd been taken in by town gossip when Edlaire shook his head. "I don't mean to disagree, but the creature reported was...of titanic proportions, Empress Regent."

"Explain."

"It was reported that the Mythos was singing a melody, haunting and aching, and there was a glowing blue light that extended over the length of five trawlers."

"End to end?" Jadzya Aphelion, Chancellor of Trade and Commerce, asked with awe in her voice.

Chancellor Koellewyn shook his head. "They'd been spread over by the Spires for the mollusks and crabs. Kept their distances to avoid the trapping lines getting tangled. Least a few boat-lengths between the fleet."

The Spires were a treacherous length of coastline to Espera's western border. Crystal from the Glass shot through the ocean waves like the jaws of some great animal left to decay in the salt sea. White foam swirled in eddies and hid the bulk of the crystal's shape beneath the waves making for the majority of shipwrecks in the area. Fisherman who hoped to just get a little closer to ease their crew's struggle in harvesting mussels and mollusks while the tide was low. That must have been *quite* the glow to be seen from deep under the night-dark waves and to have illuminated such a large area.

Elon was certain that what Edlaire claimed the fisherman saw was true and that meant something was definitely happening. Aurelia and Baelfor, now Naia. Perhaps further north there would have been sightings of Tarlix, or Zephyrus of the storms, but news from the Daylight cities was often slow to arrive. All the old makers of the world were coming together.

Eyebrow arched, nails drummed a rhythm on the arm of the throne. "Well? Out with it, Edlaire!" Hecate trilled. "You wouldn't shut up about it and now I can't get you to say more?"

Edlaire was perspiring. Familiar mahogany curls matted against his temples. "What else is there to say, Empress Regent?"

Hecate rolled her eyes, seeming more a petulant child than a monarch. "Where did Naia go? Was there anything more? What of the song? Was it a prophecy? Did she vanish or is she still out there singing with no one listening?"

Though called the Chancellor of Vox and Vita, Edlaire seemed to have lost his voice, and feared losing his life. He stammered and shook his head vigorously. "There was nothing else, your Grace. The fishermen saw her, and then she left, heading east. Naia would have gone out to sea, or gone right past us in the Bay of Prisms, but no one else has sighted her, it seems."

Hecate settled back into the throne at that, a satisfied smile on her face that felt more lethal than any blade. "Bring me word immediately if there are anymore...sightings of the Mythos. If they are in peril or seeking once again to guide the hands of men, I should be the *first* to speak with them."

Chancellor Koellewyn nodded in agreement and backed down from the throne, bowing repeatedly as he said, "Of course, your Grace. I'll see a message is sent as soon as word reaches my ear."

"See to it that it does, Chancellor."

The double doors to the throne room burst open drawing attention from all the politicians and lawmakers present. "She's been spotted, Empress Regent!" Daxios, the Post Master, charged in a scroll held aloft in one leather-gloved hand. A night hawk, an overly large species with dusky-grey feathers, most likely the bird that delivered the message, was perched with talons that glinted like onyx as they dug deep into the padding on Daxios' shoulder. Wings spread behind the hawk as it tried to keep balance with Daxios' gait, Elon noted that the outermost tips of his feathers had been painted with white markings. Was that a snake? Or a rose? The bird flapped its wings, obliterating any chance of whatever Elon thought he'd seen, and screeched as Daxios announced, "Princess Issaria is in Hinhallow! She's with King Akintunde!"

Elon's heart flip-flopped. Simultaneously, the warmth leached from the room as Empress Regent Hecate sprang from her seat on the stolen throne. She cleared the dais before she vanished, reappearing to meet Daxios in the center of the expansive hall, taking the distance in an instant with shadow-magic Elon had not seen her use in nearly a decade. She snatched the parchment from his hand and whirled away, reading the correspondence herself.

When she turned back to the throne and the gathered officials, Daxios lingering behind her like a lost child, her arctic eyes went straight to Commander Acontium's. "She's alive," Hecate barely breathed, but the words were crystalline clear as if she'd screamed it.

Issaria was alive. And she was *exactly* where she was supposed to be.

Elon looked down the hall at the Empress Regent, expecting to spy defeat in those cold blue eyes, but the placid smile that graced her narrow features made him recoil his own triumph instead. Elon glanced back to the Post Master and the hawk, still unsteady on such a narrow perch. Elon saw the paint on the bird's feathers again now that the bird wasn't squirming quite so much, he recognized the smudged markings.

A skull and a lit candle. Guild of Shadows and Bone.

This one had a pointed head, like the paint didn't dry quite as precisely as the artist would have liked. Three spikes rose out of a lopsided circle with hollow holes for eyes. A skull with a crown. A new sigil for the would-be Master of the Guild, should he only prove his ability.

Malek Wardlaw.

Elon's stomach dropped so fast that dark spots fettered the edges of his vision and he had to lean back against a pillar to keep himself from sinking to his knees. He could feel Hecate's eyes on him, Acontium's gloating grin, but he couldn't hide his horror as he sucked in gasping breaths of air.

"Sainthart? Are you quite all right?" Commander Acontium asked from where he remained by the throne.

It was over. Over so fast. Malek Wardlaw had been sent to Hinhallow with a dual mission. Find and get rid of her. And he'd proudly told his master precisely where his quarry would be.

Princess Issaria was as good as dead.

She might already have been by the time that bird delivered its scroll.

And from the exultation etched on the Empress Regent's face as Elon watched her sink back into her place on the throne, Hecate knew it too.

33

SHAIRI

Pink oleander flowers grew in tiny clusters of trumpets from arrow-like deep green leaves. Princess Shairi gently plucked the shriveled blooms from their stalks and piled the withered flowers on the workbench beside her. Sun warmed the greenhouse to an almost unbearable humidity, but as perspiration beaded on her brow, she found satisfaction in tending to the needs of her plants. Over her shoulder, the work she'd already accomplished piled around her in little harvested mounds: white calla lily trumpets lay among stalks of yellow henbane and white clusters of hemlock. Even a few greying star-shaped larkspur strayed among the more common lavender foxglove, sunshiny marigold, and indigo morning glory that graced the greenhouse.

"I thought I'd find you here, pet," Queen Emmaleigh's voice drifted into the dense humidity from behind.

Shairi whipped around, panic on her face. "Auntie Emma! Please don't come in here it's very dangerous!"

With a placid smile on her golden face, Queen Emmaleigh turned her fingertips to the silken blossoms of the greenhouse, choosing to grace the more dangerous of the princess's cultivations with her touch. "My, my, my, Shairi," she said as she strolled among the flora.

"Amaryllis, bloodroot, nightshade. You've quite the green thumb." She paused and looked about the greenhouse. "I'll be sure to get you a belladonna snippet. I see it's missing from your...stores."

Shairi blushed and cast her eyes curiously toward the queen. "You mean to say that...you *are* familiar with the commonality between my garden plants?"

"I mean to say that there is a greenhouse very much like this one in the Alcazar. Where I grew up, where *you* should have grown up. And while I may have manifested my magic in other ways a queen is not without her weapons. And as a daughter blessed of Baelfor, as *you* are, I learned certain recipes." Golden Emmaleigh turned her pale blue eyes toward the fuchsia blossoms beside her. "Oleander has such a... hesitant aroma."

Shairi glanced back at the pink plumes. "I've heard it can be a little like falling asleep in the right dosage."

"Well, maybe we want a little of the messy bits."

"What's happened?"

"There's a fox in the henhouse, pet, and she's about to make off with the crown prince," Queen Emmaleigh replied as she crossed the greenhouse with clicking heels. "King Akintunde is offering Calix to the Imperial Princess. You saw that *disgusting* display at the coronation?" Shairi nodded and didn't fight the scowl that twisted onto her face at mention of that insipid dancer-girl. "The one my darling husband sent to Calix's chamber was the princess in disguise."

"What? Why?" Shairi's heart pitched like a boat on stormy seas. "How?"

"She got caught by Coppernolle, the merchant Akintunde prefers to deal with, and faked her identity knowing she could be sold into the palace here."

"And we're certain she's telling the truth?"

The queen's blonde hair fell over her shoulder in a shimmering golden curtain as she stooped to caress the arching branches of bleeding heart flowers. "She knew that we had petitioned the Imperial Emperor for a marriage alliance nearly a decade ago. Not too long after Akin and I sent that letter asking them to consider the match,

Helios and Umbriel were assassinated. We obviously never heard about the alliance and we put the idea behind us as the Evernight made Ellorhys suffer so. And now the Mythos themselves seem to wake for her."

Shairi was silent as she fingered the withered pink flowers she'd already plucked from her oleander plant. King Akintunde hadn't even let her have a month of being engaged to Calix before revoking the promise and handing the prince out like a fancy stallion. It was revolting. More so that she still wanted badly to be the one gifted that stallion. She pinched the flowers and brought them up to examine them. "She's being housed on the other side of the pavilion pond."

"Is she now?"

Shairi nodded and put the flower petals down before rubbing the leaves of plant, selecting the firmest ones to be snapped from the stem. "We've interacted once or twice. I had no idea who she was, though it makes sense now. She was quite...insubordinate for a slave. Regardless of whose favor she'd curried."

"Yes, she just spoke out of turn to Akin as well. Asked for *time to consider* her options." Queen Emmaleigh was clearly irritated and scratched absently at her scalp as if the girl had indeed gotten under her skin. "And her aunt tried to have her assassinated, which is what brings the *poor dear* to our doorstep to begin with."

"Hm." Shairi grunted as she gathered up her oleander leaves and shed blossoms, pushing them into a woven basket on the workbench. "It sounds to me like this girl has a penchant for vexing the wrong people."

Queen Emmaleigh had retreated to the greenhouse door before she replied. "It would be so tragic if the wrong person managed to hire a competent assassin to finish her off."

"Wouldn't it just, Auntie?" Shairi said as she took her basket of oleander cuttings and escorted the queen from the stifling humidity of the greenhouse, taking care to lock the doors behind her. "I've some things to prepare, but I'll be certain to see the Princess for tea soon. Extend my most *hospitable* welcome to Hinhallow. Congratulate her on her engagement."

"Don't congratulate her quite yet dear. She has three days. She may still reject Akintunde's generous offer."

"How about...I don't give her the chance?"

Queen Emmaleigh smiled and cupped Princess Shairi's face in her hands, tilted her head downward, and laid a tender kiss to her chocolate curls. "Walk with graceful death, my sweet."

"Hand in hand, Auntie."

"So that pig thinks he can just shove you into marriage?"

"Hush yourself, Mint! That's the *king* you're talking about!"

Voices drifted out of the slave's pavilion house with careless abandon.

"C'mon Eiren. It's not like Akintunde himself is going to be wandering around the prince's pavilions. He's got his own seraglio somewhere else in the palace."

"Still you shouldn't be disrespectful," Eiren, Shairi assumed, cautioned. "What if someone heard you?"

"Who's gonna hear me, the fish in the pond?"

"What about that stuck-up princess that hates Kai's guts?"

"Princess Shairi isn't stuck up," the one called Mint said to Shairi's surprise. "She's just...in a difficult position."

"Oh yes, being a princess is *so hard*," another voice teased.

"I'm right here, Cizabet. Literally right here."

"Oh, yeah, I forgot you're a princess too. Sorry, Kai—Issaria. Am I allowed to called you that now that the king knows you're here?"

"Let's not advertise just yet," Issaria replied.

Shairi had heard enough. It was time to make her move. Loudly, but hopefully not too obviously, she stomped up the stairs from the direction of her own pavilion house. "Hello? I hope I'm not interrupting," she said as she elbowed into their cracked-open door. "It's me, Princess Shairi of Ares?" she continued to call out as she walked into their sitting area with a full tray of tea, biscuits, cakes and scones lofted before her.

"Oh, Princess! Allow me to help you," the dark-skinned girl with inky hair—Mint from the sound of her voice—said as she jumped up to help her with the laden tray.

Mint took the tray and another golden girl with blonde hair and brown eyes rose from her seat nearest the raven-haired princess to let Shairi sit. "Thank you, you're too kind. I fear...I fear I wasn't so gracious the first time we met and while..." Shairi brought her bashful gaze down to the floor. "I'm sorry for my behavior before. Toward all of you," she said as she looked up and around the room. "I was startled by your presence here. I was just told I was going to marry the Prince and then I found out he was just like his father—" She threw a hand up to cover her mouth and shook her head as she said, "No, no. I didn't mean that. I just meant to say that the king's proclivity for women is well known and I hadn't thought Calix had the same—"

"It's okay, Princess Shairi," Issaria said with a timid smile. "I wasn't very kind to you either, if you recall." Issaria's violet eyes shifted hues and shades in the light that poured in from the open garden doors in the back of the seating area. "You brought tea?"

"Oh! Yes!" Shairi leaned forward and withdrew the top from a glass teapot filled with thoroughly steeped pinkish tea. "It's from Ares. I drink this herbal blend with Princess Bexalynn all the time. Perhaps you'll join us for our next garden party, Princess?" Steam billowed in spiraling plumes from the teapot as Shairi leaned forward and poured a cup of tea for herself and another for Princess Issaria. She'd brought only two cups to minimize exposure to the toxins in her sly spread. "And ladies, please, help yourself to the treats. Marni made them fresh just for me to bring over," she said with a coaxing smile. "I told her I wanted to fix the horrible first impression I'd made on you all. It was just awful of me to treat you so unkindly."

The redhead leaned over and selected an innocent biscuit from the tea tray. One of the few untainted treats among various types of deadly toxins.

"Are you and Bexalynn close?" Issaria asked as she took the glass cup from Shari and held it, along with a clear glass saucer, in her hand. From just the right angle, it looked as though she were holding the pink tea invisibly. "I've yet to properly meet the young princess."

"Like sisters," Shairi said as she brought her own cup of tea to her lips, but did not allow the liquid to penetrate past her pursed lips. "We grew up together, and since you'll be staying a long while with us—marrying Calix and all—I was hoping that you and I, that we all could be friends."

Shairi watched eagerly as Princess Issaria smiled at her preening and brought the oleander tea to her lips, drinking deeply. "That's such a kind gesture, Shairi. However, I've not yet agreed to marry Calix. I don't quite like how King Akintunde is trying to force my hand." She paused, then set her teacup and saucer down in her lap. "I thought you'd be more upset that King Akintunde offered the marriage alliance to me when he'd only just offered it to you."

Shairi forced herself to laugh. After replacing her own teacup on the tray she tossed her chocolate curls over her shoulder and leaned across to Princess Issaria conspiratorially. "If I may be truthful, Issaria, I see Calix as a brother," she lied. Using Calix's own hurtful perceptions twisted in her heart but her aunt's implications had been clear. She had to eliminate her rival. "To marry him would be *strange*. I was only in agreement with it because it seemed like what everyone wanted at the time. I'd much rather marry someone for love rather than for a heartless alliance, wouldn't you?" She snagged a nightshade scone from the tray and nibbled the corner before frowning. "Sorry, dear. I didn't mean…Calix is a very nice man, even if he is a bit… preoccupied with the state of the kingdom. A true gentleman," she said, finding it hard to speak ill of him, even if he was stupidly breaking her heart at every turn. "You'd be lucky to end up with someone like the crown prince, truly."

Too bad she wasn't going to get the chance.

Issaria smiled and reclaimed her teacup and took another stabilizing sip before she nodded. "It is good to hear such kind things about him. I do agree with you, about marrying for love. Before…all this," Issaria said, "I hoped to marry for love. There was someone. He was dear to me."

Shairi frowned at this admission. "What happened to him?"

Issaria looked away and said, "My aunt killed him."

"Oh, Issaria, is that true?" the redhead asked with a mouthful of biscuit.

"How come you didn't tell us you were with someone? We've been talking about your possible marriage to the prince for like ever."

"Rhaminta, it's only been a day, and I..." Issaria took another bracing sip of tea and Shairi found herself hiding a smile by taking another bite of her toxic scone. It wouldn't harm her, just like the tea would find itself neutralized by her magic as well. The benefits of being Baelfor blessed, as Queen Emmaleigh had said. "I wasn't ready to admit that he might be gone. It's my fault he stayed behind. It was all to protect me, to keep her from taking over Espera completely. But...if he's gone then I've really got nothing left to hold on to with...love."

"That's so sad, Princess Issaria. I didn't mean to bring up such melancholy subjects," Shairi said.

"It's all right. You had no way of knowing."

"Are you considering it then? Saying yes?"

With all the eyes in the room on her, Princess Issaria's dark head was bowed as she considered. "I am still undecided. It's a huge choice, and one I didn't think I'd have to make quite like this, or quite so soon, truth be told." She looked up and met Shairi's intent stare. "I'm sorry, for what it's worth. I wouldn't have chosen this for me, but I certainly wouldn't have chosen this for you either. You seem kind, Princess Shairi. King Akintunde truly is wretched to use what should be precious as leverage for his own egotistical gains."

Issaria leaned over and grasped Shairi's hand with her own and gave it a squeeze. "I'm happy that from this all though, you and I can find friendship."

Then it was Shairi's turn to look away. Heat burned at her cheeks with Issaria's genuine apology. With the knowledge that Issaria had just ingested an intense concentration of oleander blossoms in the tea, guilt wrestled in her stomach. Shari had been faking her kindness toward Issaria. Death delivered by a kind, loving hand as Aunt Emma had instructed. But Princess Issaria truly was kind and forgiving of the awful way she'd behaved before. Guilt rotted the sweets in her mouth.

What had she just done?

Even before this moment, the princess had tried to be nicer despite their initial confrontation, even going so far as to tell Shairi that Calix hadn't touched her when she returned from his tower.

And what if she got caught?

Suddenly this seemed a mad, foolish idea.

She shook herself out of those thoughts before giving herself away.

"Forgive me for asking if it's another difficult topic, but I'm fascinated. I heard you crossed the Glass?" Shairi asked, changing the subject none too deftly.

"Oh, now that's a story. She almost *died*," the redhead said, eager to move conversation toward something less bleak.

"That's how Jallah Coppernolle found her," Eiren said from her seat across the room. "She was trying to come here, to talk to an assassin she met in the woods."

"When you say it like that, it becomes rather fantastical, but really I was just running away because I was told to."

"Don't be modest," Rhaminta scolded. "You were brave enough to try and lucky enough to have it work out in the most...bizarre of circumstances."

Issaria laughed and finished her tea before turning her smile back upon Shairi, who felt her undeserving, traitorous spine turn to mush beneath the Imperial Princess's orchid-hued gaze.

Some orchids, very rare orchids, were poisonous too.

The thought was so unbidden into her head that Shairi shot to her feet. The very idea that Issaria could out maneuver her *and* Queen Emmaleigh made her need to leave. The oleander would be setting in soon, and Shairi needed to be far away.

"That is fascinating, and I'd love to hear more but I just remembered that I promised the queen that I would play cards with her and Princess Bexalynn this afternoon. I can't believe I've forgotten!" She seized her tray of poisoned goodies from the table and retreated toward the door. "I'll take this back to my suite so that you don't have to worry about clean up. Thank you so much for your time, Princess Issaria!"

"Until next time, Princess Shairi!" Her voice chased Shairi from the pavilion house. "You know I think I'll have a lie down. I've got a headache forming just between my eyes and everything seems just so…bright right now."

"Well, it *is* daylight all the time now."

"Maybe you're just not used to it, Issaria. You are from the Evernight."

Glass cups rattled on their saucers as Shairi ran through slanted sunlight. She didn't stop until she was safely back across the Western Pavilions and in her own house, the oleander tea and nightshade berry scones safely disposed of and exchanged for the tea and scones that Marni had *actually* brought up from the kitchens—blueberry scones and hibiscus tea, the very same that Shari and Bexalynn were actually quite fond of.

When her alibi was set, she left the Western Pavilion and headed through the castle toward the Royal Suites, where Queen Emmaleigh and Princess Bexalynn were waiting to play cards, as promised. Shairi skipped a little as she walked and hoped there would be more of that delicious hibiscus tea. The oleander had left a bitter taste in her mouth. Perhaps, she thought as paranoia clenched her stomach, it wasn't poison that had fouled her tongue.

34

ISSARIA

I ssaria was halfway to her bedroom in the pavilion house when she felt her head crack open like someone had cleaved her skull in two. She leaned heavily on Rhaminta, who helped her to walk. Dizziness swept over her in icy waves and she heard a pitiful cry from somewhere in the room.

"What's happening to her?" Cizabet asked from somewhere far away.

"She's very pale," Eiren said as a hand pressed itself against Issaria's forehead.

She heard the sob again, as if someone were gasping for air.

"It's going to be okay, Issaria. We're here," Mint cooed into her hair as she practically dragged her down the hall.

The pitiful sounds were coming from herself.

"She's burning up! Here, get her to her on the bed."

"I can't make ice without an aquathyst!" Eiren's panicked voice sounded so distant. "I'm not that kind of magician!"

Hands helped navigate her limbs underneath the weight of blankets. Soft pillows cushioned her head. She felt as though she were lying on a cloud, drifting through the sky. Issaria opened her eyes again. Each of the girls were angels, pure halos of light surrounded their heads as they leaned in and out of focus. She giggled, reaching a hand out to touch a distant Cizabet, whose orange-red hair looked aflame with holy fire.

It was Mint's mahogany hands who found hers and clasped them tight. "Was she ill this morning? I don't recall her mentioning she felt unwell."

"I don't think so. It seems so sudden."

"Was Princess Shairi acting strange?"

"I don't think so? I'm not exactly an expert on her behavior."

"She ate and drank from the same source."

"She wouldn't...couldn't...could she?"

It was then that Issaria rolled over to the side of the bed and threw up pink-tinted stomach bile.

"Call for a healer!"

"Guards! Someone help!"

Footsteps, shouting and chaos were the last thing Issaria heard before darkness prickled its way across her vision, each brilliant halo of scintillating light winking out like thousands of little stars, leaving only the cold black to swallow her whole.

IT WAS SO HOT. SO HOT THAT EVERYTHING FROSTED OVER WITH HER thoughts.

She felt like her blood was boiling inside her veins.

This must be what the *Sanguinis Fervent* felt like as is consumed a magician. Like Prince Calix's hands.

It was agonizing.

Excruciating.

This was the end. She was certain of it. She was going to burn alive from the inside out. Her throat was raw from vomiting, or maybe she was just screaming.

It hurt so badly when they touched her.

And they were *always* touching her.

Poked and prodded. Fluffed and puffed.

Mild broth slid down her throat, a gentle relief from the acid sting of her own stomach.

A hand clasped in hers and held tight as she whimpered and darkness claimed her again.

THE MOST BEAUTIFUL SUNRISE STAINED ELLORHYS IN GOLD GILT EDGES and honey-thick warmth as the sun breached the horizon. Rosy pink blended into blossoming orange before a cloudless slate-blue sky expanded overhead.

At first she'd thought she stood atop a mountain, overlooking a lush valley sprawled with spires of verdant greenery. But upon closer inspection of her surroundings, Issaria found that she stood at the crumbled edge of a marble gazebo, beside which, a flowing stream of crystalline water was channeled throughout the garden in narrow marble rivets before emptying into larger streams to run freely over the side of the temple grounds. Beyond the garden threaded with starlit streams, pillars of moonstone and opal supported a domed temple roof. The structure was open enough, but Issaria could not spy what lay beyond the outermost promenade of pillars.

Besides, she thought as she turned her attention back to the overhang on which she stood, she wasn't on a mountain at all, but *floating* in the air. On an island.

"They made the most exquisite world, didn't they?" she said from beside her, and Issaria found that the voice wasn't as frightening as she'd imagined. "Wrought with magic and curiosities to be discovered by those brave enough to seek it. They never once considered that perhaps they'd given *too* much."

In fact, the voice she'd heard for so long inside her head, inside her heart, sounded very much like her own. An otherworldly accent lilted on her tongue as she spoke, but when Issaria closed her eyes, and just let her words wash over her like the sunlight bathing the world anew…she heard herself in Aurelia's voice.

"Who is 'they'?" she found herself asking, without really looking at the Mythos beside her.

"Why, Mother and Father, of course," she said as if Issaria should have remembered that. She gestured widely at the temple behind them, now rife with a glowing purple aura.

Issaria looked at her then, and found her heart trapped behind her ribs like a hummingbird trying to break itself free. She could have been looking at another version of herself, had she been born with her parents' coloring instead of her own inky tresses. Her small, thin nose, and the gentle pout of her lips. Even the shape of her eyes was similar. Long, white hair fell to her knees in a silken silver shimmer. Her eyes were the same mixed hue of violet and magenta, sparking the memory of an image behind a rippled pond.

"Dovenia and Chronos?" she asked, unsure if she meant Aurelia's mother and father, or if the Mythos referenced Issaria's own parents.

Aurelia tipped her head back and laughed, the sound pealing out across the realm like bells. Overhead the sky wheeled from dew-sparkled morning to diamond-flecked twilight in smeared hues of lapis, indigo and mulberry wine. "Chronos would have nothing to do with Mother after the whole *human* debacle. No, Essos created both Obsidia and myself with Mother to correct the imbalance of the world."

"The imbalance of…humans?" Speaking of the precursory species to magicians felt odd. The world was so young when humans walked the forests and valleys. Issaria looked out across the valley, dotted with yellow flecks like fireflies through the vale.

"Yes, and no. Ellorhys was out of balance. Tarlix, Dovenia, Naia, and Baelfor were ample enough to create the realm, to be worshipped as gods, but not as rulers. You know what happened there." The War of the Cities was a dark time in Ellorhys' history. Magic was emerging in favored houses, elevating some humans above others, creating castes and slavery among the magic and non-magic humans. Issaria nodded gravely and Aurelia continued, "We Primordial Mythos were conceived to embody the equal and simultaneous creation of good and evil. One cannot exist without the other; they are born of each other in the same moment. The flame and the very shadow it creates. Light and dark. Equal." Aurelia shook her head and looked out over the valley, now kissed by the midnight-arms of night. "We were supposed to be equal, sister," she murmured more to herself than to Issaria.

Stars spangled overhead and below ribbons of silver streams trickled throughout the valley, all cast off from the overflow of this one floating island above it all. The night gave way into another dandelion-veiled sunrise of tangerine and cherry-rimmed clouds. Beneath them, life in the valley stirred. Small flocks of birds winged across rivers and sang into the haze of the day. Along the riverbeds, Issaria could see the shapes of people in canoes, washing laundry in the streams. The valley was inhabited by humans. Issaria wanted to scream, to tell them to run away from this temple. To worship here would be to enslave themselves.

She did nothing of the sort.

"Why am I here?" Issaria asked as she watched this second sunrise burn off into a sapphire sky strewn with whips of cloud.

"Today is your birthday. Didn't you know?"

Issaria blinked, startled to silence by the news. "My...birthday?" She hadn't remembered her own birthday? Why was that again? Her head ached when she tried to think about what she'd been doing before she...appeared at the Vera Caelum. How had she come to be here?

"Yes, though it's a rather archaic celebration. This one's only special because it *happens* to coincide with the seal on your Curse."

"The...curse that put you inside me?"

Aurelia arched an eyebrow at her, and Issaria felt as though she were looking at a reversed image of herself. A doppelgänger. And she wasn't sure which of them existed first.

"I put the curse on myself, actually. You just happened to be the one that met my...specifications. Obsidia triggered the curse, so this is her fault, really. If she had just left well enough alone..." She sighed. "I was just suspicious enough of her to put the curse upon my soul so that if I was to meet my end at the hands of a perceived enemy, I

370

would come back to correct whatever misdeeds stemmed from my early execution." Aurelia shrugged callously. "Eclipsed no more, eighteen orbits unwinds the time spent within descended blood."

Issaria couldn't hide the horror on her face. She had been *incubating* a goddess inside her.

Darkness seemed to set with her mood. Inky twilight bled up from the horizon. A pale sliver of moon cut a path across the sky, tracking them like a slumbering eye.

"Don't look like that, *Sanguinem Descendia*, I could have been trapped in the Saros Cycle for a millennia, but *you* were just perfect. Look at us! We're more identical than Obsidia and I were. And now I can clean up the mess Obsidia made when she killed Endymion and myself to harvest our mana."

Issaria's hands flew to her mouth. "That's what Hecate did to my parents. That's how she...made the Eventide."

"I fear I should have known my sister was corrupted against me, but I hoped for the good in her, the last little bit of her shining soul to come out, even at the end."

"You cursed your own soul," Issaria hissed. "I'm fairly certain you knew she was corrupt."

Aurelia shrugged again. "I suppose I did. I hoped it wasn't so. Erebus convinced her, though it matters not what that vile creature persuaded her to do in the name of love. Either way, it's a good thing I'm here. Who would have thought that Obsidia's daughter would think to carry out her plans after seeing them fail so spectacularly the first go around?"

"And now we're here," Issaria concluded, bringing them full circle. She didn't need a full history lesson to know what had happened between and since. "But where is here? And why now?" She looked around her, back toward the temple. "Why can't I see inside?"

"Because you're not really here. I brought you here so we could...meet."

"If I'm not really here, then where am I?"

"You're asleep. You're very weak, I'm afraid. Poison. I'm doing all I can to prevent your heart from beating itself out of your chest, to keep your body from seizing, but the concoction you were given was meant to be lethal to a hundred magicians, let alone just one."

Issaria was quiet as her eyes gobbled up the silhouetted landscape of the oasis. Afraid of breaking whatever spell she was ensorcelled by to make her see such beauty, instead of feeling whatever pain her physical body might've been in at that very moment, she remained quiet. That was why she couldn't remember what she was doing before she woke up at this temple. She was probably dying right then. The only thing keeping her alive was…the Mythos inside her. She turned back to the white-haired reflection of herself.

"Why?" she asked no louder than a whisper.

"They're all very concerned about you. Even the ones who suspect I am within. They care not for me at all. It's very frustrating."

"You're talking to me because you don't like that I've had a life for eighteen years before you decided to start making an appearance whenever you feel like?"

"Well, that and I'm finally strong enough to break through and speak freely. At least for the time being. I'm still gathering my strength. It's as if I've been getting a single rain drop every day since you drew your first breath, and now that you've broken the seal on your Saros Cycle, it's pouring. I'm soaking up as much as I can, but I can only contain so much after being weakened for so long."

"That's why you need Prince Calix to take you here. To take us here."

"The Vera Caelum is the final step in restoring me to my former glory."

This time, Issaria could pinpoint the moment she saw sunlight illuminate the horizon. First, it dusted the air with gold, frosting the red sand beyond the oasis in cinnamon-spice. Trees glistened juniper green and spruce blue with the first lemony rays of light. A single white horse with a golden horn drank from a misty stream below.

Aurelia nodded. "I would prefer to be the one to join him on the journey. Tarlix's flame burns in him, and I wish to see how much of my old friend remains. But even now I find I am unwelcome."

Blue sky hung between them, endless and oppressive in its dominance.

"You can't just take over my life," Issaria said. "I won't let you."

"Yes, I see it's quite problematic that my vessel has...developed connections. It would have been better if you'd been isolated, maybe in some sort of...suspended animation. Next time, then," she said absently. "Your aura is too strong for me to push aside entirely."

Issaria snapped her attention back to the mythos. "You admit you've been trying to take over my body?"

Aurelia gave her an incredulous look. "What *else* is a vessel for, *Sanguinem Descendia?*"

"Stop calling me that!"

"What else should I call you? You *are* my blood by right of lineage. The hollow space inside you where your magic should be? I live there. *I* am your magic. Each time you've touched it you've let me see the life you've lived. I could take away all the pain, pay back all the hurt you've endured because the balance was disturbed." Aurelia smiled at Issaria and caressed her cheek. "You should be happy to let me take your place. I can fix *everything.*"

"You can't just be me! I'm a person, a *Cosmos-forsaken* princess!" Issaria's voice grew shrill as she tried to reason out to this *being* why she couldn't just take over her body now that the seal between them was breaking. "I have a life! I have a name!"

"Issaria, Issaria, Issaria. Yes, I know you've got a name," Aurelia spat as she rolled her eyes. "It's all I hear these days. They are *begging* me to give you back to them. Haven't even thanked me for keeping you alive. It's like they don't even want me there!" Aurelia pouted, and Issaria felt her realization click into place.

The air took on a rosy hue, tinting everything with pinks and corals as the sun dipped down toward the horizon. Rising up from the other side of the world, the silver sickle of the moon already ripped across the star-flecked azure sky.

"Are you...jealous of me?"

"This isn't exactly how I thought coming back to life was going to be, you know. I didn't count on you being so...so..."

"Alive?" Issaria offered, wondering how in the Cosmos she could actually *pity* a goddess.

"I thought I would…start existing one day, and everyone would rejoice that I'd returned to bring light and balance back after centuries of bickering among the rabble." Aurelia huffed and fixed a hand on her hip. "I admit it seems rather short-sighted now that I consider the cost of black magic, but I knew if Obsidia were to harvest my mana, she would be nearly unstoppable. A single mortal life for *my* life hardly seems too much to ask when I alone can correct the error of my parents' creations."

"The error?"

The darkness of night smothered the last rays of sunshine on the horizon before indigo crept through the wilderness with predatory stealth, bringing with it the song of crickets and the flutter of moths dancing in the moonlight. Just when she wasn't sure Aurelia was going to tell her what the flaw in humanity was, she heard her reply. "The free will. I've come to take it back."

"You can't just *take back* free will."

"Hm, you're right. I'll have to just raze the whole realm and have the Elementals start from scratch."

"What!? No! You can't just wipe us off the planet either!" Issaria shouted, exasperation leaching her strength.

Aurelia crossed her arms over her chest. "You're no fun. Mother would say the same thing, if she were here." She turned her back to Issaria and peered out over the edge of Vera Caelum and sighed. "I suppose you magicians have *some* redeeming qualities. Not many, mind you, but some. That knight back in the crystal city…he had a good heart." Mention of Elon had Issaria's throat clenched, her heart stuttering at mention of him in past tense. "And the ones who call to you even now have warmed the cockles of my heart."

"So, you're not going to raze the continents?"

"Perhaps, one day. Not yet," Aurelia replied. "Our time grows short, Issaria, and the cost of sparing your life has left me severely weakened in a time when I should be reclaiming my former glory. I will allow you the time it takes for your body to reach this spring, if only so I can recoup the mana I have expelled on you, *descendia*. When you bring me there, I will pass judgement on humanity and we shall see what they have earned."

"And if I refuse to bring you here? If I just stay away and ignore you?" Issaria made herself ask the question. She held her chin up as she met her own stare, foreign in its alien indifference.

Aurelia closed the distance between them and captured Issaria's chin with her pale fingers. "Then I will take your body for myself," she whispered with a lover's softness, "and you will have fulfilled your role as my vessel, *Sanguinem Descendia*." A cold smile tugged at Aurelia's lips before she pressed them feather-light against Issaria's mouth, and stomach-tumbling vertigo swallowed her in velvet darkness.

HER LIPS WERE VERY DRY. COLD SWEAT BEADED ON HER BROW AND ON the back of her neck where she could feel the tiny spirals of hair matted against her clammy skin. The sheets around her body were ringed in a cold halo of perspiration. Her limbs felt heavy with sleep and for a moment, the fear of paralysis gripped her as she prized one of her eyes open.

The curtains in her bedroom had been drawn shut, blocking out the brightness of the day. The bedside table was missing her growing stack of novellas and was instead covered with opaque glass bottles with cork stoppers and tinctures. A carafe of water sweat rings onto the oak tabletop next to a solarium crystal that gave off a peaceful, pinkish glow.

And hunched over in his chair next to her bed, face down in a wrinkled blue tunic with a blackened hand cupped around hers, was Prince Calix. Black hair spilled onto her dusky-pink coverlet as he slept. Deep, steady breathing, a rhythm she could feel in her bones. His golden skin seemed to shimmer in the shifting solarium light. Stubble prickled his jaw in a faint shadow and she wondered how long he had been sitting with her.

She glanced deeper into the darkness of her room, but it appeared as though they were alone. The garden doors were closed, shades were drawn there as well. Flowers drooped in the gloom, but the bouquets were fresh enough that she knew they'd been replaced recently. A chair in the corner had a teal blanket draped absently across it, an indication that Mint or maybe Eiren had been sitting there. Perhaps they would come back, but...until then.

Issaria looked back to the sleeping prince. She wanted to push his hair back from his face, but she didn't want to wake him. He was ruggedly handsome in a way that was entirely different from Elon. Where Calix was sun-bronzed with hair like crow's feathers, Elon was all boyish charm, russet curls, and kind eyes. Elon had been a quiet, dedicated love that smoldered inside her for years. Her heart would never forget what feeding those secret embers with lingering smiles and prolonged touches had felt like. How entirely consumed, how completely contained.

But Elon was gone.

And now she was free falling.

The safety of Elon Sainthart had been extinguished, and worse, without her having felt him being snuffed out. Another casualty of her aunt's crusade for more power. Further tipping the scales in her favor.

Issaria had to be the one to stop her. She couldn't very well let Aurelia take that from her.

Slowly, she pulled her hand out from the gentle grasp of char-coaled fingers. When she was free, she leaned over and removed the glass from the top of the carafe and quietly poured herself a glass of water.

Sweet water.

It wet her cracked lips, drenched the tundra of her throat. The groan slipped unbidden from within her as she guzzled her cup and greedily poured another.

"You're awake," Calix whispered as she swallowed down another gulp of water.

"Only just. I'm sorry, I didn't mean to wake you. I was just so thirsty." Heat flushed her cheeks as she offered a smile, then replaced the carafe and empty cup on the nightstand.

He sat up, rubbed sleep from his citrine eyes. "Don't be sorry. I'm so glad you're all right, that you're talking. Awake." He released a deep sigh and ran a hand through his hair. "I was scared we were going to lose you."

"How long have I been...asleep?" she asked tentatively.

She saw a flicker of darkness in his luminescent eyes. "Four days."

Her mind emptied. She'd been talking with Aurelia for *four days*? "What happened to me?"

"You were poisoned. We're not sure who, but *someone* knew Princess Shairi intended to share her tea with you that afternoon. They used her to deliver the poison to you."

Issaria's mind went blank. She was only alive because Aurelia had intervened and kept her body from being completely overwhelmed by the neurotoxins as they attacked her organs. Princess Shairi had no such guardian. "Is Shairi...is she dead?"

Calix shook his head. "Though Marni cleaned up the tray, she swears it was the same tea and treats she'd been delivering to Shairi and Bexalynn for years. We had alchemists and healers test the remains of the meal, but nothing was fouled. We believe the would-be assassin took a risk and tainted only one cup, placing it where they thought Shairi would be most likely to give it to her guest, instead of taking it for herself."

He pressed fire-blackened fingers into the corners of his eyes before he leaned on her bed with his forearms. The investigation had taken a toll on him. Dark circles rimmed his usually bright eyes as they found her again. "It was an incredibly calculated risk that could have gone poorly, but then the Witch was never one for damage control. We're assuming that if an accident had happened where Shairi poisoned herself instead of you, Hecate would have been just as happy with the results. We're not certain how Hecate knew you were here so quickly. Father is furious she was able to get someone inside the staff. He's having everyone interrogated. He thinks if she has an agent working here they may have infiltrated the staff long ago so that they would be in place to exact orders whenever the need arose."

Issaria's heartbeat thundered in her skull. Her aunt knew she was here. Had sent *more* mercenaries after her. How? She had a fairly good idea of how she would know Issaria had gone to Hinhallow. Elon would *never* have betrayed her, but if Hecate had tortured him, or enacted some forbidden truth magic...anything seemed within the realm of possibility when it came to Aunt Cate now that Issaria knew the truth.

"There was someone at the slave auction. Uninvited. He tried to buy me. Offered too much. Even Jallah was suspicious of him and refused his offer. I didn't think of it before but...he could have been one of hers. I thought so at the time, but I'd forgotten once I was here."

"We'll speak to Jallah for more details, and I've posted a provision of soldiers from both my own guard, as well as the Kingsguard." Calix examined the gold embroidery on her blanket. "You should rest more. I hadn't intended to fall asleep here. I must be...overtaxed," he said carefully. "I'll get one of the girls to sit with you. Rhaminta, or Eiren. They'll be glad to see you awake." He looked down on her from where he stood next to her bed. "It really is a relief to see you well again, Princess."

Calix wasn't Elon.

But perhaps she didn't want him to be.

Maybe this time...she wanted to burn from the inside out.

3 5

ELON

In the days following Malek Wardlaw's hawk, Elon spent an unnatural amount of time loitering near the aviary. The longer he went without seeing another bird, the more he dared to hope Issaria had escaped whatever foul plot Wardlaw had laid for her. And the more a second, smaller voice whispered that longer just meant he was taking his time, making *certain*, as Hecate had commanded. Elon scoured the starry skies for a predatory, black silhouette with white sigils painted on its wings, but to no avail.

Lurking near the mouth of the stables, Elon was starting to hallucinate shapes and images in negative space between stars when Safaia found him. She had been in route to the kitchens with a basket full of fresh cabbages and beets. Basket balanced on her hip, garden soil smudged along the bridge of her nose, she met his brooding stare as he briefly looked away from the aviary to acknowledge her, and heaved a great sigh. "Elon Sainthart, are you just going to stand there waiting for another hawk?"

Her honey eyes were similar to her sister's though the tone in Maiyra's voice would have been taunting. Safaia was solemn, respectful even if she was completely exasperated by him at this point.

It had been nearly a week, and still no word had come regarding

379

Malek's mission to assassinate Princess Issaria. He didn't want the hawk to come, by any means, but *if* it did, he wanted to be one of the first to prize its information. He didn't get to read the original correspondence from Wardlaw. Hecate kept the note to herself, had probably incinerated whatever incriminating contents it beheld as soon as she was able. She'd made a show of sending a rider to retrieve Issaria immediately and with diplomacy, but Elon knew that the rider would never make their destination. If there even was a rider.

His eyes were still searching the star-strewn sky when he replied, "I don't know what else I'm supposed to do, Safaia. The rebellion needs her. Otherwise, we're just farmers with grudges and Hecate will kill them all." He sighed. "I should have gone with her," he mused, then shook his head. "No, if I'd gone with her there would be no rebellion to support her when she gets back."

There he went again. Being overly optimistic. It was his fool's heart is what is was. It was going to get him killed someday.

Once, he would have been thankful for the opportunity and done so gladly.

"Or we disband," she said softly as she placed her basket against the side of the barn and leaned against the frame with him. Moonlight gilded Safaia's chestnut braid in shadows of mahogany and walnut.

"Or we disband," he repeated hopelessly as he met her eyes. "That might be worse. You haven't been out to the wood to see them, but they're *hopeful*, Saf." He chuckled. "A few of them are actually quite good. I've a mind to recommend a few for the Guard when this is all—" He caught himself and stopped. He was doing it again. Being far too optimistic for the bleak corner they'd backed into. Elon shook his head and sighed, looking back to the sky as if a hawk would come that instant and free them all from the worry and the wait. "I don't want to be the one to take that from them."

Safaia was silent for a while, the sounds of the night filling the air between them with crickets and the wings of insects. Frogs croaked from someplace nearby, loud enough for a bullfrog bellow to make Safaia start with a giggle. "Issaria *hates* frogs."

"That's probably my fault," Elon admitted recalling the incident.

He'd been maybe...ten? Issaria couldn't have been more than six when it had happened. It hadn't been too long after he'd been brought to the palace as an orphan. "I *may* have very accidentally imploded a frog while she was watching."

"You exploded a frog?"

"Imploded. There's a significant difference between the two."

"Did the frog die?"

"Ah." His face fell. "No. The um, the results were the same."

"The same as..."

"The same as when I accidentally exploded a frog the first time I tried the experiment."

Safaia held his gaze for a moment, then burst into peals of laughter. Tears bulged at the corners of her eyes where she screwed them shut from laughing so hard. Her laughter was raucous, filling the yard with obnoxious cackles and guffaws. Elon started laughing because she was so funny while *she* was laughing at him. Several minutes of trying to recover from hysterics and many rounds of falling back into giggles later, they sucked in deep, calming breaths.

Safaia was wiped her cherry cheeks of their tears. "Oh my. I haven't...I haven't laughed like that since Issaria was still here," she confessed.

"Neither have I," he admitted.

"You know who else hates frogs?"

"You?" Elon guessed, and she shook her head. "I don't know, who?"

Safaia's smile was small as she looked up at him with those familiar eyes. "Maiyra. I put one in her boot when we were kids."

Elon blinked before he laughed. "Oh, really?" He wasn't sure why Safaia had thought to tell him that little factoid, but he filed the information away for later anyway, intent on paying back some sass with a well-place amphibious scare. No explosions or implosions needed. He was already grinning at the thought of Maiyra's squeal.

"Issaria...she wouldn't want our lives to stop because of this. She'd never forgive herself if the world stopped spinning on her account."

"Not to point out the obvious or anything Saf, but..." He pointed to the moon-dark sky. "One way or another, it kind of did."

"You know what I meant, Elon." Safaia didn't look at him as she gathered her basket and turned to him with hazel eyes blazing in the moonlight. Maybe they weren't so similar to her sister's after a second look. "You know, we're still doing the right thing. *You're* doing the right thing. With the..." She left her voice trail off, but Elon knew what she meant. "Even if things don't...work out the way they should. We're not wrong to want better for ourselves. The people...they should know that. And so should you."

Elon watched her go, basket balanced on her hip as her long braid swayed behind her, suddenly seeing differences everywhere. He cast his eyes back toward the sky, still hoping and not hoping for a glimpse of painted wings against the black.

THE COPPER-RIMMED MAGNIFYING GLASS STABILIZED OVER THE GLASS LIP of the shattersphere displayed the tips of the tweezers and the small, almost grain-of-sand-sized crimson solarium crystal in alarming detail. Every nook and cranny, crevice and shining facet; it looked like a frozen drop of blood gathered between the alloy prongs. He had to be *incredibly* careful while adding the crystal to the contents of the sphere. Blackpowder, a very carefully measured combination of powdered sulfur, charcoal, and saltpeter, had been slowly added to the sphere, and one wrong move—

Elon closed his eyes and took a steadying breath.

He didn't want to think about what one wrong move could mean. Blackpowder was highly volatile and caused incredible explosions when ignited. He'd been making more and more of his creations and bringing them to the Baelforia to stock the rebellion. He hadn't been out to see them in a few days thanks to that stupid hawk, and he owed them a gift when he made it back out to the woods. Shatterspheres of silex, lux, blackpowder, projectile spheres were among elixirs and healing salves he gathered from Safaia and Abihail from the palace kitchens. Liara and Isida had been discarding more and more laundry due to "irreversible staining" as well, and the camps had been starting to resemble real encampments of actual soldiers if you didn't look too closely. He opened his eyes and refocused himself on the task ahead.

Drop the solarium shard into the black powder *without* blowing them all Cosmos high.

The door to his bedroom slammed open.

Rhori and Xenviera were both out of breath, but Elon was swearing, "ARE YOU COMPLETELY DAFT?" as his grip on the tweezers spasmed, and the solarium crystal dropped more than the advised five millimeters.

It pillowed into the mound of black powder within the shattersphere.

It sizzled and a popped like kernels of corn on the fire.

They held their breath.

Smoke fizzled from a smoldering ember, then snuffed out, black smoke turning into a white plume of feathery air that trailed up to the ceiling.

Nothing happened.

They let out a collective breath of relief and Xenviera snapped, "Shouldn't you put a sign on the door if you're...alchemizing or whatever?"

"You...you are *both* so, so lucky I messed this one up," Elon said without looking at them, eyes roving his notes for his misstep. It might have been the saltpeter. He'd used chunks the first time and it had worked better. Powdered didn't seem to be the right texture for the concoction. He'd revert back to chunks and recall the spheres he'd delivered to the Baelforia as faulty. Better to have working product than a soldier launching a dud explosive.

"Elon, there's news," Rhori said as he elbowed the raven-haired warrior out of his way.

"A hawk?" he asked, almost wishing he *had* blown them all up, rather than hear an affirmative.

Rhori shook his head. "A rider. From Hinhallow."

"Issaria?" he asked, throwing his goggles down on his desk and nearly knocking over his bum-shattersphere.

"It bears King Akintunde's seal," Xenviera replied.

"Hecate has it?"

"She does," Rhori said. "She's already opened it."

From the tone of his voice, Elon already knew this wasn't going to be good. "She's gone?"

"She was poisoned, Captain," Xenviera reported. "Badly. Akintunde claims her as his ward, says it was an attack against his crown."

"The chancellors don't know what to make of it. Hecate stepped right in it, thinking the letter would be about the assassination," Rhori said with the smug satisfaction of a cat. "They're up in arms as to how and why the Warlord of the West has Princess Issaria and is *concerned* for her safety, enough so to put out a proclamation to the cities about it."

Elon sat back on his stool, blood roaring in his ears. Poison. Chancellors upset. Proclamation.

"Did the proclamation mention an alliance between Princess Issaria and Hinhallow against Hecate?" Xenviera shook her head. "Did she recover? Is she well?"

"She is recovering; the proclamation was clear about the attempt on her life failing. The Ballentines graciously welcomed the *refugee princess* into their home, city and..." Rhori trailed off.

"And what, Rhori?"

"And their hearts, Captain," Xenviera replied, casting a sideways glare at Rhori for failing to deliver the news. "King Akintunde said that the Ballentines were opening their hearts to welcome her."

Hearts.

The word thundered through him like his own pulse.

Hearts.

Poison. Chancellors upset. Concerned for her safety.

Hearts.

"Wasn't..." Elon's tongue felt like molasses as he tried to form words, "Wasn't there a marriage alliance that was being negotiated? Hinhallow and...Ares?" He felt his world growing small, dim, as the words left his mouth.

"It's just some phrasing to taunt Hecate. Old Akin of the West is

384

just baiting the witch to see what he can scare her into showing him," Xenviera rationalized. "It doesn't mean anything."

"What does Hecate think?" Elon asked at last.

"She wants to see you in the throne room, actually," Rhori said, glancing guiltily at Xenviera, who looked smug that he'd at least delivered that lump of coal himself.

"What, she wants to gloat in person that her plot worked out? Original." Elon shucked his leather gloves and tossed them on top of his goggles. He'd come back to the faulty sphere later, maybe. But the one he tucked in his pocket...well, that one he was *certain* was live.

ELON KNEW THE REAL GAME WAS BEING PLAYED WHEN HE ENTERED THE throne room and found Hecate, draped in silver-sparkling silk and lounging sideways across the sacred seat, a goblet of wine in one hand. The Imperial Crown, a weighty thing of silver ore, black pearls, and raw crystals in an iridescent white that seemed to supply its own aura of sparkle and light, twirled between her lax fingers in the other.

Behind her, crimson-hair swiped back with sweat—Elon had seen that look in the arena as *he himself* sparred against his commanding officer—Commander Acontium held his place at attention while the loathing that slid across his superior's features relayed the message clearly. He was here, but not for Elon's benefit. He had no ally in the water magi who'd helped him complete his training in Soren Sainthart's place. It stung like betrayal, but Elon had the sinking feeling, in that moment, that Commander Acontium had instilled faults in his fighting that he would exploit later. Just like he'd planted Flynt among them as an Initiate and let their camaraderie flourish on its own. A single web of lies in an entire garden of falsities he'd been blind to all along.

"Captain Sainthart," Hecate crooned from where she luxuriated. "So good of you to join us. I've dismissed the Council, you see, so that you and I could...be friendly again."

Elon made himself continue to walk down the length of the hall, toward that vile woman who would call herself Empress, as he said through clenched teeth, "I wasn't aware we were ever *un*friendly, Empress Regent."

It was then that the red at the foot of the throne dais caught his eye. It gleamed scarlet like rose petals against the opaque crystal of the palace floor. Beads of red like the single solarium shard he'd been dropping into a blackpowder shattersphere not more than a half hour ago.

Red like blood.

And it was on Acontium's blade as well. He looked up from the splatter on the floor next to the dais and schooled his features into a mask of calm. This wasn't a meeting.

It was an execution, and perhaps not the first of the coup that was very obviously unfolding in the light of King Akintunde's proclamation.

"Oh, we were friendly once upon a time. In an orchard not so very long ago…oh, your bleeding heart!" She cried and gestured dramatically, hand with the crown to her forehead. Red wine sloshed over the rim of her cup where it bled along the seams of her fingers. "A lot has changed since then, dear Captain."

He was near to seeing red as he jammed his hands in his pockets to keep himself from doing something stupid. "I'd be remiss to disagree with you, Aunt *Cate*."

Hecate laughed uproariously, her cackle echoed off the ceilings far above. "See Galen? I told you he would bite if I showed my fangs first. He *can* play with us!" She downed the contents of her goblet and threw it down the hall at him. The alloy clattered to the floor between them. "He's been playing all along! Clever Captain Sainthart," she said with a sing-song voice, far gone from the poise and dignity he'd come to know and expect from the Empress Regent. "Thought we couldn't figure out it was *you* who helped her that night? You who caught our little infiltrator?" She leveled her arctic eyes on him and said, with the same syrupy sweetness he'd heard when she spoke to Malek, "Come now, Sainthart. After all, the game is about to get a lot harder. You're not really cut out for this sort of life, are you? You certainly weren't born to it, like your *precious* princess."

"At least I was born low-class. What's your excuse?"

"Excuse?" she echoed, sitting up at his snide tone.

"For your piss-poor attitude, Cate. Issaria *loved* you! How could you do this to her? To your own *sister?*" he shouted at her, the mask of calm shattered. "For what Hecate? For darkness? For power?"

And then her wicked smile grew. She didn't deny a thing. She only said, "Who are we kidding, Sainthart? Neither one of us *really* belonged here. That poison might not have been my doing, but it is proof that I'm not the only one who's had *enough* of the Imperial reign. Sooner or later, my darling niece will meet her end. In the meantime, it's time for something new." She gestured with her hand. "Commander, I've finished speaking with the traitor. See to it that he's dealt with properly."

Commander Acontium rounded the back of the throne, and took one massive step off of the dais toward Elon.

He only had to pull out the sphere and run.

The explosion echoed in the hall. Fire scorched and heat seared as a maelstrom of light and flame chased him back. Hecate's screams for healers could be heard as Elon cleared the entry, stifling embers that clung to his tunic, pants, and hair. He heard the clamor of armor and shields, the rattle of boots on the floors as soldiers poured into the palace to search for him.

No place was safe now. Not after he'd launched blackpowder at the Empress Regent and her loyal minion. They wouldn't have died, but he hoped it hurt like hell and the fire from the oversized solarium crystal within would burn even after there was no blackpowder left to fuel the blaze. The mixture in the shattersphere he'd brought to the meeting was a dummy sphere, a mock-up of the real deal. The first one he'd ever made. As he stole through the halls and crept out into the yard, he wished the sphere had been the one he was working on that evening. That it hadn't been a flawed sphere and he could have just wiped that bitch right off the face of Ellorhys then and there.

He took Dandelion, no tack or gear, and rode hard for the gate.

Soldiers rushed back and forth locking down perimeters and running messengers to the towers. Before anyone of real importance knew what he'd just done, Elon slipped out in the commotion and sent up a silent prayer to the Cosmos that the other members of the rebellion would follow suit and they would all see each other again in the Baelforia.

36

ISSARIA

Poison, it turned out, especially one meant to kill a small army, left one weak and in need of recovery. Healers came in and out of her bedroom amid a sea of well-wishers. Between the girls who were always flitting in and out like birds, Queen Emmaleigh and Princess Bexalynn came by. It was clear within moments of their arrival that they were only apologetic for fact that the 'incident' happened within their home and embarrassed them. *Perhaps if you'd told us of your presence within our home instead of traipsing about like a—* Issaria bit back a growl as she recalled the way Princess Bexalynn had stayed her mother's rebuke with a gentle hand.

Princess Shairi, surprisingly, had been one of the first to arrive, rushing through the pavilion in only a dressing robe and unkempt hair, having heard the news of Issaria's wakefulness from her chambermaid. Her hands shook as she had petted Issaria's hair, kissed her hand and apologized for allowing such a thing to happen to her, for being the one to deliver it to her. When Issaria had told her she was just grateful Shairi hadn't been poisoned carelessly by Aunt Cate as well, she'd only cried harder.

Issaria had yet to see the king, and since she hadn't even had a moment to consider his ultimatum, she wasn't sure if it was good or bad that he'd not been by. The other person, though she wasn't sure person was the right world for her, she'd yet to hear from, was Aurelia. Maybe she'd used too much power keeping Issaria alive through the poisoning, or maybe she really had left for the time being. Even when Issaria was alone and tried to find the white-haired version of herself in that still-pond within her...no one answered. Not even a whisper of magic

It was truly as if she were hollow on the inside.

Prince Calix, usually accompanied by Raif or Alander, visited frequently, and always with a purpose. He brought anything from a meal in place of a kitchen servant, flowers from the garden to brighten her room, or books from the library to keep her entertained while she was bedridden. Once he'd brought the tonic the healers had prescribed her to take, some charcoal sludge infused with rosemary and mint for *taste.* It was to dilute whatever toxins remained within her system and it tasted as foul as it looked: chunky grayish mud with a distinctly spearmint aroma that did nothing to hide the fact that it tasted like rocks. Rocks that had been rubbed vigorously with mint leaves. He watched her gulp it down with grimacing incredulity, then was joined by Raif and Mint in applause. She had wiped her mouth with her sleeve and grumbled, "You're impressed now. You should have seen me the first time I took it."

They never spoke of the marriage arrangement. The threat lingered over her as she healed, but her stomach churned at the thought of not knowing where Prince Calix stood with the whole thing. At the start of the meeting he was pledged to one girl, and at the end he was being offered like a slave himself to another! She wasn't sure if he was allowing her to make her own choice, or if he was so repulsed by the idea that he couldn't even bring himself to speak of it.

That morning, Calix had come in with the best gift possible: Asmy's location. Jallah had written after scouring his ledgers. She was working in a brothel in the southern districts of the city.

"And you're certain you want us to go?" Cizabet asked for the hundredth time.

"Yes, please! I'm *fine.*" Issaria had propped herself up with all her pillows and had a book open on her lap. "Go get Asmy."

"I can stay with you," Eiren offered, though her cloak was already around her shoulders.

"No, don't. Go and help Cizabet. Then enjoy the city, have some fun!"

Calix himself had offered to accompany them and negotiate with whomever owned her. The girls filed out with Raif, Alander, and another two men who Issaria didn't recognize, but seemed familiar enough with her friends as they departed. She'd missed a lot apparently.

Prince Calix paused in the doorway and looked back over his shoulder, "I promise I'll take care of them. And you." He returned his eyes frontward and added, "There will be guards at the pavilion doors outside, and here beside your door. Please shout if you need something. Otherwise Marni will be by with lunch, and we should be back before supper if all goes well." His eyes found the stack of books returned to her table and a smile tugged at his mouth. He asked, "You have enough books?"

She looked around her. At least a dozen were stacked on her nightstand alone. "I think this is a sufficient stock," she said with a wry smile. "Thank you, again, Prince Calix. What you're doing for them... for me...it means a great deal."

He had opened his mouth to reply, then thought better of it and left her alone.

That had been hours ago.

Issaria had read, dozed, and listened to the lazy-yet-persistent drone of the summer insects in the garden outside. Marni had come and gone with lunch and a healer with her afternoon tonic-sludge. Issaria had finished the book she'd been reading *and* was a good way into the sequel when her eyes grew heavy. Sunlight poured in through her bedroom window, and Issaria had to draw the thick curtains against the heat and light. She used her red paper cow from Kidalma as a bookmark and nestled deep into the blankets for a nap.

She was cocooned within sun-radiated warmth and drifting off to sleep when she heard the grunt.

It wasn't so much the grunt that woke her, though. She barely registered the noise, if she was being honest. Her hazy, sleep-craving mind integrated the grunt into whatever dream sequence was starting in her head. No, it was the sound of a sword's sheath clinking against the wall, and the final clank of it against the floor.

The sheath was empty when it hit the floor, a hollow *clank* instead of a full *clunk*.

It was that small, insignificant detail that saturated the back of her mind and forced her eyes open.

Terror shot down her spine like liquid lighting as she dove out of the nest of pillows in her bed, and skittered across the bedroom as quick and quiet as she could. Crouched behind the chaise near the hearth, blessedly darkened since its last use lest the shadows from its light give away her hiding place, Issaria's blood roared in her ears. Sweat beaded on her forehead, making her bangs stick to her cold skin as she cowered behind the couch. The tremor in her hands wasn't just from terror. Her vision swam with black spots as the door to her suite opened just enough to let a hulking shadow of a person into her room, then silently closed behind them.

The cloaked figure turned from the door, and Issaria ducked to avoid being seen. She imagined the figure taking in the shapes of the room, pitched into darkness by the drawn curtains on her window. Would the lumps of pillows in her bed make it look like she was still within the blankets? She'd fled from her bed so quickly she hadn't thought to camouflage her exit.

Their shoe squelched on the marble floor as they took a step into her room.

The thick, wet squeak made them pause, and Issaria clasped her hands over her mouth and nose to hide the sounds of her panicked breath. If the assassin couldn't hear her quickened breathing, she was certain they could hear the roar of her heartbeat as it raged in her chest like a beast trying to free itself from her ribcage. There was blood on his shoe and she could see the sheen of a puddle seeping under her door from where she crouched.

Poison hadn't been enough. She lived, and the assassin knew. They waited until they were certain she was alone.

She was going to die here.

Her aunt was finally going to win.

Water splashed on the floor, and her breathing hitched. Water Magician. Probably talented, if hired as an assassin. Mere armament magic wouldn't be enough for someone like that. Groggy, her mind tried to catalogue the magic he could use against her, from frost and ice to drowning if he was feeling simplistic—a variety of spells and mana manipulations could drown a magician easily enough. If he was feeling particularly creative, though...

The sound of fabric being pulverized by a thousand blades ripped across the bedroom. White feathers filled the air like snow and the assassin chuckled.

"We both knew you wouldn't be there," the low-voiced assassin said. "Come out and play, Princess. I've been waiting a long time to have my way with you." Her blood frosted over.

She knew that voice. She was certain she'd heard it at the auction. But now she knew it from closer to home. She'd heard that voice in council chambers, in hallways glinting with purple crystal. Malek Ward-law. She knew him from council meetings, and had seen him having many a conversation with her aunt. He was one of her closer confidants.

Issaria's mouth went dry and her ears rang with sinking confirmation. They really were enemies now, weren't they? Maybe they always had been and Issaria was just incredibly slow on the uptake. All these years, Aunt Cate had been watching her, evaluating her loyalty, perhaps waiting for Aurelia to challenge her identity.

White feathers fell into her hair, piled on the ground and furniture like little snowdrifts as Issaria steeled her spine.

Malek was here to kill her, and if she sat here, it was definitely going to happen. She could hear the trickle of water and the slow but firm steps of Malek as he scanned the dark of the room. It was now or never. She looked to the door, red highlighted like rubies in the slash of light that leaked beneath it. She probably wouldn't make it that far before he water-knifed her like her bed.

She could hide, but he would find her. If she could make it to the bed, perhaps she could crawl through the window but he would probably catch her as soon as she opened the curtain. Books toppled off her nightstand. The solarium light glowed feebly before flickering into a dim ember on the floor. A small table near the garden doors burst into splinters.

"Come now, Issaria. I thought you'd be glad to see me. Your aunt made sure to send her love," he taunted in that spine-chilling voice she swore she could feel in the air. He was enjoying this game, making her heart race and fear freeze her while he hunted her down.

Crouched where she was, she was a rabbit, just waiting for the hawk to swoop in and snatch her into his claws. Prey. If running was the only option she had, her exit had to be smart.

She glanced around the room and assessed her options. The only other real place she could hide would be in her wardrobe, and Malek was already stalking toward it. With him distracted, she turned about. The hearth was behind her, and in the old-world style, it was originally a wood-burning hearth with a chimney to allow ventilation for the smoke. Even the Crystal Palace had chimneys, slated vents in the crystal to allow smoke and vapor to exit the kitchens safely. Feathers stirred like phantom breaths as her clothes were thrown about the room in Malek's haste to find her.

She was running out of time and had already run out of options.

Issaria sucked in a breath as she stepped barefoot onto the sharp edges of the solarium crystals in her hearth and hoisted herself up into the mouth of the chimney. Strange, that she could see *better* inside the chimney than she could inside her bedroom. Light seemed to radiate from beneath her, casting a glow about the soot-covered stones as she braced her weight between the opposite walls. She looked up, curious about the darkness above her and the light from below—

"You always *were* a clever one," Malek's distant-thunder voice rumbled around her, magnified by the confines of the chimney.

Issaria looked down to see Malek's pale face in the bottom of the hearth, surrounded by glowing solarium crystals. The ones she has used as stepping stones were alight with amber radiance. She wasn't even very far up when he reached up, seized her ankle, and yanked her from within the chimney. Issaria had one last look at the straight-shot to freedom as she fell into her captor's awaiting arms and light filled the blackened hole to the sky.

The top of the chimney had been sealed off.

She thrashed and screamed as Malek's arms wrapped around her, dragged her from the hearth. "Help! Prince Calix!" she shouted until she was hoarse, screaming to call attention to her assault. In the center of the room, Malek smashed her face into the floor. A bloody footprint had congealed with feathers from her bed and tears pressed into her eyes as she squirmed against him. Her arm slipped free of one hand and she flailed harder. "Help! Please! Calix!"

"Stop fighting—" he grunted as she landed and elbow in his gut. "That's it," he cursed, fed up with her antics.

Issaria shrieked as white-hot pain sliced through her skin. All over her body, little cuts beaded with blood. Around them in the air icy arrowheads waited to strike again. Issaria stilled as she felt hot beads of blood begin to roll down her bare arms and legs, where the most exposed skin had been subjected to the ice-arrows. Stinging pain lit her skin on fire and she grit her teeth together to hold back her cries from turning into Malek's pleasure.

He fisted a hand in her hair and pressed her face into the floor again, sliding her cheek and jaw into the feathered footprint. She whimpered as the gooey-thickness of it soaked into her hair.

"Much better," he cooed in her ear as he pressed himself against her backside. "I had promised to make it quick, but she won't care what happens to you before you're dead. Little tease. You were always so damn *pure.*" Malice saturated his tongue as he leaned in and licked her neck. Issaria bucked her hips and he cackled. "Ignorant slut.

Didn't you know she hated you? Hated your stupid mother and father too."

"Get off of me!" she meant to yell, but the pleading crept into her voice through the tightness of her throat. "Please, don't!"

"That's it," he whispered against her neck. "I like hearing you beg." Malek's voice was thick with hunger when his hand snaked up her slip of a nightgown.

"No!" She keened and felt the rage pulse from within herself, penetrating her fear like a sword of light.

His grubby fingers touched her thighs, and the fury resounded again.

A fist pounding on a door.

She flung herself down to the well of her mana. The glass-like surface trembled with each strike of Aurelia's fist. Purple light radiated from her eyes like holy fire and her snarl could only be taken for divine hatred.

Like the surface of a frozen pond, cracks spiderwebbed across the splintered surface. Issaria leaned forward to meet her reflection-self, and with a feather-light touch, the fractured surface and exploded outward in glittering shards.

An inferno of purple-white light seared her eyes as feather-soft darkness drowned her in the melody of distant screaming.

37
CALIX

Asmy had not fared as well as the girls who'd ended up in the palace. She had been sold to Murtagh Ghazal, the owner of The Crimson Corset, a notorious gentleman's establishment on the southside of Hinhallow. Calix had never been to the place himself, but he'd heard many a story from soldiers who had frequented the hazy halls. Not far from the gaping mouth of the Cyth River, the backwater street that led to the manor house which served as The Crimson Corset's establishment reeked of fish guts and fetid tide pools.

Ivy crept along the pale stonework of the house and rosebushes bloomed along the walkway with cherry-jeweled petals. Sickly sweet aroma saturated the air and mingled sourly with the fish-stench from the docks. It looked, for all its hedonism inside, to be a quaint riverside estate outside. Khodri and Zakarian took up places outside while Raif, Alander, and himself escorted the four ladies up the stairs and in through the front door of the establishment.

Hazy light from crimson solarium crystals cast the interior of the building in shades of ruby and garnet. Smoke lingered like a fog, spiraling near the ceiling from curtained off alcoves where girls attended patrons with drinks and smoldering pipes for smoking.

Cizabet had lingered near Calix the entire journey, but now her green eyes were hungry as they roamed the dazed faces of the girls who ambled about, languishing between gentlemen in the smoking parlor.

A pale woman with blood red lips and kohl-rimmed eyes as dark as onyx approached their group with a feline smile. "Welcome, welcome. I am Faustina, mistress of The Crimson Corset," she said and as she bowed her head dark hair spilled over her shoulder, exposing the pale expanse of her back. Her gossamer robe left very little to the imagination. "We welcome the tastes of all—though perhaps with a group so large you only require an accommodating space?" She arched an eyebrow at them and gave an encouraging smile.

"That won't be necessary," Alander stated, his dark eyes steady on Faustina. "Crown Prince Calix has come to speak to the purveyor of this establishment concerning a recent purchase he made from Jallah Coppernolle."

Faustina's jet eyes flashed to Calix as she took him in perhaps for the first time. Realization struck her narrow features and her eyes widened. "Prince Calix, it's a *pleasure* to serve you." She clapped her hands. "Zyla. Eilin. Come make sure the prince is well cared for—"

Calix held up a hand. "Also not necessary. I am here on business purposes only."

The girls who approached, Eilin and Zyla, looked crestfallen at his lax dismissal of their services. Faustina cast her eyes around their party again. "So many people for business only, your Grace."

"Is Murtagh present?" Raif asked from his left.

"I don't see her," Cizabet whispered to Eiren.

"Master Ghazal is in his office. Please wait here while I check his schedule," Faustina replied as she turned from their group and headed toward a staircase against the far wall.

Calix looked between Raif and Alander who nodded once each, and Calix took off for the stairwell where Faustina had vanished. Silently, he took the stairs after her, looking once through the red-light and smoke of the parlor at his friends and the four girls, who were grabbing the arm of every girl who passed and asking about Asmy.

The upstairs corridor was narrow and filled with doors. Faustina's dark hair vanished behind the door at the end of the hall, and Calix followed her, ignoring the moans and overindulgent screams that issued from behind the doors he passed. At the end of the hall, he didn't knock before grasping the doorknob and igniting fire within his palm until the alloy melted into a bronze-colored puddle on the stained carpet. The door swung inward and Calix smiled at the man behind the desk.

"I figure you'd clear your schedule for the Crown Prince, right Murtagh?" Calix said as he leaned against the door frame.

The fat, bearded man glowered at Calix from beneath a greasy brow. "Faustina, see to it that Prince Calix's friends are comfortable while I see to his...requests," Murtagh said. Faustina left them alone, attempting for several futile minutes to keep the broken door closed behind her. "It's all right, love, leave it," Murtagh cried at last, and she scampered down the hall. "Jallah sent a note of your impending arrival." He sighed. "Come. Have a seat. At least make it worth my while if you're to relieve me of the girl."

IN THE END, ASMY HADN'T MADE IT INTO ROTATION AS A BROTHEL-GIRL yet. In addition to continuously failing her etiquette tests, she'd also bitten the first man who'd paid for her company. From the sound of it, the encounter ended up costing The Crimson Corset more than Asmy's asking price. Murtagh saw her as a liability after that, and demoted her. As punishment, and much to Asmy's relief, she was on dedicated cleaning duty, scrubbing bathrooms, and collecting soiled linens after a client left.

Asmy was skinnier than she'd been the last time the sisters had been together, but Asmy assured Cizabet that she hadn't been harmed too badly. Nothing beyond a lashing or skipped meals, though she'd earned a black eye from the customer she'd bitten. When Cizabet brought her sister to meet him, Calix saw the resemblance between their mossy green eyes.

"I bought your contract from Murtagh," he said. "Like your sister, you're free, Asmy. You can stay with Cizabet and the other girls in the palace, or I can help arrange passage to Snovic. Whatever you do now, the choice belongs solely to you."

She threw her arms around him and cried harder than she had upon seeing her sister.

Cizabet and Asmy clung to each other, sobbing in the parlor of The Crimson Corset for a long while before an impatient Faustina ushered them out for disrupting their business. The group emerged into the fish-scented streets of Hinhallow and meandered up the cobbled paths to burrows of stone-built shops with glass storefronts. He'd given them all Metals, and they'd been happy to start spending. Cizabet had draped her own cloak around her sister's frail shoulders and guided her into a dress shop. Like silent shadows, his men fell in behind them, following with furtive glances to establish lines with each other as the ladies enjoyed the sunlit shops and street-stalls of fried and handheld foods.

Eiren walked beside him as the other girls alternated between stalls and shops.

"Don't you want to shop as well?" he asked

"I will," the brunette said without looking at him. "I wanted to speak to you first." Blue eyes found his and she smiled a little. "I could let it slip. How you stayed the whole time she was out from the poison. The things you said. Rhaminta wants your permission, but I thought I might just tell her that you've been thinking about her since you met in the woods when she had no idea who you were."

Heat flushed his face. He hadn't known they'd heard him speaking to her, pleading with Aurelia to bring her back to him. The confession of the lingering thoughts of their meeting. How he had finally admitted to himself that he was *excited* to see her again, whenever that would have been.

"I, uh…I think things have changed for her. My father's threat to withhold the alliance is like a noose around her neck."

"She had someone. Back in Espera." He shouldn't have let the news shock him as much as it did. He might have guessed as much if he'd thought about some things she'd said. "I don't know much about him," Eiren continued, "but it sounds like he died so that she could come here and be safe. Save the world and all."

He released a heavy sigh at the news. "That's...a tragic story."

"She cries when she thinks we are all asleep."

"Why are you telling me this?"

She shrugged. "She's backed into a pretty tight corner, and we can't really help her."

"And that proclamation my father sent out is probably not going to help matters," he interjected, and she winced. King Akintunde had all but inferred that Issaria and Hinhallow were already allies.

"But I don't think," Eiren said as she gestured to Rhaminta and Cylise, emerging from a sweets shop before them. "*we* don't think Akintunde's ultimatum has to be a bad thing. Not after how you've been with her. She might be a little slow to realize it, but we've all seen."

He hadn't thought he'd been so obvious, but perhaps he had over-done it a tad when she'd been poisoned. "I...I don't want her to think I had a hand in the proposal," Calix confessed. "And as such, I agree that the ultimatum doesn't have to be a bad thing. A good man doesn't force a woman to marry him, Eiren," he said with a tone of finality.

No matter his thoughts on the matter, she had been backed into a corner. Gain access to the army that could save her city and give up her freedom yet again, or sacrifice her title, her crown...*everything.* Guilt gnawed at him, knowing he did little to protest against it, that perhaps, after hearing that they had once been intended...he wanted to marry *her.* An absurd thought, Calix knew. He barely knew the princess, and she was clearly dealing with more important things at the moment. But all the more, he *wanted* to know her. The woman who would walk across a crystal sea for the mere *chance* of freeing her people.

"Who says it has to be by force?" Eiren asked with her head cocked to one side. "Have you asked her how she feels?" Dumbly, he shook his head. He'd been avoiding the topic by discussing anything else. "I didn't think so." Then, she turned away and skipped off to join Rhaminta and Cylise who had stopped to pick out hair combs from a vendor's cart.

"This one would be lovely in the princess's hair," Eiren said as she plucked an opal-studded clip from the collection. "Don't you think so, Mint?" She asked, though her eyes found the prince, a knowing smile on her lips.

Calix remained a little dumbfounded, thinking about how to even broach the topic of the marriage alliance with Issaria *without* her jabbing her finger into his sternum again. When he finally moved to rejoin the group in a bakery, he was grinning at the prospect of igniting her again, his fire-black hand absently rubbing his chest as he walked.

UPON RETURNING TO THE WHITE PALACE, RAIF AND ALANDER PEELED off toward the kitchens, grumbling about being out too long without *real* food. Because cakes and trifles were apparently beneath them. "You could have had some lamb kabob!" Rhaminta had called after Raif, teasing him after he'd refused her skewered meat and vegetables. Zak walked as far as the hall leading to the barracks before making his exit, claiming duties Calix knew he didn't have. Khodri only said goodbye to Cylise who flushed magenta when he kissed her hand before tracing their path back the way they'd come.

Wanting to see Issaria's face when she saw Asmy and Cizabet reunited, Calix followed behind the girls, watching as they giggled and showed off the contents of their packages while they headed toward the Western Pavilion. Asmy laughed freely, eating syrup-and-fruit covered balls of fried dough from a brown-paper bag as Cizabet and Eiren demonstrated different dance moves they learned from Issaria for the coronation—the final part of the story of how Kai, the identity Asmy knew for Issaria, revealed herself to be the Imperial Princess after spending weeks among them as a slave.

"Prince Calix!" Rhaminta's voice shook as she turned her dark eyes back toward him from where she stood at the end of the hall. "Look."

Calix dashed forward, and his heart seized mid-beat. It was as though time stopped as his eyes roved the scene. Across the garden, the two guards he'd placed outside the pale pavilion house were slumped over. Scarlet blood smeared down the wall from where they'd been impaled against the white stones. The other girls gasped, Cizabet started crying immediately, and Eiren gripped his sleeve. Her blue eyes were wide with terror. "Issaria's *really* weak. She can barely stand on her own."

A scream pierced the air bringing the moment to a crushing, forward-momentum.

Calix rattled off orders. "Get additional guards. Find help immediately but do not come back here until the area has been cleared. I can't guarantee safety." He was already dashing toward the pavilion house, crushing flowers underfoot as he cleared the gardens.

Flames erupted from his hands, his scimitars forming from the fire, and he stepped into the pavilion house. Nothing seemed amiss in the seating area, but as soon as he turned down the hall he could see the secondary set of guards leaning askew in the hall, red puddles congealing on the floor.

"No!"

Issaria's panicked cry ignited his rage and sent him charging down the hall as purple light pulsed from the doorway in a white-hot surge of raw power. He felt it wash over him and carry out to sea. It bloomed like a flower, unfurling an endless tide of caustic radiance to which there was no end. Somehow, he heard the screams within the intensity of that blast. Utter pain and agony echoed before being snuffed out like a candle flame. Only the pure ringing of dazzling magic existed then, buzzing down to his very core.

The power receded, and only when a soft purple light emanated from behind the door did Calix tentatively push it open.

Haloed in her amethyst aura, white feathers surrounded her in suspension. Moon-white hair billowed around her as if caught in some unnatural breeze. Glowing white eyes stared intently at him as he approached with caution. Blood was splattered across her face and torn nightgown. At her feet, in the center of an ambiguous pile of red-pink goo, was the remains of ribcage attached to a gnarled bit of bone that Calix was certain was a spine, contorted in upon itself.

"He tried to force himself upon her," Aurelia whispered. "He would have, had I not interceded."

Calix looked between the obliterated remains of the would-be assailant and the Ethereal Lady before him. He hadn't seen it before, or perhaps he hadn't really looked at her face in his startled reverence in the woods, but she held an uncanny resemblance to Princess Issaria. The defiant tilt of her jaw, defined ridge of her collarbone, now scarred pink from her slave collar, the soft peak of her breasts beneath the remains of her shredded nightgown. His scimitars snapped and sizzled as his face heated from the very thought of it. The two were nearly identical, save the obvious hair color, midnight-black exchanged for starlit white.

"Thank you for sparing her that horror," Calix said, selecting his words carefully. "I was foolish to trust her safety to only a few guards."

"Was it not enough to save myself? Am I so unwelcome even for you, son of Tarlix?"

Calix furrowed his brow, and he extinguished his weapons with a hiss of smoke. His hands ached from clenching around his fire, and he shook them out as he said, "I don't understand? Issaria is *you*, your vessel, is she not?"

"She is," Aurelia said as she reached with a glowing white hand, fingertips brushing his cheek. "We are one and the same. I cannot be without she, and she will not be after me." Her fingers felt like grains of star-studded sky against his skin and left behind a luminous trail of dust that glowed purple in the wake of her touch before fading. "Your fire burns for her."

Calix jerked his face away from her. "What? No. She's just—you made me promise to protect her."

"I did no such thing."

"You…" Calix began, scrambling to pull together what she'd said, "You told me not to hurt her!" he amended, but to no avail.

"I had not planned on this. It complicates things." Aurelia held his stare, her expression unreadable as she seemed to examine his very soul within the expanse of their silence. "Perhaps this could be a good thing. At least for now, I permit your courtship."

"Courtship? Lady, you are *cosmically* incorrect about this situation."

"You must be more vigilant when it comes to her protection if I am to allow her to remain," she said, ignoring his protests. "I am weaker now than I was before, and it will cost us both to have summoned me here corporally. I was not ready for this merger." She looked upon him with that radiant stare and said, "More than just the Night seeks to extinguish our light, my prince of fire."

Aurelia turned, her whole body spinning away as she hovered in the air above the mutilated corpse. Her face turned toward the north, glowing eyes seemed to stare far past the walls of Hinhallow, past the churning Norvenello Ocean and beyond to a destiny he could not yet fathom. "I sense her even now. If I have returned, then so has Obsidia. Her *descendia* will know I've awakened."

Calix considered her words and frowned. "If you've awakened, where is Issaria?"

Aurelia did not turn to face him as she replied, "She allowed me to come here in her place. To stop him from hurting her."

"And where did she go if you're here?"

"She called for you." Aurelia looked over her shoulder at him. The holy fire glow of her eyes had subsided, and Calix's stomach clenched around the violet-familiarity of the forlorn gaze the Mythos cast upon him. "Even *she* didn't call for me. I came anyway, to defend my vessel of course," Aurelia whispered, "but she called for *you.*"

His heart began to pound in his chest. Aurelia was playing word games around Issaria's whereabouts. He got the sickening feeling that Aurelia, ready for the merger or not, was pleased to have come through so completely from wherever she dwelled. "Where is she?" He was through asking.

"My, my. For someone who denies they burn, you've got quite the spark when it comes to her." Aurelia simpered at him over her shoulder before saying, "She is sleeping within me, as I do whilst she walks in my place, but now I'll be watching. As is the price of my protection, yet again." Aurelia's right eye dimmed, the ethereal glow extinguished to a vacant, milk-white iris.

He had too many questions and she was baiting him with pretty words and half intentions. He ground his jaw together. "What do you mean when you say you 'allow her to remain,'?" he asked through clenched teeth.

"I mean that the princess and I have worked out a deal, and for the time-being, I'll *allow* you to keep her. She's rooted a little deeper than I imagined she'd be anyway. Prove to me that this wreck of a planet is worth salvaging, and perhaps I'll let you keep *it* too."

"Wha—that's...you're... what?" Calix's mind spiraled at the implication of Aurelia's words. She was planning on *destroying* the planet?

"Bring me to the Vera Caelum, Prince Calix. She's apt to play hero and not tell you of our deal, but you *must* bring me there. Bring me to the spring, or I will take her from you and she will not come back," Aurelia's voice raked razors across the coals in his chest.

"Where is she?" Calix roared, and Aurelia's smile grew feral across her too-familiar face.

"Right here," she said, and the light from blazing eye winked out, leaving a familiar violet iris blinking out from behind a curtain of silver-white hair.

The purple halo held her in suspension as it receded into her like the tide retreating to the sea. One by one the feathers were released from their places and they drifted around them like errant snowflakes. Gently, Aurelia's bare feet touched down on blood-coated marble and Issaria's eye seemed to gain focus as black bled into her hair from the root. She trembled like a fawn as her hair lost its billowing luster and fell around her shoulders in dark curls.

"Issaria?" Calix whispered across the room, afraid to startle her too soon.

Her name pulled her gaze toward him, and she spun to meet him. "Calix...what happened? I... I don't remember." Her eyes glistened with tears as she looked down at the mess of a body between them. Cracked ribs and contorted spine amid a reeking puddle of red and pink matter. Blood and innards were splattered on the wall, the ceiling, stuck to the floor, and pieces of furniture in chunks.

Issaria's relieved expression fell and the same horrified, lost look that Aurelia had shown him crossed her features as her already pale face drained of color. Calix sidestepped the grotesque pile as she stumbled back. Lips parted, trembling, her eye locked onto the mix of mangled shapes and colors, and he watched her try to make sense of the mess. He extended his cloak like a curtain to block the sight as he folded her shaking body into his chest.

"It's okay, Issa. You're okay. He didn't hurt you." Her hands fisted into his shirt as she shook violently. "I'm here now. It's okay," he whispered and pet her hair, cradling her against himself. "I'm here."

With her sequestered against his chest, Calix escorted her around the remains of the mutilated body and out into the undisturbed sitting room, where he sat her between his legs on a chaise. Soldiers summoned by the girls came and went as he shook his head, holding back curious parties from disturbing them. Raif entered for a moment and ducked down the hall to see the bedroom before Calix could threaten him. He left silently, his face pale after he exited Issaria's bedroom. He closed the doors to the pavilion house behind him, leaving them alone.

When Issaria pulled back, her eyes were dry. Blood flecked her cheek beneath her violet eye. The other was moon-white.

Blind.

"I...I can't see," she whispered. "She took it. My eye."

Silent, he reached a blackened hand up to the right side of her face and made to cup her cheek. Issaria flinched as his fingers touched her skin, but then she seemed to realize it was him and pressed her face into his black palm, sending embers spiraling up from his fever-ridden hand.

"When I saw the guards outside...I thought I might be too late. I thought I could really lose you this time," he confessed in a whisper. It was nearly the same thing he'd said to her when she'd awoken from the oleander poisoning, but this time he'd been concerned that *he* wouldn't see her again. She wouldn't poke *him*, or yell at *him* anymore.

He wouldn't see that fire he loved within her as she mouthed off to his father, she wouldn't smile as he brought flowers and he wouldn't learn which ones she liked by how much light shone in her eyes when she looked upon them. "I'm so sorry I wasn't there."

Hesitant fingers found his charred wrist as that brilliant, violet gaze held him captive.

Cosmos damn him, but he *was* burning.

And it wasn't the fever that consumed him this time.

Embers smoldered beneath her touch as her hands clasped around the one on her face, holding his palm against her cheek. Embers lit the air like stars between them.

"Issa," he growled, cautioning her of what she must have known stirred in him with a touch like that.

"Will you always be so kind to me?" she murmured as she raised herself up on her knees bringing her mouth within inches of his.

Shadows loomed in her eyes as she waited for his answer. It wasn't just about this moment and the molten heat her touch ignited within him. This was more than the alliance, the quest laid before them, and the bargain that hung between her and the being who would take her as soon as she was strong enough. The day was coming where Issaria would need to fight for herself, as well as her kingdom. She was asking so much of him in that small question.

He found his answer easily.

"I'll never hurt you," he replied then added with a dry chuckle, "and I'll try not to let anything else hurt you either, though you do have a penchant for trouble. Makes it hard to keep my promises."

The stars in her eyes danced with the echo of another narrow escape behind them. A small, hesitant smile pulled at the corners of her mouth as she squeezed his wrist. Calix found he could barely breathe as she whispered, "I think it wouldn't be so bad if I was your wife, in case your father is still waiting for my answer."

His hand captured her chin and tilted her face upwards to meet his kiss. He hesitated only to allow her to pull back, but her hands ran across his chest and she leaned into him. "He wasn't the only one waiting, Issa," Calix murmured against her lips.

"If you were so concerned, you should have asked me yourself," she challenged but remained within the circle of his arms. A bit of venom laced her voice, her fire returning if only for him.

Calix's mouth cut a grin. "Maybe I *would* have if you didn't almost die. Twice."

Scowling, she punched him lightly in the chest and he laughed a little as she settled back on her heels. His yellow eyes lit on her face and took in the dried blood speckled across her cheek, the tear in the pale silk of her nightgown where the assassin had thought he would take more than just her life, the full moon paleness of her eye. She had already given so much, had so much taken from her. She'd endured and outlasted, sacrificed and suffered. And he knew she would keep doing it if it meant she could free her city from darkness. She'd keep this course until it claimed her life.

"Be my wife, Issa. The Cosmos brought us together in the Baelforia, and our parents made the offer on our behalf long before that. I would honor the vows if only to give you the military aide you came for if you desire it. You may only need my army, but I want *you*, Issaria Elysitao. Your fire is one I want to burn in."

"You rock head," she murmured as she rocked forward and closed the space between them with a chaste kiss. "I said yes already, didn't I?"

"Tell me again."

A coy smile tugged on her lips. "I'm going to be your wife, Calix Ballentine."

Her declaration undid him. Calix slid his hand into the wild tangle of her black hair and tipped her head back as he claimed her mouth. Warm and inviting, she yielded to him. Soft curves of her body melded against him, and he became hyper aware of her nightgown hitched between them as he laid her back against the chaise. Her fingers mussed his hair and he held back a groan as she nipped his lower lip.

Reluctant to give her any space at all, Calix planted lazy kisses at the corners of her mouth as he said, "If we don't stop now, I'm not going to be able to."

He felt her hesitation, a momentary pause in her fingertips as they entwined with his hair, and with the utmost control, he pulled back from her, forced himself to stand and then helped her to her feet. "We don't need to rush, Issa." He draped his cloak around her shoulders, both for her modesty and for the fact that he could not take his eyes from her. The cloak dwarfed her in the ample length of black fabric. "We've all the time in the world."

And as he escorted her from the death and misery that haunted the western pavilion, nothing ever felt like more of a lie.

EPILOGUE

Shura

Mist rose out of the Ferrofrost, delineating the mountain range in gradients of fog and slate. Wind nipped at his cheeks and tossed his hair from his eyes while Shura Wintersea stared out across the snowflats toward those distant peaks. He stood atop one of the spires of the Keep in Rhunmesc, looking out across the barren tundra, windswept and not nearly as snowy as it had been in years past. The wind changed direction, pulling back toward the sea from the mountains, bringing the scent of pine and the brisk thaw of ice. Between the floods from icemelt and the landslides, the north had become a dangerous place for those beyond the safety of Rhunmesc's tall stone walls.

Disturbing rumors had reached Rhunmesc from the southern continent. Rumors of deceit, and lies, and a princess who was thought to be dead had been claimed as a refugee after showing up in a foreign city nearly a month later. Nicora Firstfrost had confirmed with a hawk as soon as she'd laid eyes on the girl in one of Akintunde's absurd alliance meetings. The southern cities needed a strong hand. They were...out of sorts. He could bring them to heel. A king of unparalleled might upon the Imperial Throne at last. Even the stars would bow to him.

He could feel it, the shift on the wind. A change in the tides.

She was coming, and soon.

Time could not have aligned more perfectly. His team of revolutionists were certain that *this time* they would perform exceptionally in the demonstration. No more explosions. No more uncontrolled blasts or automatic targeting of ally forces. This time, they would be perfect. They'd be ready.

"Prince Shura," Captain Phelix Stormgren said from the doorway behind him. "Izaak asked me to tell you that the Opifex are ready to show you what they are hoping to call the prototype for the Titan Project. Whenever you so deign to visit the caverns, my liege."

"It is not beneath me to see to my projects, Phelix. Especially this one," Shura said as he turned from the battlement and proceeded down the spiral stairs with the dark-haired captain close behind.

"They just make me...anxious," he confessed. "The things that make...what they've made...its—"

"Incredible," Shura finished for him, lest he forget that the Titan Project was only in existence because of Shura. "It's nothing short of incredible that I gathered together the brightest minds and turned them toward the future. I only gave them an idea, a nonsensical fantasy, really, and they *actually* accomplished it."

"Indeed, sire. The ingenuity behind the Titan Project could only have come from you."

Shura didn't miss the wariness that edged his friend's voice. Hesitance was to be expected. He truly had thrown caution to the wind with this plan, but that was what it took to change the Cosmos. He no longer had the luxury of keeping his ideas tame. Not when he could feel the burn in the sigil on his chest growing hotter with each passing day. The noose of fate was tightening.

"Keep faith, Phelix. The promised time is nigh."

They continued on in silence until they came to the bottom of the stairs.

"Incredible though it may be, Sire, it is also frightening."

And Shura could hardly keep the smile from his voice. "Isn't it, though?"

SHURA AND CAPTAIN PHELIX EMERGED FROM ANOTHER STAIRWELL, carved deep into the bedrock beneath Rhunmesc onto an alloy platform that had been rigged into the granite walls of the expansive cavern. Phelix lingered on the threshold as Shura strode across the platform to the balcony railing. Up this high, he was level with the solarium gems they'd suspended from the ceiling for light. Fists curled around the cold alloy railing as he took in the activities that bustled in the cavern below.

Amongst the murmured chatter of the magicians recruited to the Opifex, intellectuals and creative minds recruited from across Ellorhys, stood hundreds of mechanical skeletons. Each a collection of alloy and gears, bipedal in appearance, with massive gorilla-thick arms for focused blasts.

They were magnificent.

Every model looked a little different from the previous, so it was like seeing them for the first time whenever he entered the caverns. And at the forefront of the cavern, standing more than ten meters high, was the latest prototype.

Steam escaped from between fissures in its alloy casing. The cooling systems had been faulty in the last version, causing over-heating and implosions within the armored chest cavity. Martavius had been the one to crack that mystery. Little tubes of silex had been threaded throughout the alloy skeletons. Aquathyst was embedded along the lines to provide equal cooling throughout. Glowing aper-tures of amber, emerald, sapphire, and fiery scarlet pockmarked its chest where the elementia sources were chambered.

"Look at them, Shura," Risa's sultry voice floated on stale cavern air from the precarious alloy stairs welded to the platform. "Aren't they just *divine?*" Her storm-white hair contrasted sharply against the deep earth tones of her skin. Risa Amorelle was pretty, *too* pretty if you were wary of that sort of thing, but it was that glint of malice in her golden eyes the made Shura take her seriously, even while she wore those absurdly sheer dresses—if you could call those swaths of chiffon she sheathed her assets in a dress at all. She sauntered to the top of the stairs and went immediately to Shura's side, taking his hand in hers while she looked up at him. "You'll be so pleased," she purred and pressed his arm into her chest as she cozied up.

"You're confident?"

"Spoke with Izaak myself. Even Alianora thinks this is the right model and she's been *impossible* to impress."

Shura looked down into the cavern and found the brunette in question. Grease smeared across her cheek and a wrench in her hand, Alianora Dekastrozza had been the Opifex to route the electricity in a zephyrite crystal into the Titans as a power source. As temperamental as she'd been about his original proposal, Alianora had proven herself to be an invaluable member of the Opifex team. She might have protested these long years, but her dedication the Titan project never wavered.

"Perfect." Louder, his command filling the cavern, he said, "Demonstration!"

Below, magicians froze, looking up from their workstations, and from atop ladders propped on Titans in the assembly line, to see their benefactor lording above. "Prince Shura!" Izaak Khorsand, the lead magician on the project, called up to him. "We are so pleased by your arrival! Most advantageous, indeed." His goggled-eyes overtook his grin, making him insectoid in appearance. "Please remain aloft for the demonstration, your Eminence."

The inventor clapped his gloved hands together and began barking orders. Around the cavern, magicians scrambled to clear the demonstration space. The scraping of table legs and tools clanking into their boxes filled the air. The magicians found safe places to watch throughout the cavern: hoisted up on platforms, from within tunnels attached to the main floor, and many thundering up the rickety stair-case that lead up to Prince Shura and his team. Casualties were not unheard of on the Titan Project. He'd already paid reparations to exactly thirteen families of Opifex who'd perished in the name of progress. The mechanics and alchemists were most vulnerable as they were most exposed to the killing-aspects of the Titans. The weapons. The magic. It was the most dangerous, but also the most rewarding team to work on. Shura ensured they were all *well* compensated for their struggles.

Goggled Izaak, grease-stained Alianora with her own goggles atop her head like a tiara, and Martavius Halstead climbed the stairs until they joined Shura and his peers atop the viewing platform as several cows were led in from a doorway on the cavern floor. "No one is squeamish, are they?" Izaak Khorsand asked as he crested the last step and joined them at the railing.

"Only of failure," Risa said.

Even Captain Phelix stepped forward to watch the display, reluctant though he was.

"Begin."

The prototype remained still. A series of clicks accompanied the steady rise of humming that had started within its chest. Shura looked on, expectantly, before casting an apprehensive glance at Izaak who grimaced apologetically in reply. One of the cows brayed into the cave, its melancholy sound echoed around them.

"Sometimes it just takes a moment to start up. This one has been powered down since the testing yesterday," Alianora explained without concern for the delay. "Once they've been powered up, as long as they have a new zephyrite every twelve hundred hours, they'll be fine," she finished with a dismissive hand wave as she met Shura's eyes. "I'll keep tabs on which ones need new cores and when. We've a supply of ore ready to accompany the fleets."

A disarmingly soothing light filled the visual receptors on what would be considered the Titan's smallish head. Two cut-outs slightly rhomboid in shape filled with honey-light that leaked down its body like tears of gold, illuminating each fissure and rune etched in its armor with the same radiant glow. The whirr-and-click of gears fell into place among the hums and hisses of machinery. Steam issued from the fissures in the armor and the Titan lifted its head off its chest and seemed to assess its surroundings. The head rotated fully around its axis while the body remained stagnant.

"This is anticlimactic," Risa drawled from where she leaned against the railing, her gauzy dress revealing the ample curves of her backside as she cast an inviting glance toward the inventor. "*Izaak*," she pouted, "I thought you said this was going to be—"

Izaak held a warped and pock-marked chunk of black rock with four pillars of elementia jutting out at random angles. Runes were etched on any flat-ish surface the black rock provided. "This is the Titan's Lodestone, Sire." He said nothing else as he held it aloft in his hand. A little dramatic for Shura's tastes, but he *had* asked for a demonstration.

At once, the Titan turned its head toward the small herd of cows, now milling about the far corner of the cavern. It raised one barrel-shaped arm, now buzzing as panels opened and allowed the red light of the chosen elementia to cast a scarlet aura around the hollow end of its stump.

Fire erupted from the muzzle of the barrel in a roaring explosion of light and heat. The cows didn't even have time to complain before a maelstrom of fire spun around them, consumed them like tinder. Shura had expected it to be more chaotic, but the blast was... controlled. Directed. Precise.

Silence echoed around them as the scent of charred meat and smoke enveloped them. The grin on Risa's face was wicked. She leaned far over the railing, as if waiting for one of the scorched bovines to defy death and return to them. In stark contrast, Phelix had gone uncharacteristically pale as his blue eyes remained fixed upon the scorched spot of stone where the eight or nine cows had been standing. Embers smoldered along the rim of the blast radius and smoke churned up from blackened corpses, collapsed where they'd stood only moments before.

"There is more, of course," Alianora began, the excitement lighting her evergreen eyes. "The storm magic is particularly destructive, and then we have water and terran features as well. We can ready another demonst—"

"How soon can they be ready, Dekastrozza?"

Whatever the inventor was going to say was drowned out by a familiar humming in the back of his mind. The sigil beneath his tunic burned hot as a new brand. Shura's eyes found the cavern ceiling, and he glared at it as if he could peer up though the bedrock and the earth, through ice and out across the seas. Far beneath Rhunmesc, in the caverns made of stillness and cold, Shura felt the whisper of power pulse from the south. He scented the stale air as if he could smell Aurelia's arrival from across the seas.

He'd been waiting eight long years for her return.

The echo to his call.

The Maiden of Light awakens at last.

"Ready the armada, Phelix. Izaak, these are no longer prototypes. Dekastrozza, outfit the skeletons. I want a score of Titans on each ship. We depart as soon as we are able." His smile grew as he added, "It's time we pay my sister a visit. No doubt she'll be surprised to see me."

Shura didn't wait to see if his command was carried out as he swept from the cavern, leaving his comrades behind on the viewing platform. The final player had arrived at long last and it was high time he sought her out.

THANK YOU FOR READING!

If you enjoyed Daughter of Shattered Skies,
Please consider leaving a review
on Goodreads & Amazon

Son of Shattered Souls
Book Two of the Shattered Trilogy
Coming 2023

PLEASE ENJOY THIS DELETED SCENE

THE POISONING

Calix

"Where is she?" Calix bellowed as he elbowed his way into the crowded room. "Issaria!"

"Prince Calix!" An elderly palace healer Calix was familiar with from youthful trips to the infirmary, Magi Noemi Petaluna, turned at the panicked demand in his voice, eyes wide at his intrusion. "Please, forgive me. You must step back—"

"Magi Petaluna!"

Both the healer and Calix spun to the frail woman tangled in bed linens. Magi Petaluma launched herself back to the bedside as Issaria's prone form seized in a thrashing tremor.

Calix froze.

Foam coalesced on Issaria's lips. Healers rolled her on her side and gave her ample space to convulse after they ensured her head was cushioned. She continued to jerk and twitch as if some dark magic yanked on her bones like a twisted marionette and a breathy, ghost-like moan pealed from within her.

"Do something!" he shouted, snatching at the nearest healer and hauling the wiry-bespectacled fellow up by the lapels of his tunic. Cinders erupted from his fist, singing the healer's clothes.

"We are!" Like a deer caught in the wolf's sight, the healer's eyes were wide and panicked as he squeaked out, "I assure you, Prince Calix, we're doing everything we can, but this poison…it is unlike any we've encountered. The toxicity of the poison is…insurmountable."

"Insurmountable? What does that mean? Is she going to die?" He wasn't sure he wanted to know the answer to that, but the question had already flown free.

The frightened healer paused for a moment and Calix felt his stomach drop. Lips thinned into a quivering line before he said quietly, "It's very possible, your highness." Nervous eyes shifted to Issaria, who's convulsions seemed to have stopped for the moment. Healers swarmed her like bees at the hive. "I'm sorry, but the body can only endure so much before it fails."

The healer's words slammed into Calix like a bull.

He never felt more useless as he absently released the healer and stumbled back until he felt a gentle hand on his shoulder.

"They're doing everything they can, Prince Calix," Rhaminta said from beside him, though her voice felt so very far away.

He broke his gaze away from Issaria, his view obscured by the abundance of healers bustling around her bedside, to his charred, fire-eaten hands. Good for nothing but doling damage. The healing arts were a skill he would never know. It was beyond his talents and always would be.

Calix could do no more for her than step back and let the healers try to save her.

He closed his eyes, breathing deep. This terror he felt. It was more than fear of Issaria dying. It was anger. Rage at whoever dared to touch her. His fear hardened.

He could also find who did this to her.

Calix clenched his hands into fists, feeling the warmth of his fire burn through his body until his hands ignited.

"Prince Calix!" Rhaminta sounded alarmed.

Golden eyes open, Calix leveled his gaze at her. "I'll incinerate whoever did this to her, Mint." It was more than a promise.

It was a vow.

And his magic ached with the need to fulfill it.

"Fetch another set of linens. She's soaked these through again," he heard a healer order.

The best in the city had been called in alongside the palace's own retinue of terran and water magicians. Working individually and in tandem they were able to stabilize Issaria's condition, though Calix wasn't sure what they did to make a difference.

Now it was up to Issaria if she would wake or not.

Calix leaned against the wall near the door, thoroughly out of the way of the healers that scurried in and out. His hands were clasped behind his back—he didn't trust himself not to snatch at one of these healers again and demand they fix her, even if his demand was futile and insane.

Issaria was always pale, years of moonlight gave her skin a tone more than simply pale, but now...now her flesh was nearly translucent. Sunken and frail. The veins in her neck, and in her arms looked like black vines, throbbing in time with her frantic heartbeat. Sweat sopped her brow, her hair looked damp from it—as though the princess had been caught in a Mythos-sent downpour.

The linens, and extra, arrived in a harried stack, Eiren shoving them at the healers as if speed and efficiency would make a difference now.

"I've got her," he said with finality as he pushed the healers aside. Gently, Calix slid one arm beneath her neck, the other behind her knees, and lifted Issaria free from damp linens.

She was light. Too light. It was called dead-weight for a reason, and though Issaria was blessedly not dead, her listless body should have been more difficult to carry. Her skin was cold and clammy beneath his grip, and her head lolled against his shoulder. Calix pressed a soft kiss to her dampened brow. Beneath closed eyelids, her eyes stuttered frantically, as if she were caught in a dream.

Calix just hoped that wherever Issaria was in these moments, she was far from the agony that must wrack her body.

Prince Calix reclined in a chair he'd dragged beside Issaria's bed. Eiren and Rhaminta had been alternating sitting vigils in an identical seat on the far edge of the room, near the doors to the garden, but at the moment, it appeared that he was alone. Leaning over, elbows on his knees, Calix steepled his fervent-black fingers against his forehead and rested his chin on his thumbs. Exhaustion tugged gently at his senses, and he knew he'd pushed his limits these past few days, but he was determined to be here when she woke up.

He scrubbed his hands over his face as if to clear the fatigue from his mind. He scratched at the stubble prickling along his jawline as the haunting thought plagued him again.

Poison.

It was unspeakable.

His father was furious. Embarrassed this could happen under his nose, and that made him explosive with rage. An attack on his household may have well been an attack on King Akintunde himself for all his vehemence on the matter. He'd already sent a missive to the other cities announcing that Issaria had survived the assassination attempt, and was practically engaged to Calix already. By the time he'd read the proclamation, the falcons had already flown.

His mother was oddly quiet, but perhaps the King's outrage matched her own hidden feelings. She'd visited Issaria's bedside with Shairi and offered to sit in Calix's place, but he hadn't left Issaria's side since he'd been summoned from a dead-end interrogation to be told Issaria's heart had stopped. By the time he'd arrived, it had started again and she seemed to be doing as well as could be given the circumstances—though the hollow-eyed healers confessed they'd not been able to save her.

They'd called it a gift from the Cosmos, but Calix had a feeling he knew exactly who the gift was from. He doubted Aurelia would come this far and allow her vessel to perish. He'd have to thank the Mythos for sparing Issaria when she surfaced next.

Shairi was a wreck. Narrowly avoiding death must've pushed her emotions to the limit. The carefully crafted mask of calm she wore had shattered when news of Issaria's poisoning spread through the palace. She'd practically implied it was her fault, screaming at the top of her lungs that the tea Princess Issaria drank had been poured by her own hands. Shairi was surely Mythos Blessed to have not fallen prone herself. A stroke of luck that the cup had been tainted, obviously, and not the tea itself, or Shairi might not have been as lucky as Issaria. Only his mother had been able to quell Shairi's hysterics, and had ushered her off for some bedrest of her own. Calix couldn't say he disagreed after her hysterical confessions. The brush with death clearly rattled the Aresian princess to her core.

According to the healers, the oleander poison Issaria ingested was beyond lethal. A potency so toxic there should have been no countering it once it entered her system.

Yet here she was. Fighting it.

Calix smirked. The thought that not even poison could take her down brought a spark of pride to him. Issaria had claimed to be broken when he'd first met her in the Baelforia, but he was certain he'd never encountered anyone who intrigued him quite like she did. She underestimated herself, and from Calix's perspective, it made her triumphs even more impressive. He wanted to be by her side for each and every one.

No one could stare down a challenge like Issaria. It was in the hard line of her mouth, the way her bottom lip pinched to the side as she evaluated her options, the defiant tilt of her chin. She might look like a little princess, but Calix had seen over and over again that Issaria Elysitao was *all* Empress.

Maybe that was why he was infatuated with her. She'd make a fine ruler to any kingdom, love their people and literally walk to the ends of Ellorhys to save them. A queen that no king truly deserved.

But he'd try. Calix would toil every day to earn Issaria's heart, to be worthy of a queen that needed no crown.

Claiming her listless hand from the bed Calix pressed her fingers against his forehead as if Issaria could absolve him of his guilt. This should never have been allowed to happen.

"Issaria," he whispered her name like prayer to the Cosmos. "Issa, you're such a fighter. I knew it in the Baelforia when I first saw you." Wild eyes and snarled hair, Issa had been so unlike the enemy he'd been raised to see it had baffled him to his core to find her scraped and bloody in the forest. "You said you were useless, and I wanted to kiss you and tell you to stop being foolish."

He brought the back of her hand to his lips and pressed a kiss to her pale knuckles before placing her hand back on the bed so gently she could have been made of glass. With *fervent*-black fingers, he smoothed an inky spiral of hair near her face. "You've no idea how formidable you can be," he told her as he withdrew his hands in his lap and wrung them together.

"I know we've only begun to know one another. I've no right to want you, no right to crave you, to need you, but I *do*, Issaria." Calix confessed. "I need you so severely I fear what I'll do if you don't survive this."

But he knew exactly what he'd do. Calix would bring the world to its knees to find the perpetrator. Nothing would stop him from exacting vengeance even if he had to bring war to the doorsteps of the Crystal Palace himself.

"So I need you to fight, harder than you've ever fought before so you can come back to me, Issaria. Do you hear me?" Calix hung his head, useless hands twisted together between his knees as he pleaded, "I need you to come back to me so I can tell you myself how you've been on my mind since the Baelforia. I need to tell you that you're beautiful, and clever, and *so* stubborn." His chuckle stuck in his throat. "You're so stubborn, Issaria, you can't let this take you before I can tell you that I'm falling in love with you."

Calix offered that simple truth to the Cosmos in a plea for her life as if the fates had a care for the desires of men. "So come back to me Issaria. I'm begging you. Fight this poison and come back to me, love. Now that I know you, I don't think I can be without you."

Silence, punctuated by Issaria's shallow breathing, folded around him in the absence of his voice. He wasn't sure what he was expecting really. It wasn't as if she would hear him calling to her and wake up. He sighed and reclined in his chair.

"Just think how touching that would have been if she were awake to hear it," a voice said from behind him.

"Mythos above! " Calix exclaimed, whipping around to find Rhaminta, arms crossed over a satin, saffron-colored chiton and leaning against the doorframe. "Rhaminta? How long have you been standing there?"

"Long enough." She smiled knowingly from the threshold. "Don't worry. I won't tell her you're completely in love with her." Heat rushed to his face as he glanced back to the sleeping princess, making sure she definitely didn't hear this mortifying exchange. "I'll at *least* give you the chance to tell her first," she finished with a wink. "After she's woken up, of course."

Calix turned back to Issaria. "Rhaminta, if Issa wakes up—"

"*When* she wakes up, Prince Calix," Rhaminta interjected from beside him as she clasped his shoulder. "She's going to wake up. We have to believe in her."

She was right. They had to have faith that Issaria would pull through.

"When she wakes up," Calix affirmed, "I will bear my heart to her every day if it would make her happy."

Rhaminta offered him a reassuring smile as she retreated toward the door. "Issaria doesn't think of her own happiness, Prince Calix. It's reassuring to me that *someone* is thinking about her in all of this." Calix couldn't consider anything else even if he wanted to. "I'll come check on her later, if you're staying for a bit?"

Calix nodded. "Yeah, I'm going to stay a while longer."

"You should get some sleep, Prince Calix," she said from the threshold. "She's not going anywhere."

When Rhaminta's footsteps had vanished down the hall, Calix leaned forward and cradled Issaria's hand between his once more. Rhaminta had said Issaria wasn't going anywhere, but Calix couldn't shake the sensation that Issaria 's remaining time had been slipping though the hourglass since long before they'd met in the Baelforia.

ACKNOWLEDGMENTS

Wow, what a wild ride this has been. I've been working so hard for so long that I hardly know where to begin when it comes to gratitude. If I forget anyone, I promise it wasn't done in malice, I'm just completely overwhelmed by the fact that...this is my book, you guys. And not only is this my book? There's likely to be *another* book after this. It's surreal after so many years of dreaming and working at the story and the world. Ellorhys is here, and it is *in your hands.*

I have to start by thanking my parents. Dad, without you I would never have had the courage to take on the big dreams. You've never told me I *couldn't* reach the stars, and for that, I thank you endlessly. You taught me boundless compassion and if I remember correctly, it was also you who taught me to read. To my mother, who gave me the first book that *meant* something to me. She gave me my love of reading, and happily helped me grow my library with endless bookstore visits, midnight release parties, and never saying *no* even when I had ten books in my hand. She fed my voracious appetite for books and let my imagination grow. I would not be the reader, or the writer, I am today without that influence.

A special thanks to Laura and Andrea Drag. My sisters. Growing up with you guys inspires so much of my work, I cannot imagine a world in which we didn't misspend our youths on the internet and playing playstation. Laura, you inspire me with art and games, endless nights of comics, drawing our OC characters, and RPing on Dynasty19 (LOL. Yeah. I went there. Shout out to all the TaleDynasty gang because Ellorhys was inspired by our game) From N*sync and MCR, Sailor Moon, and video game tournaments until sunrise with our parents are screaming at us to go to sleep because its 4am goddamnit—thank you for fueling my imagination with years of creative fun. Andrea, my goddess and editor-of-the-primary-draft, your careful edits and feedback has been Mythos-sent. Your devil-magic truly is in the details. Thank you for your brain, but thank you more for your encouragement and willingness to be my first set of critical eyes. For longer than forever, I'll always be inspired by you both.

To my editor-of-the-whole-dang-thing, the great Charlie Knight, without whom this final draft would still have an excessive use of commas, randomly capitalized words and conundrums. I am so grateful to have connected with you for the final polish. You pushed me with your questions and your enthusiasm for this project, and I cannot *wait* to send you the next one.

My wonderful team of freelancers who dealt with my obsessive need for perfection and novice comprehension of the process: Ash Turner, my visionary map maker who "got carried away having fun with this map that [we've] forgotten to talk about the business side completely." You blew my mind the first time you dropped the draft into my inbox and each time we chatted the world just got better and better—you totally nailed it!

Lexie, my cover designer, I cannot thank you enough for stepping in last minute and evaporating my stress like fog caught in a beam of summer sunshine. It has been a delight to work with you and your visionary designs. Thank you so much for being part of this journey with me! I'm so happy to have found you.

To my Beta Readers, who gave critical opinions and feedback for the betterment of the manuscript: Jason DeYoung, Bianca Hicks, Dominique Cassie, Millie Hagala, Mackenzie Keefe, Elizabeth McCulloch, Jessica Payne, Katti and David Therriault, and Monica Patino. All of you had eyes on the very first version of this world. All of you had wonderful things to say, even when what you were saying wasn't *actually* all that wonderful. I cannot thank you enough for your brutal honesty and desire for more.

To my bookstagram friends who continued to push me to share

my work, Amber, Reese, Charlee, and Kat, you ladies are the best book pals a gal could find randomly on the internet. I cannot believe you guys were even interested in this work, but sharing on a broader scale with you has really inspired this journey to take root the way it has.

Thank you to *all* who have read the drafts of DOSS in all its stages. I couldn't have done this without all the thoughtful feedback and challenges that were issued in the name of a better story.

And last, but certainly not least, a final thank you to a few names that have influenced my education over the years:

Donna Decker, for telling me I should do the thing. For Creative Writing I-IV, for the Juniper nomination, the editor-in-chief position with Nevermore, and ultimately, for guiding my hand and making me believe I was worth something, in a time where I felt like I wasn't worth very much at all. I can't imagine having truly embarked on this journey of writing without that moment in your office where you told me that it wasn't just that I could. But that I *should.*

For everyone who participated in my higher education at Western State Colorado University, Barbara Chepaitis, Makayla Roessner, J.S. Mayunk, Mark Todd, and the M.T.E of WSCU (Dang it. The acronym has changed again, hasn't it? Western Colorado University now?) Russell Davis. Your collective influence in my writing, the red pen of doom, and all the lessons in between have been felt long after our classes ended. Thank you all for the wisdom, and confidence in my abilities over the years. You've always given the extra push I needed to excel beyond what I thought possible. I will always howl at the moon and feel the power in a dark and stormy on the stoop under those endless western skies.

Finally, I want to acknowledge *you,* the reader. Above all else...I wrote this book for you. I've always wanted to tell stories like a real author, and to be able to put one of mine in your hands is truly a dream come true. I can only hope you enjoyed it, but either way...I'm so happy this is real.

Dream on, dreamers.

ABOUT THE AUTHOR

Sara DeLaVergne is a fantasy author with an MFA in creative writing from Western Colorado University, a BFA from Franklin Pierce University, and a minor in fine art. When she is not writing she is likely reading, playing video games, collecting custom book-themed Funko Pops, and sniffing book-inspired candles in a totally non-addictive kind of way, though her wallet disagrees. She lives in New Hampshire with her adorable dog, Captain Hamm.

Daughter of Shattered Skies is her debut novel, but surely not the last.

You can learn more about Sara by following on Instagram, TikTok, Facebook and by visiting silverquillsara.com

Made in the USA
Monee, IL
08 May 2023

33096284R00256